Gladiator 37

Patrick Gleeson

Gladiator 37

Patrick Gleeson

Nova Orbis

Patrick Gleeson

ACKNOWLEDGMENTS

"Too many words."

Those were the concise words of my wife, Lisa, after she read my perfect first draft. I stared at her for ten seconds, my feelings alternating between fury and alarm. Then I realized something: there were too many words.

I took out 32,000 words.

As usual, my wife was right.

I just hope I took out the right 32,000 words.

Thank you, Lisa.

Gladiator 37

One

Twenty years before

The wicker man stood forty feet tall, silhouetted on the hill, arms hanging by its sides. The blood-orange sun bled through the closely woven willow branches. Short, stumpy legs supported the long, hollow torso. A crude head perched on top, its face devoid of ears, eyes, nose or mouth. Blank. Featureless.

Through the branches, Cullen saw the insides writhe.

For a moment, Cullen imagined the huge creation would come to life, its eyes would open, burning red with kill-lust.

Cullen shook his head and the writhing inside the effigy became the arms and legs of the prisoners his father had captured. Arms reached out from the spaces between the branches as if freedom could be won just by grasping the air. Their faces pressed against the holes, screaming, pleading.

One of the prisoners climbed up the inside of the giant. His hands were strong and his toes found footholds as if he'd known the contours and secrets of his prison all his life. He reached the hatch and tried to push past the guard who stood on a platform outside the wicker man. The guard–Rory, one of his father's soldiers—punched the prisoner's face. The man swung away, like a door opening inwards.

He'll fall, thought Cullen.

But the prisoner was desperate. He clawed the edge of the opening and jumped out.

His momentum carried him onto the platform. He flung his arms around Rory's neck, embracing him like a brother.

Cullen knew what would happen next. Rory raised his sword, while his other arm held the prisoner close, locking him in place. He eased the sword between the prisoner's ribs. The prisoner bucked and tried to tear away, but he hadn't eaten in days. He was weak. Before the sword was halfway in, the prisoner slumped forward, his arms slipping from Rory's neck. He rolled back through the opening and fell onto the prisoners.

Twenty captives waited at the base of the wicker man, watching in numbed horror. Like rabbits trapped by a snarling wolf, Cullen felt the fight go out of them. This was their fate. This was where they would die. They climbed the stairs obediently and allowed themselves to be pushed inside, their faces slack with terror. By the time the last prisoner fell in, two of the prisoners at the bottom of the pile were suffocating from the weight of bodies pressing above them.

Cullen felt a hand on his shoulder and looked up. His father stood beside him, impossibly tall. The five braids of red hair lay on his shoulders. Cullen's gaze shifted to his father's hand. Dried blood lay in the creases of his knuckles.

"Don't look away from this, Cullen," said his father.

Cullen looked back to the wicker giant with the writhing insides.

"In years to come, Cullen, you'll take my place as leader of our tribe. My enemies will hear about this day and they will piss in their boots."

"What's going to happen to them?"

His father smiled, and appeared almost wistful as if the relentless sobbing of the captives was a sad piece of music that stirred pangs of melancholy.

"Fire."

Two

The old man cast his net out onto the sea. It hit the water with a dull splash. His rheumy eyes watched it sink, dragged down by the weights tied to its edges. With luck, and with the help of the gods, a shoal of herring would swim into the net's death embrace.

He needed something, anything, to take to market.

His aching joints had prevented him from fishing for the past two weeks and he needed a good haul to make up for the time he'd lain on his mattress of straw, his knees and elbows swollen with fever. He still hadn't fully recovered but what could he do? If he was going to have food to eat he'd have to catch it or barter for it. So he needed the fish. That's why he'd come out, before the sun was up, rowed his boat through the fog to this part of the sea, which, in times past, had been lucky for him.

Now it was time to wait. Tendrils of mist floated around the lit candle that hung over the side of the boat. He hoped the candle's meager light would draw the fish to the surface, would entrance and bewitch them and allow him to scoop them up in his net of hempen rope, which he had sewn together two winters ago as the snow piled high outside his hut.

His wife had been alive then.

The old man wrapped the deerskin around his bony shoulders. His breath hung in the frigid air, staying close to his body, as if it wasn't sure it wanted to be outside on a day as cold and dank as this. Soon the sun would rise and then maybe his joints would cease their endless whimpering.

He pulled in his net, trying to match his actions with the slow, languid currents of the sea. His old hands felt the net flutter, much as a spider might feel the struggle of a fly on her web, a tiny vibration that told him he had snared one fish, maybe two. That would take care of breakfast and then what? He needed a boatload of herring. It was going to be a long morning if this was all he—

What was that?

A low, booming noise. It had come from out there, from the open sea. He squinted his eyes but the mist was a veil that obscured everything farther away than twenty paces. Was it a whale? He hadn't seen one since he and his youngest son had taken their boat five miles out to sea and the great behemoth, the monster from the depths, had breached the water not ten paces from their boat. His son had fallen down in horror, but he had been rooted to the spot. And he had seen the giant creature's eye. *His eye.* And they had stared at each other for what seemed like an eternity.

And then it was gone, sluicing through the water, its gray body carving through the ocean like a mountain falling into the sea.

There it was again. A whooshing noise. Closer.

"Hello?"

Even as he said it, he knew how stupid he sounded. This thing, whatever it was, wasn't human.

A cold hand of fear clutched his stomach. He was an old man and he knew that he didn't have many years left, but every morning when he woke up, he thanked the gods that he was alive. And what he was hearing now, coming toward him, was something that froze the marrow in his bones.

Whoosh.

Coming right at him now. He grabbed his net and hauled it into the boat, hand over hand. He tossed the net onto the bottom of the boat, grabbed the oars and started to row for shore.

He was dimly aware that his joints didn't hurt, not at all.

Whoosh.

Louder. Much louder. His sinewy arms pulled the oars through the water. What was happening? Why–?

He saw the shadow first, something gray speeding toward him, and before he could register what he was seeing, the eyes appeared, twenty feet above the water, bearing down on him, huge, unblinking. The old man's hands released the oars and he tumbled back into the boat, his arms flung up to protect him, his lips moving, pleading with the Gods to deliver him from this monster.

By all the Heavens it was a sea creature, a demon from the depths of the sea, heading straight for him. He had never seen anything so terrifying, so immense. The old man felt his bladder release and a warm stream of piss ran down his leg.

WHOOSH.

The old man's eyes shifted to the side of the creature, toward the sound where he saw—

—Oars?

In the blink of an eye he realized what he was looking at. It wasn't a monster. It was worse.

Romans. In one of their huge, damned warships. They painted eyes on the front of their ships so they would have safe passage through unseen and cursed waters. But he had another guess: He thought the Romans wanted to scare the shit out of poor, old fishermen.

It worked, he wanted to shout at them. But he didn't have time to shout, didn't have time to do anything except clamber back in his seat and row because the galley was close now, was so close, and it would run him down if he didn't get out of its way.

The oars were ripped out of his hands as the hull of the Roman Galley powered by, splintering them into pieces, shards hissing through the air inches from his face.

The old man threw himself against the mast that rose from the middle of his boat. His craft bounced off the hull of the Roman ship and spun around in the water. Above the old man's head the oars of the galley glided through the air before plunging down into the water, ripping through the sea with ease. He was caught between the oars and the hull, spinning out of control. He was surely dead. He careened off the galley's hull, which ran so fast through the water that it spun him around like a child's toy caught in a swirling stream.

The oars sailed overhead, huge oars, thick as tree trunks.

The oars slammed the water again, creating a swell that sent his boat crashing against the hull. It was a bone-jarring crunch and for a moment he thought his little craft was doomed. But the wicker-frame absorbed the impact and continued to spin away, bouncing off the side of the Roman ship, throwing great waves of freezing water over him and then…

…it was gone.

Almost before he could draw in a breath, the huge vessel disappeared into the mist. The noise of the oars grew fainter, their splashes swallowed up by the concealing fog.

"Gods in heaven," he said, his words wheezing out of his lungs.

He got to his feet, pulling himself up with the help of the mast. By the time he steadied himself the galley was gone. He sank down to his knees, weeping with relief. He was still alive.

Soon he would be dead.

But not today.

Three

Cullen brought the hammer down on the anvil, sending a shower of sparks onto the dirt floor of his hut. The iron took shape, as it was hammered, forced, teased into a sword. Sweat dripped from his brow and fell on his leather shirt. Each hit was precisely aimed, carefully timed. He thrust the unfinished sword into the brazier of coals, the heat of which was so great that it seared his face.

He had dreamed of his father last night. Always the same dream: The prisoners falling into the wicker man. The insides of the effigy filled with terrified, broken bodies. Finally, when it was full—*Gods, even after all he'd seen, all he'd done, it sent shivers down his spine*—when it was full his father set it afire. It burned like a demon, flames scything sideways in the fierce Irish winds.

He remembered the look on his father's face, a satisfied look, the look of a job well done.

His enemies burned.

The memories of that day haunted his dreams ever since. The details: his father's leather breeches, torn near the belt. The feel of the grass under his bare feet, still soggy from the rain. The woman who lay back in her husband's arms as he squeezed her neck, first sending her to sleep, then to her death, so she wouldn't have to face the horror of immolation.

He had been seven years old, and it was his earliest memory. It was as if that day had been so full, so important, so devastating, that it had wiped all other childhood memories from his mind.

Sometimes years passed and that dream would never surface. Other times, it would visit him every night.

He'd been dreaming it for almost three full moons.

He removed the blade from the coals and, for the next ten minutes, slammed his hammer down onto it. This sword, along with the others he had made since winter, he would trade to Uthred of Featherstone who used the weapons to defend against the Scottish tribes who attacked from across the border. Uthred liked Cullen's swords because they were superior to those of any other blacksmith in the area. The bands of steel that ran through Cullen's weapons could only be created by repeated heating of the blade, and the captured carbon fragments from the coals, mixing with the iron ore, were transformed into thin strips of steel if both elements were pounded and re-heated over and over again. It required patience and strength.

Other smiths made more swords. Cullen made better ones.

So Cullen worked and sweated, his hammer flying across the blade, coaxing the shape out of it, racing the seconds before a subtle change in the response of the metal told him the iron had lost its malleability and needed to be heated again. He worked until his muscles ached and his fingers were numb from holding the pincers he used to turn the blade of iron and steel.

By noon his stomach was growling. He glanced up at the rabbits dangling from the hook at the door of his hut. They would make a good lunch, slowly roasted over the brazier of coals.

"Cullen!"

Cullen glanced up. Coming over the hill was John the Farmer, a red-faced, muscular man whose head barely reached up to Cullen's chin. He was boar-like, with a full beard that grew in wild abandon around his face. There was a large carbuncle on his nose, a pink mound of gristle rejected by the rest of his body and exiled to this extremity. Three black hairs grew from this lump of flesh that bobbled around whenever John yelled in anger.

He was angry now.

Most of the villagers gave Cullen a certain amount of respect. Though he had never raised a fist to any of them in the years Cullen and his family had lived here, they were wary of him—and with good reason, Cullen supposed—knowing what he'd done to be accepted into the village. But John the Farmer never had a problem telling Cullen exactly what was on his mind.

"Do you know what your son did to Godwin?" screamed John.

Cullen figured it would be about Finn.

John strode through the opening of the wooden hut and planted himself in front of Cullen. Cullen could smell the mixture of sweat, feces and dried cow's blood that stained the farmer's shirt.

"My son is lying in—", began John.

"You're too close," said Cullen.

"What?"

"You stink of piss and shit. Two steps back should do it."

John the Farmer stared at Cullen in disbelief.

"Let's talk outside," said Cullen and walked past John. Even though his hut was open on one side and there was always a cold breeze sneaking down from the northern fens, the brazier heated up the hut like an oven and Cullen was glad to feel a chill wind on his body. He had built the hut in the shadow of the mountains, farther from the village than he would have liked, but the mountains and the peat marshes here were rich in ore. He could take armloads of peat and throw it in his furnace. The intense heat of the fire burned away the moss, the soil and everything else until all that was left was a clump of iron ore. Once he had enough ore for one sword, he would pound the lump of metal into a sleek, beautiful weapon. It was hard, backbreaking, lonely work and few villagers had reason to come out here.

Cullen turned to John, staring at him in what he hoped was an intimidating look. But that blob of flesh on John's nose took away any sense of danger Cullen tried to project. Cullen sighed.

"What did Finn do now?"

The short man sucked in air through his teeth.

"He was fighting with Godwin. He split his lips. Probably broke his nose. There's blood everywhere, all over his clothes. And his mother—" John leaned closer, grimacing.

"His mother is not happy. And she had no problem letting me know exactly how not happy she is. It took her over an hour." Flecks of spittle flew from John's mouth as he spoke, some landing on Cullen.

"What was the fight about?" asked Cullen.

"What is it ever about with your boy? Anything will set that brat off. One wrong word, one look is enough to start him flinging his fists around."

Cullen's eyes bored into John.

"I'll have the brat's mother speak to him."

If John detected the change in Cullen's voice he ignored it.

"His mother?" John spat in disgust. "The boy doesn't need speaking to. He needs a thrashing. And I'll tell you something: if you don't do it, someone else will."

"Meaning you?"

John shrugged his shoulders in an 'If-that's-the-way-it-has-to-be' gesture. Cullen rubbed his chin softly, trying to keep his rising temper at bay. Didn't this fool know who he was talking to? There was a time he would have gutted this whoreson with his bare hands, ripped out his entrails and fed them to the wolves that prowled the woods and shadow lands. It astonished Cullen that John the Farmer still lived if this was the way he talked to people. Calling his son a brat? Threatening to beat him? Spitting at the mention of his wife? But Cullen's family was part of the village and allowances had to be made.

A warning would probably suffice.

"If you touch my boy I'll kill you. If you spit at the mention of my wife again, I'll kill you." Cullen kept his voice low and impassive, but the look on the farmer's face faltered. Cullen noted with satisfaction a flicker of fear in the farmer's eyes. But the smaller man wasn't going to back down so quickly.

"So where does that leave us?"

"I'll talk to him."

John grunted and took a few seconds to think about this.

"When?"

"When I feel like it."

John hitched a breath in, as if to say something, but abruptly closed his mouth. *Could it be that this fool had just enough sense to live?*

John turned and stalked out of the hut, muttering under his breath.

Maybe the farmer was right. Maybe a good beating would stop Finn fighting. Rhiannon, his wife, would be against it, but *he* was Finn's father. Fathers beat their sons, didn't they?

At least his had.

His father had carried two weapons—a sword and an axe. When Cullen had first seen him in battle he stared in awe as his father swung both weapons with reckless abandon and ruthless efficiency. His enemies seemed to part before him as though they were meat for the carving. Cullen remembered how content his father was, butchering and slaughtering all who stood in his way.

The worst beating Cullen ever got was when he was ten years old. They had been in Hibernia then, and Cullen had stolen from Fiachra the Baker, a cruel slob of a man who nevertheless had a gift for making the most wonderful, sweet loaves of bread. Cullen had stolen the round loaf that was still hot to the touch, and had hidden in a hollow between some rocks down by the lake. The lake was edged with ice that reached out into the water as if trying to entice the rest of the languid currents into its frigid embrace. But the bread had been warm, so deliciously warm, and Cullen had picked it apart, piece by piece, letting it melt in his mouth, savoring each morsel.

Just as he swallowed the last glorious mouthful, his father's hand reached into the hollow, grabbed his neck and hauled him out. His father gazed at him, saying nothing, but smelling the bread on his son's breath and seeing the crumbs on his son's shirt.

He couldn't remember if his father had changed expression when the beating started, or if his face stayed blank. Cullen frowned, trying to pluck the memory from the gray mists of time. All he knew for certain was that the first blow was to the side of his head. He felt an explosion on his left cheek that slammed him to the rocky ground. For a moment he didn't know who he was or where he was. Then a birch branch whipped across his legs. The stinging pain brought him back to reality in an instant. He tried to roll away, but he made the mistake of exposing his belly and his father had driven his foot into it, kicking him hard and fast. As Cullen gasped for air, the birch branch whistled through the air, landing across Cullen's face, drawing blood from ear to mouth.

He vomited up all he had eaten. This didn't slow down his father who pummeled and kicked him even as he retched up the last of the still warm bread.

He blacked out then, because his next memory was of waking up hours later, lying in the stinking remains of his vomit. Dragging himself to his hands and knees, he had crawled to the lake and lay in the body-numbing water until he could no longer feel the pain that ravaged him. Had his mother found him lying there, or did his father come back for him? Or had his mother been dead when this happened? One thing he did know: he never stole bread again. That meant the beating worked, didn't it? Could he bring such wrath down on Finn? And he wasn't just talking about a regular beating that would bruise the boy for a few days; Finn already got plenty of those. He meant a thrashing that the boy would remember as long as he lived.

He started to walk home.

The village was built on the outskirts of the forest, which in turn was surrounded by high mountains on three sides. East of the village, and leading toward the sea, were five miles of fields, hills and scattered trees. Other villages were built on the other sides of the mountains, and trade with them was brisk, but Cullen liked the isolation of his village, far away from the tribes in the west, the Romans down south and the Scottish tribes up north. How long had they lived here now, he wondered? Four years? Five? How old had Finn been? Maybe seven years.

They'd been lucky.

When he'd led Rhiannon and Finn here, the people had been reluctant to accept them into their tribe, but had allowed them stay for a few weeks if Cullen helped them with their harvest. The villagers had been blunt, unfriendly and suspicious. They'd had trouble recently: A band of five or six scallywags from Scotland had come across the wall and were living in the hills, raiding each of the nearby villages in turn, plundering the stores and raping the women. The village had suffered their attack two weeks before Cullen and his family arrived, and one of the men had been killed trying to resist the marauders. Cullen had offered to kill the Scots. His suggestion was greeted with a disbelief bordering on derision, but the villagers readily agreed that if he could kill the bastards who had attacked them, then he and his family would have a permanent home there. Cullen had gone into the mountains, the eyes of the villagers staring at his back until he disappeared into the low-hanging mist that shrouded the mountains all year round. Rhiannon had not watched him leave. She stayed in their hut, tears streaming from her eyes. The village chief, Brendel, tried to comfort her, saying that he was sure Cullen would be safe, and that he probably wouldn't even come across the Scots. Rhiannon shook her head.

"He'll find them for you. Those thieves are already dead."

You could try to out-run the past, but it always caught up with you. Cullen had been called upon to do what he did best.

Four days later, Cullen returned. He brought with him one head, that of their leader. Judging by the size of his head, the leader had been over six feet tall. He had laid the head—and five pairs of ears—at Brendel's door, and informed the village leader that the Scots wouldn't be bothering them anymore. Brendel had stared at the head, and the ears. After he had thrown up his breakfast, he showed Cullen a corner of their village where he could build his permanent home.

Four

Cullen saw the village in the distance, nestled to the south against the forest. Fields of wheat and barley spread out toward the mountains to the west, bounded loosely by hedgerows and stone walls. The soil was rich, and the crops were plentiful. The tall wheat blew in the wind as if the spirits were caressing it, giving it their blessings as they ran their invisible hands over the heads of the plants. When Rhiannon baked the bread that came of the wheat—nothing like it in the world, especially with great slabs of butter melting into it, and a cup of ice-cold water to wash it down.

"Cullen."

Cullen turned to the voice. It was Elric the Farmer, who grew the fields closest to the forest. A big man, with broad shoulders grown from a lifetime of hard work, he approached Cullen with an easy walk.

"How many swords this week?"

"Just the one. I spent the last three days looking for ore in the mountains."

Elric scratched his chin, on which the stubble of a beard grew.

"Ore, eh? I hope you found a lot, because I need a new plough."

"What happened to the one I made you last year?"

"Stones under the ground. Chewed it up. Still works, but..."

Cullen nodded.

"It'll be a few weeks."

Elric shrugged and nodded. He was about to turn away when he hesitated, and looked at Cullen.

"Your son was in a fight today. Nearly took a couple of Godwin's teeth out."

"I know. John told me."

"It's not good to lose teeth, Cullen. What's he going to eat with?"

"I'm going to talk to him now."

He continued on toward the village. Undoubtedly, everyone knew about the fight, and everyone would have an opinion about what should be done. What else would they talk about, thought Cullen? It was a small village. Everyone knew everyone. Every word, movement, snore, fart and grunt was common knowledge. When Brendel sneezed, people knew spring had arrived as the air attacked his lungs. When Osric sang songs in the morning, people grinned to themselves, having listened to his loud love-making the night before. The huts were built close to each other, and while they kept out the cold, they allowed any noise a free and easy passage.

He could smell the village before he saw it. He caught the scent of fresh meat being cooked on a fire. A pig, a wild one, thought Cullen, catching the rich aroma it threw off. Mixed in with the smell of cooking was the fertile stench of manure, ever present because they kept all the animals inside the fence that surrounded their collection of huts. As he crested the path, he saw it, the village, his home. Twenty-two huts scattered around a clearing, none more than ten yards from its neighbor. Most of the men were in the fields, leaving the village to the women and children. Some youngsters ran between the huts, engaged in a never ending game of chase. Two women stood near the spit, turning the pig over, letting the grease drip into the fire which popped and fizzed. A weaving loom was being worked at by Ethel, a woman who—according to the older villagers—had gone through three husbands and had birthed thirteen children in her lifetime. She was the oldest woman Cullen had ever seen. She was toothless, and made herself a mixture of broth every day, in which she cooked carrots and turnips until they were nothing but mush. Sometimes when there was a feast, she would have the children chew meat for her until it was broken, then she would take it from their mouths and gum it down.

The children, believing it was good luck to be chosen for this job, fought each other for the privilege of chewing Ethel's food.

He walked down the path, noting that the fence was still unfinished. Any goat or sheep would be able to jump through the gaps between the poles and escape, and live wild off the land. Their freedom was only yards away, but they never took it. Cullen supposed they felt the village was their home too, even if their destiny was to be roasted on the spit like that unfortunate pig.

"Forgot your brains, Irish?" rasped a voice.

Cullen turned to see Morcar sitting in the shade of a cart, his leg stumps jutting in front of him. Morcar had lost his legs when he was a child, when a small cut from a submerged branch had turned his left leg putrid. To save the young Morcar's life, they had cut it off, but not before it had infected his right leg. They had taken the other leg too and Morcar had lain in the land between life and death for almost a year. The boy had grown up to be a man, and Cullen guessed that Morcar was older than he was by about fifteen years. Fifteen hard years. Morcar's face was lined with age, and pock-marked by other sicknesses that had left their scars on him. If there was an illness to be had, Morcar would find it, take it into his body, and suffer until it passed.

Morcar followed Cullen, reaching his arms in front of him, planting them down on the ground, then swinging his body through his legs. He matched Cullen's pace with surprising ease.

"Come home early to stick it to the wife, have you, Irish?"

"Piss off, Morcar," said Cullen.

Morcar fell to the ground, laughing hysterically, his leg stumps waving in the air while his arms beat the ground.

Five

Cullen stared at his sullen-eyed son. A mop of dark hair sprouted from the top of his head and fell in matted strands down to his shoulders. The hair framed a face that had sharply defined features; a strong jaw, a straight nose and eyes that sparkled when he smiled or threw off sparks of fire when he was angry. He was tall for his eleven years, and looked awkward when he moved. Right now he slouched against the wall of their hut, his eyes fixed on his father.

Rhiannon, Cullen's wife, sat beside him. Her long mane of curly, brown hair was pulled back and tied behind her head, revealing a face that Cullen still found breathtaking in its beauty. Not for the first time he wondered why he had been lucky enough to become her lover, her mate.

Aisling, their baby daughter, slept in a wicker cot near the wall. Speckles of weak sunlight snuck through the doorway and played across her face. Her mouth twitched as she dreamt.

They sat in the center of their round hut. Cullen had built it on the edge of the village, making it from the trunks and branches of birch trees. He had dug a circular ditch and placed the trunks inside, filled the ditch, and wove the thinner branches around and between the trunks. He daubed a mixture of mud, clay and dung all around the outside of the hut, and finished it off with a roof of thatched hay tied in bundles. Animal skins that hung on wooden frames divided the hut into three separate areas. It wasn't a palace but it was home, and it kept out the bitter winds that blew down from the hills of Scotland.

Rhiannon's face was set in a grim expression. His wife had seen the look on his face and knew he intended to knock Finn's brains about. She had insisted they would *both* speak to Finn. Now, caught in a staring match with Finn, Cullen didn't know who felt more uncomfortable—he or his son. Cullen decided Finn had the easier job; stand there, be defiant, give short answers, take the punishment and get away. Even though the conversation hadn't yet started, Cullen suspected that Finn felt he had already won.

"John the Farmer thinks I should give you a beating," he began.

Finn's gaze didn't waver from Cullen's face. He remained defiantly silent, determined not to let this be easy for his father.

"Is that what I should do? Take a length of birch to your back?"

Finn shrugged, a look of indifference on his face.

"I thought Godwin was your friend? Why did you fight?" said Cullen.

This time Finn drew in an exaggerated breath and let it escape out between his teeth. The boy's gaze wandered, staring at the roof of the hut, as if he were bored with the proceedings.

Cullen felt the beginnings of anger stir in his gut. In a quieter voice he repeated the question.

"Why did you fight, Finn?"

Finn cleared his throat. His voice was in the process of changing from a boy's high pitch to a young man's baritone.

"If you're going to beat me just get on with it. I don't want to stay here all day."

Before Finn or Rhiannon could react, Cullen leaped across the floor and backhanded Finn across the face. Finn spun to the floor, his nose erupting in blood. Rhiannon grabbed Cullen's arm.

Cullen turned to see her eyes flashing in anger.

"Cullen, stop!" She pushed Cullen aside and ran to Finn, who struggled to his knees and held his wrist against his bleeding nose. She tried to help him up but he squirmed away from her. Rhiannon turned to Cullen, her face a mask of fury.

"Don't you ever hit my son like that again," she hissed.

"He's my son too, Rhiannon," he replied. He had meant it to sound firm and menacing, but he was annoyed to hear a defensive note in his tone. He tried again. "He needs to learn to show respect."

"If you kill him, I don't think he'll learn, do you?"

"Does he look dead to you?"

Finn got to his feet, eyes full of anger. Cullen pushed past Rhiannon and grabbed the boy by his shirt. The side of Finn's face was crimson, and Cullen could see the shape of his hand fading from the boy's skin.

"Why did you fight?" he asked in a low voice that did nothing to hide how he felt.

"Because of his eyes," spat Finn.

"What about his eyes?"

"I saw fear in them." Cullen released Finn, staring at him.

"It was even at first. He even landed a few good blows here," Finn patted his stomach. "But then I got him good on his face. Split his cheek open. Then I got him on his neck, and then twice in the gut. He tried to yield but I saw that he was afraid. And I liked that. So I hit him again. And I would have kept hitting him if his mother hadn't seen us."

Cullen stared at his son, eyes narrowing.

"You beat him because he was scared? Why?"

"Don't you remember?" asked Finn.

"What am I supposed to remember?"

"You said there was a time in every fight when you saw the look in their eyes. When the man you were going to kill—when you both knew he was going to die by your sword. Godwin had that look in his eyes."

Cullen shook his head slowly.

"I never told you that," he said.

"You told mama," he said, nodding to Rhiannon. "I heard." Finn touched his face where Cullen hit him. A slow smile formed on his lips.

"It doesn't hurt now," he said, as if savoring his victory. "And that was a pretty good hit." Abruptly, his face lost the smile and he scowled at Cullen.

"I don't know why you're so mad at me," he said. "I just want to be like you."

Still looking at Cullen with rage in his eyes, he walked out of the hut. Cullen watched him go. He turned to Rhiannon. She stormed out past him and he cursed his quick temper. He knew he would be sleeping by himself tonight.

Six

Cullen trudged back to the forge, his heart full of regrets. His first regret was that he hadn't hit Finn harder. His second regret was that he hadn't pushed Rhiannon out of the way when she grabbed his arm. Then he could have given the boy the beating of his life. After all, Cullen reasoned, he—Cullen—had never stolen bread after his father whipped him to within an inch of his life. He hadn't hated his father afterwards. He'd been afraid of him but he hadn't hated him.

Why did Rhiannon insist on coddling the boy? Finn had that look in his eyes, an insolence that Cullen recognized as the beginnings of the same look he and his warriors had before they went into battle.

Wasn't being a warrior Finn's birthright?

Would Finn pick up the sword and become the warrior that *he* used to be, the killer that now lay dormant below the surface of his soul? Finn had never been exposed to the violence and death that Cullen had seen when he was younger. Cullen's father had not hesitated to show him the severed heads of enemies slain in battle. It had been such a part of his youth, such a mundane thing, that Cullen had no memory of being horrified by it. But Rhiannon was Finn's mother and she protected her children from such horrors. But blood was blood, and Finn was Cullen's son.

Maybe the Gods had already laid out his fate.

It was early afternoon by the time he got back to his forge and he worked steadily for two hours, fashioning the tip of a spear that he would

21

attach to a length of oak and use it to barter with Cathal the Potter. Cathal had made two clay pots that Rhiannon admired. Maybe if he gave them to her, he wouldn't have to suffer her displeasure for too long. When she was like this, it devastated him.

Rhiannon.

She had something he'd never seen before in a woman. She had a light about her, a light that came from inside, from her spirit.

Even after all she'd been through. Cullen pushed the memory away, the memory of the Roman and what he did to her.

Bile rose in his throat as the memories wound their way through his mind. No, even that hadn't destroyed what she had: It was, simply put, everything good in the world. And something in him needed that goodness, craved it. They married when Cullen turned nineteen, and a year later Finn was born. He now had a son, a boy that would carry his name into the next generation, a boy that would grow to be a man and take his place as a warrior in the tribe. Life had been good. No, better than good. Life had been great with endless possibilities for power and glory. Young as Cullen was, his name was mentioned in the same breath as his own father, spoken with the same reverence and fear. Rhiannon became pregnant again, and Cullen would soon have a family that would—

Cullen blinked, confused. What exactly *had* he been hoping for? A score of sons and daughters? A family that would reflect the glory he hoped would be his? What had his addled brain been thinking? Grainne, his first daughter, was born, and all the power he had, all the power his family had, he'd have given it all up if she could only have lived. No, not just lived. He would have traded everything for one more year.

One more day. One more moment with her.

The next four years. Dear Gods, the next four years were bloody.

He shook his head, annoyed with himself for remembering the old days. Old hurts, more vicious than sword slices, lay open just beneath the surface of his soul. Grainne was gone, and all the memories in the world would not bring her back.

"Cullen."

Rhiannon stood at the hut entrance. Finn stood beside her, his face even more sullen than it had been that morning. To Rhiannon's left was someone Cullen had glimpsed in the village over the past week. An old woman, of maybe sixty years. No, he thought, looking at her closer. Older. Much older. Her hair was knotted in a long, white braid, and it fell over one shoulder. Her eyes were lined with wrinkles and they seemed to twinkle, as if someone had just told her a joke. For some reason this annoyed Cullen. The old woman stared at him with an open, friendly expression. Cullen looked at Rhiannon, his eyes raised questioningly.

"This is Mother Miriam. She's been staying at Ethel's house for the past five days. She's traveled far."

Cullen nodded slowly, not sure how she expected him to respond.

"She saw what happened between Finn and Godwin. She saw them fighting and thinks she can help."

Cullen looked at his son, who stared back at him with a look of exasperation that Cullen was sure was on his own face too.

"Did you explain to this old witch that we don't need her help?"

Rhiannon straightened up, steeling herself.

"I did not. I welcomed her assistance."

"And I'm not a witch, Cullen," said Mother Miriam. "I'm a priest."

"What's the difference?" said Cullen, sarcasm heavy in his voice.

"Cullen, she's our guest," said Rhiannon.

"But—"

"And I want you to listen to her," she added with a finality in her voice. Cullen sighed. What harm could it do? At least they were talking now, and he wouldn't have to face her temper, or worse, her silence, when he got home. If listening to this old witch would ease the tension in their house then why not give her an audience?

They walked to the shade of an oak tree and sat down. Mother Miriam reached into a leather bag and pulled out a loaf of bread. She tore it into four pieces and handed each of them a share. Cullen realized how hungry he was and accepted the bread, annoyed that the old woman, with the smiling eyes, had anticipated his needs. Mother Miriam took out four wooden mugs and poured water into each of them. Cullen grunted, which the visitor acknowledged as thanks with a nod of her head. Mother Miriam leaned closer, squinting her eyes.

"You have many scars, Cullen."

Cullen glanced down at his arms, along which lines of scar tissue stood out against his sunburnt skin.

Cullen shrugged. "They're from a long time ago."

The old woman nodded. "Some scars take a long time to heal," she touched his chest. "Some scars never do."

Cullen managed to suppress a groan. Was this one of those ancients that liked to talk in riddles as they made their point?

"Do you always talk in circles?"

"Only when I want to annoy someone."

"It's working," said Cullen.

The old woman laughed out loud, rocking back and clapping her hands delightedly.

Mother Miriam finished her bread, drained the last of the water from her wooden cup and looked around at Cullen, Rhiannon and Finn.

"I have traveled to many distant lands. I have talked with people whose skin is as black as the night. I have seen children born and held people as they took in their last breath. I have seen indescribable horrors and felt love that would break your heart. I have this to say: there is a new God. A God of love, not war. A God of peace, not chaos. This is what I have come here to talk to you about."

Cullen groaned inwardly. Another crazy fool with a god.

At least this one had brought bread.

He tore off a bite.

Mother Miriam paused, and looked at each of them in turn.

"We live in a time of upheaval. The Romans continue to spread across the world, putting their enemies to the sword. How many times have they fought in your land? How many times have you been forced to flee from them? But hear this. There is a revolution taking place, right in the heart of their dark empire."

Cullen had to admit that the old woman had a way of demanding attention, of telling a captivating tale, the way the old *Seanachais* of Hibernia would bewitch an audience. But she had said nothing, just like all the other mad travelers that happened upon their village, raving about whatever their befuddled brains clung to.

She talked of a God from the desert.   While Rhiannon and Finn listened, enthralled by her description of this new God, Cullen's mind drifted away, her story nothing more than a pleasant buzzing in his ear, the way the distant drone of bees on a summer's day lulled him to sleep as a child. He was happy again: his belly was full and his wife's anger toward him seemed to have abated. He lay back and his eyes closed and he fell into a half-sleep, the witch's voice low and soothing.

He had no idea how long he'd been asleep when the sound of Finn's voice woke him.

"Greater than Rome?" his son had asked. Cullen yawned. He had missed what seemed like an entire conversation.

"Rome is…incidental," mused the witch. "There will always be tyrants in this world, Finn, who will seek to destroy. It is how we are inside that will determine the fate of our souls."

Cullen looked at Rhiannon who had a very strange look on her face. Tears had gathered in her eyes, which seemed to shine with a brightness he hadn't seen for a long time. She turned to him, smiling behind her tears.

"Cullen, this is what I've been waiting for."

Cullen rubbed his face and looked at Rhiannon. What had this old hag been saying to make his wife's face *glow* like that?

"Rhiannon, we have many gods already. Why do we need a God from some faraway desert?"

"This God is the only one that makes sense."

"He rose from the dead, Papa," said Finn, his face shining with an innocence Cullen hadn't seen in years.

What story had this bag of bones been weaving?

"Did she tell you that?"

Finn nodded.

"Lies," said Cullen.

"But she said—"

"Nobody rises from the dead."

Cullen met Rhiannon's gaze, and for a moment he found he couldn't speak, as a wave of memories flooded through him. No, not a wave of memories, just one. Grainne, wrapped in a linen blanket, the outline of her nose, curving up, pressing against the thin fabric as Cullen lowered her into her grave.

"When you're dead, you're dead," he whispered.

Rhiannon bowed her head. She would not meet his eyes. *Damn this witch,* thought Cullen. Twice now today he remembered his dead daughter. Over the years, he'd managed to force his mind to forget about her for weeks at a time, and this old vulture strolls in and loosens the past, giving it free reign. Enough. Cullen turned to his son.

"Finn, if someone wants to kill you and you had a choice of a sword or love as a weapon, what do you pick?"

"The sword?" said Finn doubtfully, the look on his face hardening to an expression that Cullen recognized.

Cullen smiled at the boy. Maybe they could put today's fight behind them by forming a united front against this witch.

"Are you sure, Finn," continued Cullen. "Don't you want to defeat your enemies by singing songs of love to them?"

"Maybe I do," answered the boy, picking up on Cullen's sarcasm. "I'll pick daisies and roses and they'll be my swords."

"And your shield will be? "

"A rainbow of love."

Cullen and his son started to laugh, quickly losing control as they fell on their backs. Rhiannon glared at him, but Cullen, tears streaming down his cheeks, didn't care. Rhiannon had a will of iron but she was not going to turn his son into a whimpering toadstool.

Finally their laughter subsided. Rhiannon and the old woman hadn't moved. Cullen expected to see anger in the old woman's eyes but they still twinkled at him. Maybe it wasn't so bad that his son got into fights and learned how to use his fists. Maybe he should start teaching the boy how to use a sword. It wasn't that Finn needed to be a warrior but the boy had to learn to defend himself at the very least. This was good. This conversation had cleared Cullen's head. He had let Rhiannon have too much influence on the boy. It was time Finn learned some of the lessons that a son of Cullen must know. He turned to the old woman.

"I don't know if this God of yours is real or not, but I haven't laughed this much in a long time."

"Laughter is music to God's ears."

Cullen ruffled his son's hair.

"Rhiannon, take Finn home. I've got swords to finish." He turned to Mother Miriam.

"Swords forged out of iron. Real weapons. You can't forge love."

Mother Miriam got shakily to her feet and walked over to Cullen. She tapped his chest.

"This is where you forge love. In your heart. Iron may cut flesh, but no weapon made by man can cut a soul forged with love."

"Words, witch. Words, words, words."

"Not a witch, Cullen," said the old woman. "A priest. Or if you wish, a disciple, or an apostle. An acolyte, maybe. Or simply a witness. But not a witch."

"If you're going to annoy me with your prattle, woman, I'll call you what I want."

"Then this will be a very interesting relationship, Cullen."

"Goodbye, old woman," said Cullen.

"Goodbye? Oh, we're not done yet, Cullen. I'll see you tomorrow."

Cullen forced a smile at the departing old woman. Tomorrow and the next day, and the next, he would be too busy to lend this foolish old sack of wrinkles his ears. Cullen turned back to the sanctuary of his workshop.

Seven

The Roman ship drifted in the bay. The unblinking eye painted on the brow gazed unseeing at the mist-shrouded trees that edged the water.

Gaius scanned the shore. He was thinking about lessons. Specifically, he was remembering an old schoolteacher he used to have, a Greek bastard called Cyclops, so named because he had only one eye. He claimed Romans had burned it out when he was captured and none of those nine-year-old boys felt inclined to challenge him on it. Cyclops had driven home his writing lessons with numerous and vicious beatings. Get a word wrong, three slaps. Forget a line in a poem: ten slaps. Try to give him a cheeky answer: a punch across the face. When that year was over, Gaius and his friends were the most literate ten-year-olds in the city.

Lessons.

Reading and writing were important. But they weren't the lessons he was required to teach. How to be a Roman soldier, now *that* was a lesson worth learning, especially if one desired to continue breathing until one was old, and if one's idea of dying was in one's own bed, sleeping next to one's wife, or one's mistress, preferably after a bout of good, lustful sport.

He had planned to wait until nightfall before landing his soldiers and setting up camp, but his scouts had returned an hour ago, swearing that the bay was deserted and he was impatient to start, impatient to test his men, most of whom were assigned to him straight from training camp. He wanted them to get a taste of battle. He wanted them to experience the gut-wrenching blows of iron upon iron.

He wanted to put these boys under pressure.

His men feared him. Well, not his men, he thought. The experienced soldiers—what few he had—respected him. The boy soldiers feared him. And that was good. When they boarded his ship he had worked them hard, barking orders, standing over them as the orders were carried out, punishing every infraction, the more minor the better. He had gotten in their faces, screamed in their ears, unleashing his fury at every unpolished button or speck of rust on a sword. He pushed them hard every morning, exercising them on the deck of the ship. Two hours of punishing training. His son, Lucius, was among the soldiers. Eighteen years old, full of piss and vinegar. Not the brightest lad in the world, but smart enough to know that Gaius would cut him no slack in any duty, on ship or off. He did what he had to do as well as any man, and got cuffed roundly about the ears whenever he messed up.

He would ease up when these boys had proven themselves. That would happen soon, but not today. This was a smash-and-grab operation. The village they would attack today was a village of farmers and craftsmen. It was isolated and would be easy pickings for these raw recruits. The captives would be taken to Rome where they would be sold as slaves. It would be a warm-up for the time that they would have to deal with the savages from the north of this cold, wind-swept land. Thank the gods the Emperor had built that wall to keep those sub-humans back where they belonged. Gaius anticipated no resistance, and was vaguely annoyed. These virgins of his needed to be bloodied and capturing women and children wasn't going to give these boys a taste of what a real battle should be. It might even give them a false sense of how good they were.

Which was why he had been delighted to discover one of his men dozing off during the watch last night.

What he was going to do to this boy would make his old teacher, Cyclops, proud.

It had been a raw recruit named Otho, the son of a roman merchant who had a cobbler's shop in the *Argiletum* behind the forum in Rome.

Otho should have been scanning the horizon from the back of the ship, keeping watch, doing his bit to protect his fellow soldiers from a sneak attack. Instead, Otho had decided to close his eyes. Gaius believed him when he said he'd only drifted off for a moment, but the poor youngster didn't understand. Gaius had gone out on deck looking for one of his soldiers to make an example of, and Otho had handed him the opportunity with an innocence that Gaius was going to take advantage of, the way a lecher would deflower a beautiful virgin. He was going to make an example out of Otho in a manner that would make the rest of his men piss in their pants.

All the men were gathered on the deck. They stared at Otho whose wrists were bound with rope, which was tied to hastily rigged poles eight feet apart. Otho faced the men, and Gaius was pleased to see that he wasn't blubbering or shedding tears. Yet. So many of the young ones broke down before the first lash of the whip, but it looked like Otho wasn't one of them. Gaius wanted his men to watch Otho's punishment, and he wanted Otho to look his comrades in the eye as the flesh ripped from his back.

"This man," began Gaius, in a ringing voice, "was asleep at his post."

Everyone knew this. News of the whipping spread like wildfire through the ship.

"I won't bore you with tedious ruminations of how he let down himself, how he let down you, his comrades, how he let down his family, how he let down the entire Roman army. I'm just going to show you how I feel about it, and then I want you to think about how he should have done the job assigned to him."

Gaius turned to two young men standing behind Otho. One was a tall youth, standing an inch over six feet. He was bald, electing to shave his head instead of keeping it shorn an inch above the scalp. The other was four inches shorter, with bow-shaped legs bulging with muscles. His brown eyebrows were furrowed, and Gaius couldn't tell if this was the way he always looked or if his concentration on the task ahead was such that his body felt compelled to mirror his mind's anxiety. Sweat poured from their brows, though there was a definite chill in the air.

"These two men will lay it on thick. They're friends with young Otho, but they will put their backs into it, because if I suspect they're trying to hold back, they will take Otho's place between the posts. Let's hope they understand."

From the expressions on the two men's faces, it was clear that they understood all too well. The muscles in their arms jumped and quivered as if their bodies were eager to prove that they belonged with the whips in their hands, and not their wrists tied to the posts.

Gaius looked over his men.

"If you feel you have to look away, please do. I know it's hard to look upon a friend as he receives the lash. However, if you do look away, I'll have you flogged. If I see you blink, I'll have you flogged. So please, choose wisely."

Gaius found his son, Lucius, standing on the deck. He stood straight, eyes fixed on Otho. Gaius had the feeling that Lucius knew he was being watched, but no movement or glance betrayed him.

That's it, lad. You know, don't you? You know I would have no hesitation to put you up here. You know I would not flinch from laying the lash across your back, the back your mother loves so well. The back that came from my very loins. Yes, I would have you learn the lesson most of all, since my dearest wish is to see my future grandchildren. So keep staring ahead and learn this lesson better than anyone.

Not the most intelligent boy. But smart enough.

Gaius nodded to the two soldiers. The smaller one drew his arm back and it seemed to pause in the air, as if gathering strength, the way lightning will gather on the underside of a cloud before it sends down a bolt to scorch the earth. The arm descended in a blur, and not one man looking doubted that every bit of his strength was in the blow. Otho didn't scream. His back arched and every muscle in his body tensed. His mouth was open, but it sucked in air, the way an old man might suck in a dying breath. It seemed he hung in that devilish pose for an eternity as if posing for a Roman sculptor's vision of a demon from Hades. Finally Otho's muscles let go. He fell forward, clenching his teeth as he tried to stifle the scream. The sound emerging from his mouth was a high-pitched keening that became an involuntary bark as the second whip raked across his back. His eyes bulged, and again his muscles bunched up, as if trying to expel the sudden burst of agony. Snot dripped from his nose and spit spluttered between his teeth. His body had barely lost its rock-hard tension when the third blow fell. This time Otho vomited. The wind blew toward the soldiers and Gaius knew they would catch a whiff of the nauseating smell. It would linger in their memory long after the punishment was over. The fourth blow caused Otho to have a look in his eyes that told Gaius the boy thought he was in Hell.

Not even close, Otho, thought Gaius. You're strong. You won't faint until about forty lashes in. And what do you know about Hell, boy? Try fighting in the dense forests of Germany, where the battles could go on for hours, days, where no soldier in thousands would escape without some kind of wound. Try seeing your best friends cut down on either side of you, and as you wonder how you still lived while their blood fed the fetid Germanic soil, knowing that you must fight on because ahead of you were demons made flesh, their eyes wild, their bodies painted in evil, ancient symbols, their voices uttering cries more suited to animals than men. And in their hands they yielded swords, spears and axes. They'd fall upon the Roman lines, hacking and slicing, stepping over each other the way wild dogs would chase a wounded deer. And all you could do was keep thrusting your sword forward, keep raising your shield above your head even though your muscles had failed hours ago, even though the last ounce of your strength had disappeared so long before it seemed like a previous existence.

That was Hell.

What Otho was going through was merely an appetizer, a taste of Hell sucked off the end of a finger.

He should flog all these bastards.

They knew nothing.

Otho lasted twenty two lashes before his body slumped down, his arms taking all his weight, hanging above his shoulders as if flying through the air like a great, wounded bird. He was still conscious, barely so. The two soldiers, dripping sweat, looked over at Gaius who raised his eyebrows.

"Did I order you to stop?"

Eight

Rhiannon watched Aisling as the one-year-old stirred in her sleep. She laid a hand on her cheek and felt the plump, warm skin twitch. She pulled the rabbit fur cover up to Aisling's chin. If her daughter slept for a few hours Rhiannon could bake some bread for tonight's dinner. She should go now; she should start kneading the dough. She should stoke the fire in the oven, but that would mean tearing her gaze away from her baby. *Let this one live,* she prayed. *Let this one grow to be a woman who would love and laugh and have many beautiful children. Don't take her from me. Not again.*

As always, when she watched her baby, the memories returned.

Grainne.

That winter, eight years ago, had thrown sleet and snow upon the earth, bringing a cold so bitter that her daughter caught a fever, crushing her in its insidious grip.

Cullen dug her grave under an oak tree. While Rhiannon cried for weeks, no tears passed Cullen's eyes. They remained dry and cold, as if tears were too ordinary to express the emptiness he felt inside. No, not emptiness, thought Rhiannon. Anger. Rage. Fury. Rhiannon tried to reach out to him, but Cullen grew distant. He started leading the warriors on more raids, not just on Romans but on other villages. They always returned with food, weapons and slaves, and each time he returned from a raid, his eyes lost a little more of their humanity.

But hope returned. She was pregnant again. Her belly swelled so much she suspected there was more than one baby inside her. When she gave birth to twin girls she felt sure that Cullen would find his way back to her. But her twins died before she'd stopped bleeding from their birth. She had barely decided on their names—Edra and Fern—before their lives blinked out like candles. They couldn't suckle, and their lips were unable to latch onto her nipples, no matter how many hours she coaxed them. They lost weight, they grew listless and they died. Rhiannon's swollen breasts mocked her, and they leaked milk for a month after the girls were buried.

Cullen buried the twins beside Grainne, but Rhiannon knew he had never fallen in love with the girls. He'd given his heart to Grainne and she was taken away from him. He'd learned his lesson.

So had she.

She left the tribe one night in spring, traveling north, taking Finn, and a mule carrying clothes, tools and food. She traveled for three days before Cullen caught up. He had doubled ahead of them, and was waiting at the far end of a wooded valley. He sat astride his horse, staring at her. She imagined he was daring her to run, but she knew that would be futile. How could you run from an elemental force of nature like Cullen?

The mare he was riding started to walk off as Rhiannon approached, but Cullen reined her back. The mare shook her head in protest, but did not move again.

Cullen and Rhiannon stared at each other for a long time.

"Where are you going?" he asked finally.

"North."

He nodded, and looked at Finn, who sat on the mule, huddled under some blankets.

"It's cold up north," said Cullen.

"It is cold," agreed Rhiannon.

Cullen jutted his chin at Finn.

"Boy needs a father."

"Maybe I'll find one where we're going."

34

It was a cruel answer, and something flashed across Cullen's face. It was a look Rhiannon hadn't seen in a long time. It was hurt. It was anguish.

Cullen laid a hand on the horse's mane. The mare stamped her feet again. He stroked her slowly, calming her.

"If you'd asked me, I would have come."

Rhiannon shook her head, her eyes never leaving Cullen.

"No, I don't think you would have."

Cullen shrugged, acknowledging that she was right. He rubbed his hand over the three-day growth of beard.

"Since she died..." Cullen paused, as if tasting the words as they came out of his mouth.

"Since she died, since Grainne died...I have been in a kind of fever. A madness."

Cullen's voice drifted away as he turned his hands over, studying them.

"Then I came home and you were gone. And the madness went away. Like a mist. I knew you had done the right thing by leaving me."

He dismounted, holding the reins of the horse in his hands.

"If you'd have me, I'd go with you."

Rhiannon kept as rigid a face as she could. She had wanted Cullen to say these words to her, but was it too late?

"Grainne was a beautiful girl, wasn't she, Cullen."

Cullen lowered his head and didn't speak for the longest time. Then she heard a simple:

"Aye."

"Edra and Fern were beautiful too, Cullen," said Rhiannon, still heartbroken over Cullen's rejection of his twin girls. Cullen raised his head, and Rhiannon was startled to see a look on his face that she'd never seen before. It took her a moment to realize what it was.

Shame.

"Forgive me," he said.

Rhiannon glanced over to Finn, who stared at his father through the small opening in the blanket wrapped around him.

"Suppose I told you to go, to leave us alone," said Rhiannon, turning back to Cullen. "Would the madness return?"

Cullen's mouth twisted in an awkward grin, the muscles in his face almost hesitant, as if they were unused to forming such an expression.

"I'd just keep following you until you said yes."

Rhiannon forced herself not to smile back.

"Where we're going," she said, "I don't plan on living by thievery and killing. I want a nice place, where the people farm the land."

Cullen merely nodded, saying nothing.

"I want my husband to be a fine man, respected by his people."

"I can fashion ploughs and swords. Every town needs a smith."

Rhiannon placed a hand around Finn's shoulders.

"I need Finn's father to be a father to him."

Rhiannon almost felt her voice crack as she spoke, but she bit it back. Cullen glanced at Finn.

"Show your face, boy."

Finn pulled back the blanket, revealing his untidy hair and grime-streaked face. His green eyes danced in the early morning mist as he and his father stared each other down.

Cullen shook his head.

"I don't know," he said, gesturing to Finn. "The boy barely speaks. What does he have to say that I'd want to hear?"

Rhiannon almost sputtered in shock.

"What does he have to say? He's—"

"And once you start talking to them, they'll want to be carried on your shoulders, and thrown up in the air." Rhiannon's shoulders relaxed as she realized what Cullen was doing.

"And once you give them shoulder rides, they'll want to play chasing and go swimming and they'll make you climb trees…no, Finn wouldn't like that."

Cullen looked at Finn who burst into tears.

Cullen looked at his son in surprise. This was not the reaction he expected. Didn't Finn know he was joking? He looked to Rhiannon to help him, but she only looked back at him in exasperation. With no help coming from his wife, Cullen had to do something quickly. He stepped forward and swept Finn up in his arms and brought him to the level of his face.

"Maybe I'm wrong. Maybe it's exactly what Finn would like. Would you like that Finn? Shoulder rides, hunting rabbits and climbing trees?"

Finn nodded, hiding his eyes behind his forearm.

"Then let's do it."

He swung Finn upside down and onto his shoulders, the movement so sudden and unexpected that Finn's tears stopped before he knew where he was. He grasped hold of Cullen's hair and stared around him, exploring this new perspective on the world. Cullen turned to Rhiannon.

"Ready, wife?"

Rhiannon wanted to slap him, kiss him, punch him and love him. After a moment she figured there would be time enough to do all those things—and more. She nodded.

"Ready. . . husband."

Rhiannon eased the memories from her head and stepped outside the hut. The sun was beginning to lose some of its strength as it dropped toward the horizon.

She heard shouts in the distance and recognized Finn and Godwin's voices as they yelled at the crows to keep out of the fields. Rhiannon paused. The children's voices rang with an urgency that wasn't normal. She stepped around the hut.

The two eleven-year olds ran along the dusty road faster than she had ever seen them run before. Somehow, despite their full sprint, the boys managed to keep yelling one word.

Romans.

She raised her eyes to the hill that stood half a mile up the road. What she saw made her blood run cold. An army of Roman soldiers descended toward her village at a fast run. She stood watching them, her mouth open. She wanted to run, but her legs were rooted to the ground. There were so many of them. And they were silent. Why weren't they making any noise? Why—?

Someone grabbed her arm and spun her around. She found herself looking into Finn's panicked face.

"Mama, run!"

He dragged her backward, and finally she started thinking again.

"Aisling."

"I'll get her. Run to the forest!"

Finn ducked into their hut and reappeared seconds later holding Aisling, who looked around at the now-screaming villagers, her eyes open in confusion. Rhiannon snatched Aisling away from Finn. The rest of the villagers joined them in a flat-out run. Finn had an iron grip on her wrist as he led her weaving through the slower runners. There was a forest a mile away, a forest whose trees trunks and branches went on forever. If they could reach the forest with its dense clusters of oaks and horse chestnuts and its stifling canopy the Romans would never catch them.

"Don't slow down, mama!" he yelled at her. Rhiannon picked up her pace. She was starting to breathe hard now, as her feet pounded along the dirt road.

"Let me carry Aisling," said Finn.

"Just run," replied Rhiannon. "Just keep running."

Ahead of them was Morcar, swinging his stumps forward, reaching forward with his arms, and swinging forward again.

"Fucking Romans," he yelled, as he moved forward. He stopped and reached out a hand to one of the villagers. "Pick me up. Pick me up," he screamed, and "Fuck you!" when the villagers ran by him. Morcar swiveled in a circle, eyes darting around. "Pick me up, you bastards!" Cathal the Potter ran up to him. Almost without breaking stride, he lifted Morcar up onto his back and continued running, breath wheezing through his lungs.

"Run, you prick," yelled Morcar, slapping his fists on Cathal's head. "Run, run, run."

Rhiannon felt as if the pounding feet below her belonged to someone else. Only the lungs screaming in her chest seemed hers, and they burned with each breath she took. Why did the forest seem as far away as ever?

Suddenly, one of the villagers in front of them yelled in alarm. It was young Nell, the daughter of Brendel, the village leader. Nell crashed into a heavy-set man and they both went down in a heap.

Rhiannon looked toward the forest.

More Romans, maybe fifty of them, were lined across the open field, blocking their path to the forest.

A fear spread in her stomach colder than any she had ever known. Some of the villagers turned and ran blindly toward the river that meandered beside the village. If they could swim across to the far side, they may escape these Romans. For one delirious moment Rhiannon's panic sent her a surge of strength. They could swim away from these invaders. And if they couldn't get across the river, how much sweeter to die there than be caught by these monsters?

But the Romans were upon them. Soldiers, whose armor flashed in the sunlight, wove through the fleeing Britons, knocking them off their feet. One of the soldiers grabbed Finn by his wrist and flung him to the ground.

"Bastard!" screamed Rhiannon.

Finn skidded along the dirt, grunting in pain. Rhiannon ran to him, clutching Aisling to her breast as she did so. She tried to help him up but from the corner of her eyes she saw a fist descending and her back exploded in pain. A body slammed into her. It was Cathal the Potter, the man who had picked up Morcar moments ago. She heard a thin scream. Morcar had gone flying off Cathal's back, and now tumbled on the ground in front of them, slamming into the feet of a Roman soldier, knocking him to the ground. Morcar, his stumps waving wildly in the air, heaved himself onto the back of the soldier and started pummeling him. "Roman fucks!" yelled Morcar. Bloody spittle flew from his mouth into the face of the soldier.

Rhiannon felt Cathal behind her as he tried to scramble to his feet. Blood streamed from his nose as he opened his mouth to scream. One of his teeth hung from his gums by a thin thread. For one unreal moment, Rhiannon wanted to grasp the tooth and break it off. Then a knee slammed into the back of her head as another villager tumbled over her. Siric, Gretel's husband. He yelled the same word over and over: "No. No. No!"

Aisling was screaming and Rhiannon had just enough strength left to cradle her head to her chest, not wanting to see the pain on her face, the terror in her eyes. If they were to die now, she wanted their deaths to be quick.

She brought Finn's head close to her and she prayed to her new God.

Nine

Cullen held the finished sword up to the waning light of the sun. His critical eye studied the edge from the hilt to the point. It was sharp. If used by someone who could fight it would be formidable. He glanced up at the setting sun, orange red in the fading sky. Clouds tinged with purple signaled the coming of the night.

What was happening to his family? Finn had turned from an exuberant boy to a sullen young man. Were all eleven-year-old boys like this? Is this the way they found their own way in the world, by testing the limits of what their parents told them to do?

Cullen's head hurt. His head never hurt when he had been a warrior, when life and death hung in the balance every day. But now, dealing with this domestic strife, his temples throbbed.

Bollocks. If his warriors could see him now. He was more domesticated than the goats that grazed inside their village.

He put on his belt, grabbed his spear, stepped out of the hut and started on the trek home.

He walked along a path that took him through the forest. Massive oaks grew skyward on either side, their trunks glowing red in the rays of the setting sun.

His stomach growled. Maybe Rhiannon had cooked something and it would be waiting for him when he got home. Bread, she said she was going to bake bread. And they had cheese left over from yesterday's meal. And they had that roasted pig—now that was something to look forward to. So bread, cheese and a ham hock. That was a meal. Wash it down with elderberry tea and chew on apples before going to sleep.

He looked up. He walked out of the woods wondering why there was a growing feeling of unease in the pit of his stomach. There was a curious stillness in the air. Elric the Farmer usually tilled his field until the last light of the sun faded from the sky, but Elric was nowhere to be seen. Cullen frowned. Maybe it was later than he realized. Maybe there had been a meeting in the village—no, Rhiannon would have reminded him of it. The village was still a couple of miles away and he let his gaze drift over the fields nearby.

The crows were eating the wheat stalks.

Something was wrong. And as that thought burned through his brain, someone came crashing through the wheat field toward him. In one swift motion he dropped to his knees, withdrew the dagger from his belt and rolled away from the path. He held his spear pointing at waist level, ready to kill.

A small body stumbled and fell out of the rows of stalks, landing heavily on the rutted pathway. It was Godwin, Finn's friend. His clothes were torn, and dried blood caked his face. His eyes shone with the wild, feral look of an animal. Dried spittle flecked his mouth and his chest heaved with ragged breaths.

Cullen dropped his spear and sheathed his dagger. He ran to Godwin and gently raised the boy into a sitting position. The boy looked at Cullen, relief flooding the young child's face.

"I knew...knew they hadn't got you."

Cullen clutched Godwin's shoulders tightly.

"Who? What happened?"

"They took them all. I ran...I got away."

"Godwin, who took them?"

"Romans. Romans took them all."

Cullen felt the blood drain from his face. He forced himself to ask the next question.

"They took my family?"

Godwin nodded.

"Did they kill anyone?"

Godwin suddenly turned away and vomited on the ground. Cullen cradled the boy's head as the contents of his stomach emptied. When the boy had finished dry heaving, Cullen sat the boy up.

"Elric is dead. He tried to fight. They put a spear in his gut. Everyone else, they've taken to the sea. I followed them for a bit. They're all in ropes. They're going to take them away. I didn't see you."

Godwin heaved air into his lungs. His hands grasped Cullen's shirt. Cullen squeezed his eyes shut as the blood pounded through his temples. He sank down to a sitting position, staring at the exhausted boy lying before him. If the Romans had his family, he would never see them again. No, he cursed himself. No, don't think like that. Think clearly. Find out exactly what happened.

"When did the Romans take them?" he asked Godwin.

"I don't know…I don't know," whimpered the boy. Godwin seemed to be on the verge of falling asleep now that he had found Cullen. Cullen reached over and slapped his face. Godwin startled awake.

"Point to where the sun was in the sky when the Romans took them," he said. Godwin blinked, then pointed his finger halfway between noon and sunset.

Four hours, thought Cullen. Four hours ago and he wasn't here to protect them. No, he said to himself, pushing the thoughts away. Find out what happened. Get the information you need.

"How many Romans were there?" Again, the boy shrugged helplessly.

"More than the crows in the field?"

Godwin turned to stare at the birds feasting on the unprotected wheat seeds. He nodded slowly.

"More. Lots more," he said.

So maybe one hundred or one hundred and fifty Romans took the entire village four hours ago.

"They went to the sea. Where? Which bay did they go to?"

"Near the Stone bear."

Cullen nodded. He got to his feet.

Cullen stared into the distance. A cold anger seeped through his body, spreading from his heart, flowing into every artery and vein, every pore. It was a rage he thought he would never feel again, because those days were behind him, those times of killing and murder and slaughter now only touched his life in the darkest of nightmares. His life with Rhiannon had taken him away from the charnel house that had been his existence. She had borne him five children, two of which still lived, and he had become a blacksmith. His life was normal. The only problems he had these days were domestic ones. He had not solved a problem with his sword since those Scottish raiders. Disputes were settled by talking, by endless talking and arguing and accusations and decisions and finally handshakes. No blood was spilled anymore.

But cold anger had found a home in the very atoms that made him the man he was. Its tendrils oozed through his sinews, pale fingers winding into his very core.

He picked up his spear and started to walk toward the coast, feeling the last five years of normal living fall away with each step. He had to save his family. It was that simple. And the Romans wouldn't give them back, so he'd have to take them back. But one warrior against one hundred and fifty Romans? If he went in there alone, he stood no chance of coming out alive.

So he was already dead.

And a dead man has nothing to lose.

He started to run.

Ten

It was five miles to the coast near the out-cropping of rock they called the Stone Bear. He cursed his feet: they seemed to cover the ground at a snail's pace. He cursed the Romans, all butchery, slavery and swords. He cursed himself, for building his workshop three miles from the village, wanting the isolation it brought, but telling himself and the villagers it was because he needed to be near the ore held in the mountains.

He came upon Ruane lying face up, the ground around his stomach dark with blood. Cullen saw the wound, a big tear that cut through the man's shirt and ripped open his insides. He had been killed as the Romans marched the prisoners to the coast. Cullen saw he had a deep gash in his heel. Ruane would have been forced to walk with the rest of the villagers while his heel caused him unbearable agony. He would have come to a point when the pain was too much. The Romans showed him no mercy. They killed Ruane, sending a message to the others that they had better keep up.

He ran on, breath steaming from his mouth in measured wisps of vapor. His eyes scanned the road as he ran. Footsteps, many footsteps, smudged the path. Grass on either side of the path was smashed, trampled by feet. A light rain started to fall.

He saw something up ahead, a shadow in the distance, small, about the size of a child. Cullen had the sudden notion that it was a *Bean Si*, a Hibernian spirit that would appear when someone died, to sing at their funeral. A chill ran down his spine until the shape solidified into someone that he knew well.

"Morcar," hissed Cullen.

"Fuck you, Irish," said Morcar, his voice hoarse with exhaustion.

A dagger dangled from a rope around Morcar's neck.

"Is my family alive?" asked Cullen.

"Last I saw," said Morcar, turning to Cullen, but not stopping.

Cullen caught up with Morcar and matched his pace.

"How many?"

"A hundred. More, maybe. Pricks all of them."

"Go home, Morcar. You'll get yourself killed."

"What home, Irish?"

Cullen didn't turn around as he ran past Morcar, but he sensed the crippled man has stopped moving and had lain down on the path, completely spent.

Cullen ran the rest of the way. By the time he got to the stone bear it was night. There was a fingernail moon in the sky.

Cullen climbed a hill. Below lay the field where the Romans had set up camp. He crawled forward, his eyes and ears alert to the signs of Roman guards. The grass was damp beneath him. Even though the recent rains had softened all the grass and twigs he was careful not to place his limbs on anything that might snap and give him away.

About twenty tents were set up in parallel rows on the field. Roman soldiers milled about, most having discarded their uniforms and armor now that their day's work was done, and strolled around in loose tunics. Some sat around fires that dotted the edges of their camp. Freshly killed boar turned on spits above some of the fires. He heard one group of Romans laugh as a soldier tried to strip some outer meat off one of the sizzling animals and got burned for his trouble.

Cullen's gaze fell on the prisoners and a glimmer of hope kindled in his heart. They were in a holding pen on the edge of the campsite, their hands bound with rope. All were huddled together, their faces peering out at the guards that stood nearby. Mother Miriam, her white hair lit by the light from one of the fires, sat with her hands tied behind her back. She talked quietly to some of the villagers.

He saw Rhiannon, squeezed into the corner of the holding pen, an arm around each of her children. His chest tightened, as if an invisible, malicious hand was strangling the life from it. Hot tears of fury threatened to spring from his eyes but he forced them back. There would be no crying while his family was enslaved. Let his eyes burn, but until they were free, his anger would be cold as ice.

Cullen let his gaze wander along the path to the holding pen. Between him and the prisoners were three guards. One was standing next to the villagers, his head casually scanning the darkened country beyond the fire. In his hands was a piece of wood that he whittled with a small knife. Every minute or so he'd raise his head and see if any shadows appeared where no shadows had been before, but his look betrayed no suspicion.

Twenty yards up the pathway from the whittling guard stood a legionary with a spear. He faced the pitch-black countryside, staring into its abyss. This one, while not at full alert, would present the biggest problem, because to get to him, Cullen would have to cross at least thirty yards of almost open flatland, with nothing to conceal him.

But before Cullen could even think about the legionary, he'd have to deal with the one closest to him: a hulk of a man sitting on the trunk of a fallen tree. His chest was so big that the cloak that protected him from the cold made him seem like a small hill rather than a man. His helmet lay on the tree trunk he sat on, revealing a head shorn of hair, its bald dome reflecting the light of the distant campfires. A spear was propped against the tree, held steady in the cleft of a branch. He sipped from a cup of wine and chewed on a piece of bread.

Good, thought Cullen, if this bastard drinks enough wine it would make killing him a lot easier.

Cullen studied the sight-lines of the guards. They had made the mistake of not being clearly visible to each other. This closest guard was screened from the other two by a low copse of young Oak trees.

Arrogant bastards, thought Cullen. *You thought you got the whole village.*

You missed one.

Distant laughter broke out from the camp, and the guard closest to Cullen glanced up from his wine goblet and looked down at his fellow soldiers, some of whom were slicing meat off a roasting pig. The guard looked down again, tearing off a large chunk of bread with his teeth.

Cullen moved down the hill toward the guard. The grass beneath his feet was wet from recently fallen rain. Twigs that might have snapped if they were dry instead bent silently under Cullen's weight. Sodden leaves soaked up the sound of his feet as he eased down the hill, his body low, eyes trained on the guard like a hawk. He kept to the shadows, hiding behind bushes and scrubs.

The darkness was his friend.

He had to cross forty yards, the first thirty of which had an abundance of cover. The last ten was open; the tallest plant between Cullen and the guard would be a ten-inch stalk of grass. This guard had the look of a veteran, and veterans don't stay alive by accident. This man would be good at his job, so Cullen would have to be better.

He reached the edge of the last bush between him and the Roman. He stayed still, breathing shallowly, trying to get a feel of the guard's senses. Was he suddenly a tiny bit more aware? Did he sense something was wrong? Cullen could detect no change in the man's demeanor. Time to go.

Cullen stepped out from behind the bush, his sword held in his hand like a dagger, the blade pointing directly at the guard. He took another step, his foot sinking into the damp ground noiselessly. Cullen kept his body low, both to keep his center close to the ground, and to hide his silhouette from other prying eyes. Eight paces away. Another step, seven paces. Every nerve ending in Cullen's body was focused on the guard, watching for the least change in his attitude. The slightest head tilt, the tiniest muscle twitch might signal that the guard sensed something was wrong. If he turned now Cullen would be found out because Cullen would not be able to get to him before he raised the alarm.

The guard slurped loudly from his cup, draining his wine. Cullen took two quick, silent steps and froze. The bald guard turned to his left and shouted something at his comrade down the hill. The other guard gave a short guttural laugh. He shouted something back, and the man close to

Cullen rubbed a hand over his bald head and spat forward, muttering to himself. Cullen let himself breathe again. Small, shallow breaths. He was almost at a place where he could rush the guard if he had to. Two steps closer would be better. Three steps if the Gods were generous. Four and the Roman would be dead in his hell before he could blink.

The guard belched loudly and Cullen stepped closer, once, twice. Almost there. The guard was a mere body length ahead of him.

The Roman turned around, looking Cullen directly in the eye.

It took the guard less than half a second to realize something was wrong. In an instant he had opened his mouth to scream out a warning and then all he knew was blackness.

As soon as the guard turned, Cullen drove forward with a ferocity born of hate and fury. The guard was better—way better—than Cullen could have imagined. He didn't go for his sword because he recognized his death was inevitable but he could warn his fellow Romans and had drawn the breath into his lungs to yell when Cullen plunged the sword straight down his neck, down to the hilt, at the same time clamping a hand around the man's mouth, stopping the gasp that threatened to escape.

Cullen felt the body jerk under him and he held it tightly so that the tell-tale thump of it hitting the ground would stay absent from this frigid night air. Cullen pushed the blade back and forth, severing arteries, scrambling the innards of the man's throat, desperate that this man should die quickly. The guard's fingers flexed uselessly. Cullen withdrew his sword halfway, and plunged it back down, changing the angle as he did so. The guard slumped, dead as meat.

Cullen's eyes fixed on the shape of the other guard, thirty yards down the path, waiting to see if he had noticed anything, but the second guard's body was relaxed. He had heard nothing.

Cullen pulled the dead man over the trunk of the tree and laid him down. Wrapping the dead man's cloak around him, he grabbed the guard's spear and crept over to the copse that hid him from the eyes of the other guards. He couldn't sneak up on the next Roman unseen, so he'd have to make the Roman come to him. Cullen was big, but the dead Roman was taller and wider. And Cullen had a full head of red hair, while this corpse was bald. But the cloak had a hood and there was no choice. He'd have to make this happen now. What was it that they had shouted to each other moments ago? Something about the cold? Or food? Or women? Cullen knew Latin but their words had been guttural, and in an accent that made it hard for Cullen to decipher what they had said.

He drew in a deep breath and let out a string of curses in Latin, trying best to mimic the accent of the dead guard. He stopped, waiting.

"What's happening?" called the guard on the pathway.

"There's a kid in the trees," replied Cullen. "He just threw a rock at me."

"Flavius?"

The guard was suspicious. Not dangerously so. But suspicious.

"The little bastard cut me," mumbled Cullen. He had pulled the hood of the cloak completely over his head. From the corner of his eye, Cullen saw the guard move toward him.

"Should I call down?"

"Sure, call the centurion," replied Cullen, sarcastically. "He'll be happy to know that you can't catch one of their brats by yourself."

In reply, the guard cursed Cullen good-naturedly. As the roman rounded the bushes, Cullen pointed vigorously with the spear to a large tree.

"There he is, you see him?"

The guard was staring at Cullen. He was younger than the first guard and had less of the instincts that had kept that guard alive for so long. One glance at Cullen should have told him something was wrong. But he took a few more steps forward, distracted by Cullen's rapid speech and the shaking of the spear.

"Flavius, what–?"

Cullen spun, ramming his sword into the throat of the Roman in a move so swift and fierce that the sword drove right through the spinal cord of the guard. Death was instantaneous. The guard fell onto the wet grass, the sword embedded in his neck. Cullen reached for the guard's helmet and fastened it on to his own head. He was acting on his plan as it was forming in his mind. No time to think, just let the plan happen, let it flow. If he stopped and thought about all the things he had done and was about to do, he'd drop these Roman clothes, turn and run as far away as he could, leaving his family to the whims and rages of these savages. But running was the least of his options. Guard number three. That was all he had to think about. Swift actions. Unexpected actions.

Cullen stepped around the bush. He kept his head looking at the ground, and in his peripheral vision saw the whittling guard glance up at him. Cullen strode to the spot where the guard had been standing all night, and stopped there, leaning on his spear in the same casually alert manner. He forced himself to scan the forest just like the recently dead legionary had done. Finally he risked a look at the third guard who had, Cullen noted with relief, gone back to carving. He breathed out, and waited another few minutes. He turned and walked down the hill to the holding pen. The guard still leaned against the wooden fence, unconcerned that any of the prisoners would attack him. They were all bound together with rope, where could they go?

Cullen strolled toward him, and when the guard glanced up, Cullen made a show of pulling his cloak around him as if he were cold.

"What are you doing?" asked the Roman, squinting through the darkness.

"Taking a piss," replied Cullen.

"Take a piss in your own damn place," snarled the guard.

"Fuck you," said Cullen walking on. The guard frowned, more in anger than suspicion. Cullen had the spear in his left hand, his favored hand. Fifteen paces away. The guard stood up, feet apart, as if spoiling for a fight. "Did you hear what I said, idiot, take a piss in your—"

Cullen hefted the spear up and the man stopped talking, his face blank in bewilderment. Cullen hurled the spear through the air, and it flew straight at the guard, burying itself in the Roman's chest. He crashed back against the fence and slid to the ground, clasping the shaft of the spear in both hands, his mouth opening and closing as he gasped for breath that would never enter his lungs again.

Cullen ran forward. The danger now was not from the guards raising the alarm, it was from the prisoners yelling in fright, or calling out his name if they saw him. Already he heard voices in the holding pen, frightened voices, questioning what had happened. Maybe they had been asleep and if they saw the dead guard they might scream or call out. He had to shut them up now. He ran to the fence, whispering fiercely to the villagers.

"It's Cullen. It's me. Keep your mouths shut or I will slit your throats. Anyone breathes loudly now and I will end you." Cullen bent low and stepped through the middle gap in the fence. He placed his feet carefully, not wanting to stand on an errant hand, whose owner might raise a cry of pain. "It's me. It's Cullen," he repeated, and issued a string of other threats, promising to sever heads from necks to those who didn't have the sense to remain silent. Around him he saw people waking up, and their friends clamping hands over their mouths to prevent any involuntary cries of joy. He crossed over to Rhiannon, who had each of her children's mouths covered with her hands. Cullen grabbed on to her and hugged her tightly. She kissed him feverishly on the neck, her eyes and cheeks awash in tears. Cullen took Aisling into his arms and grabbed Finn, bringing him close to his chest. They hugged him back, their actions hampered by the ropes that bound them.

"Come on, boy, show me your wrists."

Finn held out his hands and Cullen cut the binding ropes through with one swift motion.

"Legs too," said Finn, and Cullen brought the sword down, severing the rope.

Cullen drew a knife from his belt and gave it to Finn.

"Start cutting," he told his son. Finn started slicing through the ropes that bound his mother.

Cullen picked his way among the prisoners, slicing ropes, severing bonds. He cut through the ropes that held Mother Miriam. The old woman looked at Cullen with an intensity that made Cullen feel uncomfortable.

Those that he freed massaged their chafed arms and legs, then crept to the side of the fence away from the Roman camp.

"Run north. Hide in the forest. Spread out, but keep going north." Once Rhiannon was free of her bonds he handed his sword to one of the villagers who continued cutting through the ropes. Cullen pulled her and Finn over to the fence.

"Take them, Rhiannon. Take them north. Go."

"I'll stay with you, papa, I'll help,"

Mother Miriam's wrinkled hand touched Finn's shoulder.

"You need to take your mother away from here, young man," she said. "I'll help your father."

Cullen nodded to the old woman, who took the knife from Finn. She started cutting through the bonds of the closest villager.

"Go, Finn," hissed Cullen, "Go with your mother," Cullen noted the hurt look in Finn's eyes but the boy turned around and led his mother over to the fence. Already Cullen could see villagers disappearing into the darkness. If they could just have one more minute, then everyone would have a chance to get away. His heart leapt to see Rhiannon outside the fence running away to the forest. He bent down and cut ropes from one of the women of the village.

A spear cut through the air over his head, skimming the top of his hair. It buried itself into the back of Cathal the Potter who had thrown aside his ropes and stood up to run. Cathal fell face first onto the ground.

"They see us!"

A woman screamed and, like a spirit released from Hades, noises filled the night—shouts, screams, curses—and Cullen knew that their time had run out. A quick look to his left showed a score of Roman troops running for the fence. A look to his right confirmed his worst fear. Romans on that side too, and they had seen the escaping villagers and were pursuing them into the forest. Cullen ran over to Cathal, the dying villager, and pulled the spear out from his back. Cathal let out a low moan of protest, then slumped, dead. Another spear *thunked* into a wooden post beside him. He yanked that out.

Cullen dived through the gap in the fence, a spear in each hand. The villagers who had not been released screamed at him to come back and free them. They cursed his cowardice. They begged him to save them from the Romans. Cullen ignored them. He had tried to free them but that door had closed. Now he had to save his family. They didn't need much time; maybe thirty seconds, before the darkness swallowed them up and pursuit would be pointless and dangerous. He didn't have to stop the Romans, he just had to trip them up, make them think twice.

"Run!" he yelled.

Cullen rolled up from the ground with his left arm stretched back. He let loose. The spear blurred through the air, striking a Roman who ran full tilt into the deadly weapon. The Roman staggered back as if an invisible hammer had slammed into his chest. His flailing arms caught two of his companions in the face and all three of the fell down. All the soldiers turned to Cullen, just in time to see him raise his other spear. This one Cullen hurled low. It struck one of the soldiers in his thigh and exploded out the other side, dragging viscera. As the downed man started screaming in agony, Cullen was on the move, sword in hand.

He ran for the group of soldiers, desperate to get in close, where spears would be useless. Out here, twenty paces away, he was vulnerable. Face to face, he could do these bastards some damage. He prayed to the Gods that Rhiannon, Aisling and Finn were flying through the darkness, their feet skimming the ground, fear and desperation giving them the impetus to run all night.

He slammed into the first roman, his forearm knocking the man back. Twisting around, he swung his sword in a short arc. He wanted to go for their faces. He felt his sword bite into flesh. Cullen ducked low; saw a sword coming for him. He twisted aside, grabbed the soldier's wrist and sliced down, cutting through bone and gristle. Not enough to cut the wrist off, but more than enough for the Roman to release the sword. As Cullen grabbed the sword before it hit the ground, he stabbed behind him indiscriminately. He didn't have much time before one of them rammed a sword into his gut and he wanted to take as many of them with him before they got him. He twirled around, both swords slicing through the air. But these soldiers were good, trained by tough, hardened warriors to become tough, hardened warriors. They reeled back, avoiding his sword.

Something slammed into his back, propelling him forward. He crashed to the ground, tried to roll but a fist slammed into his face. He tried to jerk his swords up, but Roman feet stepped on them. Cullen shook off the pain, let go of the swords and grabbed the wrist of the man who had hit him. He bent it back and heard bones crack.

He tried to get up but another Roman fell on him, screaming into his face. Cullen drew his head back and hammered his forehead into the man's face. The soldier recoiled, his nose fountaining blood. But the Romans had found their balance and the pummeling began. Fists punched and legs kicked Cullen. He tried to wrench away but the Romans were all around him now, directing their fury onto him. Cullen fell to the ground, curling up into a fetal position, waiting for the sword thrust that would end his life. His last thoughts before he lost consciousness were of his family running through the forest with wings of Mercury on their feet.

Eleven

He jerked back to consciousness, spluttering. A bucket of ice-cold water had been thrown over his head. He was aware of pain scything through his body like a knife. His head throbbed, his ribs ached and he felt blood over his forearms.

Someone grabbed him and pulled him into a sitting position. He forced his eyes open.

The first person he saw caused his heart to plummet. Rhiannon. She sat with the rest of the re-captured prisoners, huddled in a circle, around which stood about thirty Roman soldiers. Finn and Aisling were pulled tight to her and they watched with red-rimmed eyes as Cullen shook himself awake.

They didn't make it.

He had almost done what should have been impossible. Hadn't they disappeared into the forest? They should have been safe. The position he had put his family in now was immeasurably worse that it had been before. How many guards had he killed? Three at least. Four, five? Not only would they kill him now but they would probably take the lives of half the villagers. He held Rhiannon's eyes and she looked pleadingly at him. But there was nothing he could do for them now. Undoubtedly, the Romans had let him live just so they could kill him slowly. And the villagers would be forced to watch his death as a warning to them, a foretaste of what would happen to them if they attempted escape again.

There was a slow *clap-clap-clap* sound to his right. He looked over to see four dead bodies laid out in a row, the corpses of the soldiers he'd killed. Their faces were uncovered and their eyes were open in death. Standing over them was a tall, dark-haired Roman, whose bushy eyebrows hung low over black eyes that bored in Cullen. The hint of a smile on the man's face did nothing to lessen his look of menace. His hands clapped in a slow, sarcastic rhythm. When everyone's attention was focused on him, the Roman let his hands fall to his side. He was as tall as Cullen, with muscles and sinews that stood out like rope cords on his skin.

"I have known Flavius for five years," he said, "One of the best soldiers who's ever served under me. And here he lies, his spirit wandering the fields of Elysium, wondering what in Jupiter's name just happened." He grabbed a spear from a nearby soldier and prodded the next corpse.

"This one was called Theodosius, I seem to remember his father owning a farm near the coast. Won't we have a surprise for him when we get home? Dear Father of Theodosius, your son was an idiot, an incompetent, whose ineptness killed him."

He walked to the next dead soldier, the whittler, his tunic stained dark with blood.

"This one was a Gaul. As I recall he was pressed into service with some reluctance on his part. He was barely worthy of being called a Roman soldier. His death is not a surprise. And this one," He pointed to the Roman that had been running to catch the fugitives and received a spear in his chest for his troubles, "I never knew. But he was leading the runners, he was first into battle and for that we should honor him. I want you to look," he continued, talking to his men in a booming voice, "I want you to look at these dead men. I want you to burn every wound on their bodies into your brains. They weren't killed by an army. It wasn't a band of renegades that cut them down." He looked at Cullen, gesturing to him with the spear. "It was this man. By himself. He embarrassed the entire Roman army, he made a mockery of the Roman character and he made you all look like fools." He walked close to Cullen, placed the spear under his chin and lifted his head so they were looking in each other's eyes.

"I think about lessons. Lessons that will teach my men about life and death. About enemies. Yes, I think how they can learn their trade."

He took the point of the spear away from Cullen's chin and turned to the soldiers gathered around, their faces thrown into light and flickering shadows from the torches they carried.

"Which is why I will let him live. I want all of you to look on him and see a true warrior. And one day, maybe, you will be like him." He leaned in close to Cullen, speaking to him in a whisper.

"I would know the name of my enemy."

Cullen held his gaze, saying nothing.

"Come now. Nothing will happen to you," he glanced over to where Rhiannon was sitting with the children. "Or your family," he continued, the barest hint of a threat coloring the smile on his face.

"Your wife stopped to help your son, who had stopped to help an old man, and in doing so found themselves surrounded by my men. An admirable trait in a woman, to put her loved ones' care and safety before her own. She must be very special." He ran the side of his spear down Cullen's face, careful not to break the skin.

"I was asking you your name. Or does my enemy not speak the language of his conquerors?"

"Cullen," he said. "My name is Cullen."

"Not a name I've heard before. Where are you from?"

"Hibernia," said Cullen.

"Hibernia," mused the Roman. "Nothing but savages on that island. Is it true the women fight better than the men?"

"Just better than Romans," replied Cullen.

The Roman threw back his head and laughed. Standing up, he wagged his finger at Cullen as if he'd told a bawdy joke. "My men might want to gut you, Cullen, but I like you. I really do. You risked everything to free your people. A futile act, but noble. You fought the way a Roman should fight. And I want my men to look on you, and think how you humiliated them. I want them to burn your face into their hearts. Lessons."

He walked past the four dead men.

"Bury them," he said.

Twelve

The wave crashed against the boat sending an ice-cold spray over the shackled prisoners. Drops of water, sharp as needle points, hit their skin with enough force that it seemed the sea itself was trying to rip their flesh away, and as the boat fell down into the trough of the sea and the spray receded, the wind blew against their bodies, freezing the water that clung to their soaked clothes.

They had been herded onto the battleship that morning and were chained to the deck of the ship near the bow. Cullen had begged a piece of canvas off a guard so that Rhiannon and Aisling might have some protection against the sea. The canvas was already soaked through and it would be another full day before they reached the mainland. Even the witch, Mother Miriam, hadn't spoken for a few hours and Cullen could see that her fingers were blue with the cold.

One of the villagers coughed violently. Siric, the builder, was doubled up in pain, his whole body shivering as he coughed up great globs of green from his lungs. His eyes squeezed shut as he tried to stem the racking cough, but Cullen knew that in this cold, with the rain soaking them all night, that Siric would only get worse. Gretel, his wife, rubbed his shoulders in a futile attempt to warm him.

Art sat with Brendel, his brother. They huddled with three other villagers: Sayeva, a pretty girl of about fifteen years, who was to marry one of the men from a village over the mountains. Cullen grimaced. With her long, auburn hair, piercing green eyes and pale, unblemished skin, her fate was sealed. She would be bought by some rich Roman who would give her to his son, or donate her as a present to a politician or senator, where her virginity would be taken from her, her body used for the pleasure of some rich, Roman bastard. And if that happened she could consider herself lucky. There were whorehouses in Rome that would pay handsomely for a girl like her. Her willowy looks might last a month if she was bought by a place like that. She would be brutalized and raped and in a year she would be unrecognizable from the girl she was today.

Beside Sayeva was Kinburga, Art's wife. Disease has destroyed what attractive features she had, ravishing her face, creating pockmarks and hollows over skin that had never been beautiful to begin with. But she would do well. Her skill with cooking was well revered, and if she was lucky, she'd get a job in a kitchen where her talents would be put to use.

Sitting beside Kinburga, in a catatonic state, was Aylith. She was Ruane's wife, the dead man with the cut heel Cullen had passed by on the road to the Stone Bear. They had been married less than a year. Her stomach was heavy with child. Exhaustion was etched on every line of her face, and Cullen suspected that she had tried to help Ruane keep up with the Romans as they marched to the encampment. But Ruane collapsed, no matter how much help Aylith tried to give him. They would have shoved her aside and let her watch as they ran Ruane through with their swords.

How she must have screamed.

The line of prisoners continued down the length of the boat. Bron, a youth of about sixteen years, sat with his head tucked between his knees. He was the brother of Godwin, Finn's friend. Bron rarely talked, and his silence led some people to think that he was simple, but Cullen knew that Bron had a sharp mind. The other thing that set him apart was his leg. The left was three inches shorter than the right. Cullen had a memory of some of the village boys making fun of Bron's awkward walk, and of Bron's father catching them and beating the idiots so they ran crying to their parents. That was about as serious life got in the village.

Beside Bron was Rufus. Tall and redheaded with a full beard, Rufus had a large patch of raw flesh on his face, the aftermath of trying to fight the Romans off. Rufus angled his face so that the spray from the sea fell upon his face, cleansing the wound. In all, Cullen counted sixteen from his village, and he allowed a thin smile to escape from his lips. Not all the villagers had been re-captured. At least thirty of them had escaped. But the Romans had raided another village, one called River Oak Dell. It lay ten miles south of where the Romans had landed, and it seemed as if all forty of the village's inhabitants had been taken. Cullen saw men, women and children huddled together. A baby cried weakly, its voice hoarse from having screamed all day and all night. How long would it take for the baby's tears to piss off one of the Romans and toss the little thing overboard?

"I'm going to kill them."

Cullen looked down. His son, Finn, stared at him in sullen anger.

"I thought you were asleep."

Finn moved over beside Cullen.

"I'm going to kill them. As many as I can."

"No, you're not,"

"I hate them. They deserve to die."

"I hate them too," said Cullen, "but we can't do anything now. We just have to hope there'll be a time we can get away. All of us."

One of the villagers that sat near them, a spindly youth called Twig, snorted derisively. "We're done for. Once we get to Rome they'll sell us to farmers who'll work us to death, or we'll go to one of them noblemen, and if they don't like us, all they'll have to do is lift a finger and then…"

He dragged a finger across his throat.

"Go to sleep, Twig," said Cullen wearily.

"How can I sleep? I'm freezing," replied the youth. Finn stared at Twig, impressed by his knowledge of what was in store for them.

"Is that true, papa? Will they kill us?"

Cullen put an arm around Finn's shoulders.

"How could Twig know anything? He's never been away from the village. And you know I'll not let anything happen to you, don't you?"

Finn nodded.

"No more talk of killing then."

Finn nodded again, and laid his head against Cullen's shoulder.

Finn tried to let go of his hatred, he really did, but two things happened the next morning that almost killed him.

The first thing was the chicken leg that had been his supper the previous night. The Romans had fed the prisoners leftovers, and as Finn was finishing the picked-over chicken leg, he felt the grease run down between his wrists and the manacles that bound him. Maybe because he was little more than a child the Romans had not bothered to tighten the manacles around his wrists as they had done to his father. Finn dripped more grease onto the manacles and very quickly slipped his hands out.

He stared at his free hands, pleased with himself. Then a frown creased his forehead. Now what was he going to do? His father and the rest of his family were asleep. Even if he did free them what could they do? They were in the middle of ocean and could hardly swim to freedom. And the guards were too well armed to even attempt an attack.

Finn sighed. At least the irons weren't rubbing against his wrists anymore. He lay against his father and fell asleep.

The second thing that happened was that Finn saw two of the guards staring at his mother. The first guard said something to the other guard and they both laughed. Finn had no idea of what they were saying, but he hated the tone of their voices and the way their eyes lingered over his mother. He knew that look. He'd seen the guards' eyes gaze hungrily at a girl from the other village and the Roman leader, the captain of the ship, had come down to have a look. He'd stared at the girl the way a starving man might look at a side of beef that was roasting over a fire. He'd ordered the guards to free the girl. He took her below deck, dragging her as she screamed, trying to pull away, her heels digging up splinters from the wooden deck. Her father screamed at the Roman, pleading and cursing at him.

A guard standing close by chopped down his sword.

It buried in the space between the man's shoulder and neck, parting the body the way a young child could split a plant stem. Blood had sprayed everywhere. People had screamed until the same guard raised his sword again as if to do the same thing to anyone who dared disturb his peace with their ravings. The screams of the villagers had immediately lowered to whimpers and soft sobbing. One villager still screamed: the girl who was dragged away kept up an unearthly wail for the next ten minutes. When she was finally brought back, her face was bloody and her eyes stared straight ahead, as if a night demon had whispered secrets to her that no girl should ever know. They put her back in the chains, from which they had removed the body of her father. She sat down, raising her eyes to the bright sky, unblinking, as if in trying to blind herself she'd rid herself of the unholy wisdom visited upon her.

The tunic between her legs was soaked in blood.

Finn made a vow. The Romans would not do that to his mother. The two guards came closer, one of them talking to his mother in their language. Finn's father raised his voice, and spoke to them, his eyes piercing, his tone threatening. But they just laughed at him, and when his father tried to move forward, the chains held him back as if he were a wolfhound tied to a rope.

Rain fell.

The guard took off his helmet, revealing curly brown hair cropped close to his skull. He turned his face to the sky, opened his mouth, and let the rain pour in. He rubbed the water over his face and when he looked at Finn's mother again, his eyes had that hungry look, that Finn saw on the faces of men before they took their wives into the hut, where there would be muffled laughter for a few minutes, then grunting, and then quiet murmurings before the man and woman would reappear, their faces flushed and sweaty. He knew what they did to each other. He'd seen bulls mount cows enough times to know men and women did something similar. But this man was not his father, and Finn was not going to let what happened to the other village's girl happen to his mother.

The other Roman said something to the young, curly-haired guard. His tone seemed to sound a note of caution. The young guard stared at Rhiannon with a pained look on his face, then turned away to talk to his comrade, shrugging dismissively.

Finn's hands were still free of their shackles. Incensed, he reached for the guard's sword, drew it out of the scabbard and slashed at the guard's legs. The guard turned in time to see the sword hissing toward him. It sliced a three-inch gash across the side of his leg. The man howled in pain and hopped away, avoiding Finn's lunge with the sword.

A foot came down on his wrist. The sword flew out of Finn's hand as the second guard swung a huge fist through the air. The blow caught him on the side of his face. A white-hot pain exploded in his cheek as he slammed back against the side of the boat. Screams erupted all around him. Finn felt his father grab him and pull him behind his back, shielding him from the guard's revenge.

In one blinding flash, Finn recognized both the stupidity of what he had done and the elation of stopping the guard from hurting his mother. But now the guards would kill him, his father would die trying to stop them, and no one would be left to protect his mother and sister. Well, if he was going to die, he'd die fighting. He wriggled out of his father's grip and immediately the guards turned their attention to him. A foot kicked at him. Finn turned to the side and the foot brushed past his face. He grabbed the leg and clamped his jaws over the man's calf muscle. He bit down hard, feeling the skin break, tasting the warm blood spilling over his lips. The guard screamed in agony. He whipped his leg away, leaving Finn sprawled on the deck.

This is it, he thought, and waited for a sword to rip his life out of him. Instead, there was a shout from above.

"Stop!"

Gaius was standing on the upper deck when he heard the first shout. Thoughts of the long march to Rome were swept from his mind as he turned to see one of the guards, Lucius, his son, howl in pain clutching his calf. A captured boy's mouth dripped blood.

Now his men were being attacked by children?

As Gaius descended the steps he saw that the boy's father—there was a well-muscled brute—had grabbed the boy and shoved him behind his back, protecting him from most of the punches and kicks that the guards were directing at him. At least those guards—fools that they were for turning their backs on the prisoners—had not taken out their swords. Not yet.

"Lucius. Decius. Step away."

Lucius glowered as he obeyed, and Gaius could see that the wound on his calf was in the shape of the young boy's mouth.

Gaius walked up to the prisoners. The father—the brute with the muscles, the one who had killed four of his men and severely wounded a fifth—still had his son jammed behind his back and was holding him in a grip of iron. When he saw Gaius approaching his eyes focused on the Roman leader. Gaius noted that the eyes never blinked, never lost their fixed stare. He'd seen eyes like that before.

This one he'd have to watch.

Gaius stopped a few feet away from the man. He glanced at Lucius who grimaced in pain. He let his gaze find the brute.

"You're the one who killed my men."

The man didn't respond, but kept his eyes fixed on Gaius's face.

"Cullen, right?"

The big man shifted, then nodded once, almost imperceptibly.

"Cullen," repeated the Roman. He hunkered down so he was eye-level with his prisoner.

"Tell me something, Cullen. Why shouldn't I kill you now? You and that whelp of yours?"

Gaius tried to see if his threat had any effect, but the prisoner's eyes never wavered. Indeed, something inside them seemed to subtly change, or was it the tension in the man's body? The Roman knew that Cullen was readying to attack.

"Don't do it, Cullen," whispered Gaius.

He glanced down at the chains that held Cullen in place. If his son had escaped the chains, maybe his father had as well. But the bindings seemed in place, and though Gaius was close to this man, the chains would stop this man as easily as if he was a rabid wolf tied to a post.

"Cullen."

Gaius glanced up to see who had spoken. It was the woman. She held a baby against her, and while Cullen's eyes were blazing with death, her eyes held only fear. And love. She was the boy's mother, which made her this brute's wife. Gaius shook his head in disbelief. He had not noticed before, possibly because she had been covered in mud and her hair had fallen in dank, knotted curls around her face, but he realized that she was beautiful. She had tied her hair back behind her head and it revealed a face that almost took his breath away. Even dressed in those rags, her beauty shone through. He had enjoyed that young girl early on today, but her constant screaming had finally grated on his nerves and he'd had to use his fists to shut her up. Sometimes only a woman, with a woman's knowledge, could satisfy some hungers. Maybe he'd take this bitch later when the need came upon him again. He'd love to see the look on Cullen's face when she was dragged away for his pleasure. Oh, the hatred would burn off the pores of his skin!

"Sir, you need not kill us. What happened will not happen again. We will punish the boy for his foolishness."

Gaius didn't answer for a moment, simply because he was lost in the woman's eyes. Was she a screamer or a scratcher? Would she try to bite him if he leaned too close? Would she secretly enjoy it? It was so much fun to find out. He shook his head and laughed.

"My wife," he said, as he straightened up, "would have said exactly the same thing." He turned to Lucius. "Right, son?"

Cullen's eyes shifted to the young soldier that Finn had attacked. It wasn't just any soldier. It was the leader's son he had hurt. What had Finn been thinking? If someone had attacked Finn like that, Cullen would have slain him without a pause.

A smile crept across the young soldier's face that did not reach his eyes.

"I think I'd prefer death than her punishment," the young man said. Gaius laughed and nodded. He turned to Cullen.

"You can release your son, Cullen. I will not have him killed. Once again, you have taught my men a valuable lesson. You have exposed their utter stupidity. And it will do them good to see you live, because every time they look upon your faces they will say to themselves: 'Ah, yes. I am an idiot. Indeed, my brains are in my ass,' and by such acknowledgements they may possibly learn something that will prevent their deaths on a battlefield that lies in their future. Am I correct, Lucius?"

Lucius's eyes burned with embarrassment and anger.

"Yes, father, this lesson was well taught. And well learned."

Gaius nodded approvingly.

"For your own sake, Cullen, control your son. If he does something foolish like that again I will instruct my son in another lesson: the occasional need to butcher warriors and their children. It is a lesson he is impatient to learn. He is like a hound tugging on the end of a leash. And I won't hold him at bay anymore."

Gaius turned his head aside, an almost wistful expression coming over his face. He stared into the distance, unblinking, even though the salt spray hit his face.

"I love my son, Cullen, as you love yours. I'm proud that he's a soldier, but soldiers can die like that." He snapped his fingers. "I don't ever want his mother to hear that her only son is dead. And he could have died tonight. You've provided me with an opportunity I prayed I'd never have to face, but one I knew that I must."

Gaius got to his feet, his gaze leveled at Cullen.

"He needs to be taught a lesson."

Lucius was strung up between the two posts that had been raised near the bow of the ship, only twenty paces from Cullen. The young Roman faced the villagers, but kept his eyes fixed on a point above them. His jaw was clenched shut, but Cullen could see the muscles quiver in the young man's face. It was an added humiliation: to be whipped and have the prisoners staring at you while it happened.

Gaius stood aside, leaning against the rail of the ship, the look on his face suggesting that he was passing the time away by watching two dogs wrestling in the dirt, rather than by having the skin flayed off his only son. His jaw slowly worked up and down, chewing on a piece of dried meat. His eyes betrayed no emotion as his men tied the ropes that bound Lucius's wrists to the pole.

It was time.

A soldier stood beside Lucius, whip dangling from his hands. Stripped to the waist, his muscles were taut, almost jumping under his skin. He looked at Gaius, waiting for the order to begin. Gaius pushed himself away from the railing and strode over to where Lucius stood, arms bound to the poles in a V-shape. Approaching the soldier he held out his hand. The soldier handed his commander the whip and stepped away, relief evident on his face. He disappeared down the hatch below decks. The only soldiers to witness the punishment were the guards patrolling the deck. Cullen thought this made Lucius's humiliation worse: only the slaves would look upon him as he was flayed to within inches of his life.

Silence descended on the vessel. Gaius stood behind Lucius, his head bowed, his expression unreadable. Lucius stared ahead. Gaius stepped forward and placed his head beside Lucius's ear and whispered something. Lucius remained rigid, and sweat dripped from his forehead and collected on the tip of his nose, before dripping onto the deck. Cullen's insides churned, and a deep rage that was building within him bubbled to the surface. He turned to Rhiannon.

"This Roman bastard's going to want to kill Finn."

Rhiannon drew Finn closer to her. "Then we have to—"

"You know what my mistake was, Rhiannon? Listening to you. Look at what the Roman's father is doing. He's teaching *his* son a lesson that I failed to teach *my* son."

Finn moved forward. "It's not mama's fault. That Roman was going to—"

Cullen's fist lashed out catching Finn full on the nose. Finn fell back and Rhiannon looked up at Cullen, fear on her face. Blood gushed from Finn's nostrils as he lay back dazed on his mother's lap.

"Cullen, what—?"

"You stupid woman," roared Cullen. "Do you understand Finn is marked now? I should have taken my fist to him years ago!"

Alarmed, the villagers urged Cullen to keep quiet. He ignored them. He was aware that everyone on the deck had stopped what they were doing and had turned to the domestic dispute. A distant part of him knew he should stop, wanted to stop, but a fury possessed him.

"This soldier is going to find a way to gut him, Rhiannon. His father wants him to *want* to kill Finn. He wants to drive any pity from his heart. You think by hiding him behind your skirts all these years you've protected him? You've killed him."

One of the deck guards rammed the butt of his spear against Cullen's head. Cullen's vision exploded in a burst of stars, and a searing numbness spread over his body. Through his pain, Cullen felt a surge of gratitude toward the guard, because at least it stopped him from saying anything else to Rhiannon. He'd said enough to make her hate him for the rest of her life. Gods, he was so angry with her. And why? Because she'd tried to raise Finn in a kind and loving way? That she'd allow Finn to speak his mind the way Cullen had never been allowed to as a child? Cullen knew he was wrong, knew his anger was irrational and stupid, but if he hadn't been chained up right now, he'd have strangled his wife and son.

He heard a shout. Grimacing with pain, he looked up. Gaius and Lucius were both staring at him. Through his blurred vision Cullen saw Gaius put a folded piece of leather into Lucius's mouth. The young man bit down on it. Gaius stepped back and rolled his shoulders around, loosening the muscles. Breathing in, he brought the whip back in a long arc, then snapped his arm forward.

The punishment began.

Thirteen

Gaius went easy on his boy, whipping him only twenty-seven times, and stopping before he passed out or begged his father to stop. It was still brutal, and when the soldiers told Lucius to open his mouth so they could remove the leather strap, they found that the young Roman had bitten into it so hard, they had to pry it from his teeth.

Gaius rolled up the whip as the soldiers took Lucius below deck to put salve on his open wounds.

Rhiannon had moved Finn to the other side, away from Cullen. Her head was nestled against her son's, her long hair dangling over his face, as if to shield him from the sight of any more soldiers.

She wouldn't speak to him now. Cullen wouldn't be surprised if they never spoke again. Well, she could be angry all she wanted. Finn had put them all in danger, and if Cullen had beaten the fight out of the boy when he was younger, then this wouldn't have happened.

Of course, if the Romans hadn't kidnapped them from their village they wouldn't be in this position either.

Cullen knew he was being unreasonable, knew it was fear making him feel this way. But he still wanted to pound his son to a pulp, and he wanted his wife to know that it was—what?—*her* fault? What in Hades was he thinking?

Cullen dug his nails into his palms, trying to quell a fury he hadn't felt in a long time. The boy was foolish, not realizing that those two guards would not dare have their way with any of these prisoners. Only their leader, Gaius, had that privilege, and his appetites had been sated by that poor girl from the other village. Son or no son, Gaius would have flayed the flesh off Lucius's back if he had dared to go through with so brazen and idiotic an act. That young Roman had already turned away and the danger had passed, but Finn had almost gotten them killed. Cullen wanted to beat the boy to within a hair's breadth of life. That's a lesson *he* could teach.

The only problem was Cullen knew he was wrong. He was wrong to think that anything he could have done to Finn when he was a child could have prepared him for this. He was wrong to blame Rhiannon for wanting to raise Finn to be something other than a warrior. He was wrong for hitting Finn and yelling at Rhiannon and making them more terrified than they already were.

He'd never felt more like a bastard in his life. He had to say it now while he could.

"Rhiannon, I'm sorry."

She ignored him. The only move she made was to tighten her grip around Finn, shielding him from Cullen, as if *he* were the enemy, not the Romans.

Cullen wondered if Roman wives were as bloody-minded as his wife.

Cullen looked at his son, his face hidden in Rhiannon's arms. Finn looked terrified now, but what about later? Tomorrow or the next day would he lose his mind again and strike out against their captors? Short of tying Finn up and carrying him over his shoulder, how could he control his child?

He glanced up and caught Mother Miriam staring at him. Rain dripped off the old witch's head, winding down the lines of age on her face. Mother Miriam held his gaze with steely determination.

"What?" asked Cullen.

The old woman's eyes bored into Cullen.

"It's time, don't you think?"

Cullen glanced over at Finn who had his head pressed tightly to Rhiannon's shoulder.

"He's afraid now," continued the woman, "but he'll do it again. You know it."

Cullen was startled that the old witch seemed to read his thoughts.

"And you can save him?"

"God can save him."

"God isn't here, Mother."

"That's where you're wrong."

The old woman shifted her position, leaning forward toward Cullen.

"This is a desperate situation for you, Cullen. You cannot fight them for fear of what they'll do to your family. Your son's actions are unpredictable at best. Soon we will be in a strange land, hearing languages we don't understand and told to do as they say under pain of death. Trust me when I say there is only one path you can take."

"Your God?" said Cullen.

"Your God. My God. Our God," she said.

Cullen bowed his head and closed his eyes. The sound of the boat cutting through the waves pulsed through his ears. He thought of his son and realized he didn't have a choice.

"Alright," he said, raising his eyes to the witch. "Teach him about God. Teach him love. And sacrifice. Teach him about Gods who die crucified. Just keep him alive."

The old woman touched Cullen's hand and held it gently.

"He won't listen to me."

Cullen looked at her in confusion.

"He'll listen to you," she said.

Cullen gazed blankly at the old woman.

"But I know nothing about your God," he said.

"Not yet."

The woman's eyes were steady as Cullen realized what she was saying.

"You want to teach me too."

Mother Miriam smiled serenely.

"You think if Finn sees me learning about God—"

"—that he'll listen with all his heart."

"Can you promise me we'll live?"

"You could accept God today and be dead before night falls. Nobody knows when their time on this earth is up."

"You said your God would keep us alive."

"Our bodies may die. But our spirits—our souls—will live forever."

Cullen raised his eyes to where the sun shone down upon the sea. He would gladly face an army of thousands armed with nothing but a sword in his hand and hate in his heart if he could only know that his family was safe.

How could he place his trust in a God whose only weapon was love?

"Not good enough, witch."

He turned away from her.

Fourteen

Fourteen years before

They fled Hibernia. Cullen's father's greed had consumed him, and his father tried to usurp Chieftain O'Neill's place at the head of the tribe. There was a battle, and his father lost. Cullen and his father escaped, finding passage across the sea to Britannia.

They arrived on the strange shores with nothing but the clothes on their backs. His father hired himself out to a local chief and in two years had risen to second-in-command of a small Brigantes tribe. When the chief had died Cullen's father had taken control of the tribe. Four years it had taken his father to rise from nothing to the most feared leader in Northern Britannia. Cullen was thirteen.

That was when he made his first kill.

They had chanced upon a band of raiders from a neighboring tribe who were burdened down by their plunder. Whoever they had stolen from must have had a good year because there were fine skins, swords, spears, jewels and gold. It was an incredible haul, the best they'd ever seen, and Cullen's father had quickly overcome the smaller band of thieves. After the fighting was done, five were still alive.

The survivors knelt in a line. They could reasonably expect to be kept as slaves in Cullen's father's tribe. But there was a problem. These men belonged to a tribe they never had any problems with. Yet by stealing their plunder Cullen's father had essentially declared war on them. If word got back to the tribe's leaders they could battle each other for generations.

Cullen's father, as violent and brutish as he was, did not need or want any unnecessary fighting so the choice was clear. These five men must be killed, and their bodies—along with the bodies of the fifteen warriors already lying on the ground—must be burned and buried. No trace of them must ever be found. The plunder they had stolen must be taken down south where it would be traded, far away from where this slaughter had taken place.

Five warriors, including Cullen, were chosen for the kill. It was to be done fast—a sword plunged down into the backs of the prisoners. Cullen lined up with the other four executioners behind the prisoners.

Cullen placed the tip of his sword against the man's skin. The prisoner's breath came in ragged gasps, his shoulder's rising up and down with each inhale and exhale. A droplet of blood blossomed up from where the sword touched the skin, and Cullen had a fleeting thought that he should apologize to the man.

Word was given. Heart beating fast, Cullen pushed down.

Cullen felt his sword slice through the man's flesh. He had expected to hit bone, to find resistance as the metal plunged into the man's body. There was none. The man exhaled and slumped forward. Cullen stepped away from the spurting blood, his eyes wide and staring as if the man would suddenly recover from this mortal wound and turn on him, ready to take his revenge. This didn't happen. The man stayed dead, and as his heart stopped beating, the spurting blood slowed, and simply spread in a crimson pool on the ground.

The other four warriors had completed their tasks, one prisoner dead in front of each of them. How could it have been so quick? Surely the act of killing required something more?

His father came up behind him and laid a hand on his shoulder. Cullen dragged his eyes from the dead man and looked at his father, their eyes almost level.

"Is that it?" he asked.

They worked until dark, digging a hole. They covered the grave, throwing in rocks and stones to make in harder to dig up, should anyone ever happen upon it. They scattered leaves and sticks over the ground until it matched the surrounding area. In months, the freshly dug earth would be home to sprouting trees and plants and in a year it would be indistinguishable from the rest of the undergrowth.

They rode far away that night, and when they reached their home, they had a feast to celebrate Cullen's first kill. He was now a man.

They met the Roman during the next full moon.

Fifteen

Miriam held a meeting that night. The stars shone down from an ink-black sky. A strong wind filled the sails, pulling the boat through the water and allowing the unseen rowers in the fetid hull to rest. The rain that had frozen them the night before was gone, and only occasional sprays of water were tossed up. Guards patrolled quietly. Someone far away chanted a song.

Cullen was alone in not wishing to hear her words. All fifteen of the villagers had heard Mother Miriam speak during the time she lived with them. If they had dismissed her message before, then these new circumstances put what she said in a different light. Sayeva sat huddled with Aylith, the wife of the murdered Ruane. She kept her back against the bow of the ship and had somehow curled herself against the shape of the older woman, knowing she should hide herself from these bestial Romans. Siric lay with his head on Gretel's lap. Every now and then, Siric coughed, his whole body convulsing with the effort. Art and Brendel, the brothers, sat together, their faces twisted in almost identical hangdog looks. Kinburga shivered against Art, her husband, her hands moving ceaselessly over each other, as if they were snakes playing an endless game of chase.

Rhiannon had Aisling in her lap, and Finn sat between his parents. Cullen had ordered Finn to listen to Mother Miriam and the boy had obeyed wordlessly. Since the incident that morning they had barely spoken to each other.

Mother Miriam smiled as they gathered around and settled themselves, finding a way to make their chains stretch so they were all close by. Mother Miriam turned her hands to the sky.

"Praise God for the mercy of our captors. They may easily have taken the life from one of our children, but you, Lord, stayed their hands."

The old woman bowed her head. After a few moments she raised her head and began to speak.

Cullen listened with growing disbelief. This God had rules and those rules made Cullen shake his head in bewilderment.

"If someone strikes you," said Mother Miriam, "Turn the other cheek."

At first, Cullen was confused as to why you should turn the other cheek until the witch explained that it was to let the one who hit you *hit you again*. Cullen almost burst out laughing and he looked around at the others, but they were all staring at her intently, some even nodding wisely as if what the old woman said made some kind of sense.

Turn the other cheek, thought Cullen in disgust. His mind drifted back in time to a battle. He and his warriors had come across a group of Romans, ten in all. They waited until nightfall to attack and it had been a slaughter. One of the Romans had drawn his sword and managed to slice a four-inch gash that ran down Cullen's cheek. Cullen had let that one live...for quite a while. The Roman had died screaming in agony and Cullen had definitely not turned the other cheek. He doubted whether this new God would look upon those acts with favor.

Cullen shifted uncomfortably on the deck of the ship. That soldier from Cullen's past had been a youngster, not more than twenty years old. As Cullen had been torturing him, the Roman was yelling something over and over. *Mama, mama.* The boy had been screaming for his mother and Cullen had laughed at him. He made jokes about it with his men and when the boy was dead they spat on his corpse. Let his mother suffer, they said, as our wives and our mothers have suffered at the hands of the Romans. In seven years, Finn would be that boy's age, and for a moment it was not the Roman's face that Cullen saw screaming in his mind's eye. It was Finn's. Cullen pushed the thought away. He wiped his forehead with his hand, and even though the evening was cool, sweat covered his palm.

The first rays of the sun illuminated the undersides of the clouds in a palette of purples and reds. Cullen sat against the bulkhead, his head in his arms. His family and the rest of the villagers were asleep, their gentle breathing rising and falling, the rhythm of their breaths seemingly timed to the rise and fall of the sea. Even the witch-priest was asleep, a look of serenity and peace on her lined, leathery face.

Turn the other cheek. Love your enemies. Those were the rules proposed by this new God. And the old woman had added another suggestion during her talk: Thou shalt not kill.

If the world were perfect it would make perfect sense. But Cullen knew otherwise. The world was full of people that wanted what you had, that would kill to get what you had: your money, your children, your wife. Even the Romans, they had everything they needed, they had the richest lands, the best soldiers, they came from the greatest city in the world and yet…and yet they still traveled, almost to the ends of the earth, to plunder and rob and enslave. The Romans spread misery throughout the world. Who more than Romans deserved death by the sword? They had even killed the man who was supposed to be God. They had hammered nails into his feet and wrists and left him up on a cross to die.

Didn't this God want revenge?

Didn't He want to slay his enemies with lightning bolts from the sky?

Didn't He want to kill?

A bitter smile crossed Cullen's lips. God should have gotten to him many years ago, before he'd killed the first of many men. If he'd done what God commanded and not killed he'd be dead now. No, when people had attacked him he had sent them to the world of spirits. Death had served him well.

But now…now he had Finn to think about.

Cullen had no idea what to do.

Sixteen

Cullen woke as Finn sat down beside him. He pushed himself into a sitting position.

"Are you hungry?" asked Cullen.

"Do you have any food?"

"No."

Finn huffed in what Cullen took to be a laugh.

They sat in silence for a while, listening to the rowers chant as the ship rose and fell on the sea. The other villagers stared listlessly into space. A Roman guard sat in the weak sunlight, whittling a piece of wood.

"Did you like killing people, father?"

Cullen's fingers stopped drumming their beat on his knees. He felt his son's eyes bore into him.

Like killing? he thought. *I reveled in it. I'd watch my enemies' eyes as they realized what I'd take from them. I fell upon my foes like a demon from the depths of the spirit world and when I had their lives in my hands I felt like a God.*

"Yes," he said.

"Do you believe in Mother Miriam's God?" asked Finn.

Cullen desperately wanted to say yes. He wanted to believe in a God that could deliver his family from the hands of these Romans. He wanted to believe in a God that would preserve his son's innocence. *Yes, I do. I believe her God is now my God, your God, our God. I'll follow this God to the ends of the world. I believe. To save you, Finn, I believe.*

"No," he said quietly. "Her God is weak. He makes me angry."

Finn lowered his eyes, staring blankly at the deck of the ship.

"You have to promise me something."

"What?"

"Promise me you won't kill anymore."

Cullen blinked in surprise.

"Finn, I can't promise that. Look at what's—"

"Promise me."

"But—" Cullen stared into his son's eyes, willing him to understand that what he was asking was impossible.

"If I promise not to kill anymore, Finn, we could all die."

"Promise me," repeated Finn.

"You're a child," said Cullen, his voice turning cold. "You have no idea what I might have to do to get us out of this."

Finn looked at the rim of the sun, barely cresting the horizon. Cullen was startled to see a half-smile play on Finn's lips, as if a happy memory had caught in his mind's eye.

"I had a dream last night. And in the dream you promised me. And you kept your promise and we were together. Safe. Home. But if you kill people..." Finn lowered his head. "If you kill people—even one more— we will die. We won't ever see each other again."

"This is Mother Miriam's desert God talking, isn't it?"

"Yes," said Finn. "I think it is."

"And he'll keep us safe if I make this promise?"

"I think so."

Cullen rubbed his temple, squeezing his aching skull. If he promised, if he really promised, he would keep to his word. He would have to die before killing another Roman. It was impossible and yet what choice did he have? If this would save Finn's life and Rhiannon's life and Aisling's life then he wouldn't hesitate to make the vow. But was it the right decision? What if one Roman held a sword to his wife's throat and Cullen had a chance to end the Roman's life but didn't because the vow prevented him and then the Roman slit his wife's throat before moving on to kill his children and was he supposed to stand there remembering his promise and turning the other cheek and loving his enemy and was he supposed to let the Roman kill his children too when he could have plucked the life out of the son of a whore the way a vulture tears meat from a carcass?

What horrors would befall them if he agreed to this?

But maybe it was the right thing to do. They were still alive now, weren't they? They had escaped certain death at least twice since the Romans came. Maybe their good fortune would hold. Maybe this God was already looking out for them, guiding them through this path of spears and swords. If he made this promise, would their luck hold? Maybe they'd end up working for some poor farmer where they'd have a chance to escape and find their way back home.

He felt his head would explode.

Cullen laid his head against his knees, trying to rid his mind of all thought, all feeling.

He didn't believe in God.

But he did believe in Finn.

Maybe this was the desert God's way of making a deal with Cullen: if you don't kill, your family lives.

He wished bitterly that this God was a God of hate and vengeance. It would make believing in him so much easier.

Finally, he raised his head.

Finn stared at Cullen's eyes for what seemed like an eternity.

I believe in Finn, thought Cullen again.

When Cullen opened his mouth to speak he was not consciously aware of what he said, rather it was as if somebody else was speaking and he was listening to the words as they came out of his mouth.

"Alright, Finn, alright. I promise. I won't kill any more people."

What have I done? thought Cullen.

With this promise to my son have I condemned us to die?

Seventeen

Thirteen years ago--Britannia

His name was Sulla Atticus Scaurus. He was a Roman, a centurion in the army, and he had just killed four of his comrades. They lay on the ground, all twisted and bent. He was sweating, and in the cold night air, he could feel the steam rising off his head, dissipating into the darkness in delicate silver strands.

It was done.

He had seized the moment, and in doing so, had given himself a fortune.

They had gone out on patrol two days ago and came upon a merchant with a boxful of gold coins and jewelry. They relieved the merchant not only of his gold, but of his five servants each of whom had been butchered, and his wife, who had been severely abused by the soldiers over the course of two nights, before she, too, was dispatched, to join her husband in whatever Hades he had landed in.

The five soldiers on this patrol had an obligation to turn the gold over to their General, who would put most of the haul in the legion's coffers, keep some of it for himself, and distribute the rest among the five men who had found it. The sum received by each of the men would be enough to buy whores for a year, procure a room or two above the stinking streets of Rome, and clothe themselves with a couple of nice togas. It would be a nice bonus, but it would never make them rich.

Not even close.

Scaurus knew that Sergius, the leader of their patrol, would never listen to the plan he formed in his mind. The plan, of course, was that the haul need not be turned over to the proper authorities, and should be kept among the five men. Sergius, noble, uptight bastard that he was, would reject such an idea out of hand. Furthermore, any mention of such an idea would be reported and Scaurus would find himself in the dungeons—or dead.

So Sergius had to die.

But if he died, then so must Claudius, his best friend, his inseparable partner and, Scaurus suspected, his lover. Claudius, pompous and devoted turd, would defend Sergius with his life.

So Claudius must die.

But if Sergius and Claudius both took a sword in the throat, then what might Senna do? Standing a head above Scaurus's own six feet two inches, Senna had the brain of an ox. Never had a Roman more willingly followed orders, because Senna was a man born with absolutely no imagination. Left to his own devices, he was unable to function. Give him a job to do and a time to do it in, then there was no better soldier. What might such a man do when faced with a mutiny? It would be against everything he knew, everything he stood for. No such man would willingly go along with such a heinous plan.

So Senna must die.

And then there was Titus Pulcher Albus. He was a rogue, a thief and a liar, and one of the most dangerous soldiers Scaurus had ever fought with. If Scaurus was going to have a partner in crime, then it would be Titus Albus. Together they could dispatch the other three soldiers in less than a minute, and the gold and jewelry, shared between them, could buy them each a small farm within a stone's throw of Rome and have use of all the whores in Rome until they either died or their pricks fell off. They could say that they had confronted a band of thieves on the road and despite a heroic stand, only Scaurus and Titus survived.

Of course, this line of reasoning begged a question. Why buy a small farm when you could buy a big one?

Why share with anyone?

These thoughts went through Scaurus's head as he lay curled in his blanket under the stars. He heard snores drift across the fire from three of his companions. The other—Titus—was awake, and Scaurus suspected that his brain was following the same line of thinking.

But had it led him to do what Scaurus had done before bedding down?

Had Titus hidden an unsheathed sword under his blanket?

Scaurus had deliberately lain close to Titus as they prepared for the night. He had known that if his decisions fell a certain way, then Titus had to be the first to die.

His hand curled around the sword. He allowed a soft snore to escape his mouth. Titus was three feet away and Scaurus made a motion as if turning on his side, covering the larger movement of his swift, vicious lunge at Titus. The sword sank into the man's ribs, eliciting a gasp of surprise. Titus thrashed about, trying to throw his woolen blanket off him. He made loud retching sounds, and Scaurus got to his knees, drew the sword almost out of Titus body, then slammed it back in, jiggling it up and down as he did so. Titus slumped, dead.

Senna, the oaf, woke up. He stared at Scaurus, eyes bleary with sleep. Scaurus barely had time to put the sword out of sight behind his back. Scaurus put a finger to his lips.

He quickly crossed over to Sergius and rammed the sword deep into his heart. Sergius's eyes bulged, and his hands immediately shot to the sword, which Scaurus pulled out of his body. The edge of the blade sliced through the calloused skin. The patrol leader's mouth flapped open and shut, like a salmon left to die on the shore.

A wail pierced the air. Senna. The dumb ox had no understanding what was happening, but he knew it was bad. He had screamed, and his screams caused Claudius to jump up, sword at the ready. Scaurus rushed toward Claudius, pointing his sword at the trees.

"Attack. Arrows, from the trees," hissed Scaurus. Claudius turned, and saw Sergius's feet scrabbling on the ground.

"Sergius?" said Claudius, his voice rising higher with every syllable.

Scaurus pointed to the trees beyond them.

"There they are," he screamed, and as Claudius turned to look Scaurus drove his bloody sword into his kidneys, right up to the hilt. Claudius's back arched, and he let out a terrible keening sound.

He pushed Claudius to the ground and turned to face Senna, who had thrown off his blanket and was desperately searching for his sword. But Senna's blanket had caught in his arms, and the big man was whipping his arms up and down. Scaurus picked up a spear and flung it at Senna. It caught the big man in the lower belly. Senna fell, his hands grasping the shaft of the spear.

Scaurus walked up behind him. Senna tried to track him with his eyes, but he seemed unable to do anything except concentrate on the next breath. Scaurus watched the brute's back heave up and down, up and down. He lifted his sword high and drove it down between Senna's neck and shoulder blades. Scaurus expected the big man to slump over and hit the ground with a thump and a puff of dust, but all that happened was the chest ceased to move. Senna's body seemed to settle into stillness, as if his body would remain in this position until the winds carried his crumbling flesh and bones away on this cold, wet, misty northern air.

He burned the bodies. The smell of roasted flesh filled the air, but Scaurus was too busy sifting through the contents of the box to worry about it.

He could live like a senator with this much wealth.

He felt no guilt or remorse. He'd been with these men for years, but had never felt more than a passing kinship with them. The rooms they slept in together, the food they ate, the battles they fought—all paled before the life he would have now, paid for by this treasure that cascaded from his hands.

The fire burned down, but Scaurus kept feeding it with branches, letting it burn all day and into the night. By the time the moon had risen, the ashes from the burnt branches covered the bones of the dead Roman soldiers.

Now came the hard part. He would have to go back to the Roman camp and convince them that their patrol had been attacked by a band of vicious tribesmen who murdered the others, but he, Scaurus, managed to escape. There was nothing so unbelievable about this story, but if those high-ranking bastards caught a whiff of a lie, then Scaurus would be put to the sword instead of being given a few days' rest.

The first thing he had to do was to bury this treasure in a place that he could find again. That done, he would have to slice himself up, to convince his superiors that he had fought bravely, and despite his wounds, had managed to escape the torment of his attackers. If all went well they would believe him, and if he could get himself out of the army within the year— pretend to be blind? Deaf?—then he could find his way back here, collect his loot, and be sailing for Rome and all its riches. He thought of how his life would be when he had his land and bought his whores. He felt energized, and his mind kept going back to the soldiers he had killed. Gods, but he hadn't felt that rush, that excitement, for years.

He heard a twig break.

He didn't react at once, but yawned widely, slowly, as if he'd heard nothing. He leaned forward, reaching for his cloak, but as soon as he had his legs under him, he bolted for the trees, legs pumping ferociously, his body low, eyes fixed on the thickest part of the forest. The treasure box he left behind him, his dreams of wealth evaporating in an instant. What good was a box of treasure if you had a spear up your arse?

Four men stepped out of the forest, blocking his path. Scaurus swerved, changing direction in an instant. If he could make it down to the river he could swim across and—damn it all to Hades, there were more of them. He was surrounded. He was a dead man. He knew it and the only question now was how he was going to die. He'd heard stories of these animals skinning Romans alive, slicing them up bit by bit. Better to die quickly, better to die now.

He charged at the biggest warrior he could see, a giant of a man, with red hair tied in braids down his back. A bushy mustache all but covered his mouth and in his hands he held a sword and an axe. With luck, the first blow would cleave him in two and then eternity would wrap its frigid arms around him. The man waited until Scaurus was close, then slammed his enormous calloused fist into Scaurus' face. The last thing Scaurus heard before he passed out was the sound of his nose crunching.

He awoke hours later, hands tied behind a post. It was night. A fire burned nearby and the smell of roast pork reached what was left of his sense of smell. A dull pain seemed to cover his face, throbbing gently with each beat of his heart. The background noise came into focus and Scaurus made out the sounds of laughter and shouting. He tried to open his eyes but they wouldn't budge. Had these bastards sewn them shut? He lifted his head up and was rewarded with a jolt of agony that seemed to split his face open along his destroyed nose. He lowered his head down to his chest, breathing shallowly until the pain subsided enough for him to get his bearings again.

He heard footsteps, and then a shuffle as someone sat down beside him. He heard a voice, a young boy's voice, say something to him. He didn't understand their guttural tongue but the boy's manner seemed almost tentative. Cold water splashed on his face and Scaurus jerked back involuntarily, sending spears of fresh agony through him. He realized that the boy was trying to warn him of the impending dousing. Cursing himself for being so jumpy, he relaxed. Cool, fresh water poured over his face, and he could feel the grime washing away, the icy liquid acting like a balm on his ravaged nose. His eyes unstuck, and he realized that they hadn't sewn them together; it was merely dried blood that prevented him from opening them. More cold water, and soon Scaurus was able to open his eyes to see a young man kneeling before him. Long red hair fell in a stringy mess over his dark eyes. Scaurus estimated the lad's age to be about thirteen or fourteen. The youth went away, returning minutes later with a full skin of water which he poured over the Roman's face. Scaurus opened his mouth and let the water flow in. He swished the water around and spat it out.

"Thank you," he croaked to the young man.

The youth nodded his head in acknowledgment.

"Cullen," boomed out a voice.

The youth turned, and Scaurus followed his gaze. The enormous red-haired warrior walked over to them, and Scaurus recognized that they were father and son. The youth named Cullen stood up watching his father approach. Damn, this brute was big, easily a hand over six feet. Senna, his former comrade that he had so easily vanquished two days ago, was bigger than this man, but there was no question that this red-headed behemoth would have destroyed Senna in hand-to-hand combat.

The man gestured for the youth to grab some of the roasting boar. Cullen turned to the Roman, his dark eyes boring into the prisoner. Without a word, he turned and walked away.

"My men want you to burn," said Cullen's father, in broken Latin.

Scaurus smiled.

"What's so funny?" asked Cullen's father, tilting his head to the side. "Does the prospect of death amuse you?"

Scaurus shook his head. "I thought, for some reason, they'd make it more interesting."

"Interesting?"

Scaurus nodded. "Are you a betting man?"

"Who isn't?"

"Because I have a bet."

"You've nothing to wager."

"My life."

"I already own it."

Scaurus sighed, leaned back against the tree and shrugged. "Then go ahead and burn me. My bet probably wouldn't be kindly received anyway."

"And why not?"

Scaurus shrugged.

"Are you going to skin me first? I heard you people like to make the Romans scream."

"I'm not one for skinning. It takes too long. What's your bet?"

Scaurus explored his split lip with his tongue, tasting the salty blood encrusted on it. He looked at Cullen's father.

"That I could kill your greatest warrior in combat. Hand to hand. Swords. Spears. Whatever is his best weapon, I'm better. Set me against him, he's a dead man."

"And if you won this bet, all I'd get is one dead warrior."

Scaurus shook his head.

"You'd get me."

"You? Why would I want a Roman?"

"I'd train your men. Train to be just like Romans. Train them to be better than Romans. I'd drill them without pity. I'm a fucking bastard. By the time I'm done with them, they could fight anyone and win."

Cullen's father picked at the red hairs of his beard, his eyes staring at the blazing fire.

"I'd make that son of yours into the most fearsome warrior in the land."

"He's already made his first kill," said Cullen's father proudly. "He's only thirteen."

"By the time I'm done, he'll have five hundred."

Cullen's father glanced at his son, who stood apart from the warriors, staring into the fire, the fierce, orange light dancing across his face, the shadows flickering along the fine cheekbones. His son was not one for words. Or revelry. Yes, he would be a fine warrior with or without this Roman. But the best? Why not? After all, was not his father the best now?

"Gwinn," he mused.

"Gwinn?" said the Roman.

"If you could beat Gwinn, I'd be impressed."

Scaurus smiled.

Cullen's father had planned to kill the Roman. Instead, he discovered a kindred spirit. He saw in Scaurus a man just like him: a man who would kill without remorse. A man to whom cruelty was the highest form of pleasure.

They became a team. Scaurus was able to help Cullen's father raid deep into Roman territory, stealing, plundering and raping across the land. Scaurus out-thought the Roman patrols every time. When they couldn't avoid them, they ambushed them, butchering them to the last man.

Scaurus became Cullen's teacher, his mentor, his trainer. Under his father's orders, Scaurus trained Cullen in every aspect of Roman warfare. He drilled him endlessly, harnessing Cullen's instinctive skill into something even more deadly. Scaurus incorporated Cullen's fighting style into his training, expanding it from the training an ordinary recruit would get, into a brutal and devastating fighting technique. By the age of sixteen, Cullen was standing well above six feet tall, spoke Latin fluently and was the most feared warrior in his tribe.

Eighteen

Strong winds blew the ship toward Italy and three days later the boat sailed into a port in a dust-blown town whose smell reached them before they saw it.

"Is this Rome, father?" asked Finn.

A prisoner who stood nearby snorted.

"This isn't even a flea on Rome's arse."

Irons were clamped around the prisoners' ankles and a length of chain joined all the villagers together. Escape was impossible. No one could run without all the others dragging behind.

Cullen tore off lengths from the canvas that they slept on during the voyage and wrapped them around Rhiannon's and Finn's leg irons to stop them from chaffing during the long walk to follow.

As the ship moved closer to shore, Cullen turned his gaze to the collection of sun-dried mud huts that climbed haphazardly from the shore to the top of a rolling hill.

The land looked baked.

Already he felt parched. The air seemed to suck the saliva off the roof of his mouth. Would the Romans care? Cullen thought back to when he and his men would lead the slaves they captured back to their village. He grimaced. Sometimes it was too much trouble to deal with any sickly, weak captives that couldn't walk. A cold finger of shame crept up Cullen's back.

Hopefully these Romans would show a little more mercy than he and his warriors showed to some of the people they captured.

Three mangy, black dogs ran along the sandy shore. One of them had found the carcass of a seagull and tried to protect his prize from the other two canine thieves. Half-naked urchins ran up the wooden pier, weaving around the baskets of fish and ignoring the shaking fists of the fishermen. They greeted the boat, arms outstretched, begging for anything from the soldiers hands.

"I'm thirsty," said Rhiannon.

"They'll feed us soon," said Cullen, and in that moment he would have sold his soul for a cup of water for his wife.

Aisling stirred in Rhiannon's arms. Cullen ran a hand over Aisling's dark hair as the baby snuggled against her mother.

"I'm scared, Cullen. What's going to happen to us?"

Cullen leaned nearer and held her arm.

"Just stay close. As long as we're together we'll be all right."

Rhiannon nodded.

"Will we ever get home, father?"

"No one can keep us away from home, Finn."

Reassurances. Platitudes. Empty promises. That's all he was able to give his family. *We'll be fine. I'll save us. Nothing bad will happen.*

Lies. All lies.

They walked through the town in their chains, a line of guards on either side. Behind them were twenty carts loaded with food, clothes, oils and metals that the Romans had pillaged while in Britain. The townspeople came out to watch the spectacle. Their faces were burnt brown by the sun and their hair was jet black, lightened slightly by the swirling dust that found its way between the strands.

One girl threw a tomato that caught Twig on the side of the neck and splattered all over his face. Twig turned, furious, but the guards had already chased the girl away. One of the Romans swiped the tomato off Twig's neck, flicking it onto the ground. He wiped his hand on the back of Twig's shirt. The other guards laughed.

They arrived at a field on the other side of the hill where they were told to sit down. The Romans distributed bread, skins of water and some meat. The meat, while not rotten, had begun to smell ripe. Despite that, the villagers ate ravenously, washing the food down with the brackish water. When they were done, Gaius came over to them and looked at each in turn.

"Your journey is just beginning. Today we shall rest. Tomorrow we begin our march to Rome."

He strode past the prisoners.

"It will take us a week to reach Rome. When we are there you will be taken to the market where you will be sold to the highest bidder. During the seven days it will take us to reach Rome we will feed you well. We will fatten you up because we want our buyers to like what they see. And when our customers study you, you will behave. You will be polite. You will smile and bow. Because if there is any trouble from any of you I will kill you."

His gaze found each of the prisoners. It seemed to Cullen that his eyes lingered on his, as if to see if Cullen had gotten the message. Cullen lowered his eyes, not because he was intimidated, but because he didn't want the Tribune to see the hate in them.

Cullen woke the next morning to the shouts of the Roman guards. He glanced over to Rhiannon. Aisling suckled noisily, her little hands cupping the breast gently as if guiding it into her mouth. Finn was curled under a piece of canvas a few feet away. The boy rolled over and stretched out the full length of his body. Finally he sat up, rubbing the sleep out of his eyes. He blinked and Cullen could see that the boy didn't know where he was. The boy saw the guards. His face fell as the reality of where he was came crashing down.

There was a yell behind him. Cullen turned to see a guard standing over the kneeling figure of Mother Miriam. The guard was prodding the old woman with the end of his spear. She attempted to rise, but her feet gave way and she fell to the ground. This prompted more yells and curses from the guard and he raised his spear to strike.

Cullen covered the distance in seconds, the chains on his legs stretching tautly. Other prisoners protested, as Cullen's movement tightened their chains and jerked them to the ground. Cullen ignored them. He covered the old woman's body with his own, holding his hands up pleadingly. The shaft of the guard's spear struck Cullen's body.

"Wait, wait," pleaded Cullen. "I'll help her."

The Roman's eyes flashed with anger. He raised the shaft of his spear and swiped it across Cullen's face. Cullen heard Rhiannon scream as pain seared across his cheek. The force of the blow was strong, but not enough to move him away from the old woman.

Cullen saw other guards rush over.

"I'll help her. Look."

Cullen grabbed Miriam under the armpits and attempted to haul her to his feet. Cullen felt the old woman try to help him, but she seemed to have no strength in her legs.

"What's wrong, you old witch?"

"Priest, Cullen. Not a witch," she muttered, a faint smile playing on her lips.

"What's wrong?" repeated Cullen.

"I fear the meat we ate yesterday did not agree with my stomach." The old woman turned aside and retched, dry heaving bile onto the ground.

The guard grabbed Cullen's shoulder and pushed him aside. But as he fell, Cullen grabbed the guard's wrist and pulled the guard with him. They fell to the ground in a jumble of arms and legs.

"Father," yelled Finn.

Cullen shoved the guard off him and rolled to his knees. He found three spear points pricking the skin of his throat. Cullen stopped moving and slowly raised his hands in a gesture of surrender. The guard he pulled to the ground jumped to his feet. Behind him, Cullen could hear Rhiannon pleading with the Romans not to kill her husband and to understand that Cullen was only trying to help.

What the hell have I done? thought Cullen. *The old woman's going to die anyway, sometime in the next few weeks, what made me think I had to try to extend her existence one more minute? A twisted sense of friendship?*

He cursed himself. They weren't friends, they didn't even know each other. And now he'd put his family in danger.

This is it, thought Cullen. *Spear through the throat, blood rushing in to my lungs as I flop like a fish on the ground in front of my family.*

Cullen closed his eyes, waiting for the inevitable end.

But it was not the end of a spear that struck Cullen. It was the brutal, hammer-like blow of a fist striking the side of his head. Cullen slammed into the ground, his face hitting so hard that sharp, tiny pebbles embedded themselves into his skin. Brightly colored lights flared up in front of his eyes and his cheek felt as if a red-hot poker had been touched to it. He got unsteadily to his knees and looked up at the guard.

"Listen to me. I just want to help her."

Even as he said it, Cullen cursed himself for speaking again, for pleading his case to the Romans. *Just hold your peace, idiot.* He almost prayed for the Romans to cut out his tongue so he'd be forced to stop talking, so he could retain whatever dignity he had left.

The guard, smiling now, struck the other side of Cullen's face. Cullen sprawled in the dirt. The punch sent the little shards of stone deeper into his cheek, some scraping the bone. The pain was only bearable because he was knocked almost to unconsciousness. Finn let out a cry and tried to run to his father but Cullen raised a hand and motioned him back. Cullen pushed himself to a sitting position. The Romans were laughing among themselves, enjoying this little brutality before the business of marching got underway. The guard seized Cullen's shirt and dragged him to his feet. Cullen saw a cruel smile on the guard's face and a sword in the guard's hand. He knew death was seconds away.

Cullen was saved by a shout. The guard's expression soured as Gaius the Tribune walked up. He indicated for the guard to go to him.

Gaius talked to the soldier in low tones. The soldier pointed to the prone figure of the old woman, and then gestured to Cullen with his sword. Gaius held up a hand that stopped the guard in mid-sentence. He stared thoughtfully at the old woman, then came over to Cullen.

"Why is there always one?" he asked.

Cullen looked up.

"One what?"

"One person who always gives me a headache."

"The old woman needed…"

"I understand what you were trying to do," said the Tribune. He studied Cullen's bloodied face. "I know I should kill you. I want to kill you. But there's something about you that fascinates me. Maybe it's the way my men hate you."

"I just wanted to help the old priest."

"Thank you, Cullen," whispered Mother Miriam with a smile.

"Valiant effort, Cullen," said Gaius. "You've nothing to be ashamed of. You did your best."

The Tribune looked over at the wasted old woman and nodded to his guards.

"Kill her," he ordered the guards.

Cullen watched in alarm as two guards grabbed hold of the old woman's arms and started dragging her over to a grove of trees.

She's an old woman. She's nothing. Death will be a release. Let the Romans do what they should have done days ago. And above all keep your damn mouth closed.

"I'll carry her," he said.

You fucking idiot.

The Tribune, who was walking away, stopped and turned. Cullen ground his nails into his palms so hard they almost drew blood. He could go days, weeks sometimes, and grunt fewer words than he'd uttered in the last five minutes.

"I'll carry her," said Cullen. "I'll carry the old woman."

"To what purpose?" smiled Gaius. "She's useless."

"She's not useless. She can read. She knows books. She can speak different tongues. People like her. Someone will buy her and find a use for her old bones."

Gaius considered this.

"What tongues, old woman?"

Mother Miriam licked her lips and replied hoarsely.

"I can converse with the German, and the Gaul, and some of the Ethiope's tribes. I am familiar with the tongues of the Arabs, and, of course, I can speak the language of the great Roman Empire and the tribe in the north of the country we both visited, namely the Brigantes. And, of course, Greek." Miriam's words fade to a light wheeze, as the air in her lungs seemed to give up.

The two soldiers carrying the woman looked at the Tribune awaiting his final order. Gaius raised a hand to chin, and rubbed it as he looked off into the distance.

Cullen pressed on. "She's only sick from the bad meat. In two days she'll be back on her feet. Someone will like her. She'll fetch a good price."

Gaius thought this over. He nodded slowly a few times as if convincing himself, then shrugged.

"Carry her," he said and walked away.

Cullen exhaled a breath he didn't even realize he was holding. The two guards unlocked the chains that bound Miriam's feet and brought her over to Cullen.

Rhiannon, chained in line behind Cullen, stepped forward and hugged him. "I thought they were going to kill you," she whispered.

"They were going to kill me," said Cullen.

The two soldiers dropped the old woman into Cullen's arms. Cullen helped her to stand.

"Mother, I hope you're worth it."

The old woman smiled wanly.

"Right now I don't feel worth anything."

Cullen grunted.

"Just promise me one thing."

"If I can," replied Miriam.

"Don't throw up over me."

"I will pray God gives me the strength to do as you wish."

Sighing, Cullen got down on one knee.

"Climb on, Mother."

It was, thought Cullen as the old woman climbed on his back, going to be a very long day.

Nineteen

It was cloudless and by mid-day the sun bore down on the earth with a furnace-like intensity. Most of the guards and all of the sailors had stayed behind in the garrison near the port. Escorting the prisoners to Rome was a contingent of twenty guards led by Gaius, who placed his son, Lucius, in charge of the prisoners, and the young soldier had been sending water skins among the prisoners all morning.

Miriam was small and thin, but by the time they stopped to eat a lunch of bread, water and cheese, Cullen's back was soaked in sweat and his muscles ached. Miriam had fallen asleep and snored gently as the prisoners and soldiers marched along a path near the edge of a cliff. On their right, they passed rolling fields of grass, dotted with sheep and goats. Herds of deer grazed in the distance.

By mid-morning Cullen stopped looking at the landscape and concentrated on walking. Only a constant breeze coming from the sea kept the heat from being unbearable. Cullen wished the cliffs were lower so the spray from the crashing waves on the rocks below would wash over them. Wishing would get him nowhere, he thought. One foot in front of another, that's what it would take.

When they stopped, Rhiannon gave Aisling to Finn to hold and she helped Miriam down off Cullen's back.

Miriam thanked her and gingerly felt her stomach.

"God is good," she smiled, a look of genuine surprise on her face. "He has taken my pains away."

"He didn't take them away," snorted Cullen. "He just put them in my back." Cullen rolled his arms back and forth, stretching the muscles.

"I owe you a great deal, Cullen. And it begs the question. Why did you save me?"

Cullen lay down on the grass, arms spread wide. He stared at the blue sky.

"I've found that when killing starts, it's sometimes hard to stop."

Mother Miriam smiled.

"Careful Cullen. You're giving me hope that all is not lost for you."

The next day dawned with mist so thick that Cullen could see only three people in front of him before they faded into the grey nothingness. They trudged along, Cullen, his family, his villagers, along with the River Oak Dell people with whom they had suffered their boat journey. It was a relief not to see where they were headed, and Cullen entertained a fantasy that if he could somehow free his family from their chains, they could melt away into the fog-shrouded countryside and disappear from these Romans forever.

Cullen saw Siric stumble to the ground. He lay sprawled there, his eyes wild and unfocused. Siric's cough had worsened and the front of his shirt was streaked with blood. Gretel, his wife, held him, speaking to him in ever-increasing tones, urging him to get up.

Three Roman guards prodded him with their spears. Siric attempted to rise and his muscles shook with the effort. His face, normally a strong, ruddy color, had a greenish tinge. His legs buckled, and he fell to the ground, wheezing. The guards huddled together, speaking quickly to each other. One of them walked away, returning a few minutes later with Gaius. The soldier barked at Siric to get up. Siric could only turn his head, and mumble something between breaths. Gaius regarded the prone man, then turned to the three soldiers and gave an order that Cullen was unable to hear over Gretel's pleas for compassion.

One of the soldiers unlocked the chains from around Siric's feet and dragged him to the side of the road. Gretel knew what was coming. She grabbed her husband's feet and held onto them. A soldier stepped on her wrists and broke her grip. The end came quickly. The soldier dragging Siric away withdrew his sword from his belt, placed it between Siric's ribs and plunged it in. Siric arched up as blood sprayed from his wound.

Mother Miriam whispered a prayer.

Gretel wailed, her voice rising in an incoherent scream of rage until it was cut off as a soldier kicked her in the stomach. Brendel, standing in line behind her, grabbed her and pulled her back, whispering urgently in her ear. Gretel, barely able to breath after the vicious kick, lay against Brendel. The soldiers stared, waiting to see if they'd have to kill her too, but Gretel turned away clutching her stomach, not glancing at her dead husband, a low keening coming from her mouth.

They started to walk again.

For the next two days they marched toward Rome at a pace that left their muscles burning. Mother Miriam's stomach had recovered from its illness, and she had gamely tried to walk with the rest of the prisoners, but the pace of the march soon had her stumbling from exhaustion and Cullen had to carry her. Rhiannon barely spoke a word except to whisper softly to the baby. Finn walked in front of Cullen, sweat pouring down his face. He kept silent like his mother, trying to get through the forced march as best he could. When he finally curled up with the other prisoners at night, he fell asleep within seconds.

The third day it rained.

A storm whipped up from the sea and blew across the land. The rain sliced into their faces, stinging their eyes, snatching their breath away. The Romans lowered their heads and strode into the wind, keeping a steady pace through the day.

In the afternoon the rain stopped. The sun shone through and within minutes steam was rising from the prisoners' clothes and their chattering teeth and shaking bodies finally got relief from the cold. They had marched through the day, with no afternoon rest, so when the forward scouts returned to camp carrying the carcass of a deer they had killed, the guards called for camp to be made.

Cullen guided Rhiannon to sit down on the grass. Her face was bloodless. She clung to Aisling who whimpered in a restless sleep.

"Rhiannon," whispered Cullen. "Let Finn carry her."

Rhiannon reluctantly handed Aisling over to Finn.

"Keep her against your chest. Don't let her get cold,"

Finn nodded and took his sister, cooing softly to her. Cullen spread out the girl's swaddling clothes onto a flat rock. With luck the clothes would be dry by nightfall.

"You'll kill me, won't you, Cullen?" she said.

"What?" he said, turning around.

"If they kill our children, you'll kill me, yes?"

"Don't talk—"

"Because if my children are dead. I must be dead too. I must die with them."

"No one is going to die, Rhiannon."

"If I kill myself, my soul will die, and I'll never see my children in the afterlife. So you must do it."

"Rhiannon, nobody is going to die."

But she wasn't listening to him anymore. A thin smile played on her face as she watched Finn make faces at his baby sister. But her eyes were empty, and as the wind blew her hair in front of her face, she made no effort to brush it away.

The Romans roasted the deer over the fire, turning the meat on a spit. The fire crackled and popped as the juices fell into the flames. The prisoners, woken from a two-hour sleep by the smell of the meat, gazed at the cooking food in anticipation.

"They probably won't give us any," said Twig, his wide eyes never leaving the slowly turning spit. "They're going to eat it all in front of us, and laugh at us as we watch them."

"Don't be stupid," said Art. "There's going to be lots for everyone."

"I shouldn't worry, Twig," said Mother Miriam. "They will want to fatten us for the market. The Roman said so himself. Nobody wants slaves whose ribs stick out from their skin."

Cullen agreed with Miriam, but it wasn't until Gaius himself came over with chunks of meat that the prisoners allowed themselves to drool in anticipation. Lucius came over with pieces of stale bread and hunks of cheese that was starting to ripen in the heat.

It was a feast, and Cullen made his family eat as much as they could. Their next meal might be a long time away.

Twenty

The next morning the prisoners were unshackled and taken down in pairs to behind a rock where a trench had been dug. They could relieve their bladders and bowels there as needed. Cullen and Finn went together. The previous evening's meal had each of them almost racing for the trench, their guards striding alongside them.

They grunted with relief as they emptied their bowels. Finn's head was just visible to Cullen on the other side of the rock that separated the two of them as they sat. Cullen heard Finn stifle a laugh.

"What's funny?"

Cullen saw Finn's hand point to one of the guards whose face was screwed up in disgust.

"I must be stinking the place up," laughed Finn.

"He probably thinks Roman shit smells like honeysuckle."

They laughed as Finn rose, pulling his pants up.

"Wait," said Cullen. "Did you clean yourself?"

"I used some grass," answered Finn.

Cullen looked around and saw where previous occupants of the trench had grabbed handfuls of grass. He did the same and minutes later Cullen and Finn were returning to the campsite, each feeling better than they had in days. It felt good to be out of the chains, if only for a few minutes.

The camp was on a grass verge. On the other side of the path the hill sloped away for about five yards until it reached the edge of the cliff. Down below, the blue sea glittered in the early morning sun.

One of the Roman guards came over to put Cullen and Finn's legs into their manacles. Cullen stood, following the Roman's order, when he felt the earth move beneath him. Hooves pounded up the hill behind him and Cullen turned, expecting to see a horseman ride up.

What he saw was not a horse.

It was the largest stag he had ever seen.

The enormous deer thundered to a stop at the top of the slope and Cullen heard a collective gasp from the prisoners and the guards as the magnificent animal slowly looked down on all the humans laid out before him.

Cullen watched in stunned silence. The animal was less than ten feet from him. Its chest was as wide as an oak tree and Cullen could see the muscles rippling beneath the skin. Its eyes were pools of black that seemed to suck in the light. On the deer's head grew a pair of antlers that dwarfed any pair Cullen had ever seen. It seemed impossible that the deer's head could hold up so heavy a thing, but as the animal turned its head Cullen could see the neck muscles flex and stretch effortlessly.

It continued to scan them until finally the animal's gaze fell upon a group of Romans that stood on the path. The deer seemed to tense and Cullen realized in an instant that those Romans were the scouts—the ones that had brought back the deer last night. But not just any deer, thought Cullen. They had killed the creature's mate.

The moment he made the connection, the stag moved in a blur of hoof-beats. It was suddenly in the midst of the soldiers, swinging his antlers in an arc. Three of the soldiers were flung aside with the first blow. They hit the ground like stones skipping across a river. Two of them lay moaning where they fell. The third lay still, his head split open from hitting a rock. Blood and grey matter poured from the wound, and the soldier's legs and arms twitched as if the nerve endings had been dipped in fire.

The other soldiers sprang to action and one ran behind the deer. Just as he was raising his spear, the animal backed up with three quick steps and lashed out with its hoof. It caught the soldier in the chest with a force that killed him instantly. The soldier flew through the air, rolled once on the hill sloping toward the cliff, and disappeared over the edge.

Three other soldiers rushed the animal from the front but the deer swung his antlers down, brushing the soldiers aside. Two other soldiers flung their spears from fifteen feet away. They hit the stag almost simultaneously, one hitting the animal high in the flank, the other lodging nearer the stomach.

For the first time, the animal retreated, stepping backwards to the edge of the cliff. Cullen wanted to shout out a warning to the beast, but kept his mouth closed. The deer snorted and pawed the ground as blood flowed from its wounds. The creature raised its head and locked eyes with Cullen.

Cullen felt a shiver ripple through his body. Cullen thought he saw pain, suffering and anger in those eyes, but he must be wrong. Animals didn't have emotions, did they? They didn't feel as people did. The stag moved. It walked up toward the path. Another soldier heaved a spear toward it and this one stuck deep in its chest. The stag raised its head and made a sound that was less a cry of pain than a scream of rage. Saliva spewed from its mouth. Cullen was sure that the bellowing signaled the animal's death.

He was wrong.

The stag gathered what remained of its strength and galloped up the hill. It burst through the stunned soldiers. The Romans jumped aside, avoiding the slashing antlers. The stag sank to one knee, and bowed its head as if an invisible emperor sat in a throne before it. But the animal pushed itself to its feet, turned and galloped down the path for ten yards before veering toward the cliff.

Three soldiers stood in its way. Seconds ago they were too far away to be in any danger, now they were between this crazed animal and a hundred foot fall to the rocks below. They made a fatal mistake. They hesitated a moment too long before dodging out of the deer's way. The stag, with its last remaining strength, lowered his head and charged, sweeping the three soldiers off the cliff. The stag seemed to hover in the air for a moment before it, too, dropped out of sight.

For a few heartbeats nobody moved. It was almost as if they were afraid the stag would reappear over the cliff and drag the rest of them down to their deaths.

Gaius ran forward. He was calling his son's name.

Lucius had been one of the three soldiers the stag flung over the cliff, and the boy soldier was surely dead. Cullen heard the panic, the utter desperation in Gaius' voice as he ran toward the edge and flung himself to the ground. Despite himself, Cullen felt a stirring of pity for the Roman. For any man to lose a son, and in front of his eyes, was—

"He's alive!" called Gaius. "He's—get me a rope."

Everyone, prisoners and guards, rushed to the edge of the cliff. Cullen pushed through and saw Lucius clinging to a tree that had somehow found purchase on the side of the cliff. The boy was semi-conscious and blood streamed down his face from a great gash in his forehead. Only pure instinct had allowed him to grab onto the tree to save his life. Cullen searched the rocks below and quickly saw the other two soldiers. They lay on the jagged rocks, their heads split open from the force of the fall, blood and viscera spread out from their skulls like peacock feathers. Their limbs lay at impossible angles. If they had fallen into the sea that roared into a narrow channel between the rocks they might have had a slim chance to survive, but even then they'd have been sucked under by the surging, swirling currents.

The stag must have fallen into the channel because it was nowhere to be seen. It was gone, disappeared as if it had never existed, like a creature that for one moment had escaped the spirit realm to wreak vengeance on those who would destroy his mate.

"Father."

The word croaked from the boy's throat. Blood-soaked spittle flew from his mouth and his body twisted slightly as the wind caught it. His grip, Cullen saw, loosened imperceptibly. The boy had only seconds to live unless someone could reach him.

Cullen pushed his way past two guards and grabbed the length of chain that ran through the foot shackles of the prisoners. It was thirty-five feet long and might just allow him to reach the young soldier. A voice in the back of his head screamed at him *"What are you doing?"* But he pushed it aside as he dragged the length of chain to the edge of the cliff where Gaius was yelling at his son to hang on. He was in his way so Cullen grabbed the Roman by the back of his shirt and hauled him to his feet. Gaius whirled around, his eyes enraged, but Cullen shoved the end of the chain into his hands.

"Get your men to hold this," yelled Cullen as soldiers tried to drag him away.

Cullen jammed an elbow into the nose of the guard behind him. He turned to Gaius, pleading.

"I can get him," yelled Cullen, tripping on the ground as more soldiers grabbed him. Gaius drew his sword and Cullen couldn't believe that he had been so stupid to try to help this man; so idiotic to believe that as fathers they shared a bond however tenuous. He was going to die not as a soldier but as a naïve fool trying to help the enemy of his people. Mother Miriam, at least, would be proud of him. He tensed his stomach muscles, knowing the sword would pass right through them, slicing through his bowels.

Gaius slashed down with the hilt of his sword onto the face of the nearest Roman soldier. The man fell away, clutching his bloodied face in agony.

"Release him, you fools. Let him go."

He threw another soldier away and hauled Cullen to his feet.

"Climb down, damn you."

Cullen had already wound the end of the chain around his left wrist. Two Roman guards, big and brutish, with arms that burst with muscles, grabbed the other end of the chain. Cullen pulled the chain tight until he could feel the tension in it and walked over the edge of the cliff.

He felt the soldiers brace themselves against the earth and saw three more hold the chain as he turned to the vertical face of the cliff. There was no time to look for handholds or make sure each step was safely made. One glance at the Roman clinging desperately to the tree told Cullen all he needed to know. The boy had maybe three heartbeats left before he let go.

"Father," rasped the boy again, this time too softly for anyone but Cullen to hear. Ten feet away, Cullen saw the boy's hand slip from a palm grip to a finger grip and knew what he had to do.

He jerked the chain free of the soldiers' hands with a vicious tug. As he fell he heard their cries of agony as the chain burnt through their hands, slicing them open. His life hung in the balance. Either these Roman bastards were as tough as they looked or he was about to join those two poor fools on the rocks below.

He fell past the tree and felt the sweet agony of the chain jerking to a stop. *Tough bastards, then,* thought Cullen as the chain bit into his arm, almost squeezing it to breaking point.

As he fell he knew the boy had let go of the branch, so just as he passed the tree Cullen reached out his right arm, palm open, at a point three feet below the tree. He had only one chance to guess right and felt of surge of triumph as his hand closed around the boy's wrist. For a moment Cullen felt the thrill of triumph. Then the boy's weight kicked in and a dagger of agony surged through his left arm, from his shoulder to the tips of his fingers as the extra weight made the chain cut even deeper into his wrist. He cried out curses at the guards above him, who in turn cursed him even more.

"Pull, damn you, you sons of whores and bitches."

He felt the chain jerk upwards as the five soldiers started to haul him and Lucius to safety. Cullen tried to use his feet to push himself up the cliff face, but only succeeded in spinning himself around, causing Lucius to crash into the soil of the cliff. He gritted his teeth and hung on, knowing if he could just take the pain for a few more seconds then they would both be lying safely on the grass, the sweet, sweet grass, where no chain would be squeezing his bones together, grinding them into splinters and dust.

What in the name of all the Roman Gods was taking these jackals so long to lift him up?

The seconds stretched on, endless eternities of agony until a hand reached down, grabbed his arm and hauled him over the side of the cliff. More hands reached for the young soldier around whose wrist Cullen had a death grip. The hands dragged them onto the ground where Cullen lay gasping for breath. The pressure on his left hand had eased slightly, but the chain was still wrapped around it, almost fused into his forearm.

A white-hot jolt of agony ripped through him. One of the soldiers had unwrapped the chain and his bones screamed out in protest as they returned to their normal positions. Some of his skin came away with the chain and he uttered a string of curses at the guards.

Gaius knelt between Cullen and Lucius. He took hold of Cullen's right hand.

"He's safe. You can let go now."

Cullen stared at his hand that gripped Lucius's wrist like a vice. He tried to will his hand to relax, but it seemed as if it belonged to someone else.

"I can't," he whispered.

Gaius stared at Cullen for a moment. He reached for Cullen's hand and grabbed one of the fingers. He tried to pry the fingers up but couldn't move them at all, so powerful was his grip. Gaius sat back, awed by Cullen's strength.

"You'll break his hand if you don't let go," he said gently.

Finn slipped through the guards who had positioned themselves around their commander. He knelt down beside his father.

"Father," he said. "Just relax. He's safe now."

Cullen blinked, as if just waking up. He looked down at the grip he had on Lucius and one by one his fingers let go of the young soldier's arm. The company doctor was already attending to Gaius' son.

"Is he alright?" asked Cullen, sitting up and slowly straightening his fingers out.

"No, he's not alright. He's bloody all over and he'll have a headache the size of Jupiter's Temple. But he'll live." Gaius smoothed his son's hair. "Thanks to you, he will live."

Cullen knew he wouldn't get a better chance than this.

"Let us go, Gaius," he pleaded. "We're just a family, nothing more. My wife won't last much longer. Give us our freedom, I beg you."

A puzzled expression crossed the Roman's face.

"All this does is make us even, Cullen."

"Even?"

"On the ship. After your son cut Lucius, I stopped my boy from killing your boy. He lives because I allowed him to live."

Cullen could only stare at the Roman.

"I am grateful, Cullen," said Gaius, "but your fate is determined."

Gaius turned on his heels and walked away.

Twenty one

At noon they got ready to march again. Cullen's wrists ached from his rescue of the young Roman. Rhiannon bundled Aisling into her swaddling clothes.

"Aisling's started to cough," said Rhiannon.

"I know," said Cullen. "I heard her last night."

"It was the boat. When it rained. I tried to keep her warm."

"It's just a cough, Rhiannon. She'll get better."

Rhiannon eyes bored into Cullen's, as if waiting for him to say something resembling the truth.

"It's just a cough," repeated Cullen. Rhiannon lowered her gaze and turned away.

Cullen, with Mother Miriam on his back, continued walking, the chains swishing on the dusty road. For the next few hours no one spoke. The guards were tired, but the prisoners, their strength sapped by the bleakness of their future, were exhausted. They soon settled into a steady motion, and all that mattered was putting one leg in front of the other. Each footstep caused a tiny plume of dust to rise off the ground, and with the combination of hundreds of feet making thousands of steps, the air was soon clogged with dust that found its way into every crack, crease and orifice in their bodies. Cullen, stuck near the back of the group, tried to breathe through his nose, but that did nothing to stop the dust from filling his lungs, and he found himself spitting up dark brown phlegm every hundred or so steps. Soon, even that became part of the monotony, and the entire group, prisoners and guards, trudged on.

Mother Miriam stirred, and Cullen heard her yawn widely.

"I just had an amazing dream," said Miriam.

"Me too," said Cullen. "I dreamt of a world where you didn't exist."

Mother Miriam patted Cullen on the shoulder, laughing gently.

"I do owe you much, Cullen. Not many people would have carried me this far."

Cullen grunted.

"So what was your dream about, old woman?"

"I dreamt about that soldier. The one who struck you three times."

"And that was your great dream? You enjoyed seeing me get beaten half to death?"

Cullen felt Mother Miriam shake her head.

"Of course not, my boy. The amazing part is what you did after he hit you."

"I bled. That's what happens when you get hit."

"I don't know why I didn't realize it before. Probably because I was too sick—or too concerned with my own hide—but now I know what you did."

Miriam paused, waiting for Cullen to prompt her again. Cullen tried to think about what he did but nothing came to mind, so he obliged the old woman.

"Alright, Mother, what did I do?"

"Nothing!" said Mother Miriam triumphantly.

Cullen trudged along, hefting Miriam higher on his back. Between the weight of the old woman and the word games she was playing, Cullen felt as if he could not only throw the old bitch into the sea, but jump in after her to make sure she drowned.

"I swear, you old witch, you better start making sense before I—"

"You turned the other cheek," said Miriam. She slapped Cullen's back as if she had made the argument to end all arguments. Cullen could almost feel the rosy, self-satisfied glow from her.

"You old fool. They had spears, all of them, and they were about to puncture my neck. What did you think I was going to do? Hit them back?"

"I just know what you did. You acted the way you acted because you cared more about saving me than about taking your revenge with the soldier."

"Trust me, Mother, if it was just me and that soldier with none of his friends around waiting to stick me then I may, I just may, have ripped his intestines from his body and strangled him with them."

Miriam was silent for a moment.

"I don't think you would have killed him."

"We'll never know," replied Cullen.

"I think," continued Miriam, as if Cullen hadn't spoken. "I think you value the vow you made to Finn that you will not kill again."

"I think that promise will kill me one day."

"I disagree," whispered the old woman. "I think that promise will save your life."

Twenty two

Cullen, his mind lost in the rhythm of his steps, was jerked back to awareness by a shout. He looked up to see Gaius hailing a platoon of Roman soldiers who guarded fifteen bound prisoners by the side of the road. The prisoners had their hands and legs tied. Grime and dirt caked their bodies. Roman guards were digging holes along the side of the road; others were hacking branches off tree trunks.

Sitting in the shade of an open carriage was an old man in a white tunic, around which was wrapped a purple sash. *A senator, perhaps?* thought Cullen, remembering the lessons from Sulla Atticus Scaurus how the hierarchy of Roman society worked. There must be some important business going on here. Three slaves attended him: one cooled him with a fan made of ostrich plumes, another rubbed his feet, while the third stood by, ready to be ordered about at the Senator's whim. The Senator looked miserable, his rheumy eyes shifting over the prisoners with distaste. Cullen wondered if he had ever done a hard day's work in his life. His flesh was flabby, and despite being a large man, it seemed to hang off him like loose clothes.

One of the Roman soldiers detached himself from his men and strolled over to Gaius. Cullen could see that the Roman had a wineskin in his hand. Gaius held out his hands, a smile creasing his weathered face.

"Praxis, you old drunk, the last time I saw you, you had a wine jar in your arms."

"And a wench on my lap. How are you doing, Gaius, you son of a whore?"

"If I was doing well, do you think I'd still be dragging these bastards around? I'm an old man. I should be sitting in a bright, white villa, being attended to by one of those German women."

Gaius's friend—Praxis—walked closer. Sweat drenched the armpits of his shirt. Blood spatters had dried on his legs and sandals, and Cullen noticed an open wound on his arm.

Gaius had seen what Cullen had noticed. He gestured to the wound on Praxis's arm. Praxis laughed with embarrassment.

"I swear to you, Gaius, I thought of you not an hour ago. Clear as a bell, your voice was in my mind."

"And what did my voice say?"

"Something you told me over and over when I had the misfortune to serve under you: Never underestimate a cornered rat."

Gaius glanced back at his young soldiers and smiled ruefully.

"I still say it. And there's not a skull that those words can penetrate." Gaius looked at the wound on Praxis's arm. "Not until this happens."

Praxis threw open his arms and walked closer to Gaius. The two men hugged, clapping each other on the back. Praxis grabbed hold of Gaius's shoulders and held him at arm's length. The two men stared at each other for a full five seconds, and then both burst out laughing.

Cullen recognized the camaraderie and friendship that these two men shared, and knew that they knew each other better than either of their wives ever would. If they had been in the same legion then they had seen battle together, and that would bind them closer than mere love ever could.

Praxis gestured to the fifteen prisoners sitting by the side of the road.

"Slaves. They mutinied. Killed the farmer, his wife, his children and other slaves who refused to join with them. They made it as far as the coast when they were captured by our patrol. We'll string them along the road as a warning."

Gaius studied Praxis's patrol. All of them were streaked with grime and dirt. Gaius could almost feel the fatigue from their bodies.

"You want to use some of my bastards to help speed things up?"

Praxis slapped him on the back.

"I was hoping you'd make the offer. Some of my boys have just been weaned off their mothers' teats, and it'll take me time to turn them into men."

Gaius nodded at Lucius, who motioned to two other guards. He walked along the column of prisoners and pointed to Cullen, Art, Brendel, Twig, and Rufus. The guards slipped the chains from their feet and arms, and brought them at spear point to Praxis and Gaius.

"They'll do," said Praxis, studying the hard muscles of the men. He came to Cullen and grabbed his shoulder, kneading the muscles. "They'll definitely do."

Praxis led them down the hill to where his own men worked near the bound prisoners. As Cullen got closer, he noticed movement in the forest behind the men. Five soldiers emerged, each of them bare to the chest, dragging logs behind them. They pulled the logs over to the group of Romans who were busy hacking the branches off other trees that had been cut down earlier.

"Leo! Tonio! Use these donkeys to drag the logs out."

The one called Leo gestured to Cullen and the four others with him. He was a spare man, with hollow eyes and sunken cheeks who looked as if being a soldier had sucked every ounce of fat from his body. He viewed his new helpers with distaste, and his eyes paused when he came to Cullen.

"Tonio, bring your spears. Keep your eyes on these ones."

Tonio hastened to obey him, and Leo led the prisoners into the forest, with Tonio and another guard flanking them. They came to a clearing within the forest where four Romans were busy hacking down some thin conifers. For the next two hours, Cullen and his villagers cut down the trees, broke off their branches, and dragged them through the forest to the road. It was hard work, but to Cullen it felt like a relief to be doing something so physical and normal. His family was able to take a rest, and when he compared his plight to the unfortunate prisoners who sat in the sun awaiting their fate, their arms and legs strung together, it felt as if his situation was almost optimistic.

The prisoners knew they were going to die in agony.

Defeat clung to them. Even if they closed their eyes, they could not escape the THUNK, THUNK, THUNK of the Roman axes as they hacked into the stripped logs, carving a notch in the *stipes*—the vertical trunk of the crucifix—and the matching notch in the *patibulum*, the horizontal log to which the prisoners would be nailed. The Romans worked steadily, methodically. They needed thirty stripped logs to make the fifteen crosses, and by mid-afternoon the completed *stipes* were inserted into three foot deep holes dug into the ground.

Cullen and the others who had helped drag the logs from the forest were allowed to sit in the shade, where they were given bread, cheese and a couple of skins of wine.

Cullen heard a reedy, high-pitched voice giving orders. He turned to see the Senator pointing a bloated, sausage-like finger at one of the prisoners who sat on the edge of the group. Praxis walked over to the prisoner, tapping him on the shoulder with the hilt of his sword, and looking at the Senator with a questioning glance. The Senator nodded sharply, lowering his hand so it lay across his stomach. Praxis nodded to two of his guards who walked over to the prisoner and hauled him to his feet. The prisoner kept his body limp, and the guards had to bend his arms down so they could maintain a grip on him. The dragged him over to the edge of the road. Two large poles had been placed there, about six paces apart.

Whipping posts, just like the ones on the ship.

They untied the man's hands, stretched out his arms, and re-tied his arms to the two poles, pulling them high so that his body formed the shape of an X. The man cried aloud with the agony of the stretch. Cullen could see the muscles and tendons in the man's arm vibrate with the pain of being pulled apart more than nature had ever intended.

One of the guards shoved his sword under the man's shirt. He jerked his sword up and the shirt remnants fell from the man leaving his torso bare. The man gritted his teeth and took in a number of quick, short, breaths.

Bastard knows what's coming, thought Cullen.

Sure enough, the guard called Leo, the one with the gaunt cheeks and hollow eyes, walked over to the splayed-out prisoner. In his hand he carried a whip, made up of several leather strips. Metal balls were attached down the length of each leather strap, and as Leo walked toward the prisoner, the straps brushing against each other made a *tic, tic, tic* sound. A shard of sheep bone tied at the end of each strap completed the weapon.

Leo stopped behind the prisoner, and looked over to Praxis, who, in turn, looked over at the Senator. A fly buzzed around the Senator's face, causing him to raise a plump hand to try to swat it away. Annoyed, he looked at the prisoner, arranging his body so it would appear appropriately stern and regal.

"Is this the man that led the slaughter of Publius Mons Primus and his family?"

Praxis stepped forward.

"Yes, Senator."

"His name, Tribune."

"Anders, sir."

"A wretch. A veritable wretch. Flog him hard, but make sure he lives. I don't want him bleeding out before we string him up. Is your man good, Tribune?"

Praxis looked at Leo, who stood ready with the whip.

"Very good, sir. The wretch will know what pain is."

"But don't kill him," admonished the Senator, wagging a bloated finger.

"Leo could make him live for eternity, sir, in agony."

"Unfortunately, I do not have eternity. I do not even have a day. But for the next few hours I want these creatures to suffer."

He leaned back with an audible sigh of relief. Praxis nodded to Leo, who shook the whip, causing the leather strands to dance around. *Surely,* thought Cullen, *even the snakes on Medusa's head, couldn't have sent a colder shiver of fear down a man's spine, than the sight of those strips of cowhide waking up.*

Leo stepped to the side of Anders, the prisoner, who turned his head around to the Senator.

"I'll find your mother in Hell, Roman. I'll fuck her like the dog she is." Spittle flew from the prisoner's contorted mouth, and his eyes burned with hate.

""How dare you, sir!" screamed the Senator.

"Commence!" shouted Praxis.

The whip descended in a blur. The prisoner's back arched, and Cullen could almost hear the tendons popping in his shoulders as Anders tried to escape the sudden, brutal agony that scorched his back. Spittle and snot sprayed from his mouth, and a keening whine escaped through his clenched teeth.

The Senator chuckled, and held up his hand to Leo, who brought the whip down.

"You were saying, sir? Something about my mother?"

When the whipping was done they untied his wrists and he collapsed on the ground on his hands and knees, his fingers clawing at the grass as if someone had whispered to him that relief was hidden there among the soft, verdant blades if only he could find it. His body convulsed suddenly, and he dry heaved on the ground. The Romans let him crawl around on the grass like a year-old baby, while they brought over one of the logs. They dropped the log on the ground near the first vertical post, crossed over to Anders and each of the guards grabbed him under his arms and dragged him over to the log. Anders raised his head, and through bloodshot eyes, saw where they were taking him. He twisted his body away, but the Romans had a firm grip on him.

Whatever defiance Anders had shown before had deserted him, replaced by naked fear.

"Please, no," he croaked. "Please."

"Listen to him beg now," said the Senator, his voice dripping in satisfaction.

The Romans guards grabbed an arm each and forced them to straighten, placing them outstretched on the log. The guards bore down with all their weight, holding the arms in place. Another Roman walked up, carrying a mallet and some nails.

"No, stop. Please, stop, I didn't kill anyone," said the prisoner, as the Roman placed a nail in the center of the man's wrist. He tried to catch the Roman's eye, but the soldier was concentrating on raising the hammer up high to get in a good first blow.

THUNK.

The first blow sent the nail through the prisoner's wrist and an inch deep into the wood. The two Roman guards holding him had to force their weight down more onto Anders's arms, so powerful was his struggle. Another three quick blows secured the man's left arm to the log. The Roman crossed the few steps to the other side. The process was repeated, and in seconds the man's arm was nailed to the log. Anders's head whipped from side to side, his mouth frothing.

"If you think this is pain now, you murderous wretch," said the Senator, popping purple grapes into his mouth, "then you are in for a very nasty surprise. Once they prop you upright and place you on the cross, I'm assured the agony is most dreadful."

The senator proved prophetic about the pain. Four guards lifted up the log to which the prisoner was nailed. Another guard grabbed hold of the prisoner's legs, and they marched him over to the *stipes*—the vertical pole in the ground. The Romans notched the *Patibulum* into the *stipes*. Rope was tied around the two logs where they connected, binding them to form a cruciform shape.

As Anders was turned upright, and the full weight of his body sagged toward the earth, his arms extended, his chest sank down, and Cullen could see that the position had caused the prisoner's elbows and shoulders to dislocate. The tendons strained like strands of rope under his skin. Then, in a sequence that almost caused Cullen to vomit up his meal of bread, cheese and wine, he saw the tendons pop, one by one, and slither under his skin, disappearing like malevolent worms.

Anders had no breath left to scream with, and even the muscles in his face had so little strength left that they had trouble contorting with the agony he must feel. Only his eyes managed to convey the racking, burning fire of pain that his body was going through.

Two guards twisted his legs to a ninety-degree angle so his feet could be placed flat on the pole. A third guard placed a long nail on the top of his feet, and slammed his mallet down. A high keening wail escaped from the prisoner's mouth and he tried to kick his legs away to no avail. Another hammer blow, and this time the nail went through the bottom foot and into the pole. As before, three more hits bound the prisoner to the cross.

The man hung limp on the cross, his weight hanging from his arms. His body twisted from side to side, searching for a way to get away from the pain, but he stopped this soon, realizing that any motion made the pain worse, that any movement tore into his bones and tendons, rending them apart, as if someone was holding a flaming torch to his nerve endings. In desperation the man let his weight sag and within seconds he was drawing in low, hitching breaths. Cullen thought back to the Roman soldier, Scaurus, who was a partner in cruelty with his father. He'd describe how the prisoner on the cross would try to sag forward, but this would work for only a few minutes because the prisoner would be unable to draw in a breath. He would suffocate if he remained like this. The only way he could survive was by pushing his weight up with his feet so his chest would be free to breathe properly. The Roman would tell Cullen that this was his favorite part of the torture, because the prisoner would soon realize that the only way to save himself—if only for a few more hours—was to cause himself the most unimaginable pain by pushing down on his nailed feet.

Watch their faces, the Roman would say, *you can almost see their eyes bleed.*

Cullen let his eyes drop to the ground so that he would be unable to see the prisoner put himself through the searing pain. But even with his eyes on the ground, he was unable to shut out the heart-rending squeals of purest agony as the prisoner pushed himself up, hitching in breaths and expelling them out in a piteous moan.

Miriam is right about one thing, thought Cullen. Hell does exist. But you don't have to go searching in the depths of the universe for it. Just stare at this bastard. Listen to him. Watch the Romans laugh at him. If you wanted demons, look no further than them. And where was Mother Miriam's God? What God that preached love and compassion would let this happen?

All the prayers that must float up to Heaven, all the pleadings, the begging, all of them disappeared in the mist among the stars, dissipating like morning fog on a Summer's day.

Cullen wished there was a God. He wanted Him to exist, because then he could hate Him.

The Romans made them watch.

They took Cullen and the villagers down to the road, and made them face the prisoners on the crosses. Gaius considered it an excellent opportunity for the villagers to learn what they could expect if they took it upon themselves to defy Roman rule. Cullen told Finn to keep his eyes down, but Gaius would have none of it. He looked at each villager to make sure they gazed upon the crucified men.

The Senator, having satiated himself on a meal of dried meats, fruit and bread, called Praxis over.

"Expedite this."

Praxis nodded. He turned to Leo who grabbed a large hammer. Leo walked over to the first prisoner they had crucified, the man called Anders. He swung the hammer hard, hitting the man on his knees. Anders slumped forward, his eyes widening in shock. Weakened almost to death from his ordeal, Anders only let out a grunt as he slumped forward, his eyes darting back and forth as if realizing that despite all the pain of the last few hours, all the agony that he thought was the most one person could ever endure in this world, that he still had the capacity to feel even more pain.

The blow had broken his legs, and there was no way his body could force itself to stand up. The Senator walked over to Anders.

There was no defiance in Anders face, not even a mute plea for help. Hanging forward like this meant that Anders could draw in a breath, but couldn't let one out. His breathing became shallower and shallower, his breaths mere hitches, tiny spasms of muscle movement. As the Senator watched, he slowly suffocated to death.

They made camp on the road, the corpses of all fifteen prisoners hanging from their crosses overlooking where they lay, like a legion of grotesque angels sent to guide them to the depths of hell. Finn lay with his head buried in his mother's breast, refusing to look at the dead people. Aisling was too young, and simply did not know what she was seeing. Her eyes roamed everywhere, and the dead men on their crosses were as interesting as a flurry of leaves that would blow by, or a humming bird sucking nectar from the flowers that grew wild on the side of the road. Rhiannon held Aisling in her arms staring at her daughter with an unnerving intensity.

"Feel her forehead," she said in a whisper.

Cullen put his hand on her tiny head. Heat blazed off her.

"Gods," said Cullen. He looked closer at his daughter and noticed what he hadn't seen before: her eyes were rimmed with red, and had a faraway look that wasn't like her. At that moment, her little body convulsed, letting out a huge whooping cough. Speckles of saliva flew from her mouth, and as the coughing dissipated, she cried weakly, lungs wheezing.

"We should cool her down," said Cullen.

"It was the cold that made her sick."

"We can't let her burn like this."

"I'll leave her wrappings open," said Rhiannon.

"What else should we do?" said Cullen.

Mother Miriam stepped over to them. She handed them a wineskin. They looked at her.

"Don't worry," smiled Miriam. "I asked one of the guards for some water for the baby and he put it in this. Little Aisling should drink this."

"Thank you, Miriam," said Rhiannon. "Is there anything else we can do?"

Mother Miriam placed her weathered hand on Aisling's forehead.

"Pray."

Twenty three

They marched, and the rain stung their skin. It poured down hard, each drop stinging with cold and fury. The wind seemed to come from all directions, whipping up the rags they were dressed in, flailing the hair around their faces, the rain needle darts on their faces, slapping into their eyes.

Finn walked in the shadow of his father, who blocked some of the fury of the storm. Rhiannon clutched the baby to her body as if it was her own beating heart.

They stopped at midday under the arch of a wide aqueduct. It was impossible to tell where the sun was in the sky. It was so dark it could have been dusk. The rain came down in sheets, like some malevolent curtain. Mother Miriam found her way over to Cullen. She held out some bread to Cullen.

"I begged it off a guard. They don't intend to feed us until tonight."

Cullen took the bread.

"Thanks, Mother," he said quietly.

Cullen gave the bread to Rhiannon, who gave most of it to Finn. The young boy bit into it ravenously. She kept a piece of the bread to feed to Aisling, almost crumb by crumb.

"Cullen," said Miriam. Cullen looked at the old woman.

"You'll need to be strong."

"I know that," said Cullen, a tired look on his face. "Of course I know that."

The old woman took hold of Cullen's arm and squeezed gently. She smiled sadly at Cullen.

"You'll need to be strong," repeated Miriam.

That evening they were housed in tents on a field.

As night descended on the camp, Rhiannon turned to Cullen.

"She's not taking my breast."

"Try giving her some soft bread," said Cullen.

"She won't take that either. She's had nothing all day."

"Let Cullen hold her," said Miriam.

For once, Rhiannon didn't protest, but handed Aisling to Cullen, who took the infant and held her close to him.

Where had her plumpness gone? Babies shouldn't look like this, with pale, yellowish skin and gaunt cheeks. He kissed her forehead, and the fever still had her in its grip. She hadn't cooled down. If anything, she was hotter than she was yesterday.

"*Mo chroi*," he said softly in gaelic. *My heart.*

"She's not coughing anymore, Rhiannon. Maybe that's a good sign."

"She's not coughing because she has no strength left," said Rhiannon.

"She'll get better," whispered Cullen. "She's strong."

"Why don't my daughters live, Cullen?" asked Rhiannon, in a voice flat with fear.

"Aisling will live, Rhiannon. She's your daughter, my love. She's strong."

Rhiannon took Aisling back and kissed her lips.

"I love you so much, my darling," she said, in a voice so low Cullen could only make out the words by reading her lips. "I love you always. I'll never forget you."

She looked up at Cullen. "Will you stay awake with me?"

Aisling died that night. Her chest heaved once and then emptied. No dagger had ever pierced Cullen's heart like that last breath.

Rhiannon rocked back and forth, her shoulders shaking as she sobbed. Cullen hid his face in his hands and numbness took hold of him. He felt a hand on his shoulder. Mother Miriam held Cullen and kissed his forehead.

Finn woke up and asked his mother what was wrong. Neither Rhiannon nor Cullen could answer him. Mother Miriam told Finn his sister was dead. The boy burst into tears. He went over to his mother and held her tight.

"Cullen."

He looked up to find Miriam staring into his eyes.

"We have to bury her," said the priest.

"I know," said Cullen.

"We have to bury her now. Here. In this ground."

Cullen looked at the old woman.

"Why?" he asked, his voice desolate.

"They'll throw her away, Cullen. If they find her dead in the morning, they'll throw her away."

They dug a hole in the ground, using their bare hands to scrape away the soil. Rain had softened the earth, and soon the hole they dug was three feet deep. Cullen took off his shirt and laid it on the ground. Rhiannon placed the body on the shirt, and swaddled Aisling in it, covering her entirely.

Rhiannon lifted the baby's body to her one last time. Her face was slack with grief. Cullen took the baby and placed her in the ground. He looked up at Mother Miriam.

"What am I supposed to do now?" whispered Cullen.

"You're supposed to live, Cullen."

The priest reached out with both hands and grabbed a handful of dirt. She lowered her hands into the makeshift grave and carefully placed the soil over Aisling's body. Cullen filled his hands with soil and helped the priest bury his daughter.

The sun was barely over the horizon when they started out for Rome. By noon, they were in the Slave's Market.

Twenty four

Through his grief, Cullen was dimly aware that this city was like nothing he had ever seen. White columns of marble held up buildings that seemed to reach to the sky. Statues of leaders, of soldiers and statesmen lined the streets. Houses that were lived in by ordinary citizens seemed like palaces to him. And the palaces, surely only Gods lived in them.

People. People were everywhere. Vendors peddled their wares along each road and alleyway. Citizens and slaves, low-born and high-born weaved through the streets and alleys, sometimes hooting and jeering at the prisoners trudging to the market square, but mostly ignoring them: new slaves they saw every day.

He walked beside Rhiannon. Her eyes were almost closed as if she slept as she walked. Finn walked with Mother Miriam, and Cullen could hear the ups and downs of an animated conversation between them. Cullen was grateful to the old woman for keeping his son occupied. Finn had loved his sister, but had seen three of his siblings die in years past. He had never known a sister to live past two years.

They passed by a schoolroom, not much more than a storefront, filled with children chanting lessons back to a teacher; they wound their way down streets that were crammed with shopkeepers hawking their goods. One of the shopkeepers looked at Mother Miriam and asked a Roman guard if he would take fifteen *sestertii* for the old woman. Once they were made to stop while huge gray beasts, with noses longer that Cullen was tall, walked ponderously in front of them. Cullen heard gasps of astonishment from the other captives as they beheld these creatures.

They reached the market square. Shopkeepers yelled and bartered. A herd of goats brayed in a rising cacophony as they crossed the square toward an abattoir where they would be silenced forever. Street musicians sang, played flutes and banged on drums.

Animal and human dung lay everywhere in the square. People stepped in it without care, because trying to avoid it was pointless. Rotting vegetables sent the fetid stench of decay through the air.

The prisoners were herded into a corner of the square. The guards ordered them to sit down on the cobblestones.

Mother Miriam was taken from the group by one of the auctioneer's workers. She was led over to a man with close-cropped black hair who spoke to the old woman, asking her questions and listening intently to her answers. Finally, satisfied, he nodded his head. Money was exchanged, and Mother Miriam was led away. She turned her head, found Cullen's eyes, and mouthed a word to him.

Live.

Cullen nodded once, and then Miriam was taken away and was soon swallowed up in the crowd. Cullen wished Gaius was here to see this. Mother Miriam, the old crone whom Gaius would have slain without a second's hesitation because he thought she was sick and useless, was the first of their village to be sold.

"Is she coming back?" asked Finn.

"No, Finn. She's gone now," said Cullen.

"I liked her," said Finn. "She told me a riddle."

Cullen turned to Finn. "What's the riddle?"

"She told me a story first. Then asked me the riddle."

"So tell me the story."

Finn's eyes were still looking at the spot where he'd seen Mother Miriam disappear into the crowd.

"She's gone, Finn. Tell me the story."

Finn forced his eyes up to his father.

"Do you think mother will want to hear the story too?"

Cullen glanced at Rhiannon, who sat on the other side of Finn.

"Of course. Go ahead."

Finn closed his eyes and began.

"There was this man. He was rich. Owned a big farm with lots of animals. Lots of people worked for him. He had two sons. The older son listened to his father and did what he was told. The younger son was wild and one day he went to his father and said, 'Poppa, I want all the money that's mine...' So the father gave the younger son all the money that belonged to him."

Finn glanced up to his father to see if he was following the story.

"Rich man, two sons, gives the younger son his money. Got it. But why does the younger son want his money?"

"The younger son wants his money so he can go to a city and buy whatever he wants. Drink, clothes, women."

"I see."

"He just wants to have lots of fun and do no work. So he does that. Spends three years doing nothing except having fun. He makes lots of friends. But then, the money runs out. He's got nothing. And when he asks his friends to help him, they disappear."

"I guess they weren't really his friends, then."

"Right. They just liked him because he had money. So he starts to get really hungry. Like you just want to chew your arm off. Or eat grass or snails. And he goes to a farmer and begs him for a job minding his pigs, and says all he wants is to eat the same swill as the pigs eat. The farmer agrees, and the younger son works for him, eating the swill and realizing that he misses his home a lot."

"Like you, me and your mother. We miss home too."

"Right. And he wants to go home, but he's ashamed. What will he tell his father? Will his father even forgive him for being so stupid? Finally, he's so tired of eating the pig food that he decides to go home."

A roman guard walked close to them, and stopped in front of Finn. He tapped the base of his spear against Finn's foot.

"Stop talking, son," said the guard. "Or I'll close your mouth for you."

Cullen and Finn looked at each other. Cullen waited until the guard went away, then turned to Finn.

"You can finish the story later, Finn. I want to know what the riddle is."

Finn nodded, staring fearfully at the guards. Cullen put his arms around Finn's shoulders and held him close.

The guards ordered them to take off their clothes.

Some of the women tried to cover their nakedness with their hands, but workers went up to them hitting their arms with sticks until they dropped them. They stood side by side, hanging their heads down. Cullen made sure he stood beside Rhiannon so she could at least hide behind him if she wished. But her eyes were glassy and she wore her nakedness without care, her mind far away.

The villagers lined up behind other slaves, who, group by group, were led up onto a wooden platform. The platform faced the square where potential buyers gathered. Cullen saw two distinct types: noblemen and farmers. The farmers had sun-weathered faces and stared dubiously at the first offering of slaves. Then, when a sufficient crowd had gathered, the auctioneer stepped onto the platform.

He had short, close-cropped hair and made no attempt to hide a mouth that contained a single tooth. In fact, the auctioneer beamed a wide smile at the gathered crowd, proudly displaying the front tooth, sole survivor of his ivory family.

The auctioneer waved to the crowd and surveyed the fifteen slaves with mock seriousness. He picked out the strongest man from the group— a red-faced Gaul with a hare-lip—and had him turn around. The man was bare-chested and some of the buyers nodded approval at his apparent strength.

The auctioneer pointed out the qualities that each of the prisoners possessed. One man had great strength, another was skilled in woodwork, this one could mend shoes, that one was able to carve the very likeness of Caesar in stone. And the women, oh!, the meals they could cook and serve, the chores they could do around a house that would become so clean it would shine, positively shine, not to mention the other benefits of having an extra pair of tits in the house—at this the auctioneer grabbed his crotch and pumped his hips back and forth, while his tongue snaked around the single tooth in his gums, slathering it in saliva. The crowd roared its approval.

The first bids came in and soon there was a healthy trade as the prisoners were sold, either singly or in groups. One thing that gave Cullen hope was that the auctioneer was trying to sell his prisoners in groups. If a farmer was going to buy a man to work his fields, his wife would be bought to help keep the house. The children would be put to work around the farm. It made sense to Cullen that it would be like this. A man that didn't have to worry about his family enslaved on some distant farm would be a better worker. He wouldn't try to escape to rescue them. He wouldn't try to kill his owner for fear his family would be put to death. Cullen clung to this fierce hope as the sun crawled across the sky and the slaves left the holding pen until suddenly, with the sun turning a golden orange in the western sky, only Cullen and his villagers were left and they were herded onto the raised wooden platform to be judged and sold.

Cullen led the villagers up the steps, acutely aware of all the eyes turning to them, judging them, gauging their strengths. Among this group of six men, five women and one child—Finn—Cullen could see they made an impressive show. Art and Cullen were obviously immensely strong individuals, good for farming, heavy lifting or building. The women all looked rosy and healthy. Who wouldn't want such fine slaves on their farm?

Cullen looked out at the buyers. Already the crowd was dispersing, most of them having purchased their slaves earlier in the day. Cullen listened to the auctioneer as he paraded up and down in front of the villagers, pointing and gesturing to them as he listed their abilities and strengths.

"I feel like a piece of horse-meat," whispered Brendel to Cullen. Cullen nodded, looking grim.

Put a sword in my hand, he thought. *Let me show them what I can really do.*

The bidding started, and Cullen studied the two men who were intent on acquiring them. One of them was a large man with hanging jowls and a bulbous nose. Three fawning servants surrounded him. One of these servants shaded the man's head. He had the look of a politician; one who obviously indulged in all the pleasures that a city like Rome had to offer. He reminded Cullen of the senator who oversaw the crucifixions. The other bidder could not have been more different. He had a lean face and body. His eyes were almost hidden by low-hanging eyebrows, but those eyes rarely blinked and missed nothing. White hair grew from the sides of his head and fell down onto his shoulders. His cheekbones stood out, made all the more prominent by sunken cheeks. There wasn't a spare ounce of fat on this man's body. There was a subtle strength about the man, despite his age. Cullen knew at once that the man had been a soldier.

The two bidders did not look at each other as they shouted out the ever-increasing amount of their bids. In a minute, it was done. The fat politician dismissively shook his head as the bidding exceeded what he wanted to pay.

They now belonged to the lean old man.

The auctioneer stretched and yawned, his long day now finished. He gestured for the villagers to follow him down the steps of the wooden platform so the old man could take home his purchases.

"Kind sir," said the auctioneer. "I think you got the bargain of the day. Three of these men are built like oxen."

The lean, old man studied his slaves as they found their clothes and put them back on.

"I had my eye on them all day," he said. "Some of the other slaves looked half dead. I'm surprised you managed to get rid of them."

"My powers of persuasion are legendary, your graciousness," said the auctioneer with mock laughter. The old soldier's lips curled into a thin smile, as he walked along the lines of villagers, sometimes grasping the biceps of a man, other times lifting the chin of a woman to gaze into her eyes. Cullen kept his gaze down on the ground in what he hoped looked like a subservient manner as the man walked by him. The old soldier seemed pleased with his purchases and he gestured to one of his aides, who came forward quickly.

"Settle the monies with our friend here," he said, gesturing to the auctioneer, "And then acquaint our new workers with the jobs we have in store for them. Tell them that if they work hard they will see I am a fair man and will provide…"

The old soldier's words slowed to a stop. A quizzical look appeared on his face. His eyes narrowed and he turned to face the villagers again. Out of the corner of his eye, Cullen could see that a thought had struck the old man. He could see that the Roman had lost the casual grace of moments before and had seemed suddenly to acquire a coiled stealth. To anyone else the change was undetectable but to Cullen it was as if the old man had pulled out a sword, ready to use it at the slightest provocation. Cullen forced his eyes to remain fixed on the ground as the general scanned the group.

He walked up to Cullen, his robes swishing behind him. He stopped in front of Cullen, who could feel the man's gaze burning into him. Silence had fallen on the others as the general studied Cullen.

"Everyone else looked at me," said the soldier quietly. "For some it was just a quick glance. For others they held my gaze, as if they wanted to know what kind of man I am. You are the only one who would not look. There are only two reasons that could be. Either you are a coward or a murderer. I'd like to know which one I've just bought. Look at me."

Cullen breathed deeply, trying to compose himself. *Pretend you're looking at your wife, fool. Appear meek.*

Slowly he raised his eyes and looked at the soldier. They stared at each other for a long moment. The soldier nodded and smiled. Still looking at Cullen he spoke softly.

"You'd slit my throat at the first opportunity, wouldn't you, my friend?"

Cullen shook his head, and let his shoulders drop, trying hard to act humble and defeated.

"I wouldn't do that, sir." He gathered Rhiannon and Finn close to him. "I just want my wife and children—child—to be safe. I'm glad we're going to be together." He dropped his eyes to the ground, hoping that he appeared like a docile dog, ready to jump to it at his master's bidding. Cullen felt a heat creep into his face. He'd tried to hide his murderous feelings from this man. He'd tried to appear humble and subservient. What had the General seen? How could he have known what was buried in

Cullen's soul just by looking in his eyes? Cullen cursed himself again for not fully hiding his feelings. He talked quickly to try to repair the situation.

"I'll work hard, sir. I'll work from sun-up to sundown. I'm a blacksmith. I can fix any metal for you. I'm very useful."

The Roman nodded thoughtfully, moving a little closer to Cullen.

"But what if I take your beautiful wife to be my lover? What if I want her to warm my bed at night? What if I want to give her to one of my sons as a plaything? Will just being together be enough for you? What if I decide to give your son to my nephew, who prefers the company of children to that of a woman? Will you still play the part of the humble servant or will you try to disembowel me? Look at me now."

Cullen kept his eyes fixed on the man's sandals. Even as the soldier spoke to him Cullen tried to empty his mind of all the rage this Roman was trying to make him feel.

It's just a test. Keep your eyes meek, you bastard.

"Look at me now, slave."

Cullen raised his eyes, keeping them as unfocused and neutral as he could.

The Roman smiled. He turned to the auctioneer.

"This one's a killer. I don't want him."

"No." Rhiannon held onto Cullen, who stepped forward, sweat breaking out on his face

"Please, sir, I've forsworn killing."

Two Roman guards immediately stepped forward and blocked his way. Other guards started leading the villagers away.

Finn clung to his father's arm.

"Papa, come with us," he pleaded as a Roman guard grasped the boy's fingers and prized them away from Cullen's arm. Cullen's hand shot to the guard's wrist, and twisted it.

"Don't touch my son."

The guard fell to his knees, gasping in agony as Cullen tightened his grip. Still holding the Roman guard, Cullen turned to the lean old man.

"Sir, please. Don't take my family away from me." Cullen grunted as two guards flung themselves on him, breaking his grip. They tried to force Cullen's arms behind his back but Cullen changed his grip and flung one of the guards to the ground and shoved the other on top of him. The old soldier reached to his side and calmly drew a sword as Cullen approached him.

"I promised my son, sir. I promised him I wouldn't kill again."

Before Cullen could take another step, four guards crashed into him, sending Cullen crashing to the ground.

Rhiannon fell to her knees, her arms outstretched to the old man.

"Please, sir, let my husband come with us."

A guard grabbed Rhiannon by the hair and flung her back into the group of villagers. Art tried to catch her, but she slipped past him, smashing onto the cobbled streets. A large gash opened in her forehead and immediately blood ran down her face. A cry of pain, of anguish, escaped her lips.

Anger shot through every pore in Cullen's body. He jerked his head back into the face of one of the soldiers. He felt the spray of blood on the back of his neck as he pushed his weight forward, then immediately pulled back.

The sudden shift unbalanced the guards. He rammed an elbow back, connecting with teeth, which splintered to the ground. With two guards howling in agony, he felt the soldier to his left let go of his arm as he reached for his sword. Cullen slammed his free hand up to the man's face and raked his nails down over the guard's eyes. At the same time, he dropped to the ground and rolled to his right with such force that he heard the fourth guard's knee crack.

It had taken three seconds for Cullen to free himself from the clutches of the four guards. He had no plan except to feel his hands around the face of the Roman who flung Rhiannon to the ground. All promises to Finn had been forgotten in the volcanic rage that coursed through his veins. He would feel that Roman's head in his hands, and he would rip the bastard's head from his body.

Cullen rolled into a crouch, ready to jump. Six guards who had been watching him, first with amusement, then amazement, leaped onto him. Finn ran to his father, but Art grabbed him. Rhiannon pleaded with the guards not to hurt Cullen but her cries were drowned out by the shouts and curses of the Romans as they tried to get Cullen under control.

Two of the guards, sweating and straining, managed to get Cullen's arms behind his back where they were quickly bound by ropes. Cullen bucked and snapped his head back, screaming in frustration as the battle was quickly lost. He swung his head from side to side, but connected only with arms and chests. With one last effort, he tried to get to his feet.

The old soldier watched in awe as Cullen took two steps forward, dragging the six guards with him. There was almost a thousand pounds of weight on his back, yet still he did not give up. Finally, the effort was too much and Cullen sank to his knees. Rhiannon darted over to him. She grabbed his face in her hands and kissed him on the lips, tears and blood slick on her face. She pulled away from him and looked into his eyes with a desperation Cullen had never seen before.

"Find us. Find us and take us home."

Cullen's eyes bore into hers.

"I will. I'll find you."

Two guards grabbed Rhiannon under the arms and pulled her away. He raised his eyes to look at her but a guard's hand forced his face down so his cheek pressed against the stones. He struggled, but could find no leverage. He heard the old soldier barking orders and listened as the villagers were led away. The hand kept his face pressed to the ground until the cries of his son disappeared into the Roman sky.

Twenty five

The Roman soldiers coiled a rope around Cullen's neck and tied him to one of the platform's posts, hands lashed behind his back.

Everything was lost.

Beside Cullen lay Twig, the youth from his village. When the fight had started, Twig had been nearest to Cullen and had taken a few steps back to get out of the way. One of the guards thought Twig was trying to escape and had slammed the hilt of his sword against the boy's head. Twig, his arms also bound, rolled on the ground, moaning in pain. His eyes started to open.

"Oh, my head hurts. I feel like I'm dying."

The auctioneer came over and kicked Twig in the stomach.

"You better shut up, you bastard, or you will be dying."

The auctioneer had spent the last hour trying to unload Cullen, Twig and a toothless old man, who, despite his age, still had a feisty air about him. No one had wanted to buy them.

The auctioneer sat on the platform steps, his face sullen as he weighed his options. A voice broke through his thoughts.

"This meat's for sale?"

The auctioneer glanced up to see a barrel-shaped man standing near them. He wore a dirty shirt over a pair of loose pants that looked as if they'd never been washed. The shirt hung open, revealing a stomach that bulged out over the rope that held up his pants. His chest was covered in hair, some of which was smeared against his body by what looked like dried blood. A lop-sided grin ran across his face as he surveyed Cullen, Twig and the old man. The auctioneer glanced at the prisoners, then back at the stranger.

"You want to buy them?" he asked dubiously.

"I need meat. And fast."

"Well, of course you do." The auctioneer jumped to his feet, peering closer at the man.

"Do I know you from somewhere?"

"Ever been to the games?"

"On occasion."

"I'm in charge of the animals. Name's Ari."

"Ah, yes. You keep the beasts in line."

"They're my babies."

"And babies," said the auctioneer, "need to be fed."

"Fed meat."

The auctioneer and Ari looked at the three prisoners. A roar rose from the Amphitheater. Ari and the auctioneer looked at each other.

"You need them today," said the auctioneer.

"Wrong. I need them *now*," said Ari. "Once Dracon has dispatched his foes, my babies will grace the sands of the arena. And there is a regrettable lack of food for them."

The auctioneer nodded in understanding.

"Four hundred sestertii," he said.

"Two hundred."

"Three fifty. This brute will put on a show."

"Two fifty. This old buzzard looks dead already."

They regarded the prisoners thoughtfully.

"Three hundred then?" asked the auctioneer.

"Done," replied Ari. The beast-minder spat into his hand and held it out to the auctioneer. For a moment the auctioneer looked at the disgusting hand, then spat on his own hand and they shook.

Twig looked at Cullen.

"What did they say?"

"We've been sold."

"Who is he?"

Cullen didn't answer. Twig would find out soon enough.

The heavy man grinned at them, revealing blackened teeth and swollen gums. He knelt beside Twig.

"Britons, eh?" he inquired.

Twig nodded his head, brightening at finding someone who spoke his tongue.

"Fifty thousand."

Twig glanced at Cullen, who had his eyes fixed on the large man.

"Fifty thousand what?" asked Twig.

"Fifty thousand people," grinned the man. "All of them with their eyes on you."

"On me?"

"On you. As you walk into the arena they will cheer. They will roar for you. You'll make your way into the center of the arena, their voices deafening you. It will be the most thrilling moment of your life. Then, above the roar of the crowd, you'll hear them."

"Hear who?"

"My babies."

"I'll hear your babies?"

"Do you know what my babies have?"

Twig shook his head.

"Teeth. Claws. And hunger. They're big, they are. Big as horses."

The blood drained from Twig's face.

"They're called Tigers. Beautiful bastards they are too. Sleek. Elegant. Did I mention that they're hungry?"

Twig nodded.

"Would you like to see them?"

Twig shook his head.

The large man laughed, his rancid breath nearly making Twig gag.

"But they want to see you, my friend. And fifty thousand people will be there to witness it."

"I don't want to die."

"Course you don't, son. Who does? But what can you do?"

Ari clapped Twig on the back and rose to his feet, laughing as he gestured to four soldiers who had come with him. The guards came forward and dragged Cullen, Twig and the old man to their feet.

Walking through the streets of Rome, with its incessant screeching and bestial smells, Cullen had to force his mind to focus.

He had to escape. He had to find his family. He had to take them home.

But all that was later. His first job was to stay alive.

They trudged down a narrow, rutted alley, stepped over the carcass of a pig, and came to a magnificent square. A tremendous roar ripped through the air. It was the sound of what seemed like a million voices screaming and the air itself seemed to vibrate.

They turned a corner and saw the arena.

Twenty six

Dracon stood in the center of the arena feeling his very skin vibrate with the roars of fifty thousand Romans. They cheered for him. They adored him. They loved him.

He raised his arms as if to embrace them all and they screamed even louder. Their feet stomped on the floor in front of their seats, BOOM, BOOM, BOOM, in such a rhythm it felt like the actual building had a heartbeat, and that he was the life-force of the beast.

Dracon threw back his head and soaked in the adoration of the people. He basked in it. As much as they loved him, he loved them even more. He couldn't get enough of their love and he wanted them to know it.

Today he was going to give them a show.

When the gate at the Gladiators' tunnel opened, the crowd hushed to an expectant murmur. Dracon lowered his massive arms and waited. Three warriors emerged from the tunnel: The *Samnite* came first, brandishing a sword in his right hand. His left arm held a large, oblong shield. On the shield the gladiator had painted a crude image of a warrior, presumably himself, stabbing an unfortunate victim. Covering the Samnite's head was a plumed helmet, with a visor that covered his face.

The *Thracian* walked in next. Lightly armored, the Thracian still made an imposing figure. Well over six feet tall and massively muscled; the warrior carried a small, round shield on his left arm and a curved sword in his right. Metal guards covered each leg and—like the Samnite—a crested helmet covered his head. The crest was in the shape of a Griffon, a mythological creature that was half-eagle, half-lion.

The third gladiator was a *Retiarius*. He was the most lightly armored of all, carrying only a trident and a net as weapons, with a metal guard on his left shoulder. He was smaller than the other two warriors, but seemed to have a quickness about him that the others lacked.

They walked ten paces into the arena when a chorus of boos and catcalls assaulted their senses. Did these three dare to think they could defeat Dracon?

Dracon studied the three, watching the way they walked, trying to see if they favored one side or the other, trying to smell panic—anything to give him the edge.

There was no Gladiator that could defeat him, none who could come even close. But he had never fought three at a time before and this could get very, very dangerous. In his last fight he had taken down a Nubian warrior. The man had died two minutes after the fight started and the crowd had roared its approval.

But not quite loud enough.

Had they stopped loving him with all their hearts? Had they started to feel pity for his opponents because the outcome of his fights was a foregone conclusion, their deaths inevitable?

He had gone to the Emperor, who loved him as much as any Roman and told him of his worries. The Emperor himself suggested fighting three of the best Gladiators, thereby making Dracon the underdog. Dracon liked the idea and immediately agreed.

He added one more ingredient.

He would have no weapons.

Insane. Madness.

The three gladiators turned their attention from the roars of the crowd to Dracon, who could see suspicion in the eyes of the *Retiarius* and in the body language of the *Samnite* and *Thracian*. They were looking for weapons, sure that he must be hiding them somewhere. They knew Dracon and his reputation and were not about to rush him only to discover a sword in his hands being driven into their guts. The crowd sensed their hesitation and booed loudly. Dracon smiled as he heard shouts of "Cowards!" bellow from the seats.

Dracon raised his arms and walked in a slow circle as if to emphasize his predicament. The crowd barked, their voices straining, almost whipped into frenzy by every movement, every gesture he made. It was louder than any cheer he'd ever received and Dracon smiled. They loved him more than ever and now it was time to give them a show.

The three gladiators fanned out, stepping toward Dracon, hoping to circle around him. Dracon knew they'd do that and it was the mistake he'd been hoping for. He let the *Retiarius* and the *Thracian* move behind him while the *Samnite* stayed in front. They planned to move up to Dracon and launch a three-pronged attack. If they did that, he would surely die.

But he was not going to let them get that close. The warriors had stayed twenty yards away from Dracon as they got into their positions. Dracon walked in a slow circle, keeping a wary eye on them. They had no reason to think he would make the first move. They thought he would wait for them to attack him.

They were wrong.

Dracon waited until the Gladiators were spaced evenly apart when he ran.

He sprinted straight at the *Samnite*, covering the ground at blinding speed. The sudden movement froze the gladiators for a few seconds. The Samnite's body tensed and he backpedaled once. Dracon was ten yards away when the Samnite raised his sword.

In the split second before Dracon hit, he knew the *Samnite* was going to slash sideways with his sword. It would cut Dracon in half if it connected.

The sword swung across as Dracon dropped to the ground, letting his momentum carry him into the legs of the Samnite. He heard the man's knees crack as he smashed through them. The Gladiator screamed in agony as Dracon rolled to his feet. From the corner of his eye, Dracon could see the other two Gladiators sprint toward them. Dracon figured he had three seconds, four at the outside, to do what he had to do.

He lunged for the *Samnite's* sword, but the warrior was well trained. He brought his shield up fast, knocking Dracon away. Dracon ignored the searing pain in his cheek. He rolled away. The *Samnite* was trying to get to his feet, even as his knees were broken. Dracon charged and the *Samnite* lunged. At the last moment, Dracon rolled left, letting the *Samnite's* sword graze his chest. He got to his feet, grabbed the man's wrist, chopped at his elbow, turning the sword around to point to the *Samnite's* chest, and let the *Samnite's* weight carry him forward so that he impaled himself on his own sword.

The *Retiarius* was almost on him. Dracon swung the dying *Samnite* around. Dracon grunted as the *Samnite* absorbed the full impact of the *Retiarius's* trident in his back. The tips of the spear burst through the *Samnite's* side and Dracon had to work furiously to keep his footing.

Dracon wrenched the sword out of the *Samnite's* stomach and spun around. In a move that brought a scream of awe from the crowd, Dracon swung the sword down in a wide arc, smashing through the wrists of the *Retiarius*, breaking the trident, severing both wrists, and sending a spray of arterial blood over the still thrashing *Samnite,* who was only now falling to the ground. The *Retiarius* staggered back, holding his arms in front of him as if offering Jupiter the blood that spurted from his wrists. The man's face twisted in a look of surprise. Dracon smiled to himself. While he dealt with the *Thracian,* the last remaining gladiator, the crowd would be able to watch this bastard bleed to death on the sand.

The *Thracian* dodged forward, thrusting his sword at Dracon in short, controlled movements. One of the thrusts cut a large gash on his forearm.

The *Thracian* swung his shield. Dracon ducked, but the corner cut across his forehead, sending him reeling backward.

It was all Dracon could do not to smile.

The crowd gasped in fear, seeing Dracon, their beloved Dracon, fall to the ground, blood running down his face. This was the first time they feared for his life, and he sensed their hurt and their pain as they wished him to survive. He heard grown men yell his name, he heard women weep for him as he staggered back on the sand of the arena.

The *Thracian* kicked the dying *Retiarius* out of his way. He advanced on Dracon, sensing an opportunity to kill Rome's greatest gladiator. Dracon knew his arm was cut but he felt no pain. That would come later, as the adrenaline wore off. Above all, Dracon was a showman. He grasped his arm, grimacing in what he hoped was an agonized look, and let the *Thracian* come forward.

Dracon swung his sword back and forth, as if blinded by the blood flowing into his eyes. The *Thracian* was fast, faster than most opponents Dracon had faced, and Dracon didn't see the move until it was almost too late. But Dracon was faster. He pivoted his weight so that the *Thracian's* sword slid along the side of his body, cutting the skin along his ribs one quarter of an inch deep.

Son of a whore bitch prick, that one did hurt!

His eyes watered at the sudden, deep sting and it was with immense satisfaction that Dracon drove the point of his sword deep into the Thracian's stomach. He felt the man stiffen abruptly, and let out an almost feminine sigh of surprise. Dracon leaned close to the man's ear, and could smell his last, fetid breath.

"Yes, my friend," he whispered. "This is what it's like to die." The man's mouth worked slowly but no sound emerged. Dracon jerked the sword up hard, cutting further into the *Thracian's* intestines, letting the man's warm blood spray over his hand.

"Wait for me in Elysium," said Dracon as the *Thracian* fell to the ground. Dracon released the handle of the sword, letting it fall with the dead gladiator.

The walls of the arena rocked with the booming, crazed voices of the crowd. Never had they seen such a fight as this. Never had one warrior defeated three gladiators and lived to tell about it. They knew they were privileged to live in a time such as this and see a spectacle such as the one played out before them.

But most of all they knew that this warrior, this God among men, loved them as much as they loved him, and because of this they cheered until their throats seized up and they could roar no more.

Underneath the amphitheater, in a room dank with the sweat of generations of fighters, Cullen, Twig and the old man waited. The four guards looked at the prisoners.

"We should have some fun with these," said the curly-haired Roman.

Rays of sun lit the room from a long window lined with iron bars. Benches were placed against the walls, and the wood was polished clean from years of gladiators' backsides sitting on them, waiting their turn to go into the arena. The roar from the crowd reached into the room, like the drone of a thousand hornets.

Two of the guards leaned against the wall. The other two sat on benches and regarded the prisoners with lazy contempt. Boredom hung in the room like stale breath.

"How many have we had today?" said the bald guard, picking dirt out of his fingernails with a knife.

"How many what?" asked the youngest of them.

"Gladiators," said the bald guard.

"Thirty-four," said the oldest guard.

"How the fuck do you know?" said the bald guard.

"Unlike you, I can count."

The bald guard opened his mouth like he was going to reply, but a look from the old guard suggested otherwise. He closed his mouth and turned back to the prisoners, eyeing them the way a child watches a bug squirm on a needle.

"He could be a gladiator," said the curly-haired guard, pointing to Twig.

"He's fucking skin and bones," said the bald guard.

"That's why it's funny," said the curly-haired guard.

"We should give him a wooden sword," said the young guard.

"Do you have a wooden sword?" asked the bald guard.

"No," said the young guard.

"Then don't say stupid fucking things, you little prick."

"It would make them laugh, though," said the curly-haired guard, pinching his lip.

"What do we have?" said the old guard.

The four Romans looked at each other, then turned to the prisoners, their minds pondering the problem, their boredom momentarily forgotten. The curly-haired guard broke into a wide grin.

"Decius," he said, turning to the young guard. "Grab the paint."

Twenty seven

Thirty minutes later, Dracon sat with the Emperor in the Royal Box. He had left the two dead men and the dying *Retiarius* on the Arena and entered a room under the Amphitheater where the sand was washed from his hair and body, and his wounds were rubbed with oil and bandaged. A quintet of Roman guards had escorted him to the Emperor. The crowd saw his distinctive blue and gold tunic and they roared their approval. The Emperor took him by the arm and led him to the front of the box where Dracon waved to the cheering crowd.

Dracon sat on an oak chair, adrenaline still coursing through his body. The Emperor, white hair falling in curls around his shoulders, smiled in a fatherly manner as he surveyed the crowd. Only his eyes conveyed the cunning with which he ruled the Roman world.

"I've never seen the people love anyone more, Dracon."

"I love them, Emperor."

"Not even me. You're not after my throne, are you?"

"Your throne? Of course not, I—"

Hadrian threw back his head and laughed.

"Dracon, I'm joking. I'm just glad to see you still breathing. I thought they had you out there."

"It wasn't even close, Emperor," said Dracon, settling back into his seat. He raised a silver goblet to his lips and drank deeply. He placed the cup back on the table.

"I could not be killed today." He said it simply, no trace of boastfulness in his manner, just a truth that could not be denied.

"The Gods must watch out for you," said the Emperor.

"I've never understood the Gods, Emperor," said Dracon. "There have been times when the Gods have given me more than I thought a man could possibly have in the world." He hesitated a moment.

"And other times," continued the Emperor, "when they take away your very soul."

The Emperor turned back to the Arena where three prisoners were led to the center of the oval. They had no weapons in their hands, no armor on their bodies and made a pathetic sight. One of them was an old man, whose legs were as skinny as the shaft of a spear. Around his neck hung a sign. It said 'thirty-five'. Beside him stood a youth who looked even thinner than the older man, and whose hair hung down his pale face like dark seaweed on rocks. His fingers moved ceaselessly, as if they were crabs, trying to crawl away from the death that was so very close. The sign around his neck said 'thirty-six'. The third man was a head taller than the other two. His shoulders were broad and he had the look of someone dangerous, someone who might be useful in a fight—an obvious criminal. Hadrian could only imagine what crime this fellow committed. Murder, rape, thievery—probably all three. Had the look of an ex-soldier.

His sign said 'thirty-seven.'

The paint on the signs was fresh and it dripped down onto the sand of the arena.

"Looks like one on your old legionary friends, Dracon," he said, pointing to the criminal.

Dracon nodded politely. It hurt to remember where he came from.

Hadrian turned to an old man who stood behind him in the shadows of the canopy. The man's hair was trimmed to a buzz cut and in his arms he held a roll of parchment.

"You think he's a soldier, Suetonius?"

Suetonius narrowed his eyes, staring at the prisoner.

"Hard to tell, Emperor. There's enough in the army like him."

"They're not Christians, are they?"

"If they were Christians, Emperor, shouldn't they be on their knees begging their God for mercy?"

The big man—Thirty-seven—ripped the sign from around his neck and flung it on the ground. The crowd roared its disapproval, happy to have something to cheer against. The old man and the youth looked at their companion and followed his lead. The crowd screamed louder, taking mock offense, screaming insults and laughing loudly at the petrified looks on the prisoners.

At least the petrified looks on the old man and the youth, thought Dracon. Gladiator thirty-seven doesn't even acknowledge the crowd.

Dracon felt the Emperor's hand on his arm.

"Look," said Hadrian. "Tigers."

The ropes binding Cullen's arms had been cut right before he, Twig and the toothless old man were sent out into the arena. He rubbed his wrists absently as the archway approached, a rectangle of almost blinding light that bled around the wrought iron gates. Even with his hands free, escape was impossible. They were surrounded by guards. Spears pin-pricked their backs. As the gates opened into the large space ahead of them, they could only go forward. They walked into an oval-shaped arena, sand crunching, shifting, under their feet. Two workers scattered new sand at the far end of the arena, covering blood stains. There was a weak roar from the crowd as they appeared, nothing like the cacophony Cullen heard earlier as they awaited their fate. Those voices shook the foundations of this building.

It still deafened him. He felt Twig and the old man shrink close to him. They walked to the center of the arena.

No, thought Cullen, this is more than an arena. *This is a battleground.* He could smell the death that rose from the ground. If Cullen couldn't figure something out quickly their lives would end here, soaked in the sand.

That was when he heard the tiger.

Cullen had heard stories of such beasts when he trained under that Roman bastard, Sulla Atticus Scaurus. He had listened to the Roman tell fantastical tales of these beasts that seemed to belong in the realm of the

Gods. How could a cat reach the size of a horse? And when the animal emerged from the bowels of the Amphitheater, Cullen felt as if he was looking at a beast from the spirit world. It walked into the sunlight with a tensile grace that belied its enormous size. Its coat was a rich orange that had thick, black stripes running down it. The animal's paws were as big as plates and Cullen could imagine he heard the soft *thud, thud, thud* of them as they padded into the arena.

Cullen and his companions didn't move as the tiger blinked in the bright sun. He imagined the animals were just as stunned as they were, especially as the crowd now found its true voice. They roared as one, cheering the entrance of the beast, urging it to fulfill its bestial nature and rend limb from quivering limb. The sudden burst of noise disoriented the tiger and Cullen knew he only had seconds to find a way out. The walls were twenty feet high and were impossible to climb up. To escape that way you'd need wings to fly.

A thought struck him and he shouted to Twig.

"Remember how I'd help you kids dive into the river?"

Twig's eyes were locked on the tiger but his mouth worked slowly as he tried to answer.

"The river. Yes."

"Remember how I helped you?"

Twig tore his gaze away from the tiger and stared at Cullen.

"What?"

"My hands."

Cullen interlocked his fingers together.

"Just like diving, yes?"

Twig nodded, but Cullen didn't know if comprehension had dawned or if Twig was answering blindly, not understanding anything. Cullen grasped the old man's arm.

"Can you run?"

The old man turned to Cullen. His eyes showed confusion too. Cullen pointed to Twig.

"Watch him. Watch what he does."

Cullen grabbed Twig and forced the boy to look into his eyes.

"Twig, I'm going to run. Count to three, then run after me. Run as fast as you can."

Twig nodded, swallowing hard.

The tiger saw them. Even from fifty yards away they saw its black eyes narrow on them. Cullen felt a knot form in his stomach. If this was going to be his death, it was a bad way to go. Those jaws could snap his thigh bone in two. And those claws. One swipe could—

—*Die fighting*—

—the voice cut through his thoughts. It came from inside him and sliced through his fear. Suddenly the roars of the crowd receded, becoming a dull pulse as if he listened to them through a seashell. His heartbeat slowed, and he took a breath that, for the first time in days, filled every corner of his lungs.

This is no different than facing any other warrior, he told himself. *And you've never been killed yet.* Cullen's hands were clenched so hard, the fingernails bit into his palm. He slowly relaxed them and let them hang at his side. At that moment, someone from the crowd threw a stone at the tiger. It turned away from the three men, growling.

Cullen turned and ran.

Dracon saw Thirty-seven turn suddenly, running at top speed toward the wall. He was impressed that the oaf had used the tiger's distraction to make his move but where did he think he could go? The wall was impossible to climb. Had the fool been thinking that he would let the tiger finish off his two companions, thereby leaving him alone? Didn't he know that there were hundreds of beasts that needed to be fed? But it was always like this, always before the teeth sank into their bellies they would run, believing if they could only live long enough, if they could steal just a few more seconds, then salvation would appear and they would be saved. And there goes the other one, he saw, leaving the old man to be the tiger's appetizer. It was almost humorous to—

Dracon leapt to his feet, blinking his eyes. The crowd noise stopped, as if a vortex had appeared from the dimension of the Gods and stolen the voices of each man and woman in the arena. But the crowd wasn't silent.

They had *gasped.*

Thirty-seven had stopped a few feet from the base of the wall, bent his knees and joined his hands by interlocking his fingers. He waited two seconds before the long-haired youth sprinted toward him, leapt, put his right foot in the big one's hands and then—*how in the name of all the spirits in Hades did that brute have the strength?*—the big one flung the youth over the wall into the crowd.

The crowd reached for the youth, catching him, breaking his fall.

Dracon darted his eyes back to the arena where the old man had suddenly found strength in those ancient limbs. He was tearing up the sand, and the big one had joined his hands together as before. But now the tiger was on the move, springing forward and closing the gap at a phenomenal speed. The old man was fifteen yards away from Thirty-seven and Dracon found himself gripping the ledge, urging the old man forward. He timed his leap perfectly, landing his foot in the big one's hands, who flung the old man up with such ferocity that Dracon heard the big one's cry of effort.

The old man flew over the first row of people, slamming into the second and third rows, sending Romans flying. Hands reached for the old man, helping him to his feet. Dracon wondered briefly if the crowd would toss these two back, worthless detritus of humanity that they were. He hoped not, that would ruin everything that the big one had accomplished. It would ruin the story. Apparently the crowd felt the same way as Dracon. They got the old man to his feet. The youth, disentangled now from the crowd, grabbed the old man's arm and disappeared among the surging populace.

Dracon flung his arms up in amazement and screamed with the rest of the crowd. This was a first. This had never happened before. A stab of disappointment went through him as he realized the tiger, now only twenty yards away, would kill this warrior that had done something he'd never seen before. The tiger leapt, and the warrior stood still, accepting his fate with a dignity and bravery that Dracon could only stand silently in awe of.

Except the warrior dropped and rolled under the tiger.

Dracon had never seen anyone move with such speed. The tiger went crashing into the wall as the warrior rolled to his feet. *Run*, urged Dracon, *keep away from the beast. Keep dodging it.* Dracon realized such actions would only delay the inevitable, but a warrior this brave deserved to live.

The tiger thrashed in the sand, trying to recover to its feet. The warrior ran. But he ran toward the tiger, and as the animal righted itself, the warrior flung two fistfuls of sand into its face. The tiger roared back, howling, spitting. Then it lunged forward, slashing blindly with its front paws. The warrior dodged away, grabbing more sand, flinging it into the tiger's face.

Dracon let his jaw hang open as he watched the warrior attack the tiger with only his speed, strength and grains of sand. The warrior kicked the sand, creating a cloud of dust around the beast. Always running, always circling, the beast grew confused. In thirty seconds the tiger decided it had had enough and this human wasn't worth the effort. He turned and padded away, blinking his eyes.

Cullen's knees almost buckled as he watched the tiger walk away. He could not believe he was still alive. Everything he'd done—ducking the tiger's leap, flinging sand in its eyes—had just been a last-ditch effort to live a few seconds longer. He never believed it would work. He felt the grains of sand sift through his fingers and fall to the ground.

He turned his head to the crowd and saw Twig and the old man among the throng. Cullen scanned the people and saw Roman guards approaching Twig from either side. The guards were having a hard time getting through the jostling spectators.

"Twig," yelled Cullen. "Go home. Find your way home!"

Cullen saw the wide smile on the youth's face as he disappeared into the crowd, the old man following closely at his heels.

Cullen raised his arms in triumph. He'd done it. Even if he was to die, at least he'd gotten Twig and the old bastard out. It had been four years since Cullen's lungs had opened up and let rip a war cry, but he did it now. He raised his eyes to heaven and screamed a roar of victory, of defiance. Those that heard it over the noise of the crowd felt a chill down their backs.

This was a warrior.

Dracon turned to the Emperor who sat impassively in his chair.

"Emperor, should we let the prisoner live?"

Hadrian pursed his lips as he considered this.

"He's good. He's very good," admitted the Emperor. "But also lucky. Does he deserve to live because one big cat didn't like sand in its face? Maybe. He needs to prove himself again. The people," he gestured to the screaming mob, "are understandably curious to see if he can survive again, right Suetonius?"

Hadrian's advisor nodded.

"Let's find the measure of this man."

Hadrian turned back, satisfied.

"Introduce him to the other beasts."

Cullen and the tiger had the arena to themselves. The tiger lay in a shady spot, rubbing its paws against its eyes, blinking furiously. Cullen backed up against the wall of the arena, taking deep breaths, trying to calm down his beating heart. People leaned over the edge of the wall and yelled at him, but he was so intent on watching the iron gates near where the tiger lay that he didn't hear them. Would they continue to let the wild animals attack him or would they let him go? At least let him live long enough to fight another day. Isn't that what they did here? Had he not proven that he would make a worthy warrior?

His eyes scanned the floor of the arena. Maybe in a previous fight, someone had dropped a weapon he could use. He saw some fist-sized rocks among the sand, but no telling glint of metal. His eyes rose to the crowd and he noticed the canopied royal box of the Emperor. Could that be him, Hadrian, the leader of the Roman Empire seated on his throne? Beside him were some finely dressed politicians. Praetorians stood around the box, guarding this man who wielded power like a God. They held their spears close, ready to defend the Emperor to the death.

He studied the Emperor. He was an old man, maybe sixty years. He had a head of curly white hair and a beard to match. His body still possessed the hardened muscles of a soldier. The Emperor looked at Cullen and inclined his head, smiling. Cullen nodded back. Maybe the old Roman would stop this now.

The iron gates at the other end of the arena creaked open. Cullen kept his body perfectly still, but shifted his eyes over to see two huge lions race out. Their manes flew around them as they searched for the food that usually stood in the center of the arena. But there was no motion they could latch onto. The tiger leapt to its feet, snarling. Immediately, the lions turned to it. The tiger lunged forward, then quickly stepped back as the lions retaliated, their huge paws slashing at the tiger. Cullen knew this was territorial posturing between the cats, the way wolves in his homeland of Britannia would snarl and snap at each other. It might last a minute if he was lucky. Then they'd see him, or smell him. And that would be that. He looked again at the Praetorians guarding the Emperor and his mind burned with resentment. Why couldn't they give him a spear? At least then he'd have a fighting chance.

"He's frozen," said the Emperor.

"With all respect, majesty," replied Dracon. "He's thinking. He's looking for a way out."

"Is there one?"

Dracon surveyed the arena. The lions were letting the tiger know who ruled their turf. But soon they would lose interest and search for their food.

"No majesty. He's already dead."

Cullen looked at the two stones that lay on the floor of the arena and tried to imagine throwing one so hard that it would kill a lion. He closed his eyes but all he saw was an angry lion with a bump on his head leaping toward him with both paws outstretched. And then it would all be over. He would be in the afterlife, whatever that might be.

He turned his gaze back to the Emperor.

I should throw the stones at his skinny arse. Give him a taste of what will happen to me. Better to be killed by one of the guard's spears that be eaten by those beasts. He imagined the guards flinging their weapons, impaling him in the chest. If they were good, and he knew they were, the spear would go right through his body, tearing through his heart, shredding the arteries that pumped his lifeblood through his veins. Death would be almost instantaneous. It would have the added benefit of depriving this mob of stinking Romans of their pleasure. Let the lions eat his dead body. There would be no dignity in this death, but he might be able to save some of his honor, whatever that was worth.

He paused in his thoughts, a curious expression crossing his face.

Cullen smiled.

Dracon saw Thirty-seven's face break into a grin. The warrior looked at the hissing cats and calmly walked forward. He bent down and picked up two stones that lay about ten yards from him. The warrior glanced back at the cats, the grin now gone from his face. One of the cats had turned and was watching the warrior, who stood perfectly still, not moving a muscle.

Was he going to try to fight the lions off?

The tiger leapt forward, slashing at the thigh of the lion that had turned to watch the man. The lion roared, his paws raking the tiger's face, opening a gash under the tiger's eye. The tiger retreated to the wall, his roar reverberating in the air.

The warrior was running toward them, toward the Emperor's Box. He'd used the last lunge of the tiger to buy him a few more precious seconds. Dracon was momentarily confused as to why Thirty-seven was doing this. The lions would surely see him now, and that would be the end of him. The man stopped suddenly and, with astonishing force, threw one of the stones at the Emperor.

The stone flew high, missing the Emperor by inches, striking the Emperor's advisor. Suetonius let out a high shriek and clasped a hand over his mouth, from which two or three teeth had been liberated.

The stone had missed the Emperor because Hadrian had slid to the floor, showing surprising speed for one so old. But the danger was not over yet. Dracon saw the warrior bring his arm back, ready to throw the second stone.

Dracon screamed at the Praetorians. "Kill him, you fools. He's trying to kill the Emperor!"

It was unnecessary advice. Before Dracon finished his sentence, the guard on the edge of the wall had flung his spear straight toward the warrior. It was as good a throw as Dracon had seen, and in the blink of an eye it would rip the warrior's heart asunder.

Without seeming to move, the warrior shifted his weight slightly. The spear flew past the warrior, skimming the man's chest, but it never touched the ground.

Thirty-seven had caught it.

Blood poured from between Suetonius's fingers as he let out a high-pitched whine.

"For God's sake, man, it's only a few teeth," said the Emperor, climbing back into his seat. His Praetorians moved to help him, but he waved them away.

"He caught the spear," whispered Dracon.

"He caught it?" replied Hadrian, turning to Dracon.

Dracon nodded, a slow grin spreading over his features.

The lion had not eaten for three days and the hunger was driving it mad. There was food here, he could smell it, but this other cat, this usurper, had tried to dominate him. Now the tiger had slunk back into the shadows and, from the corner of his eye, the lion had seen something else move.

There. The prey had stopped in the open, making no move to hide itself. The lion bunched its massive hind legs and lunged forward. It ran to the prey, covering the ground at blinding speed. Hunger ate at its belly, causing a feeling of almost overpowering rage. This prey would fill it up.

Even as his fingers closed on the spear, Cullen knew the lion was almost upon him. He spun, jamming the base of the spear into the sand. He lowered the spear to the ground and held the base in place with his foot. Cullen kept the shaft steady, fighting the urge to run. The beast thundered toward him, saliva spinning from its mouth.

Cullen knew he would die. But this beast would go with him. At the last moment, Cullen raised the spear to a forty-five degree angle. The lion jumped, seeming to fill the entire spectrum of his vision, and still it grew larger, until all Cullen could see were teeth and claws.

With a *thunk*, the lion impaled itself on the spear. Cullen was sure the staff would break as the lion's momentum carried it down the spear. He would be crushed by a thousand pounds of screaming beast that would live long enough to slash him to pieces with those claws that looked as long as Roman swords. Cullen fell to the ground, waiting for the animal to fall upon him, but the spear carried the beast in an arc over Cullen's head. It fell to the ground, thrashing in agony, its breath coming in short, panting gasps.

Cullen lay still, as the lion stopped moving. It wasn't dead, because Cullen saw its eyes blink twice. The spear moved gently to the beat of the lion's still-beating heart, swishing in a tight motion back and forth, back and forth. And then it was still and the lion's eyes blinked no more.

Cullen scrambled to his feet. He grasped the shaft of the spear with both hands and pulled it from the lion's body. He sank the spear deep into the belly of the lion and cut through the skin and muscles until a three foot gash was formed. He withdrew the spear and turned aside as the lion's guts fell out, steaming and writhing.

He backed away toward the wall as the other lion and the tiger approached him. They circled the dead lion, sniffing at the steaming pile of intestines. They turned their gaze to Cullen, who stood with his back to the wall, the spear held firmly.

Would the guts be enough, wondered Cullen. Would they forsake their dead friend and try to attack him, or is their hunger so great that they would eat one of their own? It didn't take long for him to find out. The other two cats buried their faces in the body of the dead lion and tugged at the skin, exposing muscle and meat. Their ravenous hunger overtook them and they began to feast.

The Emperor looked down in astonishment at the dead lion. His gaze shifted over to Cullen who now sat down against the wall of the Amphitheater.

"That was quite possibly the most amazing thing I've ever seen," he said.

"Indeed," agreed Dracon.

"I really should kill him, though. He did throw a rock at me."

"If I'm correct, majesty, he threw it to miss."

The Emperor drummed his fingers on his throne.

"Still, I am the Emperor."

"An Emperor of boundless mercy."

The Emperor stopped moving his fingers, and watched the still figure in the shadows. Dracon cleared his throat.

"If I may suggest, majesty, a contest. A fight between our warrior over there and me," Dracon gestured modestly to himself, "would create quite a stir. The Undefeated Dracon versus Gladiator Thirty-seven. It has a ring to it, yes?"

The leader of Rome nodded.

"I would watch such a battle. A battle of Titans."

"And if you let me organize these games, majesty, I will give the people an experience they will never forget."

Dracon held his breath. This was the chance he'd been waiting for. He'd gone from legionary to prisoner to gladiator to free man to rich, free man to, hopefully, organizer of the games. If he could persuade the Emperor to let him organize these next games it would put him in a position to take over the job of Procurator of the *Ludus Magnus* when that fat, old bastard, Symmachus, dropped dead of a heart attack. And if he ran the Ludus Magnus his position in Roman Society would be assured. Emperors, Senators, knights—they'd all come running to him when a show needed to be put on for the people. He'd control the flow of gladiators into the arena, pitting them one against the other. No one had a better eye for matching fighters than Dracon did.

Hadrian watched him in that curious, frank way that meant the Emperor was intrigued by his suggestion. He held the Emperor's gaze, knowing that if given the job he would put on a show such as Rome had never seen.

The Emperor smiled and turned to his advisor.

"Still whining, Suetonius?"

The old man brought a bloodied cloth down from his mouth. He tried to grin, but the blood still hadn't stopped and what was meant to be a reassuring smile turned into what looked like a grimace of death as rivulets of blood ran down his chin.

"Dracon is right, Majesty. This is too good an opportunity to waste."

Hadrian gestured to Dracon, lowering his voice in a conspiratorial whisper to Suetonius.

"As to our friend here, Suetonius, do you think a soldier-turned-thief-turned gladiator would be able to put on a show?"

"He certainly knows how to capture the imaginations of the mob, majesty," replied Suetonius. The Emperor nodded and turned to Dracon.

"The games are yours, Dracon," he said.

Dracon felt the hairs on his back stand up. *He'd done it!* Already his mind was surging ahead, thinking of all the fighters he knew, and which combinations would make for the most exciting battles.

"I believe," said Hadrian, a thoughtful expression on his face, "that I will place a bet on our friend in the shadows to win."

"Against me?" said Dracon, in mock astonishment. "Majesty, perhaps the excitement had destroyed your faculties."

"Possibly," said the Emperor. "On the other hand, maybe it's time someone challenged you for the title of Rome's greatest warrior."

Twenty eight

Cullen sat in a stone room under the arena. It must have been home to some kind of animal because the smell of musk and feces was overpowering. A physician had been in to check him, but finding no cuts, bruises or broken bones, had left him alone. The cold stones of the room were a relief after the oppressive heat of the arena. Only now had his breathing and heart rate returned to normal. He laid his cheek against the granite rock and savored its coolness.

He did not know how he still lived.

He should have been fattening the stomach of that tiger, that beast from Hades, the sight of which had chilled his blood. But he had been able to fling his two companions to safety and had overcome not one but three of the beasts. He was alive against the odds.

His continued existence was what Mother Miriam would have called a miracle. Did he owe his life to the God she'd been prattling on about? He searched his miraculously un-clawed heart, trying to find a kernel of faith that he could latch onto.

But he could find no faith. The desert God had let his daughter die and she now rotted in an unmarked grave trampled upon by Roman soldiers.

A small thought crept into his mind. What harm could it do to offer a silent prayer to this new God? He breathed a "Thank you," watching his breath mist in the air, tasting how the prayer felt on his tongue.

He remembered Aisling again.

The prayer tasted bitter.

He slept.

Cullen's eyes snapped open. He stared at a grey stone ceiling. Memory returned like an insidious beast. Aisling dead. Rhiannon and Finn taken. He pushed himself up into a sitting position.

He realized he was not alone.

Standing in the shadows was one of the biggest men Cullen had ever seen, at least a head taller than Cullen and with shoulders so wide that Cullen imagined the man possessed enormous strength. Shoulder length black hair framed a face that stared at him with unnerving intensity. Cullen massaged his arms, staring back at the stranger. Neither spoke for almost a full minute.

"Five hours ago," began the stranger, "I stood in the center of the Amphitheater. I was unarmed. I faced three of the most dangerous gladiators in Rome and killed them all in less than two minutes. It was the most incredible feat the citizens of Rome had seen in years. Possibly ever. And my glory lasted less than an hour. That was when you, an unknown slave who was meant to be meat for the beasts, did things that made them forget all about me."

Cullen saw that the giant of a man held no weapons. He tried to detect bitterness in the man's voice but found none. He flexed his fingers and toes, trying to get the blood circulating. The man waited, staring at Cullen as if waiting to hear what his answer would be. Cullen didn't want to say anything, he wanted to be left alone. He needed to think. This stranger, however, wasn't going away.

"I can hardly remember what I did," offered Cullen.

"Such is the way of war," agreed the stranger. "Mayhem, madness, blood and then it's over." The stranger blew the tips of his fingers, spreading them wide as if blowing dust from his hands. "And you find yourself standing among the dead and the dying. But you're alive. So very alive."

This bastard talks as if the words were perfumed, thought Cullen. So very alive? If shitting in your pants and avoiding the six-inch long teeth of that hungry tiger is what it takes to make you feel alive than this man was a fool to end all fools.

"Are you a prisoner here too?" asked Cullen neutrally, careful not to show this man anything until he knew who he was and what he wanted.

The man laughed gently.

"I'm not a prisoner. I'm a gladiator."

"Isn't that the same thing?"

"For most. I earned my freedom a long time ago. I choose to fight."

Cullen stared at him. *Chose to fight? Did he hear that right?* He opened his mouth to say something, then stopped, confused.

"Why are you here?" he asked finally.

The man scratched his face, brushing the stubble near his jaw and tracing a line down to his chin. Cullen saw fresh scars on his arms.

"That answer will take some time. But now that we are becoming acquainted let us exchange names. I am Dracon, freeman and gladiator, and you," said Dracon, pausing for effect, "are known to the city of Rome as Gladiator Thirty-seven."

Gods, thought Cullen, *this one should be strutting across the theaters in Athens, not fighting in the arena in Rome.*

Cullen rose to his feet.

"My name's Cullen."

"A Briton?"

"Hibernian. But one who lives in Briton."

"Well, Cullen, the Hibernian who lives in Briton, let us take a walk."

The sun shone red on the horizon as they emerged from the amphitheater. Cullen was sure his hands would be bound with rope or chains, but Dracon had told the four Roman guards who accompanied them to let Cullen remain unbound. The guards were alert, hard as bastards, and anyway, Cullen was too tired to try to escape.

The streets of Rome were almost deserted. Those attending the games were long gone and most of the merchants who had lined the streets during the day had packed up their wares and gone home. Replacing the throng of people were carts, who used the nighttime to wind their way through the city.

As they walked through the streets, Cullen could not help staring at the towering buildings, each more magnificent than the last.

"There has never been anywhere like Rome, Cullen," said Dracon. "It is a city born of the Gods. A city that makes men feel both humbled and exalted at the same time."

More flowery shit from the gladiator, thought Cullen, even as he was amazed at the view around him. He did not reply as he continued to take in the magnificent architecture. Dracon smiled at Cullen's silence.

"Are you not curious where we are going?"

"When we get there I will know."

They walked through the city and climbed up a hill. From the top of the hill Cullen turned around and looked down on Rome. Its splendor and size staggered him.

Dracon smiled, enjoying Cullen's reaction to the spectacle. Cullen glanced over to him and scowled.

"It's the greatest city on earth," agreed Cullen, correctly interpreting Dracon's smug look, "if you like your cities full to the brim of murderers, slavers and bastards. Did you bring me up here just to enjoy the view?"

"No," agreed Dracon. "It's not the city I wanted you to look at. It's the possibilities."

"Meaning what?"

"Fifty thousand people saw what you did in the arena today, Cullen. They are telling their friends, their brothers, their lovers, their wives all about what you did. By tomorrow all of Rome will know."

Cullen shrugged.

"Don't you see?" insisted Dracon, "you could become the most famous man in Rome. Gladiator thirty-seven. You could eclipse even me."

Cullen looked up to see Dracon smiling.

"You don't sound too upset about it."

"That, my friend, is because it will never happen."

Cullen's eyes narrowed as the smile broadened across Dracon's face.

"Don't worry, I didn't bring you here to kill you. Merely to tell you that your next fight will be against me."

Cullen searched the other man's eyes and saw he was telling the truth. He relaxed slightly. Dracon looked expectantly at Cullen for a moment, then clapped his hands together.

"I like you, Cullen. Whenever I tell other gladiators they are to fight me I always see fear cross their faces, even if it's just for a moment. But with you—nothing."

"I don't know you. Maybe I'm just too stupid to be scared," answered Cullen.

Dracon talked on, as if barely hearing what Cullen said.

"Three years ago I had nothing. Now I have everything I want. Everything I need. And today, Cullen, the Emperor himself charged me with the greatest job in Rome."

Cullen felt Dracon's voice fade into the distance. Was it only two days ago that Aisling fought so valiantly for her life? Was it just yesterday they ripped Rhiannon and Finn away from him? If he should live to be a hundred years old he would never forget the look on his wife's face. He let his eyes drift to the Roman guards to see if they were relaxed. All four stared at him as if he was a putrid sore on the end of a toe. They stood with swords drawn. There would be no escaping them, even if he had the energy. Dracon's voice droned back into his consciousness. What the hell had this idiot being ranting about all this time? He talked like he fancied himself to be a Greek poet.

Cullen turned to Dracon, cutting him off.

"If we're going to fight, fine. I'll fight. But I've had a long day. I'm hungry. I'm thirsty. I want to sleep."

Dracon shrugged.

"You're right. I'm being thoughtless. But my point is that you're different from everyone else. You could become as rich as me."

Cullen raised an eyebrow.

"I thought you were planning to kill me?"

"I plan to fight you. There's a difference. If you fight well and if you please the crowd and, more importantly, the Emperor, when I have my sword at your throat, you might be allowed to live."

"Why would you care whether I live or die?"

Dracon looked thoughtful.

"Good question. Interesting question." He pursed his mouth in an exaggerated manner. "Sometimes I just have a feeling about people, Cullen. When you stare a man in the face as he breathes out his last breath, you get to know people."

Cullen stared into the Roman's eyes. He had no doubt this man was as good as he claimed to be. But his arrogance was laughable.

"How many men have you killed?" asked Dracon.

"What makes you think I've killed any?" replied Cullen.

"Like I said, I know people."

Cullen shrugged, saying nothing.

"Over twenty? Thirty?" asked Dracon.

"I don't keep count," said Cullen.

"My guess is thirty," said Dracon. "That's about where I'm at."

Cullen had a sudden urge to laugh at this man, but decided it would be unwise to provoke him. He seemed like a child in a man's body, with his fixation on kills, and his bizarre desire to compare himself to Cullen, whom he'd only known for less than two hours.

"Thirty sounds about right. Maybe high twenties." Dracon nodded, as if Cullen had just confirmed that he, Dracon, had an unerring eye for warriors.

"In single combat?"

"Sometimes there was just one."

Dracon laughed. He placed an arm around Cullen's shoulders and led him down the hill. The four guards followed, leather shoes padding down the dirt road, eyes fixed on Cullen's back as if they'd personally have to answer to the Emperor if Cullen took a step out of place. A solitary dog walked by, padding softly on the cobbled roads. In its jaws was a rat, bleeding, but still alive, struggling feebly against the power of the dog's jaws. They passed by alleyways. Cullen saw shadows slink into the darkness, as if the sight of the four Roman guards were a pestilence.

Dracon led Cullen to the gladiator barracks that was nestled in the shadow of the Arena. All Cullen could see was an enormous expanse of wall. Getting closer, he saw there were windows built into the wall, but so thin that even a child would get stuck trying to escape. They stopped at a heavy wooden door near the end of the wall. Guards stood on either side of the door, staring at the approaching group with suspicion, relaxing when they realized it was Dracon returning with the prisoner.

Their only light as they entered the musty stone building was a burning torch carried by a guard. Rats leapt from their path. The black and brown creatures scurried along the wall, just out of reach of the cast light, the scraping of their feet the only clue to their existence, as if they were emissaries leading Cullen to the depths of hell. Every few yards they passed by a door, on which there was a small, iron grille. Once he thought he saw a face staring out at him, but when he looked closer he saw only the thick, impenetrable darkness. Dracon and his guards stopped at a door that was no different from the ones they'd already passed.

"This room belonged to Ferax," said Dracon. "He was good man. Always gave everything he had."

"Where is Ferax now?" asked Cullen.

"Let's just say, sometimes giving everything you have isn't enough." Dracon smirked. "You'll have to forgive the crude sleeping arrangements and the security, but I think you'll try to leave without saying goodbye."

How is it possible one man could be so pleased with himself?

Dracon continued to chuckle as the guards ushered Cullen inside and locked the door. Dracon tapped the door, looking at Cullen through the small rectangular opening.

"Don't worry, this won't last forever. In a few months you could be the talk of Rome. Or you'll be dead."

Cullen listened to Dracon's booming laugh as the gladiator and his Roman guards walked away.

The cell was small, six paces in each direction. He stretched out on the bed that lay under the window and thought about his family. At least they were with the rest of the villagers. Art would watch out for Rhiannon, he'd see she would be safe. But what of that man that bought them, the general? If he wanted Rhiannon for himself what could Art do to stop him? A feeling of resolve coursed through his veins.

He had to get out of this place and find his family.

Twenty nine

"Cullen."

The voice called him from the depths of sleep. It was a voice he'd heard before, but couldn't remember where or when. He forced his eyes open, reluctant to enter the waking world.

Mother Miriam knelt beside his bed, a warm smile on her face. Cullen sat up quickly, then grimaced as the muscles in his shoulders howled in protest.

"Take your time, take your time, Cullen. I heard you had a busy day yesterday."

Cullen flexed his muscles slowly, trying to ease them back into working order, staring at the old woman to make sure his eyes didn't deceive him. He glanced toward the door where a Roman guard stood watching him.

"I don't understand. How did you get here?"

"I was bought by the man who runs this place. A brute called Symmachus. I hear he's quite rich, but his clothes are filthy and he stinks like a crateful of rotten eggs left to boil in the sun."

"Fewer words, Mother. Why?" interrupted Cullen with a smile.

"Ah, yes. They needed me. You know I have traveled far and I have a facility with tongues. Some of the people of those lands are unfortunate enough to be here and I help them converse with the guards."

"Have you converted them to your new religion yet?"

"Please, Cullen. I've only been here a day myself. These things take time. Now how about a hug for an old woman."

Mother Miriam leaned forward and embraced Cullen.

"It's good to see you again, Cullen," she said, leaning back and holding Cullen at arm's length from the shoulders. "You're alive and that is a great gift. And God has thrown us together again. Can you imagine that? Can you imagine what great work he has in store for us?"

"Great work, old woman? The Romans took Rhiannon and Finn away from me. And God took my Aisling."

Mother Miriam grasped Cullen's hands in hers.

"He did take her. And know that she's at peace."

Cullen went to the window and looked out at the patch of gray sky visible through the small opening cut high into the wall of his cell. Drops of rain blew into his room, splattering on his face. Mother Miriam walked beside him.

"I don't have time to stay here and wait to be killed," said Cullen. "I have to find my family. What's left of it. I have to take them home."

Mother Miriam squeezed Cullen's shoulders.

"God will lead you where he needs you to be. I'll try to help. You know, they trust me so much they allowed me to go to the market this morning to buy some food for tonight's meal. I must have a pleasant face, or some trustworthy element in me. And speaking of meals, I'm sure you could use a decent breakfast."

Even the mention of the word caused Cullen's stomach to growl. Despite Dracon's promise, he hadn't been fed last night, and he realized he hadn't eaten in at least a day.

They exited the room, walking into the long, stone corridor lined with cells just like his. Two guards stood at the end of the corridor.

"Where's everyone else?"

"At breakfast. They allowed you to sleep a little longer. Kind of them, don't you think?"

Cullen looked at the old woman to see if he could detect any sarcasm or irony but her face was bright and innocent.

"I've asked myself a thousand times why I carried you on my back. Now it's a thousand and one."

Mother Miriam merely smiled at him.

Even before they reached the barracks, Cullen could hear screams, curses, grunts and the sound of breaking pottery coming from inside. Mother Miriam frowned as she opened the thick oak doors that led into the room. Thirty men, dressed variously in tunics and trousers stood around the edge of the long, rectangular room. In the center of the barracks were two men engaged in a vicious fistfight. Thick, granite columns that supported a high roof blocked Cullen's view. Stepping further into the room Cullen saw a flurry of fists flying. Blood spurted from their faces as they landed punch after punch. Roman guards stood watching the fight with amused looks on their faces. They made no move to stop the two men from pulverizing each other. The gladiators shouted encouragement to the fighters, goading them on.

"Come on, Bull. Knock his head off!"

The man named Bull smashed his forehead into his opponents face. Cullen winced, hearing the cartilage in the nose snap like a stalk of celery. Blood squirted from the injured man's nose as he collapsed to the ground. And just like that the fight was over. Bull stood over his opponent, his chest heaving as he took in great gasps of air. His hands clenched and unclenched as he waited to see if the other fighter would get up. But the other man lay groaning on the ground, his hands stuck to his face as if glued there, the blood still finding a way to escape through gaps in his fingers and run in rivulets down the back of his hands. His feet scrabbled slowly on the ground as if trying to find some way to outrace the pain.

Bull reached a hand into the man's shirt and pulled out a small leather bag. He opened the bag and emptied gold coins into his hand. He quickly counted them, then held them over his head. He turned around to the still yelling men, some of whom were handing money over to whoever they'd lost a bet to. They quieted down and looked at him.

"Eight coins, like I said. He stole them from me. Anybody want to say otherwise?"

Bull glared around the room, daring someone to dispute his claim to the coins. No one did. There was some scattered laughter and cheers as Bull shoved the coins into his shirt. He sat down on the bench and rested his arms on the table as the guards dragged the man away, leaving a trail of blood on the floor. Mother Miriam turned to Cullen and shrugged weakly.

"Welcome to your new home."

"Where are they taking him?" said Cullen.

"There is an infirmary here. They actually take care of these men. Very good care. As one would take care of a prize bull," said Mother Miriam.

There was a good deal of laughter as the gladiators took their places at the long table. They grabbed handfuls of bread and cheese, poured wine into their glasses until it overflowed the brim. They broke chunks of cheese off and jammed it into their mouths. A side of roast beef was no more than bones after the men had ripped it apart.

Mother Miriam told him to find a seat somewhere at the table. Cullen ended up sitting beside Bull. The other gladiators had chosen to give Bull a wide berth—at least until the killer's gleam had gone from his eyes.

Slaves walked around the table, clearing away the picked-apart bones and placing fresh plates of meat down. Cullen counted seven of them, and noted that all kept their eyes unfocused, refusing to make eye contact, as if trying to make themselves invisible.

As Cullen chewed on bread and cheese, Mother Miriam walked along the table with a large jar of wine, refilling the gladiator's cups. Alone among the slaves, she smiled and nodded at each gladiator that she passed, drawing looks that ranged from puzzled smiles to complete disinterest. The old woman was sweating under the weight of the jar. Cullen rose and went to her.

"I thought you were here to help decipher tongues, old woman."

"Ah yes," said Miriam, "that and other, less glamorous, duties."

"Let me help you with that," offered Cullen.

The woman grinned as she blew sweat from her brow.

"This is my job, Cullen. And the more wine I pour, the lighter it gets."

"But—"

"Sit, sit and thank you for offering to help. But you're one of them now. For you to help me would be laughable. I'll be fine."

Reluctantly, Cullen returned to his seat.

The old woman continued to pour wine as she made her way down the table toward Cullen. When she reached Bull, Mother Miriam tipped the jug forward. A drop of sweat momentarily blinded her and some wine splashed onto Bull's shirt and pants. Bull cursed as the wine soaked into his clothes. He half rose from his chair and turned to the woman with murderous eyes.

"My clothes. What the fuck?"

"I'm sorry," said the priest, "my own sweat blinded me for a moment."

Bull's hand shot out. Mother Miriam recoiled, closing her eyes. The punch didn't land.

Mother Miriam saw that she had a reprieve and stepped back.

Cullen had grabbed Bull's arm before it hit Miriam. He smashed a short, vicious jab into Bull's exposed ribs. He shot to his feet and slammed Bull's face into the table, bearing down on him.

"You'd hit an old woman," said Cullen in disbelief. He slammed a fist in Bull's kidneys. The gladiator let out a keening sound of pain.

Bull's breath whooshed out of him. He had been a fighter ever since he could remember and he had never seen anyone move as fast as this stranger. His kidneys felt as if they'd been scrambled inside his body. Fuck, this bastard was strong. He mumbled something that Cullen didn't catch.

"What was that, you bollocks?" said Cullen.

"Wasn't going to hit her," he wheezed.

Cullen had seen that Bull was going to pull his punch, but a point had to be made.

"It's still fucking unacceptable."

Bull didn't answer. Cullen rammed a fist into Bull's other kidney.

Bull coughed out whatever breath he had left.

"Yes, fuck, yes," he whispered.

Cullen leaned close to Bull, his hand pressing Bull's face into the table.

"The old woman is my friend," he said.

Interested faces watched Cullen from around the table. Not only were they being fed, but they got a show too.

"Nobody touches her. Understand?"

Bull didn't reply, but to be fair, thought Cullen, he was having trouble breathing.

"I'm going to let you go now," continued Cullen, "raise a finger against me or my friend and I'll rip your windpipe out with my fist and shove it up your arse."

Cullen let the big man go. Bull eased his arms to the front of his body and sat up, glaring at Cullen with fury glinting in his eyes, lungs heaving trying to claw air back into them. Cullen deliberately broke off a piece of bread and popped it in his mouth. From the corner of his eye he waited for the punch that he was sure would come to him, but Bull just kept staring at him with pent-up rage.

Anytime now, thought Cullen.

But Mother Miriam broke the tension. She shuffled over to Bull, carrying a new jug of wine.

"I'm sorry about your clothes, young man," she said. "Can I fill your cup?"

Bull turned to the woman and stared at her. Wordlessly he pushed his cup over to the priest who tipped the wine carefully into it. Bull lifted it to his lips and drank until the cup was empty. He slammed the cup down onto the table.

"You're the one who's going to fight Dracon, aren't you?"

Cullen nodded. "That's me."

Bull's face creased into a wolfish grin. He leaned closer to Cullen and his rank breath filled Cullen's nostrils.

"Then he'll kill you for me."

Bull shoved a slice of beef into his mouth and chewed carelessly, letting the blood from the rare meat flow down his chin from the corners of his mouth. For a moment Cullen thought this might be a time to make a statement, and pulverize this prick until he looked like the side of beef that lay on the table. He wanted to be left alone in this place and making an example of this oaf would be the way to do it. But Mother Miriam seemed to sense what was on Cullen's mind, and she laid a hand on his shoulder.

"Have some breakfast, Cullen. You must be hungry."

"Ravenous, Mother," said Cullen with a smile, never taking his eyes off Bull.

Thirty

After breakfast the Gladiators filed out of the barracks through a pair of wide doors. They emerged into a large elliptical arena. This was their training ground, a miniature version of the enormous arena Cullen had fought in yesterday. A high wall enclosed the area, and about ten tiers of seats rose up beyond that. Guards stood on the wall, spears in their hands and swords strapped to their sides, watching the gladiators with indifference.

Cullen surveyed the arena, looking to see if there were any obvious ways for him to get away from this place, but could see none. Besides, his mind was still reeling from what happened yesterday. He needed to rest, he needed to think. To the southwest, above the parapets, Cullen could see the Flavian Amphitheater, its top row of arches gleaming in the morning sun.

Cullen crossed to a section of the wall that was deep in the shadow of an overlapping ledge. He lay with his back against the cool stone. The other prisoners separated into groups. Bull had gathered a large throng of people around him. He produced a set of dice and soon they had a raucous game going on, with lots of shouting and good-natured shoving. Money changed hands at a rapid pace.

Someone tapping his feet awakened him. Opening his eyes he saw two of the prisoners sitting down in front of him. One of them was almost as tall as Dracon, but had a long mane of blond hair that fell to below his shoulders. His arms and chest were crisscrossed with scars, some white and puckered with age, others purple and more recent. Part of his nose was missing and the left side of his mouth curved down—the result, Cullen saw, of a knife slicing the muscles on that side of his face. Beside him was a dark-haired man with eyebrows that jetted out over his forehead. He was at least a foot smaller that his companion, but he had a poise about him, a stillness. Cullen immediately knew he was by far the more dangerous of the two.

The blond-haired giant cleared his throat.

"His left side's weak." He sat back and stared at Cullen as if expecting a response.

"His left side?" prompted Cullen.

"Weak," confirmed the big man.

Cullen stared at the two gladiators. His brow furrowed as he tried to catch up with them. He wondered if maybe he'd been talking to them in his sleep and had only really woken up halfway through the conversation.

"If you attack his right side," said the dark-haired man, "he'll kill you. He'll probably do that anyway, but if you attack his left side at least you'll have a chance."

"And this left side and right side belong to who?" he said finally.

"Dracon," exclaimed the blond hair. "You are the one who will fight him, aren't you?"

Cullen nodded.

"Dracon, yes, that's what he told me."

"He was cut a few days ago, right here." The smaller, dark-haired man ran a finger along the ribs on his left side. "Nice, big nasty cut that bled a lot. Of course, two seconds later he took off the bastard's head that did it. But he was cut."

"I'll remember that. Thanks." Cullen paused. "I am Cullen of Hibernia."

The blond-haired giant spoke up. "My name is Jacob from Palestine. This is Petrus, one of the Greek bastards you may have to fight. We've been in this piss-hole for nearly three years and have each survived seven fights."

A black man with earrings that hung down four inches from his earlobes approached them. In his hands he carried two wooden swords. He tossed them to Jacob and Petrus.

"You two start hitting those poles now. You—" he said, turning to Cullen. "Symmachus wants to see you."

Jacob groaned as he caught the sword. He stretched lazily in the sun. "The poles, the poles. Always the Goddamn poles. Every day of my life, the poles."

"The poles keep you alive, Jacob," said the black man, "Ask Petrus why he never complains. Because he knows this to be true."

Petrus raised his eyebrows to Jacob as if to confirm the black man's assessment.

As Cullen rose, he brushed dust off his clothes.

"It's not his left side that will defeat Dracon," said Cullen. "It's the love he has for himself that will be his downfall."

Petrus laughed and nodded, his dark eyes glinting. "Truly, if you can puncture that, you may indeed have a chance."

Cullen walked into the barracks, as more trainers entered the arena, ordering the gladiators to their feet. Before Cullen had gone back into the barracks the arena was alive with the sounds of the men hitting the six-foot tall poles with their wooden swords and shields. The trainers urged them on, alternately cursing and cajoling, reminding them that their reward would be neither riches nor power, but the simple continuance of their existence.

Cullen's eyes squinted as they adjusted from the blinding daylight to sudden darkness. Stepping inside, his eyes fixed on a large man sitting on a chair in the middle of the room. A guard stood on each side of the man, both had their swords drawn. A fourth man stood behind the seated figure. The man in the chair leaned forward.

"Are you worth a thousand sestertii?"

Cullen stepped closer to the man. His bulk filled the chair like an over-filled sack of flour, the flesh squeezing through the space between the seat and the armrest. His stomach bulged like the bladder of a sheep, filled with water to bursting point. Cullen thought that if one of the guards pressed the tip of his sword against the stomach, the man would explode. He wore a toga that looked as if it had once been white, but had collected such a variety of stains and messes that its original color was lost in the depths of time. His fingertips touched under bulbous, wet lips that seemed set in a look of permanent petulance. Fat flesh on his face pushed up from his cheeks, giving his eyes a sunken, piggish appearance.

"Are you even worth one?"

Cullen stopped in front of him. He shrugged, keeping his mouth closed. He remembered advice the Roman had given him years before; "If keeping your gob shut won't piss someone off, keep your gob shut."

The man looked him up and down, slowly taking in every aspect of his appearance. He turned to the shadowy figure standing behind him.

"What do you think, Scaevola?"

The figure walked out of the shadows and crossed over to Cullen. He leaned close enough so that Cullen could smell the rosemary on his breath.

"Open your mouth," said Scaevola.

Cullen stared at the man, an almost physical opposite of the big one sitting in the chair. Everything about this one was sharp angles and pointed joints. Even the hair on his head came to a peak just about his eyes. He waited for Cullen to obey his orders. Swallowing what little pride he had left, Cullen opened his mouth wide. Scaevola leaned forward and Cullen had an absurd image of this maggot climbing inside his mouth, poking around his teeth, prodding his tongue like some demented dentist. Scaevola's nose was so close that Cullen longed to bite down on it, crumpling the cartilage like a walnut, ripping it off the man's face. Finally, Scaevola pulled back.

"Show me your hands."

Cullen snapped his jaw shut and held out his hands. Scaevola took hold of them and turned them around, studying them intently. He then felt Cullen's arms, kneading the muscles, and making grunting noises as he did so. He walked around Cullen, pressing fingers into his back. He reached up to Cullen's neck muscles and felt the way they ran down to his shoulders. Finally he stepped back and turned to the big man.

"Pay the thousand sestertii, Symmachus, and be lucky he's not charging you five thousand. This is a good piece of flesh, and if he's as fast as Dracon says he is…" The small man shrugged, implying there was money to be made if everything fell into place.

Symmachus snorted, whether in approval or disapproval Cullen couldn't tell. He gestured to the table and Cullen saw a piece of parchment lying there. Beside it lay a quill.

"Sign it," said Symmachus.

Cullen walked over to the table, picked up the parchment and read it. Symmachus raised an eyebrow.

"A barbarian who can read. Wonders will never cease."

"It says—"

"It says that you must swear an oath recognizing you are a piece of shit, that you will endure whatever humiliation, death and sacrifice befalls you without protest. At my whim. You will dedicate yourself to Charon, the God of the Underworld. Your life as you know it, is over. You belong to my Gladiator school, the *Ludus Magnus*, best in Rome if I say so myself."

"What if I don't sign?"

Symmachus looked up sharply, as if this question had never arisen before. Cullen could see Symmachus wasn't certain if he should be vexed at this impertinent question, but in the end the owner of the Ludus Magnus merely arched his eyebrows and answered in a bored voice.

"*Damnatio ad Bestias*. Death by wild animals. Or maybe I'll just stick a sword in your gut and end this."

Cullen picked up the quill and signed his name. It didn't cost him anything, since it was an oath he would break at the first opportunity. He'd promised Finn not to kill anyone and that promise was set in stone, but he would tell a thousand lies and break ten thousand oaths if it would help him stay alive to find his family.

Symmachus studied the parchment, his small eyes narrowed in suspicion. He handed the paper to Scaevola and looked at Cullen.

"You fight Dracon in two weeks. In front of the Emperor himself. Dracon will kill you if he has a chance. Your only hope, and it's a slim one, is to give a good show to the Emperor and the people, and hope that there is a situation where your life can be spared. To that end you will train as you have never trained before. I have a *doctore* in mind to get you ready. He used to fight in the arena himself and spilled more blood there than any man I know. It will be a miracle in itself if he doesn't kill you during the training."

Cullen said nothing, refusing to ask the obvious question.

"His name," said Symmachus pointedly, "is Strabo."

Thirty one

"You fought before?" asked Strabo. They walked into the training arena in the early afternoon sun. Cullen carried a wooden sword and shield, given to him moments before by the old warrior.

"Some," said Cullen.

"Some. What does that mean? What's some?"

"It means some."

Strabo looked at Cullen.

"You ever fought Romans?"

"A few."

"Give me a number."

"Five or six."

"You're lying. How many?"

Cullen looked at Strabo in surprise.

"How—"

"You tensed up before you answered. How many?"

"Over fifty."

"How many of those did you kill?"

"Most of them."

They stopped at a *palus*, a thick, wooden pole driven into the ground.

Strabo grasped the pole suddenly, sucking in a painful breath. He clutched his back, still grimacing.

"Gods take me now," hissed the Roman. Cullen waited to see if the moment would pass. It did. Strabo slowly relaxed. Even though the attack had lasted less than a minute, a sheen of perspiration covered his face. Strabo spat on the ground, and sucked in air through his teeth. His breathing steadied, but the tension of pain never left his face.

Strabo was old, at least in his fifties. He had a long mane of white hair that he tied back in a braid. Despite twenty years fighting Germanic barbarians while in the Roman Army and later fighting men and beasts in the arena, his face was lined only with age. No sword or shield left their mark there. His body was a different story. He walked with a twisting gait, swinging his left leg forward clumsily with each step. His back, in the few hours Cullen had known him, seized up periodically, sending bolts of pain shooting up his neck. "Like a tiger raking a claw up my spine," was how Strabo described it to Cullen. His right arm still had the muscles of a man twenty years younger but his left arm was gone, cut off at the shoulder during his last fight in the arena. Strabo claimed he had died, but was brought back to life by a guard who tied the stump with strips of tunic taken from a dead gladiator, preventing Strabo from bleeding out. "It was peaceful there, in Elysium," he'd told Cullen as he chose the wooden weapons. "This beautiful woman came to me and took me by my hand, my left hand, it was miraculously back on my body, and led me to this beautiful lake. Then I woke up to a brute slapping my face, trying to force wine down my gullet. And then, when it was certain I would live, he expected me to thank him. For bringing me back to this. If there had been a sword close by I'd have run him through. Didius, get over here."

One of the gladiators, Didius, broke away from hitting the *palus* and trotted over to them. Close cropped hair revealed a face that was chiseled and lean. His chest was enormous, and Cullen imagined him holding his breath underwater for five minutes at a time.

"They still let a bag of bones like you in here?" said Didius in greeting.

"Shut up and try to kill this bastard."

Without blinking, Didius launched himself at Cullen. He struck forward with his wooden sword, slicing the air where Cullen had been a second before.

Cullen's fist sent Didius crashing to the ground. Strabo cackled as dust flew up around Didius's body.

"Get up."

Didius pushed himself to his feet and went into a crouching stance. He spat blood from his mouth and stared at Cullen, his gaze now totally focused.

Neither man moved to attack. Instead they both circled each other, Didius crouched low, Cullen straighter, his arms hanging loose by his side.

By now, the other gladiators had turned to see the two men spar. Cullen heard shouts of encouragement for Didius.

"How did you see it?" asked Cullen, his eyes fixed on Didius.

Didius frowned, but kept his mouth tightly closed.

Strabo glared at Cullen. "What in Hades are you talking about?"

"You said I tensed up before I lied. Only my wife knows when I lie. How did you see it?"

"I didn't see it, I heard it. Now fight you bastards."

Cullen and Didius kept circling slowly, each step planted firmly before the other foot rose off the ground. Cullen knew he'd have to create an opening. To his right, one of the gladiators dropped his wooden practice sword. Cullen's eyes shifted to it for a split second. Didius drove forward. He feinted left, then pivoted right, bringing his sword up toward Cullen's groin. But Cullen's glance aside had been deliberate. He slammed Didius's sword aside, then kicked him in the ribs. Didius rolled to a stop in a cloud of dust, cursing and sucking air. He got slowly to his feet and looked at Strabo.

"You see what you wanted to see?"

Strabo nodded.

"Thank you, Didius."

The gladiator spat on the ground near Cullen and strode away.

Cullen raised his chin and scratched the growth of beard that covered the lower part of his face.

"You heard it in my voice?" asked Cullen, turning to Strabo.

"You answered too quickly."

Cullen made a sound, halfway between a grunt and a laugh.

"That's what my wife says too."

Lunch consisted of barley porridge and lots of it. Having fought with the pole all morning, Cullen was famished. He drained his bowl, and servants quickly re-filled it. The gladiators sat around the long table, talking to each other between slurps in quiet tones. Once the meal was done, they went outside again where Strabo and the other trainers led them through a punishing workout of squats, jumps, sprints, and push-ups ending with a three mile run around the perimeter of the arena. The sun beat down burning Cullen's back. Everyone else in this prison was bronzed to a golden brown and Cullen suspected that his skin would soon bake to that color. The sun was relentless in this land, and, if he ever got back to his own land, he knew he would always look at clouds with a little more appreciation.

The next day Bull and nine other gladiators were taken away to fight in that day's games. While they were gone, the routine established yesterday continued for Cullen. Breakfast to start the day, training in the arena all morning, barley porridge for lunch, more training in the afternoon, a small break before dinner was served, then dinner, and then they had a couple of hours to themselves before the guards took them back to their cells.

Bull and seven gladiators returned, their eyes glassy, their faces covered in dirt and dried blood. Two of the men had to be taken to the hospital room where Scaevola washed their bodies and bandaged up their cuts. Bull, filthy and covered in grime, went straight to the table where food and drink remained from the evening's meal. He up-ended a jug of wine into his mouth. He drank greedily, letting the wine run down his chin. He shoved bread and cheese into his mouth, snorting and grunting as he chewed it up.

Cullen sat on a ledge in the corner of the banquet room. He stared at Bull. There was a manic energy to the man as bits of food flew from his mouth, and wine drizzled down his chin. Bull's eyes were wide, as if staring at a scene that played in front of him. Cullen could imagine what he saw:

His enemy under foot, sword held above the defeated warrior, roars of fifty thousand Romans in his ears. And then what? Did the Emperor allow the loser to live? Or did he turn his thumb to indicate that the man's soul be sent to Hades?

Bull looked over at him, his eyes wide and unblinking. Cullen thought Bull would scowl at him, maybe spit out a curse at him. Bull merely stared back. Cullen nodded, a move Bull was welcome to take as a greeting or as an acknowledgement that Bull must have fought a good fight. After a second's hesitation, Bull nodded back, then turned back to his food and continued eating.

Cullen thought about escape.

He watched the guards. They were alert. Suspicious. They followed every gladiator with eyes that seemed locked in a permanent squint. They were well trained and ready to fight.

Cullen knew that opportunities, no matter how small, would arise. He just had to be ready to grab them.

That night Cullen was taken back to his cell. Two Romans stood guard on either end of the gladiators' corridor. He dreamed of his family.

During the week leading up to the fight, Cullen sought out the company of Mother Miriam.

"Tell me they're alive, priest."

"They're alive," said Mother Miriam.

"How do you know?"

"A feeling."

"I keep thinking of all the times I hit Finn. A slap here. A beating there. A punch when he made me angry. Why did I do that? I can't even think of the reasons now."

"Pray that you'll get a second chance, Cullen."

"If I killed Dracon," mused Cullen, "the Emperor might grant me freedom. Rome's greatest gladiator, killed by the Hibernian warrior. If I kill Dracon, and kiss the Emperor's arse, why wouldn't he set me free? Isn't that the way this city works?"

Mother Miriam's old eyes looked directly into Cullen's.

"How many men have you killed, Cullen? In all your life, how many?"

"None that wouldn't have happily taken mine instead."

"How many?"

Cullen shook his head as he thought about this.

"Close to one hundred."

Mother Miriam pressed her lips together and closed her eyes. She breathed in heavily and exhaled.

"For the sake of your soul, you have to know. You have killed your last man."

Thirty two

Dracon listened to what the people were saying. On the streets they talked about the Hibernian that killed the lion. At the baths they marveled about how the Hibernian helped his friends jump the wall to freedom. Nobody had ever jumped the wall before. Nobody had ever thought about jumping the wall. But the Hibernian had thrown his two friends to freedom. And then he had escaped the claws of three African and Indian beasts.

Impossible, said those who hadn't been there.

My eyes saw it, was the reply. *I was there. I saw him do it. He caught the guard's spear in mid-air and before I knew what was happening he had impaled the lion.*

He caught a spear?

Behind his back, like this.

Dracon listened. Once in a while someone would mention that Dracon had defeated three men. They would tell how he had beaten the warriors despite having no weapons. There would be respectful whistles and his talents would be applauded and praised. But he had not captured their imagination. He did not set their souls afire. He did not make them dream.

The Hibernian did.

Cullen. Gladiator Thirty-Seven.

Dracon did not hate Cullen. He did not resent the people for abandoning him in favor of the new warrior. The people would always love the unexpected find, the warrior that would suddenly grab them and talk to them in unexpected ways. Dracon had been a gladiator for five years now. When he burst onto the scene and shed the blood of Cyrus the Eagle, the people had embraced him as they had embraced no one since. They had carried him on their shoulders and paraded him through the streets of Rome. Children adored him and wished to be him. Men wanted to be his friend and women desired that he be their lover. He had embraced the people and loved them with every atom in his body.

He had been their lover for five years. But now Cullen had appeared the way a beautiful woman might, in an instant, capture the heart of a man. Now they had someone else to love. Someone that excited them, someone that reached into the secret places of their hearts and affected them as Dracon never could anymore.

Which was why Cullen must be defeated. But not killed.

Dracon knew the people would not forgive Cullen's death by his hands. To have their new lover taken away from them so soon after they met would devastate them. They would blame him, Dracon. They would resent his power. No, Cullen would live, but he would live at the mercy of Dracon. Hopefully the Hibernian would put up a good fight. But there would be no doubt about the endgame: Dracon's sword at Cullen's throat.

Dracon could see it clearly: Both men would be spent and the crowd awestruck at having witnessed the greatest battle ever. All eyes would be on the bloodstained warriors, one who lay on the ground, his chest heaving as he took in great gulps of air. The other, standing regally above him waiting for the sign from the Emperor. Hadrian would take his time. He'd look at the crowd and listen to their pleadings. Some would cry "Death!" urging the Emperor of Rome to kill the Celtic barbarian. Others—most—would beg the Emperor to spare his life. The Emperor would furrow his brow and breathe out a great sigh as he pretended to weigh the decision. Finally, slowly, he'd raise his arm with his thumb pointed parallel to the ground. Neutral. And then, he would raise his thumb skyward.

The Hibernian would live. Not as the God the people longed for him to be. But as a man. Simply a man. Beaten by Dracon.

Dracon would then throw his sword away and offer the Hibernian his hand. The defeated warrior would grab the offered hand and Dracon would haul him to his feet. They would embrace. The people would see the depths of Dracon's mercy. They would marvel at the capacity for love and honor in his heart. They would see him take no pleasure in defeating this warrior from the ends of the world.

Dracon would help the wounded Cullen off the Arena's floor. Together they would walk out of the Arena to the screams and sighs of the people of Rome. But there would be only one name on their lips.

Dracon.

Thirty three

A shaft of sunlight illuminated the marble table where Dracon had scattered parchments on which he had written notes and drawn crude sketches. Suetonius sat opposite him, his gaze moving over the writings and diagrams. He opened his mouth to say something, but Dracon sat forward in his chair, fingers moving the parchments around.

"I want posters everywhere. On the temples, on every street. I want the forum covered with them."

Dracon handed Suetonius a rough sketch of how he thought the poster should look. Two crudely drawn figures were locked in mortal combat, each with a sword held high, about to stick his opponent. Written above the drawing were the words: 'Battle of Titans'.

"What do you think? Is it good? Is it terrible? What else needs to be there?"

Suetonius held up a hand, stopping Dracon's flow of words.

"Young man, we have all morning. Let's ease into this meeting, shall we?"

Dracon nodded his head in acknowledgement and leaned back in his chair. Suetonius studied the drawing for a minute, pursing his lips as he considered it. Dracon interrupted his thoughts.

"This has to be the greatest games ever. The Emperor has charged me—"

"—with organizing the games for the first time and you want to give him and the people an experience they will never forget, right?"

"Right. So we must—".

"Young man!" snapped Suetonius. "Please, in the name of all the Gods, tell me that you don't make love to your women the way you're acting now. Do you rip their clothes off before they've had a chance to memorize your name? Do you impale them with your engorged member even as they try to kiss you on the cheek to warm themselves up? Dear God, man, slow down. You're worse than a teenager."

Dracon raised his palms in surrender and leaned back in the chair.

"Apologies, old one. I'm just..." he waved his hands in the air.

"Understandably anxious," finished Suetonius, his tone softening. "And before we start, this old man would like a cup of tea, and maybe a few dates and honey bread."

"Forgive me, Suetonius. I fear the mind-set of a soldier, even removed five years as I am, is a hard one to break." Dracon turned to one of the palace servants who hovered nearby and gestured for him to come over.

"Don't apologize for who you are, Dracon," smiled Suetonius, reaching forward and touching the young man on the knee in a fatherly gesture. "Your past has made you who you are. But if you are to survive in the cutthroat world of high Roman society—and I suspect you will—then you must learn how to navigate these savage waters."

"I am clay in your hands, Suetonius."

"Good," said the old man, leaning back. "So tell me, Dracon, what's the first thing we must do?"

Dracon squinted his eyes at the ceiling.

"Well, we have permission from the Emperor," mused Dracon, "so I suppose we must fix on a date for the games?" He glanced at Suetonius, sure that his answer must be wrong, but he saw the old man nodding in agreement.

"We must fix a date, correct. Next question. What is the most important aspect to the date we fix?"

Dracon shook his head slowly.

"We must find a date that...honors the Gods?"

Again, he saw Suetonius smile, and was pleased that his answer was correct.

"Wrong," said Suetonius, his smile widening.

The old man turned to a servant who walked forward bearing a tray of food and drink. Dracon watched impatiently as the servant laid out the tray on the table in front of them, and handed both Dracon and Suetonius dishes with a selection of bread, dates, grapes and olives. Suetonius looked pleased at the food, and Dracon knew the old bastard was making him wait, testing his patience to see if it would hold.

Suetonius popped a date into his mouth and chewed slowly, savoring the taste. Dracon sat back, his elbows propped on the arms of the chair, his fingers joined together touching his lips.

Suetonius chased the date down with a swallow of wine.

"To answer the question, Dracon, let's return to the example of the impatient lover. Suppose you spend all day making love to three women. You have spent yourself. A few minutes later in walks Helen of Troy. She wants you. She needs you and she's the most beautiful woman you've ever seen. What do you do?"

"Ask her to come back tomorrow?"

"An appalling choice, yes?"

"Unacceptable," agreed Dracon.

"But suppose you'd spent not only the day but the entire week away from women, and did not enjoy their company or the heady sound of their laughter, and in walks the fair Helen. How do you feel then?"

"Enthusiastic."

"Enthusiastic is a good word. You would be chomping at the bit to please her in every way you know how. The sheer novelty of being with her would ensure a wonderful time would be had by both of you. And the problem with these blood-drenched games is that they have them all the time, sometimes for four or five days in a row. How would you feel if your games took place on the sixth day?"

"Nobody would care. They'd be satiated."

"Even if Helen of Troy—you—were there to do as they wished."

"An excellent point, Suetonius," murmured Dracon. "What do we do?"

"I asked to the Emperor to let the amphitheater sit silent for the week before our games. He agreed at once. By the time your games roll around, Dracon, the people will be hot with desire to see what you present to them."

"Suetonius, you are the very definition of genius," said Dracon.

"I have my moments," smiled the old man. "Now, to business. On the day itself we start with the animal hunt, yes?"

Dracon nodded.

"I have carpenters working on building a forest glade through which the hunters can stalk the animals."

"And the animals?"

"Ari can supply me with four lions, five tigers and twenty leopards. Plus the usual assortment of deer, bulls and bears."

"You should think about bringing the elephants in after the cats have finished."

"Yes, but I want the forest cleared first. There's nothing like the first sight of the elephant in a clear arena."

"So three elephants?"

"Three elephants, and six fighters, armed only with spears. I want some of those bastards trampled underfoot."

"Agreed. If the people don't see some heads bursting like ripe grapes they'll be disappointed. And after the animals, we bring in the condemned prisoners?"

"No, no, no. We have to slow it down a bit. Get them laughing, get them cheering, get them relaxed."

"So you're thinking...?"

"Dwarves against Amazons. I've got three of each, so we let them loose, and let the crowd get settled before the Egyptians fight."

"Those Amazons scare me," shuddered Suetonius. "I'd as soon as make love to a wild boar as mess with one of those women."

"I've had a few of those women," said Dracon casually.

"And?" demanded Suetonius.

"I was afraid to go asleep for fear of losing parts of my body."

"Then let's cheer for the dwarves. You haven't had any of those, have you?"

"I have not been so fortunate."

The servant stepped forward and filled their cups with wine. Dracon smiled, knowing his games, his first games as a promoter, his first games as impresario of the greatest mass entertainment ever seen, were going to be everything the people dreamed of.

"I've changed my mind about the elephants," said Dracon.

"Explain."

"People like elephants. They can sense a sort of…" Dracon tapped his hand to his heart. "I've been at games where they're killed. Where they hunt the elephants. They don't die quietly. They don't die well. And the people…it makes them feel bad."

"So no elephants?"

"No, we must have elephants. But for the executions."

Suetonius considered this. He shrugged. "It'll work." He swirled the wine around in his cup and looked thoughtfully at Dracon.

"Of course, none of this will matter if the main dish of this feast you're preparing disappoints."

"What do you mean?" asked Dracon.

"If this Hibernian lasts only thirty seconds and the crowd expected thirty minutes. If the skills we saw from him were only the results of panic and sheer luck. If he chooses not to fight. If he kills himself before the games. Need I go on?"

Dracon shook his head.

"I've looked in his eyes. He's a warrior. He'll fight."

Thirty four

For those fighting the next day there was a feast. Eggs, cheese and olives were brought in on platters. Lettuce and leeks were laid out. Stuffed cows udders, pheasants, chicken, antelope and hare were set down on the table.

The men ate greedily.

Cullen sat apart from the others in an alcove. He pictured Dracon in his mind's eye. He recalled the way he'd walked and talked, the way he carried his body. Was there anything in his demeanor that suggested a weakness? Was he vulnerable on his left as Jacob and Petrus suggested? Could he spin around in the blink of an eye?

Laughter erupted from behind him. Bull was standing on the table, his face twisted in a parody of bloodlust and he thrust an invisible sword into an invisible opponent, stabbing and gouging. The other gladiators cheered as Bull raised his arms in imagined victory.

Cullen turned away, his thoughts turning inward again. He had to defeat Dracon. But not kill him. Not for the first time he cursed the promise he made to his son and the priest. If the opening was there he should take it. Not doing so could easily spell his doom. Knowing Dracon and his reputation, he'd probably only get one chance to kill him. What if he pulled back and five seconds later Dracon ran him through with his sword? How would he feel about his promise then? Finn was only a boy, what did he know about the lengths he, Cullen, must go through to find him and his mother?

Damn that woman priest and damn that promise he made to his son.

The sound of giggling interrupted his thoughts. He turned to see Symmachus leading a gaggle of women through the door. They were prostitutes, and hardly Rome's finest. Their faces were painted in gaudy shades of red, as if they were actors in the theatre. They stayed bunched together as they surveyed the room, staring at the gladiators with a mixture of trepidation and excitement. The gladiators whooped and cheered as the women came in. One by one the women fanned across the room, stopping when a gladiator reached out a hand and spun them onto their laps. In the space of twenty heartbeats the room emptied, as gladiators took their whores back to their cells, where they groped and pawed each other, the gladiators' smiles hiding the urgency they felt, knowing this over-perfumed woman, this lady whose toothy smile didn't reach her eyes, could be the last good thing they felt on this earth.

Cullen went back to his cell and closed the door. His mouth had a bitter, metallic taste to it. His stomach churned as if there was a ferret loose inside. He had no real sense of how Dracon fought, but suspected that there would be no one harder to beat in hand-to-hand combat. It was very possible that he would die tomorrow.

He thought maybe he should pray for victory tomorrow, but the Desert God, this God of love, would not help him in such a violent, hate-filled arena. Maybe he should sneak a prayer to Mars, the Roman God of war. This was his territory, after all. Then he thought of his own Gods, the Celtic Gods—*Andarta, Anann, The Morrigans*—all of them powerful Gods and Goddesses, but did they know he was out here? Did they follow him across the ocean or had he been forgotten in their eyes? He thought about this but before he decided upon the correct course of action he fell into a deep, silent sleep.

A tunnel beneath the streets of Rome led directly from the *Ludus Magnus* to the Arena. It passed through the catacombs, the last resting place for many dead Romans. On a normal day the gladiators would take this tunnel. This day was not normal. Dracon had suggested to the Emperor that the Gladiators walk through the streets of Rome, so the people could glimpse the warriors that would do battle. Hadrian had agreed, and the Praetorian Guards themselves lined the streets for the short distance from the Gladiatorial School to the Flavian Amphitheater.

The crowd was thirty deep and they fought to climb any pedestal, steps, shoulders and carts just to grab a better view of the warriors. They ranged from wealthy looking landowners to ragged paupers. Their faces leered at the gladiators who walked three abreast down the cobbled streets.

The crowd yelled and screamed. Cullen turned, trying to see if something was happening behind him, but then he heard the crowd. The force of the noise assailed him and he realized what they were saying.

"Thirty-Seven! Thirty-Seven! Thirty-Seven!"

They were chanting his name—or at least the number they knew him by. Cullen's jaw dropped as the crowd surged forward wanting to be closer to him. The Roman guards on either side of the road pushed the throng back.

Cullen felt immediate relief from the noise when the gladiators were led to a room under the arena. Despite the heat outside, the stone walls shone with dampness in the light of the torches, as if the very walls perspired. The room stank of the sweat and piss of men who had to wait for the call to butchery. Cullen and Bull sat down on the stone seats. Twenty other gladiators poured into the room and stood silently around as the door was locked from the outside. Once shut in, the gladiators found a wall to sit against. Some pulled out dice and a game was quickly started.

It would be a long day, and a long time before they were called upon.

Thirty five

The leopard leapt forward at Dracon, crashing against the iron bars of its cage. It tumbled down to the wooden floor, twisting its body as it fell and landed on its paws. Snarling, the leopard padded away, its head turned just enough to see if Dracon would do something stupid like reach his hand through the bars.

Dracon did not do something that stupid. Instead, he turned to Ari who reached into a bucket and withdrew a small chunk of bloody, sopping meat. He put the meat on the end of a stick and poked it through the bars.

"You're feeding it?" asked Dracon.

"Just enough to whet its appetite, master," replied the Greek. "A little meat before the show and this beauty will pounce around like a young buck. Give you and the Emperor a grand show. A grand show."

"Pungent," said Dracon, wrinkling his nose.

"Eh?" said Ari.

"It stinks," clarified Dracon.

Ari laughed, a low rumble that came from his ample belly.

"That they do, master. That they do."

The leopard leapt at the meat, swiping its claw at it. Ari was slow to pull the stick out, and it snapped in two. The cat sank its teeth into the meat, devouring it in one bite. Its jaw worked ferociously and in seconds the meat was gone and the leopard was licking the floor of the cage, cleaning it of the fresh blood that seeped between the wooden boards.

"Vicious, little bastard," said Ari admiringly.

"Are all twenty as feisty as this one?"

"Nineteen, sir," said Ari.

"Nineteen? I ordered twenty," said Dracon.

"And I got twenty, master," said Ari, his tone hurt as if Dracon was accusing him of a horrible breach of conduct. "One died. It was sickly. It lay down two nights ago and never woke up. We skinned it, though. Kept the pelt for you."

"The pelt won't excite the people, Ari. The pelt won't sink its jaws into some poor bastard who thinks he can outrun it. The pelt won't eat people."

Ari held up his hands to stop Dracon's rant.

"You know I wouldn't let you down, master," said Ari. "I got something else for you—a replacement. Look at this."

Ari led Dracon down the corridor, past the other leopards that paced in their cage, bodies turning in slow curves, mouths hanging open so that their lower lips hung down, revealing blackened gums and long teeth. Saliva hung from those mouths, dripping, mixing with the dirt and feces that littered the floors of their small cages. Their eyes burned with some kind of inner, evil light and Dracon shuddered, thinking of the poor bastards who would have to face these beasts.

"Beautiful, isn't he?"

Dracon forced his gaze away from the leopards and looked to where Ari was pointing. A cage, big enough to house all nineteen leopards, stood at the end of the corridor. Inside, a large shape stood in the shadows, and Dracon could see glints from the chains that held the animal in place. It was enormous, and he caught a glimpse of grey, leathery skin.

"An elephant?"

"No, master. We already have three of those for you. No, they call this a Rhinoceros."

Ari held up a torch, and in the flickering light, Dracon noted the huge horn that protruded just above the animal's nose.

Gods, if he could just impale someone on that, what a show this would be.
Dracon imagined the body being speared through, and as the beast raised its head, the unfortunate victim would slide down the length of the horn, legs kicking and mouth open wide, dragging a trail of blood and guts behind him. The crowd would appreciate that.

"Is it aggressive?"

"May have to light a fire under its balls, but yeah, it'll be pissed off when the time comes."

"Nice work, Ari."

"Your servant, master."

Thirty six

Boom. Boom. Boom.

The drummer walked into the arena, his drumbeats matching his slow, deliberate pace. Following him were four trumpeters, blowing out a clear melody, heralding the start of the games.

The *Venatores*—the hunters—marched into the arena, following the drummer and the trumpeters, two lines of fifteen men; the first line consisted of men clad only in a loose-fitting tunic. Their weapon was a long spear, tipped by an iron point. The other line was made of men with various types of armor. Half of them wore iron chest-plates with flared shoulder guards. The other hunters were fully clad in armor. These hunters, however, did not carry spears. Swords were their weapons and to kill any beasts they would have to engage them in close quarter fighting. Ten archers followed behind the hunters, dressed in simple tunics, armed only with their bows and arrows.

A cheer rose up from the crowd, the sound more of anticipation than outright excitement. The people stood, hands clapping together, whistling, calling out to the hunters.

Dracon bounded into the Emperor's box, his face awash with excitement. Hadrian turned to him, and nodded a greeting.

"Impressive bunch of hunters, Dracon," said Hadrian. "I recognize some of them from previous games."

Dracon slid into a seat beside the Emperor.

"They're from the Ludus Maximus, Majesty. They'll put on a show."

"Nice mountain," said Hadrian.

Dracon bowed slightly in acknowledgement.

A hill had been built in the middle of the Arena, a wooden frame covered with fake rocks and trees, and it spiraled up to allow the animals and the hunters to wind their way to the top. With any luck, there would be some battles to the death at the summit. Other, smaller hills surrounded it. Fake trees were strategically placed around the hills, giving the hunters valuable cover from the animals. In addition to the hills that dotted the arena, the hunters also had the benefit of the *cochlea,* a tall, wooden device that could spin around on its vertical axis. This would allow the hunters to dive behind it, spinning the device to confuse the beasts that were hot on their tails. The *cochlea* was placed close to the Emperor's box, away from the hills.

The hunters strode toward the center mound and marched around it. When they encircled the hill, they stopped. The drummer and the trumpeters marched slowly back to the entrance of the arena leaving the hunters to whatever fate awaited them.

"Suetonius was right," said Dracon.

"Right about what?" asked Hadrian.

"The crowd, Majesty. They haven't had the games for almost ten days. Look at them."

Hadrian followed Dracon's glance. His people, these Romans, all seemed a little more on edge than usual. The stadium was packed to overflowing, and they seemed to lean forward, as if those extra few inches closer to the action actually mattered. There was a tension in the air, a sense of expectancy.

"He's a wily old fool, no doubt about it," said Hadrian. "He knows people. Their moods, their dislikes, their passions. If you have him on your side, helping you with all this, you may just have a very long career putting on these shows."

"That would be a good life, majesty. A good life."

"I wonder, though, if you have extended yourself too much?"

"Majesty?"

"Aren't you fighting the one they call 'Thirty-seven' today?"

"It's the climax of the show."

"And how did you prepare?"

"As I always do. I cracked some skulls, sliced some flesh and generally made a terror of myself among the gladiators of the Ludus Dacicus."

"So if I happened to put money on the Hibernian to win…"

"…you should be prepared to lose your wages, majesty."

Hadrian laughed.

"Not short of confidence, are you, Dracon?"

"If you enter the arena thinking you're going to lose, Majesty, that's the quickest way to Elysium. It's not confidence. It's *knowing*. Knowing you're going to beat the other man is everything."

A hush descended upon the crowd as the musicians walked out of the arena. The air crackled as if an invisible thunderstorm were building inside the enclosure. The hunters broke from their marching stance and faced the walls of the arena, eyes scanning the walls, waiting for the beasts to emerge.

The leopards came first, swarming out of the two southernmost gates, their movements sleek and sinuous, like fish swimming from between rocks. Assaulted by the noise of the crowd, the big cats cringed back, turning on themselves. Some tried to run back through the gates but they were stopped by Ari's men holding spears, the ends dripping with burning tar. When the last cat ran out, the gates closed, leaving the leopards outside with the hunters.

An arrow flew through the air, planting itself in the thigh of one of the cats. Enraged, it turned to face the hunters. Its gaze fixed on the closest man and in a blur of gold and black it raced to him. The man crouched low, readied his spear and waited for the leopard to leap. At the last second, the hunter planted his spear in the ground and raised it, and it looked as if the leopard was going to impale itself.

The hunter miscalculated. He had raised the spear too far and tried to re-adjust its position. The leopard skimmed past the spear tip, which sliced open a cut on the leopard's side. Spitting venom, the cat fell upon the hunter, jaws clamping around the man's face. One moment the hunter had a face, the next, the leopard ripped it off and backed away holding the bloody pulp of flesh and hair in its mouth. The man was still alive as he rolled on the ground, feet scrambling to get up, his hands reaching up to where his features had been moments before. They felt nothing. Dracon imagined that the man screamed, for the horror of what had just happened to him would terrify Mars himself. But there was no mouth left to make the shape of a scream, no muscles to stretch the face, no lower jaw to indicate the man's mouth was opening wide, no eyes to allow the crowd a glimpse into his soul.

It was exquisitely horrible.

The man's hands shook as if palsy had suddenly struck him, and his whole body went into convulsions, jerking like a puppet under the control of some demented madman, until finally he fell on his back.

The crowd, having waited for so long, yelled in horror, in approval, in excitement, in awe at what they had just seen. Dracon turned to the Emperor, whose face seemed to pale at what he had just witnessed.

"Gods," whispered Hadrian, who could not seem to avert his gaze from the dying man. Dracon smiled.

This was a great start to his games.

The bulls were released soon after the leopards. They ran around the arena, panicked by the noise from the crowd. One of them impaled a hunter on his left horn with such force the point of the horn protruded from the man's back. The hunter flopped around like a broken doll until the bull pulled up suddenly, sending the hunter flying to the ground, trailing a spray of blood that pulsed from his body in great gouts. He was set upon by two leopards. Still alive, the hunter tried to push the cats away. One of them grabbed the man's jaw in its mouth and sat down, waiting for the hunter to suffocate. The other cat feasted on the open wound in the man's stomach.

Fifteen hunters, ten leopards and a bull still lived when the lions were loosed into the arena. One of the hunters flung a sword at the first lion, baiting him. The lion rushed to the hunter who ran to the cochlea. He grabbed one of the arms of the instrument and spun it. Diving behind the cochlea, he looked up to see the confused lion swatting at the spinning machine.

The hunter rolled to his feet and raised his arms to the crowd. The people cheered loudly. The hunter put a hand to his ear, as if to say he couldn't hear them. The crowd screamed louder. The hunter appeared satisfied and bowed to his fans. He picked up a spear and walked around the cochlea, which was now slowing down, and jabbed at the lion. The big cat swatted his paws at the spear, and lunged forward. The hunter skipped back, sending the cochlea spinning again. He ran to the other side of the machine and lunged at the lion, spear thrust out ahead of him. The spear plunged into the lion's shoulder. The hunter skipped back.

He was a shade too slow.

The lion jumped on him, using its paws to hold the hunter to the ground. Before the lion could bite the hunter's face, the man twisted an arm free and jammed it into the lion's mouth, pushing forward as far as he could.

The lion gagged in surprise and clamped its jaws down, trying to sever the arm. The hunter grabbed the lion's mane with his other arm and pulled himself up, all the while trying to shove his left arm further down the lion's throat. The lion backed away, swinging his head back and forth, trying to shake loose this thing that clogged his throat. The hunter's face was a mixture of determination and pain. Blood was running down his side from the cat's bites but he kept pushing forward, jamming his arm in until the cat's teeth were grazing his shoulder. The cat swiped with his claws, and one of his blows raked across the hunter's stomach which opened as if it was a newborn mouth, complete with ruby lips.

The hunter's intestines spilled from his stomach, dangling from them like a deformed and diseased tongue might dangle from a leper's mouth.

Still the hunter pressed forward and the lion fell to the arena floor, its legs jerking, eyes open wide in fear. The hunter fell with the lion, and as the beast lay still, the hunter seemed to notice that he, too, was dying. He looked at his intestines with a dawning horror. Turning to one of the other hunters, he seemed to say something to him. The other hunter came over, placed the tip of his sword at the base of the hunter's neck and plunged it in. The man kicked once, then lay still.

Dracon was pleased with the hunt. The carpenters had done a masterful job constructing the hills and trees. The hunters had played their parts with enthusiasm and the crowd's appetite was suitably sharpened. He left the Emperor's box to the praise of the Emperor and went down to the gladiators' waiting room.

Thirty seven

He was met by Proval, the *lanista* of the *Ludus Maximus*, the gladiatorial school that had supplied much of the gladiators for this day.

"You look angry, Proval," said Dracon. "Not too happy to see me, are you?"

"I couldn't give two shakes of a goat's tit whether I see you or not, Dracon. I'm pissed because I just lost six good men in the hunt."

"You'll be well paid for them, what do you care?" asked Dracon.

"Not paid well enough. You know the Emperor. He's got hold of the purse strings like they're the soft curls of hair on a young boy's balls."

"I'll be sure to pass your concerns on to him," said Dracon mildly.

"You'll be keeping your festering gob shut," snarled Proval, throwing open a cell door. "They're in there."

Dracon walked in to the room. Two torches burned side by side, shedding a meager, dancing light across the dank flagstones. Wooden benches lined the walls, their wood old and worn. Dracon breathed through his mouth. These rooms were washed out almost daily, but you couldn't quite rid them of the stench of urine, feces and vomit, smells that seemed to cling to the walls.

There were three women in the room. One woman, with hair so red it almost seemed as if blood sprouted from her skull, was getting her hair braided by another woman whose hair was cut short so that it stuck up in spikes.

"Your name's Lidia, isn't it?" asked Dracon.

"My name's Amazon," said the spiky-haired woman. "Lidia died a long time ago." Her hand movements were slow and sensuous and she took infinite care to overlap the redhead's braids perfectly.

"Amazon, then," said Dracon, rolling his eyes. "You girls ready?"

Amazon tied a string around the braid, fixing it in place.

"Beautiful, my darling," purred Amazon. "They will fall in love with you today. Don't you think so, Dracon?"

"I can barely keep my heart in check," sneered Dracon. "Now I want to know one thing: Are you ready?"

"Why does he yell?" asked the red-haired woman, her eyes still closed. She spoke in an almost dreamy voice. "Just have him tell us who to kill, and we'll kill."

"It's not about killing," said Dracon. "It's about putting on a show. It's about you ladies entertaining the people."

"Listen to him tell us how we should act, my darling," said Amazon to the red-haired woman, who now lay her head down on Amazon's lap. "We are women. As ugly as I am, I could seduce most men if I put my mind to it."

She stroked the red-haired woman's head, tucking individual strands of hair that had escaped the braids back under the tight weave.

"He thinks we need lessons in the art of seduction," said Amazon. "Don't worry, you impatient man, we will tease the audience, we will seduce them. We will bring them to a point where they won't be able to stand it any longer and then we will release them. And as we kill the little ones, we'll feel the people shudder in ecstasy, their little moans of delight will flutter over our heads. Is that what you were hoping for?"

"You shouldn't talk so, darling," said the redhead. "You might stir his blood and he may have you. Would you like that darling? Would you like him to ravage you?"

Amazon giggled.

"I don't think he's in the mood right now," she said.

"That can change".

Dracon ignored their taunts. He turned to the shadows where the third woman sat silently on a bench. This was Xenobia, a gladiator that Dracon had specifically requested for today's games. A veteran of the arena for three years, she was still only twenty-two years old. Onyx black hair fell past her shoulders in tight curls, framing a face that was shaped in a perfect oval. Long eyelashes covered her eyes that were such a light shade of blue they seemed to glow from within. Her lips were not full, but they seemed to always be ready to break into a smile that never came. She was the most stunning woman Dracon had ever seen, she had killed twelve opponents—including the wife of a senator who thought she would scandalize her friends by fighting in the arena—and she was the one person in the world who Dracon was genuinely afraid of.

Three years ago after Xenobia's first fight, her beauty had bewitched Dracon. He had just won his freedom and had taken her back to his house. Dracon had raped her, ignoring her protests. He'd expected her to be scared, but she had responded to him, raking her nails across his back, making him pay for every thrust inside her. When he was done, his servants put salve on the long gashes that crisscrossed his skin. Coming back to the bed, Xenobia had been asleep, her face as innocent and sweet as a newborn baby. He lay down beside her, and found himself stirring again, enchanted by her beauty, but for once he hesitated to follow his urge. Next time he'd have to tie her down, and keep those daggers at the end of her fingers away from him.

Gods, she dug deep.

He fell asleep that night and awakened to the first rays of light. Straddled over him, and with a knife to his throat, Xenobia smiled.

The tip of the knife pressed against his windpipe, and any pressure at all would puncture the skin. She smiled down at him, and he returned the smile, trying to read her mind, going along with the apparent playful nature of her demeanor.

"Try to take the knife," she whispered.

Dracon didn't move.

"The knife is at my throat, lady," he said.

"Do you think you could reach it before I slam it down into your neck?"

"I think I'd almost reach it. And that's not quite good enough, is it?"

Xenobia grinned at him.

"No, it's not."

They looked at each other for a moment, both with frozen smiles playing across their faces.

"Put the knife down, please," said Dracon, his tone a whisper, his attitude pleasant and calm. He'd seen something flit across this girl's face, some specter of delight and avarice, and it had chilled him. He didn't let this thought reach his eyes, didn't let the feeling inform the expression he had fixed on himself.

Xenobia applied the merest hint of pressure on the knife and Dracon could feel the skin at the base of his neck go with it, straining to hold the point at bay.

"You're worried, aren't you, Dracon?"

Dracon made a face and shook his head.

"Why should I be worried? You like me, I like you, and we're lying in bed having a little fun. What's to be worried about?"

"Well," said Xenobia, her eyebrows wrinkling in thought. "You did rape me last night."

"You seemed like you enjoyed it."

"Not like that. You could have had me if you asked. But not like that."

"So what's——?"

"Get it hard."

"Excuse me?"

"That little plaything between your legs. Get it hard."

Dracon stared at her for a moment, then burst out laughing. He laughed loud and long, wondering if he would have a chance to swipe the knife away. Xenobia, however, had not relaxed her body, and the pressure of the knife tip on his throat neither lessened nor increased. Any attempt to get the knife away from her had less than an even chance of working.

He finished laughing and looked up at her, blinking his eyes that had watered somewhat.

"Maybe I'm not in the mood, lady."

"That's okay," she said. "I am."

"A man can't just—"

She slapped him across his face, her nails raking the skin, causing large welts to arise. He felt as if a large cat had hit him, and he could feel four separate lines of agony where her nails had gouged him. The hit had surprised him, and he'd barely seen it coming. The hand holding the knife had remained steady the whole time.

He turned his face to her, feeling the first drops of blood run down his cheek.

"You bitch," he said quietly. "You're going to do yourself a favor now. You're going to drop the fucking knife, and you're going to run as far from here as possible."

She put a mock hurt expression on her face.

"But I'm only having fun, my love."

She smashed her fist into his nose, breaking it, he roared in agony and reached for the knife. He felt the knife break the skin and tickle his windpipe. His hand stopped an inch short of hers. They held there for a long moment. Dracon knew that if he moved even an atom closer, the knife would sever his airway and he would be done. He moved his hand down.

"Very good, my darling. Wise decision. And the other thing?"

"What other thing?" said Dracon, coughing and choking as the blood trickled down his throat.

"You're still soft. And I'm ready."

And now, three years later, Dracon still felt the prick of the knife at his skin, a ghost sensation of his near-death. He had not been able to fulfill her wishes that night. His broken nose and stinging skin had prevented his member from waking up. He had tried. He called up in his memory all those women and girls he had taken, remembered all his most exciting moments, tried to hear all the moans of delight or screams of terror. He had closed his eyes and tried to summon up desire but it had eluded him.

The broken pieces of his nose scraped together causing him immense pain every time he tried to breathe. Xenobia had finally rolled off him, laughing merrily. She left his house as Dracon nursed his broken, bleeding face.

The three years had not been kind. The madness that he had only felt in her that night had wormed its way into her features. She seemed possessed by demons. He had made sure he saw her every time she fought in the arena. There was something compelling about her, and the crowd responded too, relishing not just her considerable fighting skills, but also her cruelty. She knew just how to draw out a death, how to make the end of someone unravel as if pulling on their life's thread and teasing it apart bit by bit.

Even as he looked at her now, her body seemed tensed, poised, and for a moment Dracon thought she was going to leap at him and finish the job she had started all those years ago. She had a sword in her hand and she stabbed forward, near her foot. A squeal erupted from the shadows and Xenobia raised her sword. A rat was impaled upon the end, his body still arching, his feet kicking in pathetic little motions. Xenobia held the rat into a shaft of light and watched its struggles lessen until finally in hung limp. She pulled the rat off the end and tossed it to Dracon who batted the dead creature away.

"Dracon," she said. "You're looking rich."

"I am rich. And I'm paying you a lot of money to put on a show. Don't let me down."

"Just give me an opponent who can put up a fight."

"I've got you against Buco," said Dracon. "He'll make you work."

"Buco. I like him. It's a shame," she said, her voice trailing off as if drifting into the shadows.

"So fight hard, ladies. Put on a show."

"You already said that, Dracon," said the red-haired woman. "You sound anxious. Are you anxious, Dracon?"

"I'll call you Phoebe, my darling," said Amazon to the red-haired girl. "Phoebe, after the Sun God." She turned her face to Dracon. "Sometimes when she lies down and her hair fans away from her head like a halo, I swear I've never seen anything more beautiful."

213

"She gives me a different name every day," said Phoebe. She turned to Amazon, and placed a gentle hand on her face. "But I like Phoebe. I want to keep this one."

"Then we'll keep it, my darling."

Xenobia spoke from the shadows.

"Leave us now, Dracon."

Dracon turned and walked out. Truly he would never understand women. These three would turn into demons from hell once they got out into the arena. He stepped into the hallway and realized he was holding his breath. He released it in a soft whistle. Why did she always make him feel this way? Maybe after the games he'd bring her to his home tonight and tie her down. Teach her a lesson she should have learned a long time ago. She turned him on like no other woman ever had. But if he ever had her again she'd find a way to kill him. He just knew it.

Buco, Haldorf and Valerio, the three dwarfs, were playing knucklebones in their room when Dracon walked in.

Valerio had a sour look. Buco was gathering coins off the floor, a big smirk plastered across his face.

"Hello, boss," said Buco, glancing around. "What's the news?"

"Women are looking for blood today."

"They always are."

Buco picked up the set of four bones off the floor and shook them in his hand. He raised his eyes to Valerio who tossed a handful of coins down onto the ground.

"Valerio's feeling lucky today. Don't know why. If I win any more from him I'll be able to buy him. Like to be my slave, Valerio?"

He threw the bones across the floor, and all three dwarfs leaned forward trying to read the marks on the bones.

"Two fours and a Venus," said Haldorf. "Lucky bastard."

Buco sat back and crossed his arms. There was a big smile on his face as Valerio picked up the bones.

"Cheer up, Valerio," said Buco, "You just need to be luckier than you've ever been in your life."

Valerio cupped the bones in his hand and blew on them.

"One of these days, Buco, your luck will run out."

"Is that a threat, you wormy, little toad?"

"Take it any way you want," replied Valerio.

"Easy, easy," said Haldorf. "Save it for the arena, boys."

Valerio glowered at Buco, and without taking his eyes off him, threw the bones on the floor. Valerio didn't look at what the bones showed, just kept his eyes on Buco who leaned over to read the symbols. Buco's face darkened.

"Impossible," he whispered. "Impossible. How could it be?"

Valerio blinked in surprise and looked down at the bones. Had he won? Had he finally beaten this prick and wiped the grin off his face? He glanced down at the bones and saw that he had...nothing. He looked up at Buco, who had a slow smile spreading across his face.

"Can it be that I've actually won again?" said Buco. "Is it possible I've beaten you for the seventh time in a row?" Buco rocked back on his heels and laughed, beating the ground with his hand. Valerio looked up, a low whine coming from his throat, and threw himself at Buco. They met in a flurry of fists punching and feet kicking. Haldorf scooted back, trying to avoid the flying limbs.

Dracon ran forward, grabbed Valerio's shoulders and hauled him off. He threw the dwarf against the far wall of the cell. Valerio grunted with the impact and fell to the floor. Buco put a hand to his mouth and wiped blood away.

"You'll pay for that, you bastard," said Buco to Valerio. "We'll talk about this after."

Valerio got to his feet, straightening his tunic. He flexed his wrists and studied a gash that had appeared in his arm.

"After? What are you talking about after? You'll be dead, and I'll go through your rotten corpse and take all my money back. You think I give two shits about you beating me? Right, boss? Tell him what's going to happen. Tell him he's fighting Xenobia."

Buco turned to Dracon, a questioning, almost accusatory look on his face.

"How the fuck does he know that?"

"He's guessing," said Dracon.

"So it's not true?" asked Buco.

"Actually, it is."

Buco stared at Dracon for a long moment. He slowly crawled over to the coins on the floor and started picking them up one by one.

"That's not fair, boss," said Buco quietly. "I fought her last time. It's his turn." Buco glanced up at Valerio, who now had a smirk on his face.

"I wouldn't last two minutes against her," said Valerio, "She'd cut me like a side of beef. And besides, everyone knows you're the best fighter we've got. Only you've got any kind of chance against her." Valerio's mouth had curled into a sneer as he said this.

"It's not fair, boss," repeated Buco.

"I want you bastards to put on a show," said Dracon, ignoring Buco's protests. He stepped aside and nodded to the door. "Now, get the hell out of here and start slicing."

Thirty eight

Valerio was matched against Phoebe, and the flame-haired lady was the first to die.

Lunging forward with her weapon, she left her side exposed and Valerio drove his sword in deep. He was exhausted, as she had been pressing him hard for almost ten minutes. He collapsed to his knees, his chest heaving, his forehead sweating from the exertions. Gods, she almost had him a few times. New scars crisscrossed his upper arms. But even as he thought he'd had enough, she'd made that mistake and he'd pounced. He fell across her, as her legs twitched beneath him.

He heard a scream behind him, turned with great effort, and saw Amazon rushing toward them, her face a mask of anguish.

"My darling," she screamed, over and over again. Valerio rolled off Phoebe just as Amazon reached Phoebe's body and cradled the dead woman in her arms. Haldorf followed her, his sword raised, ready to strike. He screamed like an animal, spittle flecks caught in his wiry beard.

Amazon turned and drove the sword through his neck.

It didn't reach his spinal cord, and so he stood upright, sword still raised, body still, as if not moving would somehow turn back time and this whole misunderstanding would somehow sort itself out.

Amazon pulled the sword out of Haldorf's throat and a spurt of blood followed it. It was undeniable now, and Haldorf's hands dropped the sword and flew to his neck, trying to stem the blood. It spewed from between his fingers, spraying Valerio with crimson droplets though he was a full body length away. Haldorf fell to his knees and his arms dropped to his sides. His eyes had a look of supreme concentration, as if by force of will he could close his wounds and breathe fresh air once more. Amazon drew back her arm, sword glinting in the sun. Her mouth curved into a rictus of anger, and Valerio had a glimpse of her gums, veins crawling from inside her mouth, down to her teeth which seemed to glow with her white-hot fury.

She swung the sword, decapitating Haldorf.

A huge cry rose up from the crowd as Haldorf's head rolled on the sand. His body remained upright for a moment, blood pumping from the stump, drenching the sand around him. Valerio scrambled away, his stomach heaving. He turned and vomited on the sand, the image of his friend's last moment forever etched in his mind. The horror of it gave him a jolt of energy and he got to his feet, turned and faced Amazon.

The woman had turned back to her friend Phoebe, whose face was pale in the harsh sunlight. Her eyes were open, their brilliant blue hue incandescent. Amazon lifted her head up and freed the two long braids trapped under her body. She undid the braids and spread out her hair so that it fanned out from her head like the radiating lines an artist might paint to symbolize the sun. With this done, she bent down and kissed Phoebe on her lips.

Amazon turned to Valerio, her eyes brimming with tears.

"Is she not beautiful?"

Valerio's chest still heaved and his legs felt as if the muscles had turned to cheese. He staggered slightly.

"Very beautiful, my lady," said Valerio.

She got to her feet, sword held in her right hand. Gazing down at Phoebe a slow smile creased her face.

"Is she not beautiful," repeated Amazon, a smile crossing her face, a smile that held only madness. The woman charged at Valerio. She came at him swiftly, her sword raised and Valerio had a quick impression of what a devil in hell would look like. He ducked under her charge and drove the sword deep into her belly. For a moment he was sure he would die too, expecting her sword to plunge into his back, but he heard the soft sound of the sword dropping on the arena sand. He felt her hands grab on to him, and now he thought she would try to scratch his eyes out before she died, but her embrace was almost gentle and Valerio knew she meant only to kill herself. Her bosom filled his face and he caught her sweat scent from the soft flesh.

She slid down to her knees, and her face pressed close to Valerio. The dwarf could see her eyes lose their life. Amazon's hands fell away and her body collapsed in a heap in the sand, kneeling with her legs splayed out and her head bowed forward as if in supplication.

He heard a cry above the din of the people's cheers. He looked up.

Xenobia had severed Buco's sword arm off at the wrist. Buco backed away, holding his arm against his stomach, trying to staunch the bleeding. Xenobia was bowing to the crowd, her bloody sword held out, accepting their cheers.

Buco knelt down in the sand, and with his intact hand, opened the fingers of his severed arm and grabbed the sword still held in its grip.

He struggled to his feet and ran over to Valerio. The crowd laughed and yelled, enjoying the dwarf's side-to-side run, his legs making half-circular strides as he crossed to his friend. Valerio watched Buco turn to the crowd and saw him mouth the words, 'Fuck you' to them. Valerio bent down and pulled at the thick leather strap that belted Amazon's tunic at the waist. As Buco came forward, his face twisted in pain, he thrust his bloody stump forward. Valerio wrapped the leather belt around Buco's arm, pulling it tight, ignoring Buco's high-pitched scream. The flow of blood shut off immediately and Valerio knotted it as tight as he could.

"Shut that fucking noise up," growled Valerio.

"Let's kill that bitch," screamed Buco.

With his sword held in his left hand, Buco charged at Xenobia, who still bowed to the crowd. Valerio was right on his heel. It seemed to Valerio that it took them forever to cross the sand to Xenobia. She stood up to face them. Valerio saw, to his dismay, that he was outpacing Buco and would reach Xenobia first. He knew this would probably be his last breath because he was beyond exhaustion and she seemed to have a sweet smile on her face.

Nothing. He had nothing left.

With the last of his strength he lunged forward. His sword met air as she easily avoided him. Her foot slammed into his stomach sending him head over heel along the sand. Every last breath was knocked out of him. He landed on his knees, face buried in his arms, trying desperately to suck in air. He felt his bladder loosen and piss flowed down his legs turning the sand under him dark. Gods, he had nothing left. His stomach heaved but nothing came up.

The clash of swords caused him to look up. Buco swung wildly at Xenobia and she laughed as she parried his pathetic thrusts away.

Laughed.

A surge of anger welled up inside Valerio. He tried to use the surge of adrenaline to get to his feet, but his muscles were like milk curds and would not obey his commands. Frustration welled inside him and all the impotence and humiliations he suffered came back to him. He raised his sword above his head and flung it at Xenobia, knowing it was a futile gesture, one that would probably spell his own doom.

The sword drove into her back. She arched suddenly as if a thousand wasps had descended upon her. With her free hand she tried to reach around but it was no use. She spun in place like a cat chasing her tail. Valerio stared in disbelief at what he'd done. He had to blink sand out of his eyes to make sure he knew what he was seeing. Buco backed away, mouth open. He watched Xenobia spin some more, her movements becoming more frantic. She slipped and fell backwards, and the sword hit the ground and drove all the way through her body. Again, her body jerked. Buco dropped his sword and sat on the ground, watching her die. He turned to Valerio with glazed eyes. They nodded to each other, sand plastered on their faces, bodies hurt, beyond exhaustion. They did not hear the crowd anymore.

Dracon, watching from behind one of the iron gates, saw Xenobia die. That little bastard, Valerio, was at best a mediocre fighter, and when he flung his sword it should have gone anywhere but right into Xenobia's back. He dragged his gaze from her prone body to the crowd. They were in full voice. Xenobia had been a favorite of theirs but they didn't seem upset. On the contrary, the fact that the tables had been turned and the three women were dead seemed to invigorate them, as if they realized that in these games—Dracon's games—anything could happen.

And the games had barely started. Dracon suspected that by the end of this day's battles, people would talk about him in a whole new way. His attention shifted to a new figure that walked across the sand of the arena. It was a tall man, very thin, dressed in black from head to toe. A bird's beak mask covered his face. His shoes were long, and curved up, tapering to a point. In his hands he held a long hammer. The crowd's cheers changed to a hushed "Oooh!" as he strode slowly across the arena.

Two Roman guards stood behind Dracon and one of them muttered an invocation and touched his mouth and heart. Dracon looked at him and raised an eyebrow.

"It's not the real Charon, you idiot," said Dracon.

"You tempt the Gods if you want to, Dracon," replied the guard. "As long as I'm alive, I'll be respectful."

"Even images of the Gods have power," confirmed the other Roman.

"That bastard scratches his balls like the rest of us," said Dracon.

Following the figure dressed as Charon was a smaller man, clad in a costume with wings on his ankles and helmet. He wore a white tunic trimmed in gold. In his hands he carried a poker with a white-hot tip. This was the God, Mercury. The figure dressed as Charon, God of the Underworld, stopped at Amazon. He gestured expansively to her and stepped aside. Mercury walked forward, raised the poker in the air and lowered it to Amazon's bare leg. Dracon saw a whiff of smoke rise up from the burning flesh. Amazon didn't move. Confirmed dead. He took the poker away and stepped aside as Charon moved closer. Charon raised his hammer, his black clad figure making a striking silhouette against the white sand. He brought the hammer down with theatrical slowness, tapping Amazon's head. He now owned her soul. She would return with him to the underworld where she would live out eternity.

They repeated the process, going from corpse to corpse, touching each with the hot poker to make sure they were dead, then touching the hammer to each one, to lay claim on their eternal souls. As they approached Xenobia, Dracon had a strong feeling that her body shouldn't be treated like the others, and for a moment he considered going into the arena to carry her body away in his arms. But the crowd might not appreciate his interference, and the job of Charon and Mercury could not be ignored or cast aside on a whim. And why should he do it for her anyway? Hadn't she tried to kill him? Were not his feelings for her just the lust and longings that any man has for a beautiful whore? And yet, one time, she had consumed him. If it was just lust, why then did he feel like he should spare her this final humiliation? Even in death he could do something for her.

Too late. They had reached Xenobia and a curl of black smoke rose from her leg where the poker scorched her skin. For one heart-stopping moment Dracon was certain she was going to get up and send her sword through the two actors portraying the Gods.

She didn't move. Dracon had a moment of crushing disappointment and loss. It hit him unexpectedly and his head swirled as he fought the emotions down. He'd always thought he'd try her again, devil-soul and all. But she was gone.

Arena staff ran out onto the sand carrying long hooks. Each of them curled their hook around one of the dead fighters. They waited. Charon and Mercury walked slowly toward the south gate of the arena. One by one the arena staff followed them, dragging the dead behind them. Valerio and Buco, the two remaining fighters, got to their feet and shuffled behind the dead. Buco raised his bleeding stump to the crowd, and Dracon couldn't tell if it was a gesture of acknowledgement or defiance.

Thirty nine

Dracon turned to the two guards standing behind him. "It's time." The guards nodded, and walked back into the dark shadows under the arena.

It was noon.

It was time for the executions.

He'd been looking forward to this part and had come up with some very creative ways to kill these scum. He'd found thirty criminal and condemned slaves, and was determined to put them to death in ways that would not soon be forgotten. He wanted the audience to know who these men were and what crimes they had committed. To that end, he had signs on which were written in large letters that could be read from the highest point of the arena, the words: "Murderer" or "Escaped Slave" or "Thief" and as each of the condemned was led to where they would die, the arena staff would walk around them holding the signs up. The more the crowd knew who these wretches were, and what they'd done, the more they'd enjoy seeing their slow, agonizing death.

There were chained together, standing in a tunnel that led to the arena. Dracon walked the length of the tunnel, barely hiding his satisfaction at having such a wonderful bunch of cut-throats to execute. Criminals all of them. Their faces, grimed with dirt, looked past Dracon, through the bars of the gate to the arena beyond.

This was their fate.

"All present?" asked Dracon.

"Almost all, sir," replied the guard.

"Almost all?" repeated Dracon.

"One of them stuck an ass-wiping sponge down his throat. Stick and all. He choked."

"He stuck it down his throat?" asked Dracon in disbelief.

"Yes. He's still down there if you want to take a look. The stick's coming out of his mouth."

Dracon stared at the guard for a second. The guard shrugged his shoulders.

"You should take a look, it's really funny."

Dracon held up a hand. "I believe you." He turned to the rest of the prisoners. A bearded man met his eyes, and he leaned forward, brows furrowed in supplication.

"Please, sir. Please. They got the wrong man. I didn't do anything."

Dracon turned to him in mock surprise.

"What do they accuse you of?"

"Murder, sir. I've never killed anyone in my life."

Dracon turned to the Roman guards.

"Why hasn't this man been shown justice?" he demanded.

The guard rubbed his chin and raised an eyebrow at the prisoner. He shook his head.

"I didn't realize he was innocent, I suppose. Shall I let him go?"

The prisoner's eyes seemed to glow with a surge of hope. He looked from the guard to Dracon, his eagerness palpable in the shadows.

"We could," mused Dracon. "It would show them I'm merciful."

The prisoner nodded, clinging to this one straw of hope that kept him from falling into the precipice.

"Yes, sir. Merciful. It would show them."

Dracon turned to one of the arena staff who waited near the iron gates.

"Open it," he ordered.

The man opened the gates.

"These five," said Dracon, pointing to the first five prisoners closest to the gate. The bearded prisoner was in this group. He looked wildly at Dracon as the guards separated them from the rest of the prisoners.

"But, my mercy, sir. My mercy."

"You have my mercy, it's given. You shall be freed. Or rather, your soul shall be freed from your body. What more would you wish from me?"

"But I'm innocent," said the man as he was dragged with the four other prisoners into the harsh sunlight.

"So am I," said Dracon.

The bearded man's name was Apicius, and he was far from innocent. Roaming the streets of Rome as part of a gang, he had robbed, beaten and killed since the time he was fifteen. Now, ten years later, he found himself being forced onto his back in the arena, his arms and legs splayed out, tied with rope to four stakes so that he looked like a slaughtered bull ready to be butchered. Twisting his head, he could see the other four prisoners bound in the same way, splayed out on the sand on their backs. The sun beat down on him and he narrowed his eyes, and called to the guards.

"Please. Mercy! Please."

They ignored Apicius, and he doubted they heard him, so great was the roar of the crowd. He caught the eyes of another prisoner, and realized that the other man's wild and insane look must match his own. He had thought in the past few weeks that if he had to die he would meet his fate with dignity, but not only had he begged pathetically for mercy, but he had just soiled himself, and he imagined the crowd caught the stench of his humiliation and jeered at him. When he heard that the prisoner had choked himself on the ass-wiping sponge he had shuddered in disgust. Now he envied him beyond measure.

The guards finished tying the last prisoner to the stakes. They hurried from the arena.

A sense of expectation hung in the air. Apicius craned his neck up to see what was happening. The five of them lay on the sand, arms and legs spread-eagled. They looked at each other, fear etched on every face. One of the prisoners was sobbing.

The scraping of iron against stone caused him to look up. He saw one of the massive gates rising up, until it *clunked* to a stop. Something moved in the darkness, something huge. It was as if the shadows themselves were coming to life. He shook the sweat out of his eyes and blinked, trying to clear his vision.

He wished he'd kept his eyes closed.

An elephant walked out of the darkness, its slow steps covering as much ground as quickly as a man could jog. The elephant's head bobbed up and down with each step, and its ears flapped in the air as if they were eagle standards from the legion. The animal's prehensile trunk swayed from side to side. Dust billowed up from around the elephant's foot with every step it took and Apicius could actually feel the ground tremble.

He heard a scream beside him. Turning his head he saw another prisoner, a Gaul, one whose name was guttural and unpronounceable, stare at the elephant with eyes that bugged out of his head. He jerked his arms back and forth, trying in vain to free himself from his bonds. Apicius saw one of his shoulders pop out of its socket but this didn't stop the Gaul from continuing to struggle.

The elephant stopped, confused by the high-pitched screams. It turned its head toward the screaming Gaul. It raised its trunk and appeared to sniff in the Gaul's direction. Apicius saw it blink slowly, lower its trunk and step toward the Gaul. Realizing, perhaps, that his screams had attracted the attention of the elephant, the man stopped yelling. He froze in place, and seemed to stop breathing. It was too late. The elephant crossed over to him, body lumbering, huge and inevitable. Now the Gaul started to shake. The elephant's trunk reached forward, exploring the man's body, sniffing him, tasting him. Satisfied, the elephant took one step closer and raised his front foot over the man's head.

Apicius wished he had the willpower to turn his head away from what he knew was going to happen. He couldn't do it. The Gaul's fear was so deliciously horrible that Apicius had to watch. As the elephant's foot descended, the Gaul turned his head sideways, pressing it into the sand, trying to put off for one more second what was unavoidable. Apicius found himself staring into the Gaul's eyes as the elephant pushed his head down into the sand. The Gaul's body started to shake uncontrollably and

Apicius saw the fear turn to abject terror until suddenly the elephant's foot came down fast. The Gaul's body bucked and Apicius tried to convince himself he'd only imagined the sound of a melon popping under the elephant's foot.

The elephant remained standing there for a full minute, while the Gaul's right leg twitched as if teased by a handful of biting ants. When the leg stopped moving the elephant looked around and met Apicius's gaze. The man was struck by the sadness in the creature's eyes and for a moment was certain that a creature that obviously felt such deep emotion could not possibly want to kill anyone else. The elephant swayed to the side, then walked toward him. Apicius's gaze was drawn to the head of the dead Gaul. It was as flat as a dead bird trundled over by the wheels of carts. The elephant lumbered toward him, its huge bulk looming larger and larger until it blotted out the sun. The creature stopped and raised his foot high over his head. Apicius, terrified beyond measure as he was, could see each line that was etched in the bottom of the elephant's foot, and as it descended he imagined for a moment that he was looking down onto some ancient, unknowable landscape, pitted with valleys, and he was falling toward it from a great height.

Apicius screamed.

Forty

The feathers tickled Themistocles.

They brushed against his face, just below his eyes, teasing the skin with a maddening softness, making him want to grab a handful of stones and sand and rub it on his face to get some relief. But there wasn't a damn thing he could do about it. His hands were tied behind his back and if he moved too much the guard beside him would give him a poke with his sword.

His mouth tasted of vomit. Watching from behind the iron gate he had seen the five prisoners squashed by the elephant. That had been bad, especially the fact that it took them quite a while to die, bouncing and shaking under the elephant's foot, but that wasn't what made him lose the contents of his stomach. What horrified him was what happened afterwards. They had tied a prisoner to two vertical posts; his arms and legs spread wide, his toes barely touching the ground. The man had been silent, accepting his fate with whatever dignity he could. The ropes holding his arms to the posts had been pulled tight, and Themistocles could see the pain on the prisoner's face as the ligaments stretched to their breaking point. All but one of the guards left the arena. The remaining Roman held a red sheet and a handful of stones. He stood a little ways apart from the bound man.   The crowd felt the unbearable tension grow and started jeering the prisoner who had killed a well-known shopkeeper on the Aventine. This was a man who deserved whatever horrors lay in store for him.

The gates opened and a monster appeared.

It was enormous, a great, grey, armor-plated beast with a giant horn on the end of its nose. Themistocles had never seen anything like it. More to the point, he'd never imagined in his worst nightmares anything like it could exist.

The remaining guard walked in front of the prisoner and waved the red flag. The creature turned toward the movement, but didn't move. It stayed rooted in one spot, and Themistocles thought the noise of the crowd disoriented it. Two arena staff emerged, each with burning straw on the end of a long stick. They approached the animal and prodded it with the fire. The creature turned, enraged, and seemed ready to charge them, but the heat of the fire made it back away, further to the center of the arena. It turned around, and this time seemed more focused on the red flag that the Roman waved furiously. The Roman threw a stone at the creature, hitting it on the side of its body. The creature snorted furiously, and shook its head. The Roman threw another stone, hitting the animal in the face, and this time there was no hesitation.

It charged.

It covered the ground almost as fast as a horse, aiming straight for the red flag. The Roman backed away, moving behind the prisoner, still waving the flag. He dropped the flag on the ground five feet beyond where the murderer started to quickly lose his composure. The murderer, arms and legs spread out like a star, was as vulnerable as a newborn baby.

The creature ran right through the prisoner, impaling him through the stomach, ripping his arms off at the shoulders, and skidding to a stop on the red flag, which it promptly trampled into shreds.

Themistocles swore that the man did not die right away. He saw the eyes blink as the blood spurted from the two stumps where once his arms had been. So great and violent were the creature's actions that the man actually rotated in a complete circle around the horn.

Having destroyed the red flag, the beast lowered its head then flung it wildly up. The man—now dead, Themistocles was sure of it—flew into the air, turning slowly like a circus performer. The man landed on the creature's back, then bounced off. The beast turned, incensed, and did to the man what it had just done to the flag. It trampled the man into the sands of the arena with such venom that Themistocles was sure there would be nothing for the God of the Underworld, Charon, to take back with him to Hades.

Themistocles thought he must have blacked out then, because when he woke up he was sitting down, cold water running down his face mixing with the vomit that dripped down his bare chest. He was still in the same place, sitting beside the iron gate. A Roman guard leaned close to him.

"Didn't want you to miss this," he said, pointing to the arena.

Three bound prisoners were rolled toward the center of the arena on what looked like miniscule chariots. Rising from the center of these chariots were poles, around which the prisoners were tied. The guards lined the three chariots in the center of the arena, tying the handles of the vehicles to pegs in the sand. *So they won't move*, thought Themistocles. The guards shook the chariots to make sure they were solidly in place.

They ran out of the arena.

A full minute passed before another gate opened. The leopards emerged. Themistocles hated leopards. He reasoned that if he were being chased in the street by an elephant or that damnable creature with the horn on its nose, then at least he could run down a narrow alley, or hide in a small space and they wouldn't be able to get him. But leopards could go anywhere he went, they could follow him into any crack that might be small enough to hold him and he had an awful vision of having got himself stuck in one of these small places, unable to move, and the leopard sliding toward him, ears flat against its head, starting to feast on his toes, biting them off one by one, the way his master used to bite off the head of the field mice that Themistocles would serve to him every full moon. Hated, hated, hated leopards. Hated them. Themistocles turned his head away, but the Roman guard slapped him hard and ordered him to watch.

So he watched and these leopards had none of the hesitation of the monster. They ran to the three prisoners and leapt onto them, jaws biting, claws slashing. Themistocles kept his eyes forward, just like the Roman ordered, but he unfocused his vision. The images became a blur of red, and yellow, and black, and if it weren't for the prisoner's bone-chilling screams he'd have almost been able to imagine that what he saw was a pageant, with performers throwing red roses in the air, their petals falling to the ground in a glorious crimson shower.

He was the last of the condemned prisoners. Twenty eight had already perished, twenty eight horrible deaths, twenty eight screams and yells of terror and shame. Ever the optimist, Themistocles had held out for a last minute reprieve. After all, he wasn't a murderer, hadn't stolen anything, hadn't desecrated any temple, hadn't harmed anyone, and hadn't done anything except run away. And then, only because he'd been pushed to the limit by his master. All Romans were cruel but this man, his master, had taken cruelty to the level of an art form. Oh, the abuses he'd suffered at his hands! The depravity, the humiliations. Beaten daily, Themistocles had lost most of his teeth. It was all he could do to chew a piece of meat—if he ever got meat. His arms and legs were covered in bruises from his master's white hot temper. But that wasn't the worst. The worst came at night, when his master's carnal appetites seemed to rage within him and no slave was safe, neither man nor woman. And these foul and unnatural attacks would occur within earshot of the master's wife.

How was a man supposed to endure such degradation? Themistocles could have killed him, but then all the slaves at his master's house would have been killed in retaliation, and to serve as a warning to any other slaves contemplating such a heinous act.

So he'd run. And for three glorious months had slept under the stars, living on fruits and small vermin, hiding in trees and bushes as he made his way north where he would leave this hellish world and get back to his beloved Greece. He had been free for the first time in eight years.

He dreamed of seeing his father again. His father! What high hopes he'd had for his son! No doubt wishing for a warrior to bring honor to the family, his father cursed him with the name Themistocles, after the great Greek general, hero of the battle of Salamis. But in his youth he had shown neither the passion nor the inclination for the life of a soldier. Instead, he grew up with his face buried in scrolls and books, his slight and pale body more suited to his calling as a teacher than following in the impossible footsteps of the historical Themistocles. Oh, yes. If he could see his father again, he'd make him see that there was honor in teaching. That there was honor in knowing who you were, however modest it may be.

He'd never see his father again.

He'd been found and questioned by a Roman patrol who didn't believe the story he'd spun that he was a teacher to a young Roman family, who was traveling home to visit a sick father. Under torture he'd confessed everything. They'd taken him back to his master and the sick, demented man had wanted him to end his days here, in the arena.

Themistocles used his shoulders to brush the feathers out of his face. And now this final humiliation. He was not just going to be killed, but the Romans were going to make him put on a show first. He was going to be the lead actor in a drama whose finale would be his death.

Dracon, that brute of a gladiator, had dressed him up as Icarus, the tragic figure who had flown too close to the sun, so much so that the wax binding his feathers had melted and he had fallen to earth, to his death.

A hand grabbed his shoulders and pushed him into the arena. This is it, he thought, and all hope of a reprieve faded. This is where his unfortunate, unlucky life ended. The soldiers brought him to the side of the arena where there was a large pole stuck into the ground. It must have been about forty feet high.

Strung out from the pole and across the arena was a rope, tied to an equally high pole on the other side.

Along with the huge wings that covered his back, they fitted him with a special harness around his waist. They tied a rope to the harness and hoisted him up until the tops of his wings were touching the rope that was strung between the two poles. He was so high now that if he fell he'd surely break his legs on the sands of the arena.

He started turning slowly in a circle. He was so high above the ground that when his body rotated toward the seats he found himself staring into the faces of the crowd. They stared back at him with curiosity, nothing more. No avarice, or bloodlust. He had an absurd desire to nod and smile at them, as if they were friends passing on a street. After all, there was no excuse to be impolite, even if they had come to see him torn limb from limb. He kept turning and the faces moved out of his field of vision and he was staring across the arena again.

His attention focused on a cage that hadn't been there before. When had they brought that in? A sudden wind whipped up the top layer of sand and the interior of the cage was obscured by the slowly dissipating dust. When the dust cleared, Themistocles saw the occupant of the cage.

It was a bear. So bright was the sand that he could only see the animal's silhouette but that was all he needed to see. Sharp claws, almost a foot long. Wide mouth, yawning, crammed full of curving teeth. And bulk. Lots of bulk.

The next ten minutes were a blur. Some idiot actor entered the arena, and was shouting out the story of Icarus to the crowd, using many effusive hand gestures to get his points across. Imbecile, thought Themistocles, with a weary detachment. They'd left out Daedalus. He was Icarus's father, everyone knew that. *He* was the one who had tied the wings to both him and his son and both of them had flown toward the sun. Themistocles couldn't believe they'd ruin a good story by not paying attention to details like that. And there was no shortage of prisoners to play the part of Daedalus. Laziness, pure and simple. Themistocles couldn't abide laziness.

As the actor talked and gestured, Themistocles was pulled slowly across the rope, an iron pulley squeaking above him. He refused, absolutely refused, to look at the cage again. He concentrated on the rope ahead, where another actor stood waiting, balancing on the rope. This buffoon was dressed in a yellow suit and around his head was attached a golden halo, meant, he supposed, to represent the sun. It was obvious, too obvious. Themistocles prided himself on his Grecian heritage. His were a people that knew how to put on a show and they didn't need caged bears with long claws to spice things up. The actor portraying the sun brought his hands close to his face, then gestured out, fingers splayed, representing, Themistocles supposed, the heat rays of the sun. The actor continued making this motion and his balance never wavered, despite the fact that the rope was only a couple of inches thick. Themistocles grudgingly admired that, but knowing that the actor's role was to send Themistocles to his death, his admiration could only go so far.

The crowd noise was getting louder now, and he heard the people urging Themistocles forward. Bastards, he thought, as he reached the actor portraying the sun. He was now directly over the bear cage. Using broad gestures, the "Sun" reached down and plucked a large white feather which he held up to the crowd. He opened his hand and the feather flew away, see-sawing down and finding its way into the bear cage. The animal inside snatched at the feather, and Themistocles couldn't help himself. He glanced down. The animal had speared the feather and shoved it into its mouth. Having been around animals all his life, Themistocles knew one thing: the bear was hungry. No, it was starving. Saliva walls formed and broke in the bear's mouth. The sun glinted off the massive incisor teeth. The bear's tongue worked ceaselessly.

Shouldn't have looked. Shouldn't, shouldn't, shouldn't have looked.

With a big gesture, the "Sun" reached down and pulled a string that Themistocles didn't realize ran down the center of his wings. He felt a soft ripping along his spine as the wings fell down, one wing on either side. The left wing hit the edge of the cage and bounced to the sand. The crowd roared its approval: the sun had successfully melted Icarus's wings. Now for the fall to earth.

It happened slowly, as an actor on the ground and two of the Arena staff dressed in black took the weight of the rope and started lowering him down into the cage. The bear, sensing that he was going to be fed for the first time in over a week, stood up on his hind legs and sniffed. He sneezed, sending a spray of mucous into the air. Themistocles watched this with a sense of disbelief. It felt as if he was watching himself from a distance. In less than a minute this beast would be tearing him apart. In two minutes he would be dead. With his hands tied to his side he could do nothing to prevent this slow journey to the afterlife. He felt the wind from the bear's first unsuccessful strike on the base of his feet—he was still too high to grab. Two things crossed his mind: The first was that his face didn't itch anymore. Those damned wings were gone and the feathers that had tortured his face with their delicate touch were no more. And the second? It wasn't much comfort but at least it wasn't leopards.

He hated leopards.

Dracon smiled as the bear's claws hooked onto the runaway slave and pulled him down into his cage. There was a flurry of motion, some screams and the slave somehow rolled away from the bear, his left cheek flayed open and blood spurting from his right leg. Despite his wounds, the slave tried to climb up the bars of the cage—his arms had been freed of their bonds. The bear grabbed him and dragged him down to the ground. The end came swiftly after that, but the crowd had been very entertained by the slave's refusal to go easily. All in all, a superb morning at the arena.

Forty one

Cullen and the gladiators waited. The tension had long since soaked into the room, becoming part of the very atmosphere they breathed. Dice games had been put aside, conversations ended. This was their time and they had to be ready.

Cullen glanced up at Bull and saw that he had a broken stick in his hand. Unconsciously, Bull was digging the stick into the back of his hand. His eyes had a glazed, faraway look as he stared into space, preparing himself for what lay ahead.

The door opened and a guard entered the room. He gestured to the gladiators.

"Let's go. Everyone but you." He pointed a sword at Cullen. The warriors got to their feet and filed out of the room. Bull got up and walked to the door.

"Bull," said Cullen.

Bull turned.

"Stay alive."

Bull's eyes locked with Cullen's. He nodded, then left Cullen alone in the room.

There was a small window near the ceiling of the room that looked out onto the arena. Cullen heard the trumpets and the screams of the crowd greeting the gladiators.

They wanted more spectacle, more fighting, more blood. If fear was a food, the Roman people ate it up as if their stomachs were bottomless wells. Cullen loathed the people that fed on this diet of entrails and severed limbs. And yet, hadn't *he* lived on the same sustenance for many years?

Cullen heard the crowd roar as Bull and the other gladiators walked out onto the sands of the arena. The room shook as the people above him stomped their feet as they chanted their favorite's name. Some called: *Bull! Bull! Bull!* The cadence, dulled from its full power by the dank, stone walls, was almost hypnotic. The cheers lessened and rose as other warriors were introduced. There were some boos and catcalls.

The crowd hushed expectantly. Cullen imagined the two warriors circling each other, looking for the advantage. Bull must be one of them: he could hear the Romans chant his name.

The sound of swords clanging was almost drowned out by the cheers of the crowd. Cullen strained to hear what was happening. The citizens of Rome urged the fighters on. Cullen heard a quick series of metal striking metal and then the crowd gasped, a collective *OOH!* Someone, thought Cullen, had joined the spirits.

The ceiling above him shook with the stomping of feet again as the crowd chanted Bull's name. Cullen let out a breath that he hadn't realized he'd been holding. Bull lived and would see the sunrise tomorrow. The only question now was whether Cullen would welcome a new day too. If that were going to happen, he'd have to fight for it through Dracon. And that was fine, because he had a rage building in him, an anger that was as cold as the ice that covered the rivers in winter. He welcomed his rage into his heart, opened his arms to the adrenaline that began to seep into his muscles. The anger would help him fight even if blood poured from wounds all over him. The fury would keep him alive, and he needed to stay alive, because his wife and two children—*no, one child, his wife and one child*—needed him to find them.

The door opened and a guard appeared.

It was time.

Forty two

Surprisingly, for Dracon, the least successful part of the day was the afternoon's gladiator fights. Oh, they had paraded in well enough, the arena trumpet blowers declaring them with all the pomp they could muster in their instruments. They showed off their muscles, caused the young girls in the audience to dissolve into either faints or fits of giggles. The ten sets of fighters had paired off and given it their best efforts. Two gladiators had died from their wounds, one had been killed after the fight was over because Hadrian had correctly seen that the man had spent most of the fight running away from his opponent's sword. The rest lived to fight another day, with only superficial scars on their bodies. But the audience seemed restless, and toward the end of the fights Dracon knew why. They were waiting for his fight with the gladiator called Thirty-seven.

Good, thought Dracon. I've got them thinking. I've got them wanting something they haven't seen. They may think they're hoarse now, but wait until my fight with Cullen is over. They will never have yelled like this before.

Cullen followed the guard down a low corridor that caused him to walk hunched forward. They stepped into the weapons room. Laid out on tables and propped up against the wall were swords, shields, spears, tridents and helmets. Nets with weights on them hung from hooks on the walls. The armorer stood beside a table waiting for him.

"Said your prayers, Hibernian?"

Cullen ignored him and walked to the table. He ran his finger along the row of swords. They were all short blades, good for close quarter combat. He picked one up, spun it around his hand and decided he liked the weight of it.

"Thirty-seven."

Cullen turned to catch the helmet that the armorer threw at him.

"This will protect what little brain you have."

Cullen grabbed the rusty, blood-stained helmet and put it on his head. He hated it. He'd never worn a helmet to battle and it made him feel constricted. He began to reach for it to take it off but the armorer walked over to him.

"You've got to wear it, it's the rules. You're a Thracian. Be proud."

The man shoved a metal guard over his right forearm. It was a series of overlapping metal plates that protected his sword arm. How was it supposed to protect me, thought Cullen, if I can't move my arm in the first place? The armorer strapped it tight to Cullen's arm.

"I want two swords."

"Against the rules. The Thracian's got a shield and a sword."

As if to emphasize the point, he shoved a large shield into Cullen's left hand, then bent down and tied a *greave*—a leg guard—to his right leg.

It was almost laughable, all this metal meant to protect him, when all it would do would slow him down.

"I'm not fighting with this shit on me."

"Shut up," growled the armorer. "You fight and live at the Emperor's pleasure—and mine."

He stood up and cast a critical eye on Cullen. His expression soured when he saw how awkwardly Cullen carried himself in his battle gear.

"You're not going to last ten heartbeats, are you?"

A guard appeared at the top of the steps that led into the arena.

"Time."

The armorer moved to grab Cullen, but Cullen leaned back slightly and fell against the sword table.   Swords clattered to the floor as Cullen regained his balance.

"By all the demons in Hades, you'll impale yourself before you even get out on the sand. Get up."

He hauled Cullen to his feet and shoved him forward up the stairs. Cullen stumbled, but managed to keep his footing. He climbed the stairs, flanked by a guard. In his left hand, hidden by the shield, was the sword he had snatched from the table when he pretended to lose balance.

Now he had two swords and the Emperor would get his show.

Dracon waited on the opposite side of the arena, just behind the iron bars of the gate. From the shadows he watched the crowd. He had never seen their faces so excited, so expectant. They came to see combat the likes of which they'd never seen before. What the Hibernian had done last week had spread through the city like the fire that had been started by the madman, Nero, decades before. The citizens had lapped the story up like dogs digging in the entrails of a bloated cow. How they'd 'oohed' and 'aahed'. How they'd imagined themselves accomplishing the same feats. Yes, the Hibernian had captured their imaginations. No, not captured. The Hibernian had stolen their imaginations from *him*. But that was fine. Now Dracon had a job to do. He had to steal it back.

A fanfare of trumpets interrupted his thoughts and quieted the crowd. The Emperor, his lean figure straining forward, was as caught up in the excitement as the lowliest peasant.

Dracon put on his helmet, tapped the forearm guard on his right shoulder, hefted his small shield and felt his pulse quicken as he waited for the gate to rise. He fought as a Samnite today, as he always did.

And here came Cullen, striding across the arena. The roar of the crowd hit Dracon in an almost concussive wave. Even now Dracon was shocked. How they loved this man! How ready they were to worship at his feet. Dracon laughed mirthlessly. How great their disappointment will be when their hero falls.

The iron gate in front of Dracon rose and he strode out into the arena. His heart warmed when the crowd's roar seemed to increase. The very sand on the ground trembled as he strode toward the center. Cullen had stopped at his place and faced the Emperor. Dracon halted ten yards away. He tried to read the Hibernian's face, but the helmet he wore hid any expression. Despite that, Dracon could see that Cullen was uncomfortable. His weight kept shifting as he tested the armor.

"Cullen."

Dracon had to almost scream the word for it to be heard. Cullen turned his head toward Dracon.

"The salute. To the Emperor."

Dracon thrust his sword into the air and the crowd hushed with an inward gasp. He glanced over at Cullen and was annoyed to see Cullen slowly—*insolently?*—raise his sword toward the Emperor.

"We who are about to die," yelled Dracon, "salute you!"

The crowd roared its approval and Dracon sustained his salute in what he knew was a suitably heroic pose. As the crowd quieted down again, Dracon stepped closer to where the Hibernian stood.

"Cullen, remember. Give it all you've got. Fight hard and we can make this last. If you do well the Emperor will let you live."

Cullen raised his face to Dracon with eyes that seemed almost detached, as if Cullen's mind was far away. *This Hibernian better not lose his nerve.* The arena could do that to people, even the best of them. But if this fight disappointed, then all the great show that had gone on before would have been for nothing. He needed Cullen to be brilliant.

Dracon grimaced behind his helmet.

"Fight hard, my friend. Or I will kill you."

The trumpets blew in a fanfare again and Dracon stepped back into position. He flexed his muscles and waited for the trumpets to cease. That was the signal, then he would attack and—

—*What in Hades was the Hibernian doing?*

Cullen had removed his helmet and was walking toward the crowd. *What? Was he refusing to fight?*

The crowd roared and Dracon could hear their confusion.

"Where are you going, fool?" he hissed. But the words couldn't carry more than two feet from him above the crowd's cacophony.

Cullen stopped fifteen feet from the edge of the wall and flung his helmet into the crowd. People surged to where the helmet fell, hoping to be the one to own the souvenir. Cullen walked back to the center of the arena. Dracon expected to see the terror that surely must have overcome the Hibernian but instead Cullen was smiling coldly. Cullen cast his shield aside and Dracon saw that he held a sword in his left hand too. He used the sword to slice through the leather strap that held his forearm guard in place.

Dracon heard the crowd's confusion.

He could use this to bring them onto his side.

Dracon straightened up and walked in a circle, his arms gesturing to the crowd as if asking: "What's going on here?" He got an immediate response. There was laughter and cheering as Dracon expressed what the crowd felt. Had the Hibernian lost his mind? Dracon made a big deal of scratching his neck, and shaking his head as he attempted to make sense of what Cullen was doing.

Now Cullen was cutting off his greaves—his leg guards. He kicked off his sandals and finally stood still, barefoot, no armor but with a sword in each hand.

Dracon let the crowd look at the two of them facing each other. Finally he made a gesture that said: "Are you done?" The crowd howled with laughter, appreciating Dracon's theatrics. Cullen nodded and waited.

Dracon reached up and took his helmet off. He flung it aside and it rolled across the sand. The crowd went wild, stomping and clapping. Dracon quickly cut the straps that bound his leg and arm guards. They fell away. The Roman citizens screamed their approval. Now the two warriors faced each other, Cullen with his two swords, Dracon with a short sword and rectangular shield. Neither of them moved and a hush descended on the crowd.

Dracon liked the way Cullen was playing this. He knew how to use the crowd, knew how to let the drama play out. Now if he could just fight long enough to make the fight the best this crowd had ever seen then—

Cullen attacked.

Dracon had never seen anyone move so quickly. In a heartbeat, Cullen had crossed the distance between them. In the moment before they clashed swords Dracon realized that there was no fear in Cullen's eyes.

Cullen's swords rained down on Dracon, driving him back, his feet frantically trying to find purchase in the sand. It was all he could do to use his sword and shield to deflect the attack. Blow after blow fell and Dracon backpedaled, his arms lashing out, fending off the attack.

Dracon's feet slipped on the sand. Cullen's fist smashed into his jaw, sending him crashing to the ground. Dracon lashed out blindly, expecting Cullen to try to finish him off, but his sword met empty air. He blinked his eyes furiously as he leapt to his feet. Cullen had backed away, and was twirling his swords around his hands.

For the first time in weeks, Cullen's spirit felt free. What sweet and honeyed delight he took in the look on Dracon's face. He had seen a look of surprise. Had no one, in the last few years, managed to lay a hand on him? Or maybe the ones he fought cowered before him, believing that they had no chance, defeated before the fight was even started? Whatever it was, Dracon now knew that he fought a warrior. Cullen spun the swords around his hands, letting the sun glint off them. He stalked around Dracon as the other man blinked and spat sand. The crowd roared their approval and urged Cullen to attack again. But there was no rush.

He had nowhere else to go and this was turning out to be fun.

Dracon wiped his sword arm across his nose. Blood smeared across the hairs on his forearm and dripped down, mingling with the sand.

"How am I doing so far, gladiator?" yelled out Cullen. Dracon looked up.

"The show," continued Cullen. "Am I putting on a show for them?" He gestured toward the screaming crowd.

Dracon banged his sword and shield together.

They ran for each other, smashed together and bounced apart. Dracon snuck in a sword thrust that opened a gash in Cullen's side. Dracon grinned as he backed away. He didn't think he'd hit anything vital but it was a cut and it did bleed. That's when he realized that his shoulder hurt like a son-of-a-whore. He glanced down at it. The skin was sliced open and the two sides of the cut looked like the plump lips of a fish.

Cullen's side stung. He couldn't afford many more skirmishes like that one. If he was going to live he didn't want to be torn up and bled out. Dracon was a warrior. After the surprise of Cullen's initial attack, the Roman had given it right back to him. Maybe better.

Dracon leapt forward and slashed down with his sword. Had it connected, it would have cleaved Cullen in two, but he rolled away and rose to his feet in one continuous motion.

Dracon spun, using his shield to hammer Cullen, spinning again, his sword cutting through the air, aiming for Cullen's midriff. With any luck the Hibernian's guts would grace the sand of the arena.

Cullen's sword blocked the blow. Instead of retreating, Cullen stepped forward and smashed his forehead against Dracon's already injured nose. Dracon's head exploded in agony. He wanted to fall back and clutch his face and weep in frustration. Instead he pivoted, bringing his shield around in a blur of motion. Cullen didn't even see it coming. The shield slammed into the side of his face. He flew backwards, tumbling end over end.

Where had that come from? He tried to focus his eyes but bright sparks taunted him. Cullen rolled away, thrusting blindly with his swords. If Dracon was anywhere near him he was a dead man. His sight cleared and Dracon stood twenty feet away, nose pouring blood. Cullen felt a wet stream down the side of his face. Blood trickled down his cheek onto his shoulder. Dracon and Cullen circled each other again.

"Remember I told you," said Dracon, "remember I told you if you fought well I wouldn't kill you."

Cullen remained silent, his swords sweeping lazily in front of him, ready to repel the next attack.

"Anyway, just so you know, I will kill you. First chance I get. I don't like you anymore, Cullen."

Cullen said nothing. He was searching for an opening, some sign of weakness. He had cut open Dracon' shoulder, but the wound was superficial and would do very little to slow him down. He needed to break Dracon down more. He'd have to take some chances. He launched another assault, running straight at Dracon, raining down blow after blow on him. The key to staying alive was to keep the blows coming so fast that all Dracon could do was block them. Cullen drove the Roman back along the sand, both warriors' arms moving in a blur of violence. Cullen was stunned at Dracon' speed. Everything he threw at him was blocked and parried, and the Roman even managed to sneak in a few blows of his own that Cullen had to avoid if he was to remain alive. For a full minute, Cullen pushed forward, chopping down, punching, slicing and each time his swords hit Dracon' shield and sword.

Finally, Cullen stepped back, breathing heavily. He looked at the Roman with renewed respect. Never mind about trying not to kill this bastard, he thought. If I can even get near him I'll be doing well. Gods, he's as fast as I am.

Dracon knew he had miscalculated. He'd assumed that Cullen was good, but had taken for granted that no matter how good he was, there was no way this barbarian could defeat him. Taking in great gulps of air, he realized he'd been guilty of underestimating his opponent. This bastard had driven him back about thirty yards and Dracon didn't know how he still lived. The assault had been furious. It was all he could do to parry the blows. Another attack like that and he'd surely find a sword in his belly.

Finding his voice again, he laughed at Cullen, shaking his head.

"If that's the best you've got," he paused, chest heaving to take in more air, "then it's not going to be very long before that bastard, Charon, hooks you and drags you off to Hades."

Bastard, thought Cullen. There had been that one moment, early on in the fight, when for a split second Dracon had left his side unprotected. He could have tried to stick him then. But he'd pulled back, had stepped away. His promise to Finn had stayed his hand. He tasted bitterness in his mouth, angry that the promise prevented him from ending this fight quickly. Angry that the promise may have sealed his fate.

This time Dracon attacked, sword and shield swinging, driving Cullen back. Cullen tripped and fell on the sand. He lashed out and kicked Dracon's feet from under him. Rolling away, Cullen was glad to see that Dracon landed face first in the sand. *Breathe in a lungful of that*, thought Cullen, *and let's see how you fight then.*

Cullen rolled to his feet and launched himself at Dracon, but the other man turned holding his sword forward, ready to impale Cullen. Cullen knocked the sword away, but not before it sliced a gash in between his ribs. Cullen yelled in pain as he fell on the ground.

That fucking hurt!

He lashed out with his sword, trying to block a follow-up thrust. He heard a grunt, and as he rolled to his feet, he saw with satisfaction that he had opened up a deep gash in Dracon's forearm.

Dracon leapt to his feet and faced Cullen, eyes blazing with fury. And as angry as he was, Cullen realized he detected an element of fear in those eyes. What did Dracon fear? Death?

Death, thought Cullen, *is only the second worst thing that could happen to Dracon today.* If he, Cullen, won, then he'd do something much worse to Dracon.

He'd let him live.

Cullen, breathing heavily, stopped pacing. This fight was not going to end quickly. Before it was done, it was going to get bloody.

Dracon ran, raising his sword and shield high, ready to smash them down on Cullen. For a moment his stomach was unprotected but Cullen sensed a trap. He faked a lunge for the bared stomach, then twisted away as Dracon sliced the air where Cullen's arm would have been if he'd continued his move. Cullen dropped to the ground, and in one fluid move kicked Dracon's feet from under him and hopped back up. Dracon lashed out blindly with his sword, finding nothing but air. He pushed himself up and they faced each other.

No one was talking now. Dracon attacked again, crouching this time, showing nothing. He launched himself at Cullen and both men fell back into the sand. Dracon landed on top of Cullen, knocking the sword from his right hand. Cullen balled his fist up and smashed Dracon in the face, once, twice, three times, his punches relentless and devastating.

Dracon tried to hit back but his shield prevented him from making contact. Cullen grabbed a fistful of sand and jammed it into Dracon's face, twisting and gouging. Dracon rolled off, howling in anger and pain. Cullen rolled with him, sensing he had the gladiator in full retreat. Now that Dracon was on his back, Cullen jumped on him, one sword raised.

Cullen wanted to impale Dracon in the chest. How sweet it would be to kill the man who saw Cullen as nothing more than a slave, whose death would bring him praise and riches. The thought left Cullen's mind almost before it found purchase there. Cullen up-ended the sword and smashed it down onto Dracon's face. At exactly the same moment Dracon summoned every ounce of energy and drove his fist into Cullen's face.

Cullen felt his face explode with white-hot pain. He flew off Dracon and fell back into the sand. He tried to hold onto consciousness and his one, coherent thought was that this must be how it felt to be hit by an anvil. He was dimly aware of the crowd's screams and roars. *Move*, he told himself. *Move!*

All he could do was open and close his fists, and let the sand spill from between his fingers. His eyes refused to open, as if the soul-taker had already stitched the upper and lower lids together in preparation for his life in the underworld. Any second now he would feel the hot blade of Dracon's sword slip through his ribs and that would be it. His life would be over and his family enslaved forever. But the moment grew longer and the roars of the crowd changed swiftly into a rumbling chant.

With a superhuman effort Cullen forced his eyelids apart. He couldn't see the other warrior. He turned his neck until, from the corner of his eye, he saw Dracon lying on the sand, trying to pick himself up.

Cullen gathered whatever reserves of strength he had left and pushed up into a kneeling position. The crowd erupted in cheers. Dracon was still feebly attempting to get to his knees as blood streamed from his broken nose. A sword lay half buried in the sand. Cullen grabbed it. With a supreme effort he got to his feet.

Dracon turned his face toward Cullen, aware that he was about to lose the battle. A groan of fury escaped his clenched teeth as he tried to heave himself up. Instead of rising to his feet, he succeeded only in pushing himself onto his back where he lay, his eyes half closed.

Cullen staggered toward Dracon.

The spectators, who until now had shouted themselves into a frenzy, fell silent. The people knew they had witnessed history—the defeat of Dracon. Would this warrior, this Hibernian, this Gladiator Thirty-Seven, look to the Emperor for the life or death decision? Or would he take it upon himself to end Dracon's life now?

Dracon rolled his head toward Cullen. The two men stared at each other. Their faces were unrecognizable: bruised, bloody, eyes barely able see from beneath swollen eye-lids.

Cullen raised his face to the Emperor's box. Someone from the crowd yelled, "Death! Death to Dracon!" Immediately another cried, "No, let him live!" As if released from a stupor the crowd burst out into cries of life or death, the individual words drowned out in the tumult of noise.

The Emperor stayed in his seat, slowly turning his head from side to side, as if listening to his subjects and weighing their desires. He stood up and walked to the edge of the wall. The Emperor raised his arm out from his body, keeping his hand in a fist. The crowd hushed. When the final cry of "Death to Dracon!" was swallowed by the silence, the Emperor extended his thumb and pointed it toward the sky.

Dracon would live. Cullen dropped his sword and walked away.

Forty three

Cullen woke up in a cool, dark room. His eyelids seemed unwilling to open. It felt as if a demon from the underworld had swabbed his eyes with pitch, and the hot, sticky substance had glued his eyes together. With effort, he managed to pry them apart, just enough to see a blurred image of an empty room in front of him.

He let his head roll left and instantly regretted it. Pain exploded on his cheek and he had a flash of recollection—Dracon's fist smashing into his face, the scarred knuckles visible for the briefest of moments and then the searing pain. He turned his head forward. The pain receded and he felt himself slipping out of consciousness.

Dark, dreamless sleep.

He awoke in a different room. He was back in the barracks, staring at the stone walls of his cell. He thought about moving his head but remembered the pain that had sliced through him when he had moved before. He lay still for a while, but decided he'd have to move eventually so it might as well be now.

He sat up slowly, and had to grit his teeth so he wouldn't cry out. The pain was bad, but not as bad as—when? Yesterday? Two days ago? How long was he out? He forced himself to his feet, using the wall to help him. He took one step forward, then another and gingerly walked around the room, his fingers touching the wall, using the rough texture to ensure he stayed connected to something that would stop him from falling.

Dracon wanted to scream in frustration. He wanted to rage and smash at anyone who came near him. He wanted to twist necks and rip entrails out of stomachs but he couldn't. He was in so much pain. Everything hurt. There wasn't an inch of space on his body that didn't seem to be bruised, cut or beaten, and all because of the Hibernian. Cullen.

Worse than the pain that racked his body was the memory of what happened at the arena as Cullen stood over him, the Hibernian's sword at his throat. Yes, the humiliation of defeat was bad enough. Being at the mercy of the whims of the Emperor was terrible. But what really devastated him was the crowd. The people, his people, they were cheering Cullen's name.

Cullen! Cullen! Cullen!

Not just a number anymore. Not Gladiator Thirty-Seven.

They had learned his name.

The slave defeated him and won them over. The love that belonged to him was gone and given to another.

How dare they?

After all he'd done for them, and all the love he'd returned. Scum. Filth. Well, they had better enjoy their precious slave, because the moment that Dracon could hold a sword again, would be the moment Cullen died. And how the people would weep then. How they would mourn for their new hero.

Forty four

Cullen sat on the edge of his bed while Scaevola, the physician, poked and prodded him.

Mother Miriam stood behind Scaevola as the physician took Cullen's head in his hands and tilted it back, staring into his eyes and nostrils.

"Open your mouth," he ordered. Cullen did as he was told and Scaevola peered inside, muttering to himself. He lifted Cullen's left arm and ran his fingers along a large scar below the elbow.

"Close your mouth," snapped the doctor. "Don't leave it open like a gawking schoolboy." Cullen closed his mouth and glanced over to Mother Miriam. *Have patience*, said the old woman's look.

Finally, Scaevola stood up.

"Three broken ribs, mending nicely. Two teeth, lost forever. Some concussion that seems to have dissipated. Two broken fingers, a sprained left wrist, left elbow and left shoulder. Extensive bruising everywhere, especially in the face, but even that seems to be calming down now. No permanent damage done."

It was two weeks since the combat with Dracon. Scaevola attended him daily, applying poultices to his wounds and splints to his broken fingers. He fussed over Cullen like a cranky old woman, muttering to himself as he designed cures for Cullen, and in the next breath questioning whether he was doing the right thing.

He had ordered Cullen confined to the small cell during his recovery. He was not even allowed to walk into the yard and soak up half an hour of sunshine.

"Scaevola, I'm going mad in here. Let me walk around outside."

"My judgment," said Scaevola "is that you remain inside."

"But—"

"When I first saw you Cullen, I thought you'd been trampled by a herd of oxen. I suggest that your organs are still very delicate. You will stay in this room. Good day, Cullen. I trust next time we meet you will refrain from questioning my judgment."

Scaevola gathered his bag and left. Mother Miriam turned to Cullen.

"He's supposed to be one of Rome's best doctors. You should heed his advice."

"Why would one of Rome's best physicians work on someone like me?"

"Since you defeated Dracon, the citizens of Rome speak of you as almost a semi-deity. The Emperor wants to be sure you recover."

"He's got an empire to run, and he thinks of me," said Cullen. "Madness."

"He has plans for you, Cullen." Mother Miriam shook her head and laughed quietly to herself. "He thinks they're his plans, Cullen. But the plans are God's alone. Can't you feel His hand at work here? He has brought us far from home and here we stand, prisoners in Rome, and the Emperor himself taking a personal interest in you. He must have some astounding work for you to do." Mother Miriam patted Cullen on his shoulder. Behind the smile, Cullen could see something was troubling her.

"What is it, old woman?"

Mother Miriam's brow creased in thought.

"Don't forget your promise to your son. You will be faced with terrible choices in the days and weeks ahead. You must be strong."

Forty five

Four guards escorted Cullen and Symmachus through the streets of Rome. The sun still hung low in the eastern sky. Merchants were setting up their stalls, shopkeepers rolled out the awnings over their shops, laughing and cursing at each other. The smells of cooking mingled with the aromas of animal and human waste, unwashed bodies and rotten meat. The day was going to be hot and by midday the stench would be unbearable. Everything about this city, thought Cullen, the people, the smells, the buildings—it all seemed so unreal. So unlike his village. Gods, it seemed like years since he'd been there. It seemed to be a life he'd had in someone else's body. All around him the citizens moved, but not just Romans. There were people from every corner of the Empire, thrown together in these few square miles, a seething mass of humanity, so great and vast a number they seemed to flow as one entity rather than individual people. The people seemed to feed off all the energy and turbulent activity as if each person was both a parasite and a host to someone else.

His thoughts were interrupted when they turned a corner and rising before him, in impossible majesty, was the palace of the Emperor. They had walked north from the Flavian Amphitheater, through the arch of Titus and along the Via Sacra. They came upon a large, paved space—the *Area Palatina* according to Symmachus—and Cullen looked upon the massive palace, built up on the Palatine, its façade stretching across the hill in a seemingly unending, unbroken line. It made the arena seem almost homely by comparison.

An Administrator waited for them by the entrance. He bowed to Symmachus and wordlessly led them inside. Symmachus bowed low, gathering the folds of his toga as he did so. Gone from his clothes were the splotches of food, and drizzles of grease. Instead, Symmachus's toga gleamed as if the sun itself shone from it. Cullen noted how nervous he was.

Cullen was staggered at the enormity of the building. Huge marble pillars lined the walls, which were covered in mosaics depicting sumptuous landscapes and heroic Romans. Drapes cascaded down from ceiling to floor like a crimson velvet waterfall. The floor, also marble, was polished to a high sheen. Dignitaries and politicians walked along the corridors, their heads close together in deep conversation. Soldiers, servants and slaves were everywhere, bustling about, and each doing their part to make sure the machine that was Rome kept turning.

They walked into a room with ceilings so enormous that Cullen thought they were higher than any tree he had ever seen. This was the *Aulia Regia*. At the far end of the room—*and it was very far*, thought Cullen——was a large throne set inside a shallow apse. He let his eyes drift across the walls of the room and saw twelve enormous statues, carved from black basalt, standing in niches. Between the statues, and covering the marble walls, were paintings of Roman soldiers defeating a horde of hairy-looking peasants. Typically, the Romans were given faces of stalwart heroes, while their adversaries—*his people, Cullen's people*—were depicted as savage and uncouth, with red-rimmed eyes, blue-painted bodies and wild hair. Cullen shook his head in amusement. Maybe an artist would arise from his people one day to paint the picture the way it really was.

He heard someone clear his throat. Cullen turned to see three men standing beside a table at the other end of the room. One of the men was the Emperor Hadrian, resplendent in a purple toga. Despite his age, and Cullen could see that his body stooped forward, and his hands trembled as they held a stylus, Hadrian's eyes seemed sharp and the mind behind them finely tuned. Another man, with wide protuberant eyes was drumming his fingers unconsciously on the table around which they stood. He gazed at Cullen with an almost insolent amusement and Cullen took an instant dislike to him.

The third man was Dracon.

He stared at Cullen with cold fury in his eyes.

The guards led Cullen and Symmachus over to the three men. One of the guards indicated that Cullen bow toward the Emperor. He did this, but the Emperor waved an impatient hand. Symmachus, sweat dripping from his forehead, bowed his head low toward Hadrian, and was unaware of the Emperor's hand waving him up.

"Yes, yes," said the Emperor, his voice surprisingly soft, almost delicate. "I meet with some Senators in an hour and I wish to get the cart rolling on my plan. Burrus?"

Cullen now had a name to put on the man who stood slightly behind the Emperor, his hands raised to the level of his stomach. Burrus. The fingertips of each hand touched each other lightly, as if he was always on the verge of making a delicate point. Burrus made a small bow toward Hadrian, his voice rumbling out "Majesty."

Burrus turned to Cullen, a smile on his face.

"I watched you fight, Cullen." He inclined his head to Dracon, whose gaze had not wavered from Cullen's face.

"The most exciting games I've ever seen." He paused, the side of his mouth twitching minutely in a smile. "And from Dracon's point of view, the best start to his career as an Organizer..." Burrus's smile widened and he shaded his voice with a hint of false empathy, "...with the obvious exception of his defeat at your hands."

A muscle in Dracon's face twitched. Burrus laid a hand on Dracon's shoulder. "And look how upset you made him. I swear if he looked at me the way he's looking at you I'd faint. Positively faint."

Burrus walked behind Dracon as he talked.

"Those Romans who were fortunate enough to see you two wage the battle of the Titans are still talking about it. And those who didn't see it, well, they hold their lives a little cheaper because of it."

Burrus continued to walk around the table toward Cullen, placing his feet as carefully as if crossing a stream on stepping-stones.

"But this is Rome," continued Burrus. "And our Emperor does not wish to see Romans regret one moment of their lives. And he does not wish that Dracon frown so. Do you know," whispered Burrus, leaning close to Cullen's ear, "I think the man has not smiled since you held your sword inches from his throat. Therefore, in keeping with his majesty's endless compassion, he has decreed that Dracon will get another chance to defeat his nemesis—-that would be you—and the people of Rome will get to witness what will simply be the greatest battle ever seen by the eyes of men."

Burrus grabbed the edge of the cloth that covered the table, and with all the drama of a stage actor, whipped the cloth up to reveal a beautiful model of the Flavian Amphitheatre. Carved from wood, it was intricately detailed, right down to the grooves in the stone wall that surrounded the arena. Fine salt had been laid in the bottom of the arena floor to represent the sand that would soak up the blood from those destined to die within its walls.

"Rome," continued Burrus, "has the greatest engineers in history. Reason wins over modesty so that I include myself in such hallowed company. We have built roads that span out from the city like a spider web. We have buildings that inspire grown men to fall to their knees upon seeing them. We have built bridges that span chasms, so it is a relatively simple matter..."

Burrus reached for a lever and pulled it down.

"...for a river to be diverted..."

A gate on the model opened and water gushed in, fanning out across the arena, sloshing against the sides.

"...so as to fill the arena with the very ocean itself, setting the stage for a sea battle."

Cullen blinked and looked up at the engineer to see if he was joking. But Burrus's eyes shone as he gazed at the water on which he placed four small boats. Cullen glanced at Dracon to see what he thought and for a second their eyes locked. For a fleeting moment Cullen could see an expression of awe on his face, then it was gone, replaced by the hatred that Dracon seemed determined to have toward Cullen. The Emperor smiled at the looks on the two gladiator's faces.

"Tell them the story, Burrus."

The old man cleared his throat delicately.

"His majesty," said Burrus, "came up with the story himself: A slave, who used to be a great warrior—that's you, Cullen—leads an escape from Rome, having murdered his owner's family, women and children included. They are plundering villages all along the coast of Rome, burning houses, ravishing women and men alike, stealing gold, silver, jewels and generally making a damned nuisance of themselves. But so far none of Rome's legions can match this warrior-slave for ferocity and blood-lust. What is to be done? It falls upon Rome's greatest soldier to defeat these rapacious beasts, these gluttons of death."

Burrus stepped back, an actor backing away from the candlelight at the foot of the stage. He looked at Cullen with a grin.

"You know, we had to calm Dracon down before you arrived. He was insisting that if he and his men won the day, that he should then be allowed to crucify whomever of your crew remained alive. Rather unsporting of him, I said. Well, he capitulated. He compromised and reasoned that by the end of the battle, there would be no warrior of yours left alive."

Dracon's eyes bore into Burrus, who continued to speak.

"When the slaves have been defeated, as is their destiny, Dracon will lead a celebration that will spill onto the streets of Rome and will be spoken of in tones of awe from now and for all times hence."

"Unless we win," said Cullen.

All three faces turned to Cullen. He looked at them with a smile on his face.

"You do want the citizens to witness a battle, not a slaughter?" asked Cullen.

"We want them to witness both," smiled Burrus.

"They'll get both," said Dracon through clenched teeth. "I'll give it to them."

"You see, Cullen," said Burrus, pointing to two of the model boats. "These boats will be filled with you and the Gladiators from your *Ludus Magnus*. These two," he pushed the other two boats forward, "will be filled with the finest Roman sailors and soldiers. All volunteers. All promised six months wages if they defeat you. Yes, the battle will be mighty and many of our fine young men will undoubtedly perish, but the outcome is inevitable."

"Your majesty, I must protest!"

Hadrian turned his head toward Symmachus, whose face had grown beet red.

"Must you?" he asked, an amused smile on his face.

"Majesty, let us fight other gladiators. Let us fight warriors from the *Ludus Gallicus*, or the *Ludus Dacicus*. Giving Dracon the pick of Rome's best soldiers puts us at an insurmountable disadvantage. We will be butchered."

"We have a prophet," laughed Burrus.

"Soldiers have never fought in the Arena," blustered Symmachus. "This goes against the...the..." His eyes looked around wildly.

"The rules?" suggested Burrus. "The rules are made by the Emperor. And if he decrees that the games will be fought thusly, then *those* are the rules."

Symmachus put up his hands in recognition of what Burrus said, but he continued on.

"If these games are allowed to go ahead in their present form, I will lose all—not most—all of my fighters. The *Ludus Magnus* will be empty in the days, weeks and months after the games."

He glared at Burrus, since he did not dare glare at the Emperor.

"You exaggerate," said Burrus simply. "There are legions of men who will voluntarily enter into your school to be trained as fighters. There are legions of prisoners who can be conscripted into your school to be trained as fighters. Yes, the experienced gladiators will be missed but fresh blood, fresh muscles—in time they will find their way into the hearts and minds of the people."

"My men are fighters, not sailors. Most of them have never been on a boat, never mind—"

"That's why we're giving you the Cilician Pirates," said Burrus, holding up a hand to stop Symmachus's protests.

"Cilician Pirates?" asked the procurator.

"Captured near Rhodes as they tried to plunder a fleet of trading ships. By all accounts they are excellent sailors. They should do a fine job for you. Give you a fighting chance and all that."

"According to who? I don't know if these Cilicians can do anything except pick their toes and—"

"The discussion is over," said Hadrian simply. Symmachus clamped his mouth shut. Any further protests would be taken as treason. He bowed slowly toward the Emperor.

Burrus clapped Symmachus on the back, causing the leader of the *Ludus Magnus* to grimace with distaste.

"Don't worry, Symmachus. Think of it as a challenge. You'll soon have a whole new set of bastards to fill the rooms of your school."

"Unless we win," said Cullen.

Burrus's grin grew even wider, and Cullen sensed that the more annoyed this man became, the wider his smile would be, the heartier his tone of voice would become. "You think a bunch on northern savages and some pirates can even think of competing against the cream of Roman soldiers? Fight as hard as you can, yes, let your swords sink deep into the bodies of your enemies, lop off as many heads as your swords can handle but do not delude yourself that you will win. Just pray that your death comes quick."

Cullen nodded absently to himself and bit his lip, as if he were seriously thinking about what Burrus just said.

"Your reasoning makes perfect sense, sir. I'll tell my men they must be prepared to meet their fate with bravery and a sense of duty."

Burrus relaxed and smiled.

"Unless we win."

Burrus' body tensed and he locked eyes with Cullen, who kept what he hoped was an insolent and amused twinkling in his gaze. Without breaking eye contact, Burrus purred to the guards. "Take him back to his cell."

Cullen smiled as the guards surrounded him and led him away. He caught Dracon's eyes, and noted that the Roman's mouth had turned upward in a murderous grin. They were all grinning—he, Dracon and Burrus—all grinning and smiling, and each wanting nothing more than to see each other's blood spilled in the arena.

Forty six

There was silence as the gladiators stared at Symmachus with looks that betrayed little emotion. The director of their *Ludus* had just told them what would be in store for them four weeks from then. He had talked, and Cullen, standing to one side, watched the gladiators' faces, and despite their stoic demeanor, saw them register what this plan would mean, he saw them calculating the odds of making it through alive, he watched their eyes narrow as the truth about their predicament sank in. This would not be just a regular day at the arena where the chances of walking away with your life were good. This was going to be a master class in butchery.

"Let me get this clear," said Bull finally. "Two boats full of Roman soldiers will attack two boats full of us. And we're supposed to try to defeat them?"

"What else are you supposed to do?" said Symmachus, unable to hide the misery in his voice. It was not sadness for the men who were doomed to die, men whom he'd trained and given the skills to survive the arena. His misery was for all the money he'd lose when the Romans slaughtered his men.

Cullen's mind drifted away. All the complaining and moaning wouldn't change what would have to happen. He glanced up and froze.

The auctioneer—the man who sold his wife and child—walked into the room. Gladiators glanced over to him and looked away again, disinterested. Symmachus nodded toward him and held up a finger as if telling him to wait a while.

Cullen guessed Symmachus had summoned him here so the auctioneer could channel all the likely gladiatorial candidates to the *Ludus Magnus*.

One of Symmachus's servants led the auctioneer out of the room.

"I don't think we're supposed to defeat them," said Petrus. "We're supposed to put up a good fight and then roll over and die. It's to the death."

Jacob, the gladiator from Palestine, spoke above the noise.

"Where does this leave us? We don't fight, we die. We do fight, we die. What are we supposed to do?"

Petrus, his short, stocky friend, gestured to Cullen.

"You've fought him. You've fought Dracon and you've beaten him. Have we got a chance?"

Cullen was so intent on trying to figure out how to get to the auctioneer that he didn't realize that every eye was upon him. Startled he glanced around the room.

"What?" he asked

"Bloody hell" said Bull. "At least pretend you give a fuck."

"Maybe we could petition the Emperor to have another gladiator school fight instead of the soldiers," said Didius, taking the attention off Cullen.

There was a chorus of agreement from the gladiators when an older voice cut through the air.

"Cowards," said Strabo.

The gladiators turned to their trainer, who sat on a chair against the wall. He stood slowly, bones creaking and face grimacing in pain. "The lot of you, cowards." He put on a high falsetto voice. "It's not fair. We shouldn't fight Roman soldiers. We're going to die." Strabo crossed to the table. "Bollocks." He glared at all the gladiators around the table. "Anyone who doesn't think they have a chance should fall on their swords now. Save the Romans the trouble. If you're going to fight, then fight like men. Take the glory. Kill the Romans. You've got four weeks before this happens. You can all handle weapons; you've all killed before. The arena belongs to you, not to any bastard of a Roman soldier, no matter how good they think they are. In four weeks I can make you twice the warrior you are now. It just takes commitment. And pain. Lots of pain."

He walked over to Bull.

"Get a good night's sleep, Bull. Try to finish crying in your milk by tomorrow, because when I'm done training you, your tears won't have the strength to drop from your eyes."

Bull shrugged Strabo's hand off him. Strabo grinned and turned to the gladiators.

"Grab the glory, boys. This battle will make you famous."

With all eyes on Strabo, Cullen slipped out of the room.

Cullen walked down the corridor toward Symmachus's room. The door was closed. Cullen pushed it open and walked straight in, pulling the key out of the lock as he did so.

The auctioneer raised his head. He sat on a stool and leaned against the table Symmachus used for his work. His mouth broke into an automatic grin. Cullen was vaguely surprised to see that the lone tooth in the auctioneer's mouth still clung tenaciously to the man's gums.

"My dear Symmachus," began the auctioneer. He stopped when he saw Cullen. "My apologies, I thought you were someone else," he said, confusion on his face.

Soon you'll be more than confused, thought Cullen, *especially if you don't have what I need.*

Cullen put the key in the door and locked it. He turned to the auctioneer who was rising to his feet.

"You locked the door. Why?" he said, the faintest tremor of fear in his voice.

"Do you know me?" asked Cullen.

"I do not," said the auctioneer.

"Look closer," said Cullen, stepping into the light.

The auctioneer peered at Cullen. Recognition dawned on his face.

"You're the one they're talking about. Cullen. You're the one that defeated Dracon," said the man, an awed smile playing on his face.

Cullen waited, letting the man's memory catch up. A look crossed the man's face.

"I sold you," he continued, "and…" The auctioneer stopped, as if biting back a forbidden word.

"Finish your thought," said Cullen softly. The auctioneer hesitated.

"And your family," he said.

The auctioneer took a step back, but was stopped by the table. Cullen didn't move from where he stood.

"I'll scream," said the man. "I'll scream and they'll come running and you'll be dead."

"You could scream," agreed Cullen. "You'd die, but you could scream."

"Then what do you want?"

"The name," said Cullen.

"What name?"

Cullen merely cocked his head at the auctioneer. The man grimaced, shook his head as if trying to convince himself of something, muttered 'bad for business, bad for business', all the while glancing up at Cullen trying to read him, then glancing at the door as if salvation was on the other side.

"You have no weapons," said the auctioneer, desperation now evident in his high-pitched voice.

"I could cut your balls off with a knife in one second. If I use my hands, it will take seven. You'll wish I had a weapon. Either way I'll have your balls."

The auctioneer paled and his hands seemed to creep of their own volition toward his groin.

"And if I give you the name?"

"I walk away. You keep your little friends."

It was a good deal, and the auctioneer recognized its value.

"His names Sulla. He's a general, or he was. He owns a farm north of here. Don't ask me where, I don't know. Buys slaves from me to work his land."

Cullen kept his eyes on the man's face. He believed him.

"Are you going to tell anyone about our little talk? Anyone at all?"

The auctioneer shook his head.

"Because I own your balls now," said Cullen. "You can have them because I'm lending them to you. But they are mine. And if you fuck me over, I'll take them back. I'll fucking rip them off, and I'll do it slowly. You believe me?"

The auctioneer nodded, his face a pale circle of dough.

"Wise," said Cullen. He unlocked the door and walked out.

That evening, Cullen sat on a stone ledge looking out a window crisscrossed with iron bars. Outside, the hawkers tried to sell the last of their wares for the day. Dust kicked up from the street, making the air near the ground seem like a dirty, yellow mist. The grit found its way into his room, coating his hair, skin and teeth with a thin film of grime.

"I wish it would rain," said Cullen.

Beside him, Mother Miriam took a sip from the cup of sour wine in her hand.

"Where we came from, the village," continued Cullen, "it could rain for weeks at a time. When the rain was done, there'd be this mist. It would roll down from the mountains. The land would have secrets." He brushed dust off his clothes and stared at his hand, streaked with ochre.

Mother Miriam rubbed her knees and shook her head.

"I've suffered through those rains in that land of yours, Cullen. My joints have never been the same. Forgive me if I say I enjoy the warm weather of this country."

"This land is cooked."

"Maybe it is," said the priest. She drew in a breath. "I'm proud of you, Cullen. Proud of you keeping your promise to your son."

Cullen turned to the priest.

"We need to escape, Mother."

"Indeed we do. Do you have a plan?"

"I have some ideas."

"Good ones, I hope."

"Insane ones, unfortunately."

"Good plans rarely work anyway."

"And insane plans hardly ever work, but when they do, it's a beautiful thing."

Mother Miriam chuckled.

"Then let insanity prevail."

The priest stood up. Cullen could hear her joints creak like the timbers in a patched-up trading boat.

"I need you to do something for me," said Cullen.

"A task," said the old woman delightedly. "I'm good at tasks. What would you have me do?"

"Find out where General Sulla lives."

She raised her eyebrows.

"He has Rhiannon and Finn," explained Cullen.

Cullen told the priest everything that the auctioneer had told him. Mother Miriam nodded.

"I'll find out what you need," she said.

Forty seven

It rained torrentially the next day. The gladiators, having trained hard for the previous five days, remained inside. Bread, cheese, wine and meats were provided generously for them. They needed to be in the best fighting condition of their lives.

Cullen was restless. The loud, raucous yelling of his fellow captives grated on his nerves. He sat by himself in an alcove, trying to shut out the incessant shouts and laughter. One of the gladiators, a Gaul, was barking out a story in a language that Cullen couldn't understand. Throughout the story, the Gaul would bray with laughter. Cullen stood up, picked up one of the wooden swords and went outside.

Cullen found he wasn't the only one out in the practice yard. Bull, rain running in rivulets down his face, circled one of the wooden stakes, alternately lunging at it with his sword and slamming it with his shield. Judging by the heaving of his chest and shoulders, and the way his leg muscles quivered, Bull had been out here a long time.

Bull glanced up as Cullen stood before another of the wooden poles. Cullen nodded curtly at Bull, who raised his jaw a fraction in return. Bull turned back to the stationary opponent and continued his training. Cullen dropped his two swords onto the ground and for the next ten minutes stretched his muscles until they started to burn. He could still feel the bruises where Dracon pounded him like a carcass of beef. When his muscles were somewhat loose, he picked up his swords and faced the dummy. If this was a real warrior facing him, Cullen would know only one way to fight: a relentless, overpowering, vicious attack that would not end until his opponent was dead. He stared at the dummy for a full minute, clearing his mind. From stillness, he lunged forward, thrusting, slashing, pummeling in a blur of motion. All the while he circled the dummy, making sure that his sword movement didn't follow any pattern but changed so that no one could guess where the next attack would come from. He kept this up for ten minutes and by the end of it, if it hadn't been raining, he would still have been soaked thoroughly in his own sweat. At the end of his ferocious attack, Cullen stood panting in the rain. Most fights he'd ever had ended within fifteen seconds. Some even lasted as long as a minute. But Dracon was different. Very different. He would need to build up his stamina if he was to give himself an even chance of surviving their next encounter.

"So the priest has got you believing in God, Hibernian?"

Cullen turned. Bull stood near him, a hint of a sneer on his face.

Cullen shrugged.

"I don't believe in God. I only made a bargain with Him."

Bull looked at Cullen, and in his gaze Cullen could see something different about him.

"Do you know why I'm here, Cullen?"

Cullen shook his head.

"We were thieves, my wife, my kids and I. I thought we were the best at what we did."

"Thought you were the best?" asked Cullen.

"We got caught, didn't we?" said Bull. "Then we became common criminals, like everyone else. But I was Bull, nobody could fucking touch me, could fucking out-think me and I'd find a way to escape. But that night…"

Bull grinned, but there was no mirth in his smile.

"A bargain with God. Let me tell you about a bargain with God, Cullen."

The rain hit Bull's eyeballs but Bull didn't blink.

"That night," he continued in a whisper, "they took my wife away from me. For six hours my two sons and I listened as she screamed and fought and cried. And I prayed, Cullen. Oh, how I prayed. I swore allegiance to God, whoever or whatever He is. I swore my undying loyalty to Him if He would only stop those bastards from raping her. Then...her crying stopped, like that."

Bull snapped his fingers in Cullen's face.

"I wanted to slice all their throats after what they did to my beautiful Sonia. I would have tried, but I had my two boys to think about, so I had to be smart. I told them that we would wait until the time was right and we would escape. They nodded and held my hand and said, 'Yes, Papa. We will wait for the right time.' And I prayed to God to keep my boys safe. But they were angry. That night they waited 'til I had passed out from exhaustion, they cut their bonds and attacked a Roman guard."

The rain ran down Bull's face as he stared at Cullen.

"Do you know how beautiful my boys were? Do you have any idea what they were like?"

Cullen said nothing. Bull's voice suddenly lost its power and in a whisper he continued. "Do you know what they did to my boys? They were only twelve. They loved their mother so much. Do you know what they did to them?"

Bull spread his raised his hands to the sky. The rain danced along the length of his arms.

"They crucified them," said Bull. "The Romans, they crucified my boys. My beautiful boys. They made me watch."

Bull dropped his weapons on the ground and turned his face to the sky. He let the rain wash over his face. Cullen's chest burned. Why would a loving God let the Romans kill them like that? But if he didn't believe...if *he* rejected God, would *his* family die?

Why were there people like the Romans in the world?

Why were there people like *him* in the world?

"You're praying that your family's alive, aren't you?" asked Bull.

"What makes you think I've got a family?" said Cullen.

"Because the look on your face is the same look I had on mine."

"What look?"

"You're terrified."

Forty eight

Two days later the Cilician pirates arrived. They were led into the *Ludus Magnus*, iron collars around their throats, all joined by a length of chain. Cullen did a quick count. There were thirty-five of them. They looked haggard and worn. Their clothes were dirty and ripped. Eyes looked out from hollow, gaunt faces. Their skin was burnt brown from the sun, and almost all of them sported long, wiry beards. Cullen, standing beside Strabo, turned to the veteran gladiator.

"They'll need to be fed."

Strabo looked dubiously at the ragged line of prisoners.

"I was hoping they'd be..." his voice trailed off.

"Me too," said Cullen. They looked as if they'd marched all the way from Greece.

Strabo shrugged. "They're what we've got. Let's see what a few days rest and some bellyfuls of food will do for them."

Strabo left Cullen and joined the Roman guards who were taking the iron collars off the prisoners. Cullen hoped the pirates were as good as the Emperor's engineer had promised.

Cinna, the servant, watched Dracon spar with unbridled fury. Dracon's opponent, a tall, barrel-chested soldier from one of the local garrisons, stumbled back under the assault. His face dripped sweat as he used his shield to deflect the blows Dracon rained down upon him.

The soldier stumbled under the vicious assault. That was all it took for Dracon to exploit the weakness. Two lightning fast sword hits, barely blocked, pushed the soldier to the ground. Even before the soldier's head slammed into the soft grass, Dracon's knee drove into his chest and the point of his sword almost broke the skin of his neck.

"I yield, I yield," coughed the soldier, dropping his shield and sword, holding his hands palm up.

Dracon, breathing hard, stared into his opponent's eyes, his face a mask of controlled fury. For a moment, it seemed that Dracon would run the sword through the soldier's neck, but then the gladiator let out a slow, shuddering breath and laid his sword aside. He got to his feet and the soldier gasped as Dracon's knee left his chest.

"Tomorrow," said Dracon. "Be here at sunrise."

"Yes, sir," gasped the soldier as he rose slowly to his feet, his face dripping with perspiration.

Dracon brushed dust from his shoulders as the soldier walked away.

Cinna held out a cloth to Dracon.

"I think you may have scared him off, master."

"I think I did, Cinna," said Dracon, wiping his face. "Soon there'll be no one left to fight. Except you."

Cinna smiled slyly.

"I couldn't do that, sir. I'd be afraid of hurting you."

Dracon allowed himself a smile. Cinna was barely five feet tall, and had only three fingers on his right hand, the legacy of an accident in his childhood. His body was thin to the point of emaciation, and his hair hung over his withered, ancient face. He was almost seventy years old.

"Cinna, I have a job for you," said Dracon.

"Yes, sir."

"You know the Hibernian called Cullen. The one who…"

"…defeated you. Yes, sir."

Dracon regarded the slave coolly.

"The one who defeated me, yes. The one who had his sword at my throat. I need to know…who he is. Where did he come from? Was he

"She gives me a different name every day," said Phoebe. She turned to Amazon, and placed a gentle hand on her face. "But I like Phoebe. I want to keep this one."

"Then we'll keep it, my darling."

Xenobia spoke from the shadows.

"Leave us now, Dracon."

Dracon turned and walked out. Truly he would never understand women. These three would turn into demons from hell once they got out into the arena. He stepped into the hallway and realized he was holding his breath. He released it in a soft whistle. Why did she always make him feel this way? Maybe after the games he'd bring her to his home tonight and tie her down. Teach her a lesson she should have learned a long time ago. She turned him on like no other woman ever had. But if he ever had her again she'd find a way to kill him. He just knew it.

Buco, Haldorf and Valerio, the three dwarfs, were playing knucklebones in their room when Dracon walked in.

Valerio had a sour look. Buco was gathering coins off the floor, a big smirk plastered across his face.

"Hello, boss," said Buco, glancing around. "What's the news?"

"Women are looking for blood today."

"They always are."

Buco picked up the set of four bones off the floor and shook them in his hand. He raised his eyes to Valerio who tossed a handful of coins down onto the ground.

"Valerio's feeling lucky today. Don't know why. If I win any more from him I'll be able to buy him. Like to be my slave, Valerio?"

He threw the bones across the floor, and all three dwarfs leaned forward trying to read the marks on the bones.

"Two fours and a Venus," said Haldorf. "Lucky bastard."

Buco sat back and crossed his arms. There was a big smile on his face as Valerio picked up the bones.

"Cheer up, Valerio," said Buco, "You just need to be luckier than you've ever been in your life."

Valerio cupped the bones in his hand and blew on them.

The broken pieces of his nose scraped together causing him immense pain every time he tried to breathe. Xenobia had finally rolled off him, laughing merrily. She left his house as Dracon nursed his broken, bleeding face.

The three years had not been kind. The madness that he had only felt in her that night had wormed its way into her features. She seemed possessed by demons. He had made sure he saw her every time she fought in the arena. There was something compelling about her, and the crowd responded too, relishing not just her considerable fighting skills, but also her cruelty. She knew just how to draw out a death, how to make the end of someone unravel as if pulling on their life's thread and teasing it apart bit by bit.

Even as he looked at her now, her body seemed tensed, poised, and for a moment Dracon thought she was going to leap at him and finish the job she had started all those years ago. She had a sword in her hand and she stabbed forward, near her foot. A squeal erupted from the shadows and Xenobia raised her sword. A rat was impaled upon the end, his body still arching, his feet kicking in pathetic little motions. Xenobia held the rat into a shaft of light and watched its struggles lessen until finally in hung limp. She pulled the rat off the end and tossed it to Dracon who batted the dead creature away.

"Dracon," she said. "You're looking rich."

"I am rich. And I'm paying you a lot of money to put on a show. Don't let me down."

"Just give me an opponent who can put up a fight."

"I've got you against Buco," said Dracon. "He'll make you work."

"Buco. I like him. It's a shame," she said, her voice trailing off as if drifting into the shadows.

"So fight hard, ladies. Put on a show."

"You already said that, Dracon," said the red-haired woman. "You sound anxious. Are you anxious, Dracon?"

"I'll call you Phoebe, my darling," said Amazon to the red-haired girl. "Phoebe, after the Sun God." She turned her face to Dracon. "Sometimes when she lies down and her hair fans away from her head like a halo, I swear I've never seen anything more beautiful."

Mr. Adams had to agree with Jake, though he didn't say so. Moved by the boy's forlorn slump and his pleading eyes, he also let his use of the F-word slide. Plenty of time later for hard-talk. No, now was for holding open his arms to Jake. Mr. Adams's heart went out to him as he sensed the desperate yearning coming from the skinny, shivering body pressed tightly into his. Neither his own drenched jacket nor Jake's soggy sweatshirt and jeans offered much warmth. But Mr. Adams suspected Jake was shivering, likely from more than the cold.

"You're alright now, boy," he said repeatedly.

Would that he could whisk away whatever it was that held Jake so profoundly in its damaging sway. Mr. Adams directed his attention to the trembling boy collapsed into his arms, until his eye caught a flickering candle coming out of the darkness under the stage.

"What's under there?" Lotte demanded.

Mr. Adams sighed, sorry to lose his momentary connection as Jake stiffened and stepped away. With his customary disdainful shrug, Jake withdrew behind a mute, tough veneer. Mr. Adams knelt to get a better look under the stage but Allegra blocked his way.

"That's Zorro's Snail Palace. You can't go in there!" She batted her fists against his back.

"Chill," mumbled Jake, and Allegra looked confused. "It's done. Over."

The four of them stood wordless in the pouring rain. Mr. Adams looked to Jake for an explanation, but couldn't catch the boy's eye.

Lotte broke the silence, demanding an answer, "What's this all about Jake? Allegra?"

Allegra turned and crawled into the dank space under the stage above. She motioned for them to join her. Mr. Adams crouched down and followed, then Lotte, and lastly Jake.

At least it is a little drier inside, thought Mr. Adams, relieved for the flattened cardboard boxes under him and for the inch leeway above the top of his head as he shifted to a more comfortable sitting position. He stretched his long legs and surveyed the scene, so recognizable to him as a lonely boy's hideout—a hideout that held much that was familiar from his own childhood. The candle's faint light illuminated small mounds of now-hardened melted wax, candy wrappers, and a jumbled sleeping bag—all clues that Jake spent a great deal of time there. Books were piled neatly by the candle, their titles unreadable in the darkness. Mr. Adams noted by her silence that Lotte also must have been touched by the sadness of the place.

He heard Allegra speak into darkness, "Look at all the snails. See..." His eyes tracked the arc of her flashlight to hundreds of shiny black and brown snail shells crowded into a damp corner of the structure.

"A perfect habitat, of course," an elated Mr. Adams concluded, his scientific mind automatically replacing concern.

Then, embarrassed, he glanced at Lotte to see how she was taking his obvious excitement. His concern melted at the sight of an eyebrow raised quizzically and lips pursed to suppress a smile. She was softening, the distrust disappearing.

Over the next half hour, managing to place some order to the two children's confused recounting, Mr. Adams realized what happened. It seemed that Jake mentioned the Snail Palace to Allegra, along with a rabbit foot in a box he hid there. He swore Allegra to secrecy, which of course only magnified her interest. Allegra implored Jake to take her there to collect snails so she could get more prizes at the holiday party. So, when Mr. Adams wasn't looking, she'd grabbed Jake's hand and pulled him from the park to go see it.

"The foot's dead, but you can kiss it with your lips. It's soooo soft." Allegra's voice was hushed as she explained. Mr. Adams saw she was obviously in awe as she held up a small, hinged wooden recipe box that was closed with a rubber band. Jake slumped forward, folding into himself, his arms clenched tightly around him. He seemed helpless to stop Allegra from opening the box and revealing his secrets. "He keeps the rabbit foot in here, look. A knife that folds, too." In each hand she held the precious items for them to see. "His dad gave them to him before he died." Mr. Adams motioned with his head for Allegra to look at Jake. As he hoped, she grasped the boy's dismay and whispered an urgent apology. "Oh, Zorro, I'm soooo sorry. I forgot I wasn't 'sposed to tell."

"Doesn't matter," mumbled Jake, shrugging. "It's junk."

"Not true, son," interrupted Lotte softly. "Allegra, put the knife and rabbit's foot back inside the box and hand it to Jake." Mr. Adams swallowed hard as Lotte slowly inched closer to Jake's side until her arm barely touched his. Jake's eyes stayed focused on the box cradled protectively in his lap. Lotte whispered, "It's a box of...treasures. Treasure is in the eye of the beholder. Meaning our treasures are always with us, no matter where we are. Hmmm...Jake? Just like your dad is always with you. And...your daddy is too, Allegra." Mr. Adams leaned in to hear Lotte's voice. Her face was luminous in the faint light as she spoke. "Jake, thank you for keeping Allegra safe from the rain. You are a treasure, a most special kind of treasure."

For Mr. Adams, the next minutes turned magic. Jake's slim body straightened, his posture softened, and he held out a hand to Allegra.

Allegra piped up and asked Lotte, "Can he can come to the pageant and party, pul-eeese?"

How would she answer? When Lotte replied, "Of

course, Jake. You are welcome in our family anytime," Mr. Adams wished he could show Lotte how crazy in love he was with her. He almost reached to touch her hand, but the gesture felt too forward with the children watching and the sting of her recent rebuke too raw. He could only trust another opportunity would soon appear.

"Now can we go to Flying Sauce? I'm starving," said Allegra, tugging on Lotte's coat sleeve.

Mr. Adams held his breath. Taking Lotte's nod as a yes, he invited her to join them. With Allegra holding firm to Jake's hand and urgently waving Lotte and Mr. Adams to walk faster, off they went.

-

Noting Jake's hesitation as they entered the warm, bright restaurant, Mr. Adams beckoned with an inconspicuous nod for the boy to accompany him as they followed the maître d' toward a corner table. *Maybe Flying Sauce was a mistake,* he wondered, surmising from the panicked look on Jake's face that this was likely his first time in a white tablecloth establishment. Mr. Adams wished he'd chosen instead one of the many less formal taco restaurants in the neighborhood where Jake might have felt more comfortable. Too late now. The least he could do was not bug Jake about removing his sweatshirt hood.

Once they were seated, Mr. Adams made a big gesture of spreading the ironed napkin onto his lap. Then, so Jake would know what else was expected of him, he pointedly explained they were to choose what they wanted from the daily menu board on a nearby wall. But he needn't have worried. In Allegra, Jake had the perfect ambassador for this new experience.

"I already know what I want," she announced. "How 'bout you? Have the bean and banana pie, like me."

When the restaurant's heavily tattooed waitperson came to their table to get their orders, Allegra pointed to two blue-green snakes intertwining around the woman's upper arm and then demanded that Jake take off his hood, insisting, "Come on. Show her your tattoo." Jake complied, and to Mr. Adams's relief, the wait person rewarded him with high praise for the tattoo artist's workmanship. Jake responded with the hint of a smile.

The waiter went on to explain the day's fare. "All our ingredients are locally raised and fresh. Yes, young lady, you're in luck—we do have the bean 'n banana pie for our vegan option today. But you might want to consider our fish of the day. It's fish 'n chips made with lingcod that was swimming in the Bay five hours ago, served with sweet potato fries and rosemary vinegar that we brewed last week. Homemade bratwurst and alone or was he with friends or family? If so, are they alive or dead? Does he have children? Does he weep for them or is his heart made of stone. I need to know…"

"…everything about him?"

"Everything about him," repeated Dracon slowly.

Cinna bowed to Dracon.

"I will do your bidding, master."

"As you always do, Cinna," murmured Dracon.

The old man excused himself and limped away. Dracon raised the sword and ran his finger slowly along the metal. It was sharp, but not sharp enough. It would need to be honed to a razor's edge.

"Right now," said Cullen, "the only question we need the answer to is this: Can the Cilicians be trusted?"

Mother Miriam sat beside him in their usual alcove in the main room, where the hustle and bustle of the streets went on only a few yards away. The recent rains had turned the normally dusty streets into a muddy quagmire, and Cullen was glad he didn't have to breathe in dirt with every breath he took.

"Well, they are pirates," said Mother Miriam. "They murder, steal and plunder with no conscience. If we tell them too soon, what's to stop them making a deal with the Romans. We can't tell them yet."

Cullen grunted and pulled a face.

"I need to know if I can trust them. But they need to know they can trust me too. If I wait to tell them when the Romans are shoving spears into our throats, then I'm not sure they'll be in a listening mood."

"Just the leader, then," said Mother Miriam.

"And the Christians? Have you talked to them yet?"

"Tomorrow, Cullen. We'll know tomorrow."

"If they say no, then our plan will not work. We need them."

"I shall use all my powers of persuasion," smiled the old woman.

"Tell them I know my plan is ridiculous," said Cullen. "I don't want them thinking I'm a fool who doesn't know what he is doing."

"Trust me, Cullen. If the plan weren't ridiculous, it wouldn't have a chance of succeeding. Ridiculous against Romans is the only way to go. The Christians will see that."

Cullen nodded.

"So, do you speak the pirates' language?"

Forty nine

The leader of the Cilician sailors faced Cullen across the floor. His name was Kaseem, and Mother Miriam spoke to him in low tones. Kaseem listened intently, nodding every now and then. As Mother Miriam finished, Kaseem tugged absently on his short beard, a hint of a smile on his face. Cullen noted that the man's forearms had muscles running like whipcords up to his shoulders.

Mother Miriam turned to Cullen.

"I told him of the Emperor's ambition to have you and his men wage battle against the Romans in the arena."

"So why is he smiling?"

"They were captured by Roman sailors. He wants revenge."

Kaseem turned defiantly to the old woman. He spoke to her and folded his arms across his chest as if to drive home the point. Mother Miriam looked a little pained and started to speak in a cajoling manner to Kaseem.

"What did he say?" asked Cullen.

The priest ignored him as she continued to plead with the Arab. Kaseem shook his head and spat on the ground.

"What are you telling him?" said Cullen, an edge creeping into his voice.

"I'm telling him that revenge is a sin against their God and our God."

Cullen snorted.

"Mother Miriam, just because I listen to your idiot ramblings doesn't mean anyone else will. You've just told him that he and his men are about to die but they're not supposed to take any Romans with them. Of course, he doesn't want to hear it."

"But—", began the priest. Cullen interrupted her.

"Tell him this: my name is Cullen and I have killed more Romans than anyone I know."

Mother Miriam turned slowly to Kaseem who stared at Cullen as he spoke. Kaseem listened to Miriam's translation.

"Tell him," continued Cullen, "that I hate the Romans too and there's nothing more I want than to separate Roman heads from Roman necks."

Kaseem chuckled as Mother Miriam relayed this information.

"But," Cullen spoke again, "my wife and child have been sold into slavery somewhere in this cursed land. I do not wish to die even if I take a hundred Romans with me to the next world."

Cullen paused as Mother Miriam translated these words. Kaseem listened to her, but stared at Cullen.

"You have someone you love, family left behind. You think that you may never see them again, but I have a plan that might make it happen."

"Are you talking about escaping from this place?" asked Kaseem. Cullen nodded, after listening to Miriam's translation.

"The plan will work only if you and your crew are the equal of the Romans."

Kaseem shook his head sadly, and spoke to Cullen in gentle tones, as if informing an idiot of a very simple concept.

"We are the greatest sailors in the world."

Kaseem spoke this in Latin, not his native tongue. Cullen and Mother Miriam looked at him in surprise. Kaseem shrugged. "If you weren't worth talking to, you didn't need to know I spoke the language of the Romans."

"Fine," said Cullen. "You say you're the greatest sailors in the world, but you were captured by the Romans."

"Four ships against one. And we almost escaped."

"My plan requires that we do more than 'almost escape'. The worst thing that could happen to us is if we 'almost escape'."

Kaseem bowed.

"What is your plan, Cullen?"

Cullen spoke in low tones, his eyes locked on Kaseem as the plan unfolded. When Cullen was finished, there was a smile on Kaseem's lips.

"Cullen," he said, "your plan is madness. In all likelihood it will not work and the Romans will butcher us. But it is as daring as it is stupid. I like it. My men," he gestured to where his men sparred in the courtyard, "...will make our boats sing for you."

They shook hands and Kaseem walked away. Cullen and Mother Miriam looked at each other.

"We'll see," she shrugged.

Cullen snapped his fingers.

"I almost forgot."

The old woman looked at him quizzically.

"Something you should have told Kaseem?"

Cullen shook his head. "Something I've been meaning to ask you. Finn started telling me a story that he said you told him. But he never got to finish it."

Mother Miriam squinted in puzzlement, then her eyes lit up.

"The riddle!" she said.

"That's the one. The rich farmer and his two sons."

"How far did Finn get with the story?"

"The younger son—the one who spent all his money on wine and whores—he was going back to his family in disgrace, hoping to beg his father's forgiveness."

"Ah, yes. Yes. The younger son. Let's sit down."

They crossed over to the alcove. Cullen settled in to listen.

"You can imagine his shame," began Miriam. "He's squandered his father's money, foolishly thought his so-called friends would stand by him when he needed them, and is reduced to eating the food that not even the pigs will eat. The boy is at the end of his wits. And as he makes his way back home, he can only imagine what his father will do to him. Will he banish him from his sight? Will he pretend not to know him? Might he even kill him? The son expects nothing but anger and bitterness and rejection.

"Many weeks of walking through sun and rain finally brings him home. He can see his father's house in the distance. Servants in the fields. One of them sees the younger son, recognizes him and rushes in to the house to tell his master. The younger son drags his thin body and bloody feet toward the house. Suddenly, the door bursts open and out runs the boy's father. Well, the sight of his father is too much for the younger son. He falls to his knees, sobbing. As his father approaches, the boy says: 'Father, I am not fit to be called your son. I've have sinned against heaven and against you, I am no longer worthy to be called your son. Please take me back as one of your servants.'"

Mother Miriam paused and looked into the distance. Cullen waited for a few moments,

"Mother Miriam?"

"Hmm?"

"Have you forgotten the rest of the story?"

The priest smiled and shook her head. "No, I've not forgotten it. It stirs memories, that's all."

"Would you like a cup of wine?"

"The father, Cullen," continued Mother Miriam, not even hearing Cullen's question, "ran up to his son and wrapped him in his arms, holding on as if he could never let go. He kissed his son, and his tears fell on the boy's face. He ordered his servants to dress the boy in the finest robes in the house, to put rings on his fingers, to put sandals on his feet. He ordered them to prepare a huge feast that night and to kill the fatted calf in celebration. The father was so happy that his son who was lost had been found. Can you imagine the father's joy, Cullen?"

"I can," said Cullen.

The priest looked at her hands, a smile playing on her lips.

"I've always thought that was the happiest moment of both their lives," she said.

"I imagine it would be," agreed Cullen.

Silence stretched between them for a minute. Cullen waited, studying the priest.

"It's a nice story," said Cullen.

"Yes," said the priest.

"So where's the riddle?"

"That's not the end of the story, Cullen. You see there's another son. The older one. And he's working in the fields, working hard as he always does, always has and he hears...music and laughter and cries of joy. He sees people dancing in the house. He asks a servant what's going on. He's told that his brother is back and that his father has killed the fatted calf and has ordered a great feast to be prepared. They are going to celebrate the safe return of the younger son.

"Now, this makes the older brother angry. He refuses to go into the house. His father, hearing this, runs out and begs him to come into the house. But the older son turns on him, eyes blazing, furious and he says 'I've worked for you all these years, I've done everything you said, and tried to be a good son. And in all those years, you've never even given me a young goat so I can have a feast with my friends. Yet when this son of yours comes back after squandering your money on prostitutes, you celebrate by killing the finest calf."

Cullen shifted his position. "He's got a point."

"Yes," said the priest. "I can understand his anger."

"What happened then?" asked Cullen.

"The father stares at his older son for a moment. Then he puts his hands on his son's face and looks into his eyes. He says 'My dear son, you and I are very close. Everything I have is yours. We have to celebrate this happy day. For your brother was dead and has come back to life. He was lost, but now he is found."

Cullen nodded slowly.

"You have to be a father to understand that."

"Yes, I agree," said the priest.

"And the riddle?" said Cullen.

"The riddle is this. Which son are you? The older or the younger. Which one?"

Cullen shrugged.

"Don't answer yet," said Mother Miriam, "think about it. And now," she said, stretching her arms, "it's time for me to return to my duties. Goodnight, Cullen. May you have pleasant dreams."

"Goodnight, priest," said Cullen.

"But before you sleep," said Mother Miriam, "you must tell the other fighters of your plan."

"That's a lot of people who have to keep a secret, Mother."

"And yet, they must know."

Cullen went around to the groups of gladiators, and talked to them quietly. He explained the plan as simply as possible, told them to be ready for anything and gave them hope that the sea battle in the Arena may not, in fact, be their last day on earth. They listened intently, swore to keep their mouths shut, and went back to what they were doing.

Bull nodded in appreciation at Cullen's plan.

Any plan was better than just turning up to be slaughtered.

Fifty

Cullen waited for Mother Miriam to return with news from her meeting with the Christians. If they all believed in peace and love and turning the other cheek, then Cullen doubted they'd have the inclination to put themselves in danger just to help a bunch of violent, murdering bastards escape from prison.

In the far corner of the courtyard, Kaseem had his crew of twenty out on the ground, lined up as they would be in a boat. Each man carried a thirty-pound sack of stones and as Kaseem barked orders, they "rowed" with the sacks of stones that they held at arm's length. They pushed and pulled in unison, reacting to Kaseem's shouts as one entity. By the end of the morning, the Cilicians dripped sweat onto the sand of the courtyard. Kaseem walked among them, clapping his men on the back, encouraging them, and urging them on. Cullen was impressed by the unity of the crew and he allowed a small kernel of hope to grow inside him, hope that this ridiculous plan of his might actually work.

At noon, the warriors left the baking heat of the courtyard for the coolness of the barracks. When Cullen entered, Mother Miriam sat at the table wiping sweat from her face.

"What happened?" asked Cullen as he slid in next to Mother Miriam. "They said no, didn't they?"

Mother Miriam drank some wine and continued to mop her brow.

"They said no…" confirmed the priest. Cullen uttered a snort of disgust. Mother Miriam held up a hand.

"…until they meet you."

"Until they meet me? How can they meet me? Don't they know where I am?"

Mother Miriam grabbed Cullen's arm.

"Let an old woman wipe her brow for a few moments. Those streets were very hot and I ran into a band of roughnecks who chased me down an alleyway. I guess they figured out I had no money. They let me alone."

"Well, if they hadn't let you alone," muttered Cullen, "I'm sure you'd have turned the other cheek."

"I'd have been too tired to do anything else."

Cullen slumped forward onto the table.

"So if the Christians won't help, we'll just have to do it without them. We'll…"

"They want to help," interrupted the priest. "They will help. We just have to meet them."

"But…"

"Tonight."

"Tonight? How?"

"We'll walk out."

Cullen stared at the priest for a long moment.

"You can get me out of here?" he asked quietly.

"To meet with the Christians, yes," confirmed the old woman.

Cullen leaned forward and lowered his voice.

"How?"

The priest waved her hand at Cullen. "It's not as simple as that, Cullen. There's a guard who's…" Mother Miriam paused and studied the ceiling, "…one of us, and he's willing to let us slip out for a short while."

"Woman, listen to what you're saying. We can get out of here, you and me. We can escape and find my family."

Mother Miriam shook her head sadly.

"We can't, Cullen. If he does this for us, we must promise him we will return. That's the only way it can happen."

Cullen reached over and grabbed the priest's robe and pulled her close.

"So we promise him," said Cullen.

"He has to believe us," said Mother Miriam.

"I can be persuasive," said Cullen.

"It must be the truth."

"No. It must be whatever it takes for him to let us out."

"It must be the truth," persisted the priest.

"We lie if we have to," said Cullen, his voice soft.

"No, we don't."

"This could be our only chance."

"We don't lie," said the priest, her dry, withered hands prying Cullen's grip from her robe.

Cullen released the priest, took a deep breath and sat back, seemingly resigned to doing it the priest's way.

"So when do we go?" asked Cullen.

"Tonight," said Mother Miriam. "If."

"If what?" said Cullen.

"If I believe you when you promise me you'll return here after we talk to the Christians."

Cullen threw his hands up in exasperation.

"Alright, you old hag. I promise I'll return here. I'll come back."

Mother Miriam stared at him with hooded eyes.

"You're lying."

"I'm not lying. I'll come back."

"No," said the priest slowly, "you won't."

"If we don't meet these people, then we're all dead tomorrow."

"Exactly. So promise me you'll return. And mean it."

"It seems as if you won't believe anything I say."

Mother Miriam unconsciously drew a pattern on the table with her fingernail. She pursed her lips and glanced up at Cullen.

"I was afraid this would happen. For your plan to work, Cullen, we must meet with the Christians. But if we meet with them, why should you return? You'll be free." The old woman rubbed the bony knuckles of her arthritic hands.

"So there's nothing I can say to make you believe me?"

The priest said nothing for a moment, and kept her gaze fixed on the table, as if studying the whorls and splinters that ran through the aged wood.

"Swear on your son's life," whispered the priest.

"What did you say?" said Cullen, leaning toward the priest, his voice flat and dangerous.

Mother Miriam looked up at Cullen. "I'm sorry, Cullen. It's the only way I'll believe you."

Cullen looked at the priest, anger building in his eyes. He rapped a finger on the table as the muscles in his face clenched and unclenched.

"Go to hell, priest," said Cullen.

The old woman held Cullen's gaze, and her eyes hardened.

"Swear it."

"Let's just walk out the gate," pleaded Cullen, "and never look back. This is our chance."

Mother Miriam's gaze didn't waver, even though Cullen could see the priest's eyes were red-lined with exhaustion, and the whites of her eyes were blood-shot with capillaries that crept like spiders' legs to her irises.

"Damn you, priest. Damn you. Damn your God and all His arrogance and—"

The slap came so fast that Cullen only saw the hand as it left his face. The priest was standing, her body shaking with anger.

"Arrogance?" spat the old woman. "You, you who have butchered your brothers and made widows of your sisters dare to call Him arrogant? He has given you a gift. He has given you a chance to redeem yourself and all you can feel is self-pity. Of course this is hard. Of course you are required to make impossible choices. You fool. If you could see what I see you would throw yourself on your knees, beg His forgiveness and swear on the lives of all you love."

The priest paused, breathing heavily, her eyes never leaving Cullen.

"Swear it, or neither of us walks out that gate tonight."

Cullen felt the hot sting of the slap fade away. The priest's face had gone pale, but it only accentuated the crimson hue of her eyes. It seemed as if all the blood in her body had collected there, so she could focus all the power of those broken, filmy orbs on Cullen.

"On my son's life," began Cullen, each word deliberate, "I promise I will return here after meeting with the Christians."

"Then we leave after dark," said Mother Miriam.

They stared at one another and the silence stretched between them. Mother Miriam turned and walked away.

.

Fifty one

The guard's name was Quintus and he'd been a soldier for twenty years. He campaigned as far east as Turkey and as far north as Germania. He'd endured blistering heat and bone-numbing cold, and had never lost faith in the Empire of Rome. He had killed men by the dozens without blinking an eye. He had worshipped the Emperor without question.

Quintus was the perfect soldier, until he met a Jew by the name of James, son of Peter the Farmer. James was one of hundreds who had been captured and brought to Rome. At Rome, he would be thrown to the lions, providing a minute or two of pleasure for the people of the city. While in captivity, James and Quintus had talked to each other through the bars, captor and captive. They had struck up an almost-friendship. James was a Christian which was a minor cult that had sprung up some generations before. James talked to Quintus about the prophet—the Christ—who they believed to be the Son of God. Quintus, bored almost to distraction by the guard duty, listened to James speak of this God/Man. He scoffed at James's description of how this prophet preached love. James never took offense, but spoke on in his calm, quiet voice and Quintus was genuinely sorry when, two weeks later, James stood shaking in the middle of the arena as a lion leapt upon him. Within seconds the lion had ripped James's head clean off his shoulders, and spilled his insides onto the hot sand. James body jerked spasmodically for almost ten heartbeats, even after the lion had buried its face in the man's stomach. Quintus turned away from the spectacle, chiding himself for letting himself get close to a prisoner that he knew was doomed.

For the next year, Quintus refused to allow any prisoners to speak to him and this had the interesting effect on Quintus of re-playing all the conversations with James over and over in his head. After a year of hearing the echo of James's voice, Quintus sought out some other Christian prisoners. He had a long list of questions he wanted answered. Mainly he wanted to find reasons to reject the ideas—*the crazy ideas*—that James had planted in his brain. But the Christians he found had the same effect on him that James had. He was growing to respect them, to love them.

One day he woke up and it was as if a light from a candle burned in his eyes. He got out of bed and fell to his knees. He raised his eyes to the sky and asked the question: "Are you real?"

Even though he was inside the barracks he swore a soft wind blew across him, raising chilblains on his skin, and causing the hairs on the back of his neck to stand up. He felt as if the wind had carried away every sin, every secret evil in his heart. He felt as if God had scoured his soul with the gentle brush of forgiveness. Already on his knees, he fell forward so his body lay on the ground, prostrate before something bigger than himself. He wept.

Quintus secretly attended meetings with the Christians that were held in the back alleys of Rome and other cities. Wherever he went he sought them out. He learned more of the Prophet, how He lived, how He died…and how He lived again. For Quintus it was a miracle that seemed as fresh now as it did then. He stayed in the army of Rome—all he ever did these days was stand guard duty. And his current job was to stand guard over the school of gladiators assigned to the *Ludus Magnus*. He had to guard the gate behind the stables, a bitch of a post as it was out of sight of any other guard. He couldn't even have a decent laugh with one of his comrades. It proved a stroke of good fortune, however, because the old Christian priest, Mother Miriam, needed his help and Quintus was in the perfect position to oblige. It was dangerous and Quintus knew he was gambling with his life. It wasn't the first time he'd helped the Christians and one day he was sure he'd be discovered and then he would be food for the tigers. But so be it. He would not refuse the Christians. Maybe in doing so it would help expiate the sins he had committed during his life. *So many sins, so much killing.* But the Christians assured him that God's love was boundless and his forgiveness limitless, so maybe his soul was saved.

Tonight, his job was to let the old priest and the warrior, Cullen, out of the gate. They promised to return within a few hours. Quintus could only guess the reason they wanted to be away for so short a time. If they did not return, Quintus would have to confess that he let them out and the guards would be decimated—one in every ten would be summarily executed. Quintus grinned to himself. He almost looked forward to declaring who he was and let the sword fall where it would. Maybe, after this winter, he would take off his sword and armor, throw it in the river and run away with some Christians. He could help them spread the Word. First, he'd have to survive the next few weeks. He had a feeling that momentous things were going to happen.

Fifty two

When Dracon returned to his home on the peninsula, he eased himself into a bath. He had trained for two hours that morning, enough to hone his body to perfection for tomorrow's games. Now the hot bath would loosen his muscles, get the blood flowing. When the time came, no one would be in better shape than he was, not even the Hibernian.

Dracon was impressed at the way Cullen had molded the different gladiators into a team. The Cilicians—stinking scum that they were—rowed extremely well and even the rogues that made up the rest of the warriors seemed to have developed some sense of brotherhood. Not that they could hope to defeat the superbly trained Roman sailors and soldiers, but it would make for a spectacular fight.

But something had bothered him since watching Cullen that morning and he was unable to put a finger on it until now. Cullen had seemed a little too…content? Distracted? A little too at peace with himself or the world. What did that mean? Had he become a fully-fledged Christian? And if so, would he do the worst thing he could possibly do to Dracon tomorrow? In other words, would he roll over and die without putting up a fight? That would be unacceptable. It would turn what should be Rome's greatest ever games into a farce, and Dracon did not want to be part of anyone's farce. He imagined the chorus of boos and catcalls if Cullen and the rest of his warriors laid down their swords, closed their eyes and let Dracon and his soldiers gut them without putting up any kind of fight. What a disgrace that would be, what a travesty to foist upon the people of Rome, upon the Emperor of Rome. Hadrian would no doubt find some way to blame him for it. No, no, no, it could not be allowed to happen.

What Cullen needed was a little touch of hate in his heart.

"Master?"

Dracon shifted his gaze to his servant, Cinna, who stood in the doorway, his travelling cape wrapped around his shoulders.

"Cinna, tell me you had an interesting journey."

Cinna smiled.

"I believe, Master, I have outdone even myself."

Dracon smiled broadly.

"Do tell."

"Hello, Quintus."

The guard turned to see Mother Miriam emerge out of the shadows of the stable. Behind her was a tall man whose face was hidden by the cowl of his cloak. Quintus knew this would be Cullen, the Hibernian Warrior.

"Hello, priest."

"I believe you will be helping us tonight."

Quintus nodded. He glanced around, straining his ears and eyes for any sign that others were taking note of their meeting. Satisfied that they were unobserved he faced the priest.

"Two things," he said, squinting at them. "First, be back in two hours."

Mother Miriam bowed her head.

"And second?"

"Just so you know, if you don't come back I'm a dead man."

"We will return, Quintus," said Mother Miriam, cutting off Cullen who seemed about to argue the point.

The soldier opened the gate and stepped back as the priest and Cullen walked outside. There was a fingernail moon in the sky and Cullen knew that with the clouds blocking what little light shone down from the moon, they would blend in with the shadows of the Roman streets.

"I hope you know where you're going," muttered Cullen, as they wound their way down streets and alleyways. After fifteen minutes Cullen was hopelessly lost.

"Do not worry, Cullen. All is as it should be."

Cullen looked around at some of the houses and frowned. "Haven't we walked down this street before?"

"Yes," replied Mother Miriam. "The Christians here are very careful. They have to be. They've watched us since we left the *ludus* and are making sure we're not being followed."

Cullen darted his eyes from side to side. He had not realized he was being followed or watched. Either he was getting old or these Christians were good. So far the only people he'd seen were beggars sleeping in doorways and a couple of drunkards weaving their way home, stumbling and laughing.

They walked on in silence as the sounds of the drunkards faded into the distance. Cullen glanced at the priest, sensing that the old woman was troubled.

"Spit it out, Mother," said Cullen.

"I shouldn't have hit you, Cullen. I'm sorry. I let my temper get the best of me."

"It didn't hurt," said Cullen.

"That's not really the point, is it?" said the priest.

Cullen shrugged. "The things you said, about what I've done..." Cullen's voice trailed away and he felt the priest glance at him.

"Cullen, it's not for me to judge you. I was wrong to hit you."

Cullen held up a hand to stop the priest.

"What you said reminded me of things I haven't thought of in years. Things I've been trying to forget. I've told you of making my first kill, haven't I?"

"When you were thirteen, yes," said the priest.

"That kill didn't make me a killer," said Cullen. "Neither did the next eight kills. Those deaths were in the heat of battle, and how I wasn't the one choking to death with a sword in my throat I'll never know. They happened so fast, and I was so scared and young and I pissed in my pants during the battles. Those deaths meant nothing." He paused, thinking the priest would have something to say about that. But the old woman merely nodded and squeezed his arm.

"It was the ninth death that made me what I am today."

"What happened, Cullen?" asked the priest.

"He raped Rhiannon," said Cullen, his voice catching in the cool, night air.

"Who?" asked Mother Miriam.

"The Roman. Sulla Atticus Scaurus. The man who trained me. The one we let live."

A scurrying noise beside them betrayed the presence of a group of rats. Cullen glanced over, to see them crawling out of the belly of a dead dog. The mongrel's stomach heaved and pulsated as the vermin chewed in a frenzy of feeding.

"She was sixteen, a year younger than me, daughter of one of the men in the tribe. I wasn't the only one who thought she was beautiful. She caught the eye of Scaurus, and as much as she tried to avoid him, once he got it in his mind to do something, then that's what he'd do."

"Was she your friend at the time? Your wife?"

Cullen shook his head. "Hadn't even talked to her then. Hadn't the courage. Every time I thought I'd say something to her, my tongue would fill my mouth, and my spit would dry up. My heart would race faster at the thought of talking to her than it would in actual battle. Isn't that something?"

"Love will do that," said the priest.

Cullen grunted as they walked on. Above them, the moon was blocked by the three story tall *insulae*—apartments—that rose on either side of the street. A baby's wail escaped from one of the windows above, and was quickly swallowed in the night's air. Cullen had a quick image of Aisling in his mind, her plump little hands reaching for him.

He pushed the thought away, replacing it in his mind's eye with the image of Rhiannon, seeing her for the first time all those years ago, her face lit by the flickering light of a fire, laughing with her friends as burning embers lifted into the air, twisting and turning in an updraft. He had noticed her in passing before, but had never really *seen* her. That image of her, the sound of her laughter, the way she placed her hand on the forearm of her friend and pointed to the tiny lights as they rose higher in the night air until they vanished in the blackness—it was as if someone took hold of his heart and sent a cool breeze over it. The hair on the back of his neck stood up and all he could do was gaze at her. And as he looked, her eyes shifted directly to his. And he was taken.

"For a month, I gathered my courage to speak with her. But our camp was large, and it was easy to put it off until the next day. I wasn't in a rush. I enjoyed just feeling the way I felt. Then one day, I'd had enough of just dreaming about her. I decided to go to her. She'd work in the fields every day..."

Cullen's voice trailed off, and he could feel the blood draining from his face. An all-consuming hatred rose up from the depths of his memory, and he was dimly aware at how fresh that hatred was, as if the years in-between had not diluted those feelings at all.

"I went to the fields and the other women told me Rhiannon had gone to the river to fetch some water. I followed her there. When I reached the clearing beside the river there was no sign of her. Then I heard a cry near a rock outcrop. Like a puppy being hurt. I ran around the rocks and that...that bastard was on top of her. She was trying to scream but he had his hand over her mouth. She tried to bite him and he just slammed his elbow into her face, not enough to knock her out, just enough to shut her up. She was bleeding from her nose and mouth. And Scaurus was grinning. He must have heard me, because he turned around. He laughed when he saw me. And he said I could have a go after he was done."

Even in the light of the crescent moon, Cullen could see his breath form in the air ahead of him.

"And then she looked at me, Mother. Those beautiful eyes looked at me, and through all the pain, and all the humiliation I could see hope in those eyes. I had to look away, because Scaurus's sword was within reach of his hand and I was twenty paces away. I couldn't rush him. And in that moment I became a killer. My heart, Mother, my heart went cold as ice. This feeling come over me. A calmness. It was as if night descended on my soul, giving me this gift. So I didn't look at Rhiannon, because one more glance at those eyes now might take this feeling I had away. I kept my eyes on Scaurus. I smiled at him and told him to take his time and I'd just watch. He turned away from me, back to her, so he could look in her eyes and drink in her pain. I strolled up behind him, took out my sword and sliced it across his back. He rolled off, screaming, and tried to grab his sword, but I kicked it away. The bastard actually looked confused, as if I had somehow betrayed him, especially after he'd been so generous in offering to share her. I sliced down again, opening his face. I stepped back as he went for me, slicing again, and again. Rhiannon had jumped up and she was screaming at him, or at me, I don't know. I kept slicing and cutting. I cut everywhere. Finally I cut his heels, slicing his tendons, crippling him. By this time he was covered in his own blood, and he was screaming too, begging for mercy one second, and swearing to cut my balls off the next. I just kept circling, slicing and cutting. And I was enjoying every moment of it. At one point Rhiannon stopped screaming and started sobbing. I kept hacking away at him, bit by bit. Eventually, his arms were useless. Both hung on to his body by shreds of muscle. I climbed on him, sitting on his chest. Before he bled out I wanted him to feel agony. I placed my thumbs in his eyes and drove them in. He wriggled underneath me like a trapped fish. After I was done with his eyes I cut off his tongue. That was a good day. That was a good, good day. Everyone looked at me differently after that day. Even my father."

Mother Miriam walked in silence beside him.

"Don't try to find words, Mother. You know as well as I do that if your God really exists, and if I really do have a soul, then there is a pit in hell waiting for me. Because even if Scaurus's death was justified, there were dozens of others that weren't. It's my fate, that's all. I just want my family back. I want them safe. If hell is the price I pay, then that's the price I pay."

A candle flame emerged from the darkness of a small alleyway. Cullen heard a soft word in a language that he did not recognize. The priest veered toward the person holding the candle, who turned and led them down a pitch-black alleyway that was so narrow that Cullen had to shuffle sideways down it because his shoulders were too wide.

They climbed down some steps that led into an inner courtyard, which was surrounded by a shabby, two-story building. From the shadows he heard the low growl of a dog. The candleholder whisked them through the house, down another alley, followed by some fast turns that left Cullen totally confused.

They arrived at an open doorway that they immediately entered. As soon as Cullen's foot cleared the threshold, the door was closed noiselessly behind them and many hands grabbed Cullen and held him immobile.

Fifty three

Dracon arrived at the Ludus Magnus with a retinue of forty soldiers. It would be interesting, he thought, to see the prisoners' faces when they beheld some of the men they would fight the next day. More importantly, he needed the protection because of what he was about to do. It would be highly embarrassing to be torn apart by the mob the day before his greatest triumph.

The gladiators were enjoying their evening meal—*their last evening meal,* thought Dracon—when he entered the room. Dracon saw that instead of the gladiators' usual meal of barley porridge, the table was resplendent with a large variety of dishes. This was a special meal, the traditional supper before the games. Cheese, olives and eggs had been laid out, and the gladiators continued to reach for them even as the Roman soldiers spread out around the room. Later, if these bastards still had an appetite, they would be treated to wild fowl, chickens, hare and antelope. They would fill their bellies tonight, and tomorrow this half-digested food would spill from their guts with the help of Roman swords.

Those with their backs to Dracon turned, and to a man, he saw their brows furrow and their eyes narrow. Good, he thought. These men were ready to fight. No point putting on a show unless both sides showed up and it looked as if Cullen had prepared them well. His gaze swept the room and he frowned slightly when he did not see Cullen among the men. He turned to a gladiator.

"Where's Cullen?"

The man, Petrus, popped an olive into his mouth and surveyed the room. Turning back to Dracon, he slowly worked the pit of the olive to the front of his lips and spat it out at Dracon's feet.

"Don't see him," said Petrus.

Dracon felt like slicing his sword across the brute's insolent face. Instead, he stepped past the man and walked over to the table. Some of the warriors had deliberately turned back to their meal, ignoring the Romans.

"What's all this?" barked a voice. Dracon turned to see Strabo limping toward him.

"Where's Cullen?" asked Dracon.

"What are you doing here?"

"Whatever I want. Where's Cullen?"

"You don't come into the *Ludus Magnus* with your orders. Get these bastards out of here," he said, pointing to the soldiers.

There was a shuffling sound and Symmachus appeared in the doorway, out of breath and looking haggard, followed by two of his servants.

"Strabo, stand down," he said.

"Symmachus, what's all this?" said Strabo, gesturing to Dracon.

Symmachus wheezed to a stop. He raised a hand and waved away Strabo's protests.

"Just answer his questions and he'll be gone. Gods, I want done of this. Dracon say to Cullen what you need to say and be gone."

"Then find him for me."

Another candle was lit, allowing Cullen to make out the shadowy outlines of the people in the room. There were about seven of them, four of whom had him up against the wall. Two others held Mother Miriam. A woman stood quietly in the middle of the room looking at Cullen with sparkling, green eyes. Her brown hair fell loose around her shoulders, framing a face that was beautiful yet remote. There was an authority to the way she carried herself. Maybe, Cullen reasoned, it is because she stands still while all the others are nervous and twitchy. The others looked at her expectantly, waiting for her to say something or do something.

She bowed to Mother Miriam who inclined her head back. The woman turned her gaze to Cullen, walked up to him and held the candle up to his face. For a long moment Cullen and the woman looked into one another's eyes. Cullen found the woman's gaze disconcerting. He didn't want to look away. Should he say something about himself? Should he talk about how he wanted to find his wife and child? Maybe—

"He's not a spy," said the woman quietly.

Cullen blinked as the people holding him loosened their grips. Still looking into Cullen's eyes, the woman spoke to the priest.

"We will help you, Miriam. We will do our part."

She smiled at Cullen.

"When Miriam first told me of your plan, Cullen, I thought either you were a Roman spy that had tricked her, or a warrior who had taken one too many blows to the head. But you are neither. I hope you find your family, Cullen. I wish you a long and happy life."

She turned and walked away.

"You'll help?" said Cullen. He was mystified. This woman had looked at him for less than ten seconds and she was willing to risk all she had to help him. He wanted to say something, to tell her how grateful he was but he found all his words inadequate.

"Please," he began, "what's your name?"

"Ruth," said the woman.

"Thank you, Ruth," said Cullen.

"By the way, we know where General Sulla lives," she said.

Fifty four

Strabo returned from the cell block alone. Dracon looked at him.

"Well?"

Strabo popped a stuffed egg into his mouth and chewed it slowly. He regarded the Roman as a slow smile formed on his lips.

"He's not sleeping." He swallowed the egg and chased it with a cup of wine.

Symmachus frowned. "Then where is he?"

"I don't know. I haven't seen him since the afternoon training session."

Symmachus held up his hands.

"Wait. You can't find him? Did you check the other cells?"

"Why would he be in the other cells?" asked Strabo popping another egg into his mouth.

"Did you check them?" asked Symmachus, pronouncing each word separately.

"No," said Strabo.

Symmachus turned to two men and snapped his fingers at them.

"Find him," he ordered. The men scuttled away.

Two minutes later they were back. No sign of Cullen anywhere.

Dracon looked at the gladiators' faces to see if they knew what was going on. Most seemed genuinely puzzled by the turn of events. Some were grinning, but appeared to be just as surprised to find that Cullen was missing, as they were delighted that Dracon was losing his temper.

Dracon felt the blood drain from his face. If the Hibernian had somehow managed to get away, to escape, then tomorrow's games would be a joke. An expensive, bloody, brutal joke. It didn't matter how many of these useless thieves and slaves he killed, if Cullen wasn't among them, it would all be for nothing.

Dracon felt a cold, icy anger course through his veins. How dare Cullen cheat him of a chance to get his revenge? This could not happen now. Not today. He turned to the gladiators at the table. Some looked back at him, smirking. Others, old warriors, kept their faces neutral. Push a man like Dracon too much and heads could be separated from bodies.

"Someone knows." said Dracon. He looked up and down at the gladiators' faces.

"And if that person who knows tells me where he is, I will give that man their freedom, and a purse of one hundred gold pieces. So I ask again. Where is he?"

A murmur rippled around the room. Dracon listened to the tone of the voices and heard the undercurrent of greed as the gladiators whispered to each other. If any of them knew where Cullen was, they would tell. If you offered freedom and money to men who had neither there could only be one outcome. But despite the interest no one raised their voice to declare they knew where Cullen was.

Dracon looked at the gladiators in disgust. These men would last no longer than twenty minutes without Cullen. It would be a slaughterhouse in the arena tomorrow. He turned to go when he stopped. One of the gladiators had kept his back turned to him ever since he had stepped into the room. The gladiator had not turned or spoken, even when Dracon had offered the reward. Dracon pointed a sword at the two men who sat beside this warrior.

"Get up," he said.

The two men slid off the seat and Dracon sat down, turning sideways to face a large, heavily muscled man. The man continued to chew slowly on some dried meats, refusing to look at Dracon.

"I know you," said Dracon. "You've spilled some blood on the arena's sand. What's that they call you?"

"Bull."

"Bull," repeated Dracon slowly.

Dracon lifted a sword to Bull's face and drew the point down the scar that ran from Bull's hairline, down past his eye, around the contour of his cheek, through the ravaged lip and ending at his chin.

"Looks like you've had some close brushes with the afterlife, Bull." Dracon lowered his sword. Bull stared stonily ahead. Dracon whispered conspiratorially. "I know you know where he is. I can tell by the look in your eyes. And I appreciate your loyalty. I respect that. So I'll offer you this. Your freedom and five hundred gold pieces if you tell me where he is."

Dracon saw a muscle tighten in Bull's jaw. This could mean two things. Either he was incredibly insulted that Dracon would try to buy his loyalty or—more likely—he was trying in vain to stop himself from betraying Cullen.

Bull drank thirstily from the cup of wine in front of him.

"Five hundred pieces of gold," whispered Bull, wiping his mouth.

"Yes."

"And my freedom. Just to tell you where Cullen is."

"Just to tell me, yes."

Bull pointed to the doorway leading to the practice yard.

"There he is."

Dracon whirled to see Cullen and the old woman standing at the doorway, startled eyes darting around the room, taking in the Roman soldiers that stood nearby, weapons in hand. Both the Hibernian and the old woman wore cloaks as if they had just returned from a stroll around Rome's streets. Dracon's surprise turned to relief and anger. He started to get up when Bull's hand closed on his wrist.

"My gold. My freedom."

"What?"

"Five hundred pieces of gold and my freedom just to tell you where he was. I told you. Give me my gold."

Dracon shook Bull's hand off him. Bull threw back his head, laughing hard.

"Behold a Roman's promise. Not worth the steam off my piss."

The other gladiators roared with laughter as the tension broke. Dracon had been humiliated and if they were going to die the next day, then they would enjoy his humiliation now. Dracon stepped in front of Cullen and his eyes burned with anger.

"Out for a little night air?" he said, through gritted teeth.

Cullen and the priest glanced at each other. Cullen considered four or five lies and chose the one that seemed the least full of shit.

"We were praying."

"Liar," said Dracon, "you left the Ludus."

"We prayed in the shadows." said Cullen. "Your men are blind."

Dracon turned to the Centurion.

"Bring in all the guards who were—"

Just then, one of the guards from the courtyard rushed in, breathing fast.

"Quintus is gone. He dropped—"

"Who's Quintus?" said Dracon.

"He dropped his shield, spear and armor and ran away."

The Centurion stepped forward.

"Chase him down, sir?"

"Chase him. Find him. Gut him."

Dracon turned back to Cullen. His anger still roiled inside him, but mostly he felt relief that Cullen now stood before him. He forced his mouth into a grin.

"You took a walk out of here. Perfectly understandable. Who wouldn't have done that?"

Cullen remained silent. Dracon continued: "But you came back to your inevitable death. That I don't understand."

Dracon turned and walked away, his lip pinched between his thumb and forefinger, his brow furrowed.

"I think," said Dracon, "I think you have a plan. And I think that plan is that you won't fight tomorrow, and that…" he wagged a finger at Cullen as if admonishing a naughty child, "…is unacceptable."

Dracon nodded at two guards who stood behind Cullen. They each grabbed an arm. A third guard approached Cullen and put a sword tip against his throat. Dracon's grin spread wider now. The gladiators stopped their murmurings and sat still on their benches, trying to guess what Dracon was up to.

"You Christians," said Dracon, "you'll just roll over and die tomorrow? Is that what you plan, Cullen?"

Dracon chuckled to himself as he walked over to Mother Miriam.

"But we're soldiers, Cullen. You and me. So how smart could we be? It's people like this," he put his arm around the old woman, "that are able to entrance us into being sheep, with their talk of love and redemption."

"It's not just talk, Dracon," said Miriam in a soft voice. "The love of God is real, and He loves you as much as He loves me, or Cullen or any of the…"

Dracon ruffled the old woman's hair, and clapped her on the back.

"See what she does," said Dracon, laughing. "Even now she's trying to convert me, even as my soldiers twist her arms." Dracon's laugh became a chuckle. "I don't want to fight a bunch of old ladies tomorrow, Cullen. All this talk of love—it makes me worried, that's all I'm saying."

Dracon withdrew his sword and plunged it deep into Mother Miriam's stomach.

The old woman grunted in surprise and her mouth formed an almost perfect "O" shape. Dracon glanced over to Cullen who bucked trying to throw off the guards, but they held him fast. Dracon turned back to the woman, whose eyes were still wide in shock.

"You believe in Paradise, don't you, priest? I think you'll find out quite soon if you're right."

He pulled the sword out. Mother Miriam collapsed to the floor. Immediately, blood soaked the priest's white tunic, as if a crimson flower opened its petals wide.

"No," screamed Cullen. "No. Why? Why?"

Cullen let out a stream of curses at Dracon, who appeared to be mildly amused by the commotion.

"I'll kill you!" yelled Cullen as he heaved and pulled against the Romans' grips. Dracon nodded to the third guard who drew back and landed a punch in Cullen's gut that dropped him to his knees. Dracon walked over and grabbed Cullen's hair. He lifted the Hibernian's face to him. Cullen's eyes were closed.

"Open your eyes, Cullen."

Cullen's eyelids rose until he looked Dracon full in the face. Dracon laughed in delight.

"Oh, there's hate in there. There's enough hate in those eyes to kill an army."

Dracon stood up, backing away. He motioned to the guards to follow him. Cullen's handlers dropped him to the ground.

Fifty five

Mother Miriam's breath came in short, painful gasps. Blood seeped through her fingers and pooled on the floor in an expanding, red circle. Cullen, still trying to catch his breath after being hit, struggled over to the priest.

Miriam gasped and flecks of blood sprayed from her mouth. Cullen knew she did not have long to live.

"Mother," he said.

Cullen laid a hand on Mother Miriam's head and brushed long, white hairs away from her eyes. She looked at Cullen, her mouth struggling to say something. Cullen leaned closer, bending his ear to the priest's mouth.

"I've been waiting to die...for a long, long time, Cullen. God was waiting for me to meet you." Her voice came out in short hitches, her breath the merest whisper. She touched his face.

"Remember...your family."

The priest's grip on Cullen's wrist loosened and the old withered hand sank to the floor. She was dead.

A thought crossed his mind, so horrible and delicious that he almost physically recoiled from it.

He wished his family were dead.

He wished he knew for certain that they had been slain and he alone lived. What freedom that would bring! If they were dead he would never again have to listen to the lies of this God, these empty promises that He made to His children. If they were dead, then all hope was dead, all love destroyed. And, oh, how he would grasp his freedom! He would embrace the almost carnal desire for slaughter that he felt waking in his bones. He could use the hate and the anger to visit destruction on his foes in ways they could never imagine, strike at them with his sword and send them to Hades.

If he knew they were dead. If he could be certain.

But...

...No matter the rage and hate he felt for Dracon, if there was a chance his family was alive he would cling to that hope. And if that required his belief in a God who allowed evil to run rampant with only the hope or promise of love in the afterlife then so be it. Besides, if he really wanted to hurt Dracon, escaping would be far worse than sticking a dagger through his heart.

He would do as the dead priest said.

He would swallow this bitter poison.

He would hope his family lived.

Fifty six

Cullen and the gladiators walked into the depths of the arena. Oil-soaked torches, braced in iron brackets, lit the tunnels.

They reached the room where they would wait until called to their ships. Outside the room was a man Cullen had seen once before. It was Burrus, the Emperor's engineer.

"There you are," he said, smiling expansively, his gnarled hands grasping Cullen's shoulders in greeting as if they were old friends. "I've been waiting to show you what we've done. I think," he said, with a twinkle in his eyes, "that you will be amazed."

The engineer turned on his heels and walked away. Two of the guards prodded Cullen to follow the engineer up a series of steps. They emerged from the darkness of a stone stairway onto the top level of the arena. Below him, the streets of Rome were waking up with the first rays of sun.

"This way," said Burrus.

Cullen followed the engineer up to the forth tier of seats. They were still on the walkway that looked over the streets of Rome when the engineer turned and walked through an archway that led toward the interior of the arena. Cullen followed him, curious about the engineer's evident excitement. Cullen walked from the shadowed arches out onto a platform that overlooked the interior of the arena. His breath left him in an involuntary gasp. The engineer smiled. This was the reaction he'd been expecting and Cullen didn't disappoint.

Water filled the arena.

It rose to a level ten feet below the first tier of seats, sloshing against the walls. Four boats were tied against the edge of the stadium, each at opposite points: north, south, east and west. The shape of the ships told Cullen that they were galleys—what was it the Roman marines had called them? *Quinqueremes?* But Cullen immediately noticed that these were smaller. The galley that had taken them over from Briton had been longer— —much longer—and had five banks of oars. It had held hundreds of Romans and almost a full village of prisoners. The galleys that Cullen looked at now boasted one level of oars, ten on each side of the ship, twenty in all. The prow of the ship was a miniature version of a Roman attack vessel. The bottom curved outward into the water, rose high above the level of the sailors, curving inward at the top. Each of the boats had its own colors. The one furthest away, at the north end of the arena, was purple. Cullen knew this was the color of royalty, and he was surprised to see the flag that blew from its mast was small. Opposite the purple boat, on the south side of the arena, the boat was painted black, as was the larger flag that flew from its mast.

Whoever is in that boat has been cast as the villain, thought Cullen.

A crimson boat was moored on the west side of the arena and Cullen knew this was the color of the Roman army. Romans would fill the crimson and the purple boats. The last boat, bobbing on the east side of the arena was a dirty yellow color. Mustard, thought Cullen. The color the slaves wear. It was obvious to Cullen which boats he and his comrades would fight in.

The engineer smiled, pleased at Cullen's obvious awe at what he was seeing.

"They built this arena on a lake. But the water is only held in abeyance by the drains. So when the need arises, the drains are opened, water floods in, and now all of Rome can witness a sea battle a mere stone's throw from their own bedrooms."

He grabbed Cullen's sleeve and led him to the edge of the top tier. A rheumatoid finger pointed at the boats.

"Smaller than a regular attack ship, as you've no doubt noticed. Shallower too. Draws only four feet of water when loaded with men. Wider too. Why? So that the citizens of Rome won't be craning their necks, trying to look around masts or shields. If a ship should be boarded, every arm that's hacked off, every throat that's sliced open, will be as visible as if the Greeks themselves staged the drama."

"You must be very proud of yourself," said Cullen.

"You have no idea."

Cullen let his gaze drift to the north end of the stadium. His plan depended on a lot of things happening at the right time. There was no room for error, but there were so many opportunities for it.

The engineer's voice broke into his thoughts.

"I can see in your face that you're wondering if this will be the last sunrise you will see." It was not what Cullen had been thinking, but now that it was mentioned he wondered if indeed it would be his last. "Well, let me tell you something that might amuse you. The Emperor's priests cut open a chicken, laying bare the entrails inside it. Apparently after a few moments of "oohing" and "aahhing" they came to the conclusion that these games today would be the talk of Rome for days or weeks to come. Which means—of course—that the fight will be a tremendous one. Roman soldiers against gladiators led by the Hibernian warrior, Cullen, the so-called Gladiator Thirty-Seven. A warrior as mysterious as the land he came from."

The engineer rubbed his bony knuckles together, caught up in the passion of his story. "If I wasn't so good at my job, I should love to be the organizer of more of these games. I have a feeling for the drama, don't you think?"

"Like you were born to it," said Cullen. "Is Dracon ready?"

"He's not a marine. So fighting on a ship might throw him off. As it might you. Which will make it all the more entertaining. Now," he clapped his hands together and rubbed them heartily, "are you ready to go back to your men? Tell them what's in store. Rouse them to fight for victory?"

"I'm ready," replied Cullen. He turned away from the water, his mind already making plans, strategizing and discarding tactics. It was very simple really. He had to lead his fellow prisoners into battle against a superbly trained enemy, avoid death from any number of ways, hope that the Christians were able to do more than talk and he had to do all this without killing anyone.

God help him.

Dracon walked along the ranks of men that would fight with him today. Forty sailors, twenty to a ship, and ten marines in each vessel, whose only job was to board the enemies' ships and rip as many bellies as they could. The scowl on Dracon's face belied the satisfaction he felt because these men were tough, battle-hardened warriors, veterans of many campaigns from Arabia to Germania. Their swords had spilled guts from one end of the empire to the other. They would do.

And what did Cullen have? Good sailors, he had to admit. Those Cilicians could handle a boat, but how long could they stay out of reach of his Roman sailors? Minutes maybe, if they were lucky. But once the marines boarded the ships it would be nothing short of wholesale slaughter. Probably. Because the Hibernian was different from any other warrior Dracon had ever faced, and to underestimate him was to invite catastrophic failure. To that end, Dracon addressed the sailors.

"No mercy will be given to you by these thieves and murderers. No pleas will be heard. If you leave yourself open you will be killed. You will look down at one of their swords thrusting into your belly. There will be no pity in their hearts, no hint of regret in their eyes. So show them no mercy. Squeeze all love and kindness from your spirit. Revel in their pain and rejoice in their deaths. And when you are done and their blood flows around your ankles, turn toward the Emperor, raise your swords in salute and know that you will have done something that even an Emperor cannot do."

Dracon sensed the men stir, felt their sinews tighten. They were ready now. By the time the battle started they would be consumed with rage and bloodlust. And not even Cullen would be able to stop it.

In the dark room under the arena Cullen searched out Kaseem. He found the bearded man sitting in a corner, his face pale and gaunt. On Cullen's arrival he forced a weak smile.

"Is there nothing worse," whispered Kaseem, "than waiting to die?"

"Dying isn't our plan, Kaseem," replied Cullen.

"We must be like tigers when the fight starts, Cullen."

"Yes, my friend. Like tigers."

Both men glanced up as a faint rumble sounded in the arena.

"The citizens of Rome arrive," said Kaseem. He put his head into his hands and exhaled deeply. Cullen watched him, wondering what words of encouragement he could say to the man.

"Do not worry about me, Cullen," said Kaseem, reading his thoughts correctly. "Once I climb into that boat I shall be ferocious. But now I must let my fears course through me. It has always been so with me. Before my first battle I moaned and cried so much, my father thought he had raised a woman for a son. He hit me and tried to get me to stop bawling, but I couldn't. His men were embarrassed for him, watching me snivel and rock back and forth. He tried to throw me off the boat, but I hung on, and out of sheer horror he left me crying at my oars, trying to ignore the commiserating glances of his men as I made a fool of myself. Then the battle started and that day I killed my first man, plus two more. After the first stroke of the oars my fears disappeared and—well—what happens will happen? My own men have been similarly patient with me. Isn't that right, Razoul?"

A razor-thin man with a sharp, pointed beard turned to Kaseem.

"It is true, Cullen. He acts like a howling monkey before a fight, and a savage during it." He shrugged. "It is our burden to bear."

Kaseem turned to Cullen, a smile broadening on his face.

"See? Coming from Razoul, those are fine words indeed. Fine words."

Three hours later the door opened and the gladiators walked out. In single file they trudged along the tunnel where Roman guards were posted every five paces and all looked alert and suspicious. It was not unknown for prisoners to try to make a break for it, even under so heavy a guard. What did they have to lose? Either die now or die later. Why wait?

But there was no escaping now and all the prisoners knew it. So they marched up the steps to the first tier. They had been divided into two groups of thirty: twenty oarsman and ten warriors. Kaseem and Cullen led the first group. Bull was leader of the second group of warriors and the lead oarsman was Kaseem's thin friend, Razoul. Cullen, Kaseem and their crew lined up inside a dark tunnel on the south side of the arena. The end of the tunnel opened up into the arena, and the crushing murmur of fifty thousand Romans pulsed into the hearts of the gladiators.

Bull, Razoul, and their crew walked around to the east side of the stadium to their boat.

The two Roman galleys were moored opposite the gladiators' boats on the North and West side of the arena.

The crowd was deafening, their screams and cheers crashing into the tunnel and echoing down its length. Cullen tried to block out the noise and focus on the job that lay ahead.

Beside him, Kaseem dry-heaved. Spittle dripped from his mouth, dangling like the rope of a bell.

It had come to this time and place, thought Cullen. Two months ago his life had been simple and plodding and if he had not exactly been happy, he had found peace of mind. Now every day was turmoil. He wondered how he had never fully appreciated what he had back in Briton and why he had never felt joy. If only he could have that life back again. How he would savor the love of his wife and child. Maybe he and Rhiannon would have more children. He thought about the comradeship of his friends in the village—why hadn't he talked to them more? Did he enjoy being thought of as the battle-hardened warrior who intimidated even those who lived near him?

Was he really that arrogant?

Rhiannon had never feared him. Ever since they first met, her eyes had seen through him. She knew who he was, right down to the darkest corner of his soul. He had thought he would frighten her away, by telling her of the horrors he had perpetrated on his enemies, but instead of being repulsed by his stories she had held him in her arms and shared the burden of the killings he had done. And he had wept. The tears flowed for the first time since his childhood and she had held him tight. She was an island in the middle of a treacherous ocean and he had been fortunate to land upon her shore. Since then the memories of his brutal years faded into the grey mists of time.

All because of the love of a woman.

Please keep her safe.

"Did you say something, Cullen?"

Cullen looked up. Kaseem watched him curiously.

Cullen shook his head. "Praying," he explained.

Kaseem nodded. "For victory?"

"For redemption."

"Do you think your God heard you?"

Cullen hesitated. Every person he'd ever killed seemed to flash before his eyes.

"I hope."

A centurion strode over to Cullen and nodded at him.

"It's time. Gather your men."

Cullen walked to the other side of the tunnel and looked down at his men lined up single-file against the stone walls. He let his gaze find each one of them and let the moment lengthen. He felt like he should make a great speech, one that would stir his men's blood and get them ready for the carnage that lay ahead. He wanted each of them to know that right here, right now, they were brothers in arms, that by going shoulder to shoulder into the abyss of war they would be closer to the man next to them than to any blood brother they spent their entire childhood with. He wanted to say this, but he saw in their eyes that they already knew, already felt it. There was nothing to say.

"You bastards ready?"

Their eyes never left Cullen.

They followed Cullen into the blinding daylight.

Fifty seven

The crowd surged toward them as they appeared from the tunnel. The already deafening babble rose to a monstrous roar as Cullen and Kaseem led their crew over to the wall where their boat was docked. The noise of the crowd hit them as a physical force. Hands reached out toward him, trying to grab pieces of his clothing. It was a relief to reach the wall where two soldiers guided him to the rope ladder that led to the boat. The black boat. Being cast as the villain didn't bother Cullen. Was it not how he saw himself?

Cullen scaled the ladder and moved to the front of the galley. Kaseem and the rest of their crew followed. All their movements were quick, hurried, bird-like, utterly at home on the ever-changing tilt of the surface of the water. Adrenaline surged through their veins. Their eyes were narrow and unblinking. The rowers found their places at the oars. The warriors picked up swords and spears that were arranged in rows down the middle of the boat. There were plenty of weapons.

Cullen looked at the other boats. Bull, Razoul and their crew took up positions in their mustard-colored boat. Bull glanced up and Cullen raised a hand in greeting. Bull pumped a fist in the air in response.

Opposite him, and to his left, the Romans swarmed into their boats. Their movements were organized, fast and proficient. On the purple boat, the figure of Dracon was plainly visible, towering over the other soldiers. Cullen could see him bark orders and the men responded instantly. The ten warriors in the Roman boat were in full armor, lined up in the center of the craft. Another relayed a command from the officer and, as one, the men reached down for their weapons and brought their swords up across their chests. Then, on orders from Dracon, thrust their swords up into the air three times, shouting *Victory! Victory! Victory!*

The crowd roar swelled and Cullen sank lower into the boat just to escape the punishing violence of the noise. Glancing back at his crew, he saw the same mixture of awe and fear on their faces.

"Cullen."

Kaseem had to scream his name just to be heard over the concussive force of the crowd. Cullen turned. Kaseem looked pointedly at his men and Cullen understood. The fight would be over before it began unless he could focus his warriors on the fight ahead. He stood up in the boat and banged his two swords together. His crew looked to him, their eyes wide.

"Stand up," shouted Cullen, gesturing with his hands. The men got unsteadily to their feet. Cullen pointed down the center of the boat with his swords.

"Make a line."

The men made a shaky line along the center of the boat.

"Where I come from," yelled Cullen, "we have a special way of greeting our enemies before combat starts. It is a gesture to show how much we respect them."

"Respect them?" shouted a warrior, his face twisted in a mixture of fury and fear. "They can go to Hades and freeze!"

"I agree. But before I send them there I want one of their last memories to be of my big, hairy arse."

Cullen turned his back to the Roman vessel opposite him.

"Turn around," he yelled at his men.

Half of them now had smiles on their faces and they turned their backs to the Romans. The Cilicians looked at each other in amazement, but on command from Cullen they grabbed the waist of their trousers.

"Ready?" yelled Cullen.

Everyone nodded. One or two of them were laughing.

"Drop britches!"

As one, the men pulled their britches to their knees. The roar of the crowd turned to laughter and whistles. Scattered applause rose from the opposite side.

"Bend over!"

Cullen's crew bent forward at the waist.

At first Dracon wasn't sure what he was seeing. When the prisoners in the black boat stood up, he thought it was a pathetic attempt to copy the Roman victory cry. Their line was ragged and without discipline. Half of them couldn't speak the other's language. It was a last desperate attempt to gather some courage. But then he had to blink because the men across from him lowered their trousers. The crowd understood what was happening before he did. Their hoots and ribaldry made him realize what the prisoners were doing. The gladiators bent over, showing their bare backsides to the elite Roman soldiers he commanded. His men responded by yelling back and making obscene gestures with their hands. And so, in fifteen seconds, Cullen had taken back the initiative from Dracon

When Bull saw what Cullen was doing he laughed until his sides hurt. He urged his men up into a line and together they showed their arses to the Romans in the crimson boat across from them. The tension that had hovered over his crew since last night was gone. The fog of indecision and fear melted away in the coarse laughter and fluent curses of his men. Now it was simply a fight to the death—or maybe an escape if Cullen's plan came together. He was ready. Live in freedom or die here today. He knew he had seen the last of the *Ludus Magnus*. He would never stare up at the dripping ceiling of his cell again, he would never feel the heel of a Roman's boot on his face, and he would never be a prisoner again. With the weight of a mountain off his shoulders, Bull hauled up his britches and grabbed his sword.

A hush descended upon the arena. Hadrian walked into the Emperor's pavilion and waved at the crowd. The people responded with cheers and cries of "Long Live the Emperor!" Hadrian raised both arms as if to embrace the crowd. They cheered even louder and the Emperor bowed. He lowered his thin figure into the chair.

An old man, garbed in a white robe, walked to the edge of the arena near the Emperor. Cullen glanced at Kaseem.

"This is it."

Kaseem nodded. Above them the Roman guards got ready to cut the mooring rope. The old man near the Emperor raised an arm that held a white cloth. With an actor's flair, he waited for just the right moment and let go of the cloth. It spread out like a bird's wings and fell down to the water, where it settled, buffeted by the small waves. The Roman guards sliced the mooring rope and Cullen pushed the boat away from the wall.

Kaseem stood beside Cullen at the prow of the ship.

"They'll expect us to run. To try to evade their ships."

"I know. Which is why we must do the opposite."

"Attack?"

"Attack," confirmed Cullen.

Kaseem barked out orders to the sailors. The rowers on the left side pushed their oars through the water and in seconds the black boat was pointing directly across to Dracon's purple boat which aligned itself to point at them. Now both sides of rowers pulled their oars and the boat glided across the water. The rowers were so perfectly in syncopation that the wake they left behind looked as if it had been drawn by a straight edge. Kaseem called out the rhythm to the rowers who increased the tempo of their efforts. Cullen could see Dracon's face watching from the prow of his ship, which closed the distance between them on a direct collision course.

"Kaseem, which way will they break?"

"They won't break. They'll count on your nerve to fail."

"Thirty yards, Kaseem."

"Right side ready!" bellowed Kaseem to his rowers.

"Twenty yards."

"One more stroke, right side!" screamed Kaseem. His men heaved back one more time, their bodies already covered with a thin sheen of sweat.

"Ten yards, Kaseem," said Cullen.

"Right oars in now!" barked Kaseem. "Left oars push forward, push forward!"

The men on the starboard side of the ship hauled their oars into the ship as fast as they could. At the same time the rowers on the port side reversed the direction of their oars, pushing mercilessly against the water.

The ship curved away from the center, brushing along the left side of Dracon's ship.

Dracon's marine commander saw what they were doing, just in time.

"Oars up!" he ordered, and the Roman sailors pulled their oars in.

The sides of the two ships scraped by at a speed that blurred the faces of each of the boat's crews.

Someone from the Roman boat threw a sword and it struck one of the Cilician rowers in the side, burying itself up to the hilt. The pirate gasped and fell forward, dead. One of the Roman rowers was too slow in hauling in his oar. It smashed like a twig against the gladiators' boat, splintering violently. A twelve inch shard flew into the rower ahead, impaling his throat. He stood up, clutching his neck, spluttering blood over his crewmates. Dracon strode forward and pitched him into the water. The boats parted, gliding away from each other.

Bull's mustard-colored boat tore through the gap between the black and purple boats, the rowers heaving back on their oars. It sliced through the water faster than a man could run. Cullen turned his head to follow it just in time to see the crimson Roman boat smash headlong into it. There was an almighty smash as the prows of both boats shattered into pieces. Bull was thrown halfway back into his boat and the men on both ships were a tangle of bodies and oars.

"Kaseem, bring her around. Now, while the red boat is open to attack."

"Cullen, Dracon has the same plan."

Kaseem pointed to Dracon's boat. It was turning too, planning to attack Bull's boat. Some of Bull's crew lay slumped over their oars, either dead or unconscious from the jarring crash.

"Get between them. Try to ram her side."

Instead of stopping the boat, Kaseem guided her in a looping circle so that the boat never lost speed. However, it had to cover a lot more water than Dracon's boat, which had done an abrupt about face. Dracon's problem would be picking up enough speed to beat Cullen's boat to the damaged, drifting ships. Cullen watched in frustration as Dracon's boat, only forty yards from Bull, started to close the gap.

"Kaseem."

"We'll get them, Cullen."

As Cullen's black boat continued to loop around, Dracon urged his rowers to pull faster. The gap closed to thirty yards, then twenty, then ten.

Kaseem brought his vessel around so that it pointed directly at Dracon's boat. Frustration seethed within him. They were gaining speed, but were fifty yards away from Dracon's purple craft.

While the Roman boat carrying the crimson flag floated adrift on the water, Dracon's boat pulled alongside Bull's boat, hulls only feet apart. Didius launched himself at the first Roman who leapt across. His sword slashed down, severing the soldier's arm.

Soldiers from both boats stood up now and spears were flung across the short distance. In seconds, five of the gladiators were dead, and only one Roman. A gladiator swung a sword at a soldier. It almost severed his head. The soldier disappeared into the water.

"Faster, Kaseem."

"Four seconds, Cullen."

Dracon glanced over his shoulder. In the heat of the battle he had forgotten about Cullen's boat—for a few seconds—and now he saw it, a black beast bearing down on his ship at an incredible speed.

"Brace for impact!" he yelled.

Cullen's boat smashed into the side of Dracon's vessel. The Roman hull collapsed, killing at least six Romans. But the crash pushed Dracon's boat further against Bull's boat.

Dracon and his Roman soldiers took full advantage of what should have been a disastrous situation. They leaped from their sinking vessel into Bull's boat and engaged the gladiators in battle.

Cullen cursed violently when he saw Dracon's men abandon their purple ship and leap into Bull's vessel. What could have been a deathblow to the Romans had turned to a potential catastrophe.

Bull's ship was now enemy territory.

Dracon's teeth still rattled in his head from the bone-jarring impact. He kept his footing as the left side of his boat was destroyed. But all was not lost. The crash had knocked his boat onto Bull's boat. Ten of Rome's finest soldiers leaped into the gladiators' dirty-yellow boat, swords slashing and thrusting. Dracon jumped into the boat, twirling to avoid a spear-thrust from a wild, red-haired warrior. Dracon rolled to his knees and sliced at the man's ankles. The gladiator screamed in agony as he fell, his partially severed ankle refusing to hold him. Dracon thrust his sword forward, traveling deep into the red-haired man's chest. The man put his arms up to the sword, as if to check that it was really there. He stared into Dracon's eyes.

Dracon saw the eyes lose their life, as if a candle had been blown out.

Bull saw Dracon leap onto the other end of the boat and knew that if he wasn't able to hold off this attack he and his entire crew would be dead in minutes. Right now, Dracon was the least of his problems: a huge Roman leapt from the sinking purple boat, sword drawn back, ready to drive it deep inside Bull's body. Bull turned to move but two of his shipmates stood on either side, trapping him. The Roman shoved his sword forward and Bull tightened his stomach muscles, knowing it would be useless, but braced himself anyway for his certain death.

But the pitching boat caused the Roman to lose his footing and his sword plunged into the side of the man standing next to him. The man screamed and pulled back, freeing Bull's arms. Bull drove a spear deep into the Roman's chest, driving it in so hard the point of the spear went clean through the Roman's body, embedding itself into the hull of the boat.

Someone screamed ahead of him.

A soldier pulled a sword from the neck of a dead gladiator. The Roman, high cheekbones with low eyebrows, turned to Bull and raised his sword. Bull reached for the sword stuck in his comrade's side, and as the Roman sliced his weapon down through the air, Bull pulled the sword out, and sliced upward. Sparks flew as the swords met. Bull's free hand grabbed the Roman's wrist. He pushed the arm up and drove his weapon into the Roman's armpit and heaved the dying man into the water.

Fifty eight

Cullen's black boat careened sideways after smashing into Dracon's hull. For a few seconds it was dead in the water and Cullen found himself on top of a tangle of limbs and groaning bodies. His initial hope that Kaseem's craft might have irreparably damaged Dracon's vessel was true. The Roman boat was already sinking to the sands of the arena. But that was where Cullen's fortune ended. At least ten of the Romans had jumped across to Bull's boat and there was a furious hand-to-hand battle taking place. The Romans were a more disciplined fighting force and only the pile of corpses between the Gladiators and the Romans stopped the immediate slaughter of Bull's crew. With the weight of ten extra Romans the edge of the boat had sunk to within inches of the surface. If it started to roll side to side, everyone on board would fall into the water.

Cullen grabbed some of the fallen men in his boat and half-dragged, half-flung them back to their place at the oars. Kaseem was doing the same thing, slapping dazed men awake, cajoling them, threatening them.

"Kaseem, get them ready!"

"I know. I know."

Cullen threw one of the dead sailors overboard to make room for those able to row. Kaseem pushed sailors into their seats and shoved oars into their bruised hands. He moved in front of the sailors.

"We row around to the other side of their boat. On my orders: Oars up!"

The sailors raised their oars out of the water, keeping them within an inch of the surface.

"And now, everyone together!"

The sailors slammed their oars into the water and pulled.

Kaseem glanced at the crimson boat. It had come off worst when it crashed headlong into the mustard-colored boat. In the two heart-beats he had given himself to assess the situation, Kaseem saw the Roman soldiers throw three dead sailors overboard. It would be a few moments before the crimson boat was anywhere near battle ready. Kaseem turned his attention back to his own vessel. Even though the boat sliced quickly through the water, it seemed like an eternity before their vessel looped around to the other side of Bull's boat.

Cullen couldn't believe that Bull's boat was still afloat. The entire deck was covered with standing warriors. The dead did not have space to fall. As their ship skimmed the back of Bull's boat, Cullen screamed at Bull, trying to make his voice heard above the ear-splitting noise of the crowd, and the shouts of the combatants.

"Bull, when we're alongside you, jump!"

Kaseem guided the boat around. Cullen's warriors stepped to the edge of their boat and as soon as the Roman soldiers were in reach, they stabbed at them. Several Romans leapt across to Cullen's boat, but the attempt, which had worked so well on Bull's boat, failed now. They were met by fresh warriors who cut them down before they could gain a foothold.

Cullen, at the back of his boat, stepped onto Bull's vessel and shoved whatever men he could find onto his boat. There were not many left, maybe seven in all. It had been a slaughter. One by one the remaining gladiators and sailors jumped across to Cullen's boat as the Romans fought furiously with Cullen's warriors.

"Quickly, Cullen," yelled Kaseem.

Cullen grabbed Bull who used a Roman spear to jab at any Romans who tried to climb over the fallen bodies. They fell back into Cullen's boat and Kaseem had his sailors push away from the other vessel. The deft strokes of the rowers took the galley out of danger.

Cullen struggled to a sitting position in the middle of the boat, out of the way of the rowers. He looked around at the gladiators they had rescued. All of them were injured and bleeding. One of the sailors was doubled-up near the bow of the boat, his hands clutching his sides. Blood seeped through his fingers, drenching his tunic. The man's face was pale and his lips were white.

One of the Roman sailors threw a sword. It embedded into the side of the hull with a *thunk*. Kaseem screamed at his rowers to work harder, pull faster. The sailors doubled their efforts, and propelled their boat toward the southern end of the arena, leaving the crimson and mustard-colored boats adrift in the center of the water.

Dracon straddled the sides of the hull of the captured mustard-colored boat near the back where the hull narrowed.

"Drop the bodies into the water," he bellowed. The order was unnecessary, as the soldiers had already started to fling the dead and dying men overboard. A Roman soldier, bleeding profusely from a wound in his neck, clutched the tunic of a soldier who tried to heave him overboard, but his grip was too weak and he hit the water where the weight of his armor dragged him under like a stone.

It took two minutes, but finally the deck was cleared. Blood pooled under the feet of the surviving Romans as they turned to Dracon. Dracon gestured to the empty oar seats on either side of the boat.

"Fill those seats, you bastards."

As the men shuffled to their places Dracon made a quick head count of how many were left. When all the seats were filled, he had fifteen sailors and four marines. They could afford to take five men from the other Roman boat commanded by—*what was his name? Cyrus? Crassus?*—whatever his name was he had certainly taken his time getting his crew organized. As the crimson boat pulled forward Dracon yelled across to him.

"Where's Cyrus?"

"Crassus, sir? He's dead," yelled a young soldier.

"Who's second in command?"

"Junius, sir. He's dead too."

"How's your boat?"

"Seaworthy, sir."

Dracon counted the men left on the crimson ship. Twenty six, almost a full complement. *Four dead,* he thought, *and two of those dead were the commander and his second-in-command. Piss poor luck.*

"Pull alongside us."

Dracon turned to one of the soldiers from his sunken purple boat. "Gnaeus."

"Sir?" said Gnaeus.

"Go with them. You're in charge of the crimson boat now. But give us two sailors and two soldiers from it."

Gnaeus climbed aboard. Men switched boats until both the mustard and crimson galleys each had an equal complement of warriors.

That's when Dracon looked at the boat he was in.

"Fuck," he said quietly.

He was in a mustard-colored boat. A boat the color of what a slave might wear. He had been given the honor of commanding a purple boat, a color reserved for Emperors and kings, and that boat now lay at the bottom of the arena. The flag that flew from the mast had cost a small fortune, dyed as it was in purple. Purple was expensive to make. One of his whores told him the pigment had to be extracted from the veins of Murex snails. He didn't know how you'd do that but it sounded really fucking boring and time-consuming. And, of course, it was Cullen who'd ruined that honor for Dracon, by crashing his black boat into Dracon's purple one.

Dracon had only dropped his guard for a few seconds and in that time the great Gladiator Thirty-Seven had taken advantage of it.

Goddamn him.

Dracon looked toward the southern end of the arena where Cullen's black boat drifted near the wall. He forced himself to forget about the loss of his regally-colored galley and concentrated on what had gone right for him. Not only had the gladiators lost a boat, but over half of their men had been killed. He wondered what trick Cullen was hoping to pull out of the bag this time. If everything went the way it should, the gladiators would be dead within the quarter-hour and Dracon would be celebrating a glorious victory, purple boat or no purple boat. Dracon was in no hurry to finish off the prisoners. The people, adulterous with their affections though they were, had come to see a battle. If Dracon wished to win back their love, he must woo them with such a fight as they had never seen before. Their seduction must be slow, gentle to start with. But it must end with his sword penetrating Cullen's belly. The Hibernian must die in his arms.

Fifty nine

The man clutching his stomach bled to death on the floor of the boat. Cullen lifted him to the side of the boat and dropped him overboard. They had twenty seven men left, including the seven rescued from Bull's boat. They drifted at the southern end of the arena, while the two Roman galleys held the center.

"At least we'll move faster," growled Bull.

"So will they," replied Cullen, glancing at the Roman boats. Bull leant close to Cullen's ear, speaking to him in a fierce whisper as if afraid the Roman guards ringing the stadium would hear him.

"So where are they? Where are your friends?"

"North end of the arena," Cullen replied, keeping his voice low as Bull did, even though he knew that unless someone was standing within two feet of them there was no way they could be overheard.

"So let's go over to them now," hissed Bull.

Cullen shook his head. "We've got to do this right. If we allow the Romans to get close while we're there, they'll cut us down. We'll die with swords in our backs, seconds from freedom."

"You're saying we've got to take the Romans out?"

"At least one of them."

Bull grabbed Cullen, speaking fiercely.

"We got close to them once. Out of thirty on our boat, they killed twenty three. We can't attack them. It's suicide."

"One of their boats must go," repeated Cullen.

Bull let go of Cullen's shirt. "If you've got a plan, let's hear it."

"We ram them."

"And then what?"

"Then we run to the north end and hope the other boat hangs back. Hopefully we're half way up the wall they'll realize their mistake."

"And if they don't?"

Cullen reached over the side of the boat to grab a spear floating on the surface. "You know the answer to that. Kaseem, are we ready to go?"

Kaseem nodded.

"Take her around the edge of the arena. Let's see what happens."

"Let's see what happens," muttered Bull, as the boat started to move through the water. "That's your plan?"

Cullen ignored Bull and moved toward Kaseem, who watched the two Roman boats intently. He drew in a breath.

"They're moving."

Cullen's black boat pushed through the water, hugging the wall of the arena. The crimson galley, with Gnaeus in command, headed toward the eastern edge of the arena on an intercept course. The crowd noise, which had abated somewhat as the combatants gathered themselves, now rose up in cheers at the prospect for another skirmish. Cullen and Bull watched the crimson Roman boat drive through the water. If both boats continued on their present course, the crimson boat's brow would smash into the side of Cullen's boat, breaking it apart like tinder wood. Cullen's boat was so close to the wall of the arena that any collision would send them smashing into it.

Above them, Cullen could see the Roman citizens leaning out, desperate to see what was going to happen.

"They'll hit us, Kaseem."

Kaseem clapped him on the back. "If you believe that, my friend, then they certainly think the same thing."

Kaseem waited until the Romans were three boat lengths away when he roared orders to his sailors. The oarsmen immediately doubled the speed of their rowing. The boat shot forward.

When the gladiators' boat picked up speed, Gnaeus exhorted his men to double their efforts. The crimson boat's speed increased, but the gladiators' boat sped by in a blur, inches from the wall. Gnaeus, a veteran of many wars, had never fought on water and was a few seconds late in ordering his men to slow down. By the time the order was relayed and the men slammed their oars in the water to reverse direction, it was too late.

The boat smashed into the wall with bone jarring force, throwing Gnaeus off the boat and into the water.

The armor that so far had saved Gnaeus's life three times today dragged him under. He called out for help, but his lungs filled with the blood-tinged water. Breaking the surface, he vomited up the water and took a lungful of air. He reached out for the boat, but a swirling eddy, pulled him away, inches from the hull. The weight of his armor pulled him mercilessly under again. He struggled frantically for fifteen seconds, furiously holding his breath, trusting that one of his soldiers would see his hands clawing above the surface of the water. His toes could even touch the ground beneath his feet but he could not get enough leverage to push up. He felt a current pull him even further from the boat and he knew he had seconds to live unless someone grabbed his hands, but all they grasped was air. Gnaeus drowned, his fingertips dragging through the surface of the water as his toes kissed the mud bottom.

Dracon watched in disbelief as the crimson boat smashed into the arena wall. What had Gnaeus been thinking? He had seen Gnaeus fall into the water and yelled at the Romans in the crimson boat to fish him out. But they were either stupid or dazed and Gnaeus died within inches of safety. In the meantime, Cullen's boat continued its long looping movement along the wall of the arena.

Dracon ordered his boat forward, planning to engage the gladiators at the north-east corner of the arena. There was a limit to how long those pirates could keep up the pace of their rowing.

Kaseem barked orders. They black boat shot toward the center of the lake.

Dracon saw the change in direction and thought that the gladiators meant to ram them. He ordered his rowers to turn their boat so that the gladiators would hit the prow of the ship, not the hull. But instead of ramming his ship, the gladiators skimmed past his boat.

Kaseem guided his oarsmen into a sweeping loop around the water. He noted with satisfaction that Dracon's maneuver had caused him to come to a dead stop. It would take him precious seconds to get up to speed again, and by the time he realized what they were doing, it would be too late.

The oarsmen pulled as they had never pulled before, their muscles burning, sinews straining.

Kaseem guided the boat into a long arc until their black boat was pointing directly at Gnaeus's crimson galley. Now the rowers gave it everything they had. The boat shot forward, doubling its speed in the space of three seconds. Gnaeus's crimson galley bumped lazily against the wall of the arena as the crew tried to shake their heads awake. Some of the Romans lay unconscious at their oars, other moaned in an agony of bruised bodies and broken limbs.

The gladiators' boat bore down on them with deadly intent.

The crowd above the Romans surged forward, desperate to look at the dazed and bruised soldiers.

Dracon stepped toward the front of his boat, gesturing frantically for the other boat to move, but it was already too late. The Cilician pirates were accelerating at an unbelievable rate and were now only twenty yards from the Roman boat. With every pull of their oars, they covered ten yards. Dracon saw a young Roman who had taken it upon himself to lead, strike at his men, urging them to their seats and begin rowing. He cuffed his men on their heads, screaming words that only he could hear. It was too late. With their final heave, the Cilician sailors lifted their oars out of the water and let the ship's momentum carry it directly into the middle of the crimson hull.

There was an almighty snap and crunching of wood as the crimson Roman vessel was slammed against the wall of the arena. Those Roman soldiers that were waiting to jump onto Cullen's vessel were flung overboard like rag-dolls. They hit the water and were at once dragged under by the weight of their armor.

The effect on the Roman boat was devastating. Seven men were killed outright, their bodies a jumble of torn and broken limbs, their bones smashed by the force of the crash. Gladiators leaped from the black boat onto the floundering Roman vessel. Years of anger, hatred and desire for vengeance came to a head as the prisoners drove swords and spears into the bruised and battered Romans. The young Roman managed to stay conscious. Grabbing a sword, he thrust it forward blindly. Immediately, Bull and three other gladiators drove their weapons into the young Roman, killing him instantly.

The crowd above leaned over the wall, screaming in horror and fascination at the slaughter being played out below them. Some urged the gladiators to show no mercy, other screamed for the Romans to fight back.

One of the spectators—a bearded Roman dressed in the clothes of a successful merchant—leaned over too far and fell directly into the midst of the slaughter. He tried to rise to his feet, but his hands could find no purchase on the blood-slick bodies of the dead soldiers. He scrabbled away from the slashing swords to the side of the boat near the wall.

Jump, thought Cullen. *Jump into the water away from these killers.* So far, his men were concerned with killing anything in a Roman uniform, but their blood-lust wouldn't stop when the soldiers were dead. Some of the man's friends leaned down, trying to reach him, but their hands were yards apart even when the merchant managed to find his footing on the crushed body of a Roman soldier.

Someone in the crowd—his wife? His brother?—lowered a length of cloth down. The merchant's panicked hands grabbed the material, and he launched himself up the wall, his feet scrabbling wildly and ineffectually against the stones. Somehow he got within reach of the many hands stretching out for him and he swung his free hand up. Just as it seemed he would escape, the cloth tore. Frantic hands in the crowd grabbed at him but he plunged down into the sinking boat. He knocked against a gladiator who, incensed, drove his spear into the bearded merchant's stomach.

He let out a high-pitched wail.

Other gladiators descended on him, swords hacking and slashing. Arterial blood sprayed out and he tried to block the swords with his arms. His screams, if anything, grew louder, until Bull rammed a sword into the man's neck. Frothy bubbles of blood sprayed from his mouth and his hands grabbed the sword. His fingers made a movement as if he was trying to ease it out of his throat. His eyes had the look of an animal who knew it was dead, but whose mind refused to acknowledge the fact. Cullen couldn't believe the man still lived. *Die, you bastard*, he thought. *Just die.* As if to oblige Cullen, the man let his hands drop to his side, and slowly keeled over, his body slumping over the headless corpse of a gladiator.

Over the roars of the crowd, his wife screamed.

Bull pulled his sword out of the man's neck and looked around for more Romans to kill. Blood swirled around his ankles mixing with the water that filled the Roman vessel. Any Roman that remained on board was a corpse. Bull's men stood, chests heaving, eyes wide as clay bowls.

They had won this battle in devastating fashion.

Two of the men grabbed the body of the merchant and flung him overboard. His tunic, once white, now soaked in blood, floated on the water for a moment before following the merchant under the surface.

This final act by the gladiators did something that struck Cullen as an almost physical force. The crowd went silent. Only the shrieks of his wife pierced the air. The crowd watched the merchant—one of their own—sink beneath the bloody surface, red tendrils following him down into the depths. He was already dead, already wandering through the demon-haunted afterlife.

As the noise of the crowd seemed to be swallowed by an invisible God, Bull gathered air into his lungs and let out a bellowing cry of victory. He seemed to yell with every pore of his body. Sinews popped out from his neck and sweat flung from his face as his head shook in the aftermath of the battle. The other gladiators in the boat drove their bloody swords up into the air, joining Bull in his primal scream of defiance.

Sixty

Kaseem maneuvered the boat sideways to the half-sunk crimson vessel. Cullen leaped on board. Grappling hooks lay on the deck of the ship and Cullen thought they might be useful.

"Help me, Bull," he called.

Bull didn't hear him. He seemed to be in a semi-catatonic stupor, his eyes half closed, a guttural whimper still escaping his lips. Cullen grabbed Bull's wrists and dragged him down to his knees. Bull's eyes snapped back into focus and he tried to raise his sword arm, but it was trapped in Cullen's iron grip.

"I need your help, Bull. Are you with me?"

Bull nodded numbly. Cullen let go of his wrists and together they heaved the dead soldiers overboard, freeing up the grappling hooks. The other gladiators saw what they were doing and followed suit, pulling the hooks free and tossing them into Kaseem's boat.

"Cullen, hurry."

Cullen looked up. Dracon's boat moved toward them, their rowers straining with effort. Cullen turned back to the task in hand. One of the grappling hoods was lodged in the wood at the bottom of the crimson boat. The bloody water was up to Cullen's elbows and he couldn't tell if the hooks would come out. He only had one chance and he heaved with all his might. The hook broke free, wood splinters following it up, and Cullen fell back against Bull. The two of them lay sprawled over the bodies of the few Romans that hadn't been tossed overboard. Hands grabbed at them and helped them up. Dracon's boat was only fifteen feet away and Kaseem was already pushing away from the Roman vessel. Bull, Cullen and two other gladiators leapt into Kaseem's boat, landing in a heap on the bottom of the hull. The force of their landing gave their boat some much-needed momentum.

Kaseem's rowers pulled away as Dracon's boat passed by the bow of their ship, missing it by inches. Another pull of the oars and they could row to the other side of the arena and catch their breath.

TWAK!

Cullen whirled around as something whistled past his ears and embedded itself into the prow of the ship. One of Dracon's grappling hooks was lodged in the wood. From the hook trailed a thick rope that Dracon tied around an iron toggle near the prow of his vessel. The rope lifted out of the water and snapped into a straight, taut line between the boats. Kaseem's boat jerked to a stop. Cullen yelled at the man closest to the hook.

"Cut that rope!" he yelled.

Gundar, a massive German, leapt toward the rope and raised his sword. Suddenly, his body jerked back, a spear protruding through his throat. Dracon raised his arms in triumph. Beside Dracon stood the spear-thrower, a gangly, sharp-faced man with eyebrows that hung low, making it look as if he had dark holes where his eyes should have been. He grinned as Gundar's knees gave way and fell dead to the deck.

Dracon's rowers dug in, propelling their ship toward the gladiators' vessel. The rope slackened and Dracon quickly tied the extra rope around an iron toggle, shortening the distance between the boats. Another gladiator jumped up to the prow of the boat, using it to shield himself from the spearman. He hacked at the rope and his sword went about a quarter of the way through the thick strands of fiber. As he raised his sword again the Roman boat swung around in the water. Most of the gladiator's body was still hidden by the prow of the boat as his arm swung up, ready to finish the job.

The warrior launched a second spear. His aim again was deadly. It slammed into the gladiator's chest, ripped apart his heart and killed him instantly.

Kaseem's rowers were taken out of their rhythm and the rope slackened again. Dracon tied the rope around the toggle, decreasing the distance again. At this rate, the Romans would be upon them in less than a minute.

Bull rushed past Cullen, running to the prow of the boat. He crouched low, shielding his body from the deadly aim of the spearman.

"I'll cut the rope, Cullen," he shouted hoarsely, "but you'll have to deal with him."

Cullen stepped across to the dead gladiator and wrapped his hands around the spear in his chest. He pulled it out sharply and turned to Bull.

"Show yourself, but duck back."

Bull nodded. He leapt up, his sword high as if he were about to slice down on the rope. The spearman leaned out from behind the prow and threw his spear. Before the Roman spearman darted out, Cullen flung his own spear, aiming it just to the side of the prow of the Roman ship. As the Roman appeared, Cullen's spear slammed high into his hip, just as the Roman loosed his weapon. The Roman grunted in surprise, and fell back. His spear flew wide of Kaseem's boat. Bull jumped up and sliced the rope holding the grappling hook. The rope ends snapped back.

Kaseem's boat leapt away as the rowers dug their oars into the water. Cullen braced himself against the side of the boat looking for the man he had injured. He saw him writhing on the deck of the ship. In agony, but alive. If the spearman continued to survive this day, he would never again walk without a limp.

And Cullen still hadn't killed anyone.

A movement behind Bull caught Cullen's eye.

"Bull, look out!"

THUNK.

A grappling hook slammed into Bull's shoulder. One of its spikes drove clean through the muscle under his shoulder blades and through the skin above his chest, protruding about eight inches. Bull lurched forward, a look of surprise on his face.

Cullen grabbed a sword from the deck of the ship and ran toward Bull. On the Roman ship, Dracon pulled the slack rope hand over hand, a look of triumph on his face. Before Cullen could reach Bull, Dracon gave one final tug, yanking Bull over the side of the boat. Bull disappeared under the surface. An almighty roar filled the arena. Bull had easily been the most visible and vicious of the gladiators and his death would turn the tide of the battle.

Cullen didn't break stride, but kept running, planted a foot on the hull of the boat and dove after Bull.

It was like suddenly being in another world. The noise of the crowd disappeared and Cullen's eardrums rejoiced in the silence. The coolness of the water washed the filth, grime and blood from his face and body. He had flashes of memories: diving into the river back home, swimming with Finn, shivering in the almost freezing waters of winter in Briton.

There he was.

Ten feet ahead of him, pulled through the water toward the Roman boat. Bull's left hand clutched his right shoulder in a vain attempt to dislodge the hook. Bubbles trailed from between clenched teeth and Cullen knew he had only seconds to free Bull.

Kicking hard, Cullen gained on Bull. In the distance, he saw the dark shapes of the oars dig into the water. If the Roman boat was able to build up momentum, Cullen would be left gasping in the water, ripe to be picked off by one of the Roman spearmen.

Cullen reached out, grasping Bull's ankle. He switched the grip on his sword and used both hands to climb up Bull's body. He could feel Bull kicking in agony as this new pressure tore at his wounded shoulder.

Just a few seconds, Bull, thought Cullen.

Cullen's lungs burned as he lunged for the rope. As his fingers wrapped around it he could feel Bull's struggles ease, whether from the release of pressure or from starting to drown, Cullen couldn't tell.

The Roman boat was nearer now. Cullen hefted his sword and looked at Bull. To his relief, Bull was watching him. Cullen gestured with his sword, pointing up, then pointing down, trying to communicate with that simple motion that they would have time for one breath while he cut the rope before they had to dive back down into the water. Bull nodded to show that he understood something of what Cullen meant and then they were dragged to the surface.

Cullen saw two pairs of hands hauling the rope over the side of the Roman boat. He had one chance to save both their lives. Using the rope as a lever, he kicked with his feet and pulled his body out of the water, exploding from the surface like a water demon. He sliced through the air with devastating force.

Dracon and another soldier were pulling the rope up and Cullen had only a moment to appreciate the look of surprise on both their faces. Dracon jerked his hands away from the rope as soon as Cullen erupted from the water. The other soldier hung on, whether from courage, slowness or just stupidity. Whatever the reason, the end result was the same. Cullen's sword, aiming for the rope's tightest point, sliced through both of the soldier's wrists and the rope. He saw Bull's head come up and suck in a lungful of the putrid arena air, and as they both fell back down into the water, Cullen had a moment to see the soldier rearing up, staring in disbelief at the two stumps of his hands spraying blood into the boat.

Cullen and Bull sank straight back down. As their feet touched the sand at the bottom, he saw spears slice through the water, trailing bubbles. Cullen led Bull sideways, away from the top of the Roman boat. The one breath they each took wouldn't last long. Blood trailed from Bull's shoulder, misting dark and foreboding in the depths of the water.

A shadow passed over them. *Kaseem's boat.*

Cullen planted his feet on the floor of the arena and pushed up, dragging Bull's weakening body behind him. They broke the surface of the water, shielded from the Roman vessel by Kaseem's boat. They barely had time to suck in a lungful of air before hands grabbed them and hauled them on board, dumping them unceremoniously on the bottom of the deck.

Cullen heard Kaseem barking orders to his men and he felt the frantic energy of the rowers digging their oars through the water. He wanted to help them. He wanted to grab an oar and give that extra effort that would propel the boat to safety. But he couldn't. The air filling his lungs tasted too sweet. His muscles refused to budge, compelling him to lay still as they sucked the oxygen into their starved sinews. Somehow he had saved Bull and they were both alive. For now. Bull's shoulder was still impaled by the grappling hook. For him to live the hook would have to be taken out, but pulling the hook out would cause more damage than it had going in. If Bull hadn't already severed an artery by now, surely the act of yanking the hook out would complete the job. Death would follow within minutes as his blood formed a pool of crimson in the cradle of the hull.

Cullen got to his knees, his chest still heaving with the joy of breathing.

How had he ever taken air for granted? Was there anything more delicious?

The Cilicians had rowed the boat to the south side of the arena. This seemed to be their corner, their eye of the hurricane. Cullen expected Dracon to chase them, but the Roman must have decided that his rowers, as good as they were, would never catch up to Kaseem's ship. They waited at the north end of the arena and gathered their strength.

"Kaseem, I need three strips of cloth, this wide, this long." Cullen held out his hands to show Kaseem, the dimensions he needed. Kaseem pointed to one of his men who pulled the robe off a dead oarsman. He tore the material into the lengths Cullen needed.

Cullen turned Bull on his side. Bull hissed in a sharp intake of breath and directed a stream of profane curses at Cullen. Kaseem knelt down beside him.

"You're going to take it out?" he asked doubtfully.

Cullen closed his eyes.

When all this is over I will love my wife, Rhiannon, and my child, Finn. We will plant wheat and barley and oats. We will bake bread and after supper I will chase my son around the village, letting him escape from me, and we will bathe in the river and shiver when the sun sinks below the mountain. My wife will hang my wet clothes near a fire and I will tell her I love her. This hell will end. This abattoir of death will be forgotten, as nightmares flee in the bright light of day. I will see my Finn's children grow up in freedom.

Cullen opened his eyes, grasped the hook and pulled it cleanly out of Bull's shoulder.

Blood sprayed out of Bull's wound, following the iron hook as air might flow into a lung. Cullen did not know if this meant Bull was mortally wounded. The Fates—or God—would decide. Cullen jammed a wad of cloth into the wound and commenced to wrap the injured shoulder with the lengths of cloth.

"So how long will they keep the Romans away?" asked Kaseem, his eyes gesturing to the north end of the arena where the Christians waited, ready to help them attempt an escape.

"They said they'd come up with a diversion."

"How long will we have before the guards descend on us?"

"With luck," said Cullen, as he finished tying a knot on the makeshift bandage, "a minute. Maybe two."

"Maybe none," grunted Kaseem.

"Then our deaths will be mercifully quick."

Kaseem chewed his lip, his gaze dancing from the Roman vessel to the crowd at the north end of the stadium.

"How many hooks did we take from the Romans?"

"Seven," answered Kaseem.

Cullen glanced up and made a quick head count. He saw Pugnax, a German whose wide jaw was covered with a thick red beard. Pugnax held a bloody axe, and stared at the Roman boat as if he expected it to charge over to them at any second. Bull sat beside a Gaul named Listor whose mouth was clenched in what looked like a permanent grimace. Jacob, the Palestinian giant, stared at him and Cullen almost counted him as living, until he realized that Jacob stared at him through glazed, lifeless eyes. The Palestinian was dead. Maduro, a Spaniard, who, despite being an inch over five feet tall, was blessed with amazing speed and prodigious strength, was covered in blood, but it must have been other peoples' blood, because Maduro's head flicked side to side, birdlike, while he cleaned his crimson sword on the shirt of a dead gladiator. Didius, Cullen's sparring partner on that first day, sat on a dead Roman, his chest heaving up and down, trying to draw in some air. Cullen recognized one other gladiator, a man he never had any dealings with. Close-cropped hair framed a determined looking face. Their eyes met.

"What's your name, gladiator?" he called over the din of the crowd.

"Marcus," said the man, sucking in air through clenched teeth. "Are we getting out of this shit-hole?"

Cullen nodded. He turned to Kaseem. "I've got seven, including me."

"Ten of my men are left," said Kaseem.

"Seventeen then. I hope the Christians brought some ropes with them. If we have to double up, some of the second men up the rope won't make it."

"And if ...after...we get out of this charnel house, what then?"

"They said they'd have horses."

"And if they don't?"

"How fast can you run?"

"I pray," said Kaseem, "that these people are worthy of your trust."

"Kaseem?"

"Yes?"

"It's time to get out of here."

Sixty one

Dracon's boat waited in the center of the arena, bobbing gently on the water. In his vessel were twenty-three men. Twenty-two if you didn't count the idiot who got his hands sliced off by Cullen and was right now crouching at the far end of the boat keening like an old woman. One of the other soldiers had fashioned a tourniquet around the man's wrist to stem the worst of the bleeding but Dracon knew if they didn't soon get the man to a doctor he would bleed to death.

He'd be better off, thought Dracon, if he did die. Who would want to live as crippled as that? What woman would want a man with stumps where there should be two, strong Roman hands? The poor bastard wouldn't even be able to pleasure himself properly. He'd have to resort to the cheapest, dirtiest whores to relieve himself.

Dracon shook his head, blinking away the look of contempt he realized he had on his face. He let his glance drift over the other men in his boat. The reason they had not pursued Cullen's craft was that after expending what was left of their energy and enthusiasm, they would, in all likelihood, not be able to catch up with the other boat. Maybe in a few minutes, when their muscles reclaimed their strength and their battered bodies recovered slightly, then they could make a move. Dracon wondered if he could add some other incentives for his men.

"Two extra months' pay to every dog one of you if we kill these pigs."

The men looked up, and Dracon could see the beginnings of fire in their eyes.

"And whores," continued Dracon. "I will keep you in whores for a year. Or until your wives find out."

There was generous laughter, and Dracon could see them forgetting their aches and pains and re-focusing on the job at hand. A low rumble of enthusiasm greeted his offer.

At least, thought Dracon, he had the men's attention. He had no intention of paying them money, or providing them with whores. When all this was done—whether Cullen was killed or not—each one of these bastards would find themselves marching to the far ends of the Empire away from the glories of Rome. They were supposed to be Rome's finest, yet they had allowed a group of thieving Cilicians and a barbarian from a land he hadn't even known existed, to exact a stalemate here on the waters of the great arena. But this stalemate would not last. There would be a victor. Dracon meant that victor to be him.

Pugnax, one of the surviving gladiators, picked up a bloody sword from the deck. He would take on the Romans with an axe in one hand and the sword in the other. He would not die easy. His eyes appeared unfocused as he stared at the Roman boat.

"You hurt?" asked Cullen.

Pugnax continued to stare straight ahead, as if he hadn't heard Cullen. Then he blinked, and turned to Cullen.

"I'm good," he said.

Pugnax turned back to stare at the Romans. Cullen felt a hand on his shoulder. Kaseem stood beside him.

"They're moving," said Kaseem.

Cullen nodded. Dracon's boat was coming toward them in a vaguely zigzag pattern. Its rowers were holding back, not yet rowing at half-speed. The wanted to see which way Cullen's boat would break. Kaseem barked some orders at his men, who turned the boat ninety degrees so that it's prow pointed directly at the Roman vessel.

"It's very simple, Kaseem. We're here, on the south end of the arena. We need to be there," Cullen pointed to the north end of the arena. "And we need time, as much as you can give us."

"Then we must let them come a little closer."

He walked down to his men and gathered them close. For half a minute he spoke to them, explaining what he needed. They listened intently, nodding as he spoke. Cullen watched the slow, seemingly random progress of the Roman vessel as it meandered toward them. They were closer now, enough so that he could see the look of concentration on Dracon's face. For a moment their eyes locked together, then Dracon let his gaze drift away.

Kaseem appeared at Cullen's shoulder. The Roman ship was almost one hundred yards away, directly ahead of them. Kaseem turned to his men, uttering a single, sharp word. Immediately the rowers pulled their oars through the water and the ship leapt forward. It quickly built up speed, closing the gaps between the two boats.

"It comes down which way they think we'll break," said Kaseem. "If they guess correctly, they'll destroy our boat."

"Which way will you break?" asked Cullen.

Kaseem shrugged. "The way to freedom, I hope."

Forty yards away, and the Romans were rowing faster now. Kaseem grabbed the prow of the ship.

"You'll want to hang on, Hibernian."

Cullen crouched low and grabbed he hull. Ten yards away.

Kaseem yelled something. It didn't even sound like a word, just the kind of sound you'd make if you stubbed your toe on a tree root. Cullen expected the rowers to do something maybe lift the oars out of the water and turn the boat but they ploughed straight on. Cullen experienced a moment of panic until he realized what Kaseem's ploy had done.

Dracon, thinking Cullen's boat would turn on a command, guessed they would break right. He ordered his rowers to turn the boat, hoping to smash into the prisoners' vessel. But he saw that Kaseem's plan was not to evade Dracon, but simply to plough right through where his boat had been. Dracon yelled for his men to straighten the boat but momentum had been lost. Before his men could adjust to the new orders, Kaseem's boat flashed by, its wake causing the Roman boat to bob in the water like a children's toy.

"After them, you fools!" yelled Dracon, cuffing the soldier next to him. The Roman marines pulled on their oars and maneuvered the boat around. Kaseem's boat already seemed impossibly far away. *They can't run forever*, thought Dracon. He expected to see the boat slow down and play a waiting game, while each side pondered its next move. Maybe Cullen's boat would try to ram Dracon's craft, hoping to end this tedious cat and mouse game.

Dracon squinted. *What in Hades was Cullen doing?* He had taken a red cloth out of his clothes and was waving it frantically above his head. *Was he trying to rally his Cilician comrades?*

Ruth gave the signal to the two men. They stood sixty yards apart, and each carried a jar full of oil. Immediately the men, who waited at the wall overlooking the water, started to pour the contents of their jars on the edges of the wall, bumping people out of their way, cursing loudly at them if they refused to budge. They walked toward each other from opposite sides of the arena. They stopped, twenty yards apart, emptied the last drops of oil onto the wall, dropped their jars into the water and ran into the crowd. Roman guards were already on their way to intercept them when a yell of fear erupted from the crowd. Unseen by them, two more of Ruth's comrades had put hot coals on the oil, one on each side. A wall of flame erupted up. The Roman guards, distracted by this new commotion and jostled by the crowd, lost sight of the oil spillers.

And then it hit Dracon in a blinding flash.

The prisoners were planning an escape. Everything in the way they fought today was not so that they would kill the Romans but that they would *survive* the Romans. Subtle difference. Big difference.

Dracon shifted his gaze to the crowd. A fire had erupted along the edge of the wall and the crowd seemed to be jostling each other, trying to avoid the flames. Two lines of flame had sprung up and Cullen's boat headed directly for the place in the wall that remained free of fire.

Lost amid the incipient panic, ten men among the crowd took out bows from under their cloaks. Oil-soaked cloth took the place of the arrowhead. The cloth was quickly set alight, and the ten archers aimed their bows high. The burning arrows flew, each of them landing on the awnings above the top row of the amphitheater that protected the Roman crowd from the heat of the sun.

Within seconds, flames spread across the canvas, feeding on the dry cloth.

The crowd started to push toward the exits.

"Turn the boat around!" Dracon screamed at the Romans. Slowly, ever so slowly, his Roman marines ploughed their oars through the water, picking up speed at what seemed to Dracon an incremental rate.

"Row, you curs. You sons of whores and drunkards!" Dracon picked up the end of a rope and slashed wildly at his oarsmen, causing welts to blossom on their backs like rose petals opening to the sun.

Kaseem's rowers slammed their oars deep into the water, causing the boat to almost skid to a sideways stop. The timed it so perfectly that their hull gently bumped the north wall of the arena.

Even before the boat settled, Cullen, Kaseem and five others threw the grappling hooks up in perfect arcs. The hooks grabbed the edges of the wall.

From above, the Christians threw down more ropes.

"Climb, you bastards," yelled Cullen.

The men grasped the ropes and climbed to the top, their exhaustion forgotten with freedom so close. Cullen saw Maduro and Listor reach the top in seconds, closely followed by five of the pirates.

Cullen forced a half-conscious Bull to stand. He tied one of the ropes around his waist. By the time this was done, six more men had climbed up. That left four: Cullen, Kaseem, Bull and a small pirate whose beard almost touched his waist. Cullen waved his hands to the men above. They pulled Bull's body up.

"Cullen!"

Cullen turned. Kaseem had grabbed a rope and was frantically pulling himself up, hand over hand. And Dracon's boat was fifteen feet away and heading toward them like a missile. Cullen and the short bearded man each leapt for ropes. The ropes jerked upwards.

The Cilician sailors above hauled both men up just as Dracon's boat smashed through the hull of their ship with such force it continued into the granite walls of the arena. A shudder went through the wall, and an explosion of planks, wood splinters and iron shot up into the air as Cullen and his companion crested the wall and flopped on the area in front of the seats.

Hands grabbed him, dragging him to his feet. He sensed, rather than saw, more of the crowd moving away from him, creating a path through which he half-ran, half stumbled. Ahead of him, Pugnax and Maduro dragged Bull. Kaseem and what was left of his crew were already at the edge of the arena. Kaseem sat down, took hold of a rope that was tied around a pillar hear the edge. Kaseem disappeared over the edge, down the rope. The Christians had tied ten ropes around the pillars. Pugnax and Maduro tied a rope around Bull and lowered him over the edge. Cullen was muscled through the retreating crowd to a rope. Hooded figures yelled at him.

"Climb down as fast as you can!" Cullen couldn't see who spoke, such was the commotion going on around him. Obediently, he grabbed the rope and turned. Before he climbed down he stopped, used the sleeve of his left arm to wipe the sweat from his eyes and looked up.

Ruth stood before him, serene and ageless. Her grey eyes twinkled and a thin smile crept along her lips. Despite all the screaming and yelling and shoving going on all around her, she seemed to exist on a different plane from everyone else. Time seemed to slow down, and Cullen heard each word that she spoke to him.

"God go with you," she said.

Even though the air was full of shouts, screams and curses, Cullen heard her words as if they stood alone, inches apart, in the middle of a vast, empty plain.

"And you," he replied.

Then he was gone, half climbing, half sliding down the rope, and in seconds his feet touched the ground. He found himself staring at a horse, a chestnut brown stallion with a black mane. Bull slumped on another horse, groaning in pain. Cullen slipped his foot into the stirrup and swung himself up. He turned to thank the people who had saved his life but they had scattered. Three horsemen, dressed in hooded robes, rode up to the gladiators and whipped the flanks of their horses. The horses bolted, ploughing through the melee, scattering through people who had gathered, attracted to the commotion. The three mysterious horsemen galloped to the front of the pack, their cloaks flowing behind them, leading the escaped gladiators away.

The horses ran hard down the cobbled streets of Rome. Glancing left and right, Cullen saw Bull, Pugnax, Maduro, Listor, Didius and Marcus riding hard. Seven gladiators left. Kaseem and his sailors rode with them, past merchants pedaling their wares, past houses through which stunned faces watched them, along alleyways and under arches they rode, tears streaming from their eyes as the wind whipped into them. And then there were fewer houses, fewer cobbled streets. They passed by one or two people instead of ten or twenty. The air seemed to become cooler, less pungent as the stench of the city gave way to the rich, fertile smell of fields and hedges.

A final corner was turned and ahead of them were fields and rolling hills. Cullen risked a look behind and saw no pursuers. He turned forward to drink in the glorious sight of a world without bars and dark cells. For the first time since he could remember, he smiled.

Sixty two

Blood thundered in Cullen's head in time with the pounding of his horse's hooves on the packed dirt road. He was the last rider and the horses ahead of him kicked up dust which found its way into his eyes, nose and mouth. He didn't care. The grime tasted of freedom and the possibility of seeing his family. Until his horse had galloped past the last street in Rome he had not allowed himself to hope that this freedom was real. And if he was free, then…his family. God in Heaven, he could be re-united with his family before the sun had dipped below the mountains.

Cullen urged his horse forward toward Bull.

"Can you keep going?" asked Cullen.

Bull turned his bloodshot eyes toward him.

"Try and stop me."

They rode, winding around low hills. They kept to the path until they were about ten miles outside Rome. The three robed figures led the gladiators off the path, along a low valley toward a forest that seemed to cover the distant hills for miles in a dense, verdant growth. The horses were panting now, and, impatient though he was, Cullen forced himself to slacken the pace along with the other riders. If the horses pulled up lame or dropped dead because their hearts burst, then their freedom might be over very soon. The forest drew closer at a maddeningly slow pace. Right now they were exposed, and any citizen who happened to see them could alert the Roman patrols. For now they'd been lucky—*very lucky*, he reminded himself—but it wouldn't take much for their luck to run dry.

They entered the forest, and Cullen almost moaned in relief as the shadows of the forest caressed him in their cloak of anonymity. He experienced what seemed like physical pleasure as the darkness descended on him. They rode on, weaving through the trees, the sunlight dappling on their horses. After about twenty minutes the rider at the head of their group stopped, and one by one the rest of the horses caught up to him.

Cullen cantered his horse to the front of the group where Kaseem rode with the leader.

"This is Phillip," said Kaseem, gesturing to the man who led them. The man's face was hidden by a cowl. When he turned, Cullen almost flinched away. The left side of Phillip's face was a mass of scar tissue, his skin was an ugly mess of wrinkled, pink crevasses from which sprung clumps of black, wiry hair. There was a black patch over his left eye.

"You are Cullen?

"That's right."

"Your family's being held on a farm, a day's ride by horse. I'm to take you."

Cullen's horse whinnied nervously and shook its head. Cullen reached forward and patted its neck. Sweat ran down the horse's skin, soaking Cullen's hand.

"Has anyone seen them?" he asked quietly.

Phillip shook his head. "It's a big estate, but if General Sulla bought them, then that's where they are." Phillip urged his horse closer to Cullen, and the breath from the two horses mixed in the cool afternoon air.

"Ruth asked me to tell you something."

Cullen looked quizzically at Phillip.

"She prays your family is alive and well."

"Why shouldn't they be alive?" asked Cullen. "They're slaves. Bought and paid for. Why kill them?" But even as he asked the question, a hundred different reasons as to why they shouldn't be alive flooded into his brain.

Phillip shrugged.

"My family is alive," repeated Cullen stubbornly. "I've done everything God asked of me. We had a deal."

"You made a deal with God? Why didn't you say so?" said Phillip, with a bitter grin Cullen didn't like.

"They're alive," said Cullen.

"Of course they are," said Phillip, his voice ripe with sarcasm.

They rode on in silence. Afternoon turned to evening, and the small amounts of sunlight that filtered through the leafy trees dimmed. Phillip led the horses on, winding through the trees in a pattern that seemed random, but the cloaked man seemed sure of where he was going and never stopped to check his surroundings. As the darkness descended fully, Phillip stopped and dismounted. Everyone else did the same, tying their horses to the nearest tree. Phillip produced dry bread and skins of water, and having satisfied their hunger, they settled down for the night.

Bull's moans kept Cullen awake for most of the night. He could hear the injured man roll around in pain and he was certain that Bull would die soon. Loss of blood, infection, fever—something was bound to take hold of him and end his life. Finally, Cullen managed to drift off to sleep. When he awoke, the only sounds were birds calling through the forest, greeting the early morning grey mist that crept through the trees like a silent thief. He realized that Bull had stopped moaning, and quickly crossed over to him. The gladiator was breathing slowly, having fallen into a shallow sleep. Cullen moved away, careful not to wake him.

They continued their journey as soon as the trees were visible through the gloom. The forest seemed endless, and curiously still. Once or twice he glimpsed a deer, but most of the time the only creatures visible were birds, which swooped through the forest cawing and screeching, the sun and shadows hitting their wings in rapid patches of light. Bull was on a horse, his waist tied with a rope to help him stay upright. He rode doubled over, the pain constricting his body, contorting it into a hunched-over shape. Cullen tried to keep his mind blank. He blocked all thoughts of his family from his mind. They were too close, too maddeningly close, and if he dwelled on them he'd go crazy. Instead, he concentrated on the forest, scanning the trees in the distance, making sure the Romans weren't stalking them like animals. And then, almost within the space of a couple of blinks, the forest ended.

A road appeared ahead of them, branching off in three directions. The main road continued on, gently rising and falling following the contours of the hills. Another road branched west, disappearing between two forested hills. The third road wound inland, weaving around groves of oak trees before losing itself under a canopy of tall, gnarled chestnut and beech trees, with roots that spread out, staking their claim to as much ground as they could hold on to.

As they approached the crossroads, Phillip raised a hand and the column of horses came to a gradual stop. Steam rose off the horses' bodies and their heads hung low.

"To the west," said Phillip, pointing that direction, "is the port of Centumcellae. There are boats there. A merchant who is one of us is willing to take some of you home. Kaseem, he is making a journey to Palestine. That is close to your homeland. If you wish—"

"I will stay with my brother, Cullen. I will help him take back his family."

Cullen turned to Kaseem, moved by the Cilician's loyalty. He hesitated before speaking.

"Kaseem, your friendship will forever live in my heart. But it is time for you to go home."

"But—" began Kaseem.

"Bull, Pugnax, Listor and Maduro have all agreed to go with me. Any more will be too much. Take my friends, Marcus and Didius, with you."

Kaseem stared hard at Cullen, then broke into a smile.

"So I am going home?" he asked, almost as if he expected to be denied the opportunity.

"You are going home."

Kaseem leant across his horse and the two men embraced.

"I shall tell my children's children about you. What a story they shall hear."

"I wish I knew the end of it, Kaseem."

"My family shall hear a happy ending."

Cullen shook hands with Marcus and Didius. No words were exchanged. There was nothing left to be said.

Kaseem dug his heels into his horse and rode down the path leading to the sea, his men following close behind. Marcus and Didius urged their mounts forward, following Kaseem. In minutes the only evidence of them was the slowly dispersing cloud of dust that hung between the trees.

Patrick Gleeson

Sixty three

It was only when the tall figure walked over to the stream that Cullen knew it was Bron. With his left foot three inches shorter than his right he had a distinctive circular motion to his walk. He looked closely at the other people in the field, squinting his eyes, trying to recognize traits or shapes that would tell him who they were. He studied them, looking for Rhiannon and Finn, but the figures were too far away.

Bull had drifted into a sleep, his body perched awkwardly against the roots of a beech tree. Blood seeped through the wrappings tied around Bull's shoulder, attracting a swarm of flies. They buzzed around the drying blood, driven to a frenzy by the rich, coppery smell. Soon the bugs would lay their eggs in his wound, the wound would turn putrid, his blood would become poisoned and Bull would die. Unless he didn't. Bastards like Bull were hard to kill.

They sat at the top of a hill that overlooked the farm. A copse of trees and bushes hid them from view and shaded them from the burning rays of the sun.

The other three gladiators hid in a forest whose edge circled a collection of low mountains. They were to wait there until Cullen waved a white cloth to summon them. Cullen looked at the shadows on the ground and figured it was mid-afternoon. Another two hours, maybe three, and the work would end for the day. Then, as the General's family ate their evening meal, that's when Cullen would make his move.

Bull was snoring now, reminding Cullen of how tired he was. It felt as if he had been awake forever. Was it only yesterday morning that he had

350

fought in the Flavian amphitheater? He closed his eyes and rested his head on his knees. He felt his eyes grow heavy and was powerless to stop himself drifting off to sleep.

His eyes jerked open. He mustn't let himself sleep now, he thought. He wouldn't wake up for a full day. A soft laughter broke through his thoughts and he turned to find Bull awake, a smile on his pale face.

"So you woke up," muttered Cullen, yawning.

"I've been awake for two hours," replied Bull. "I'm surprised your snores didn't bring every Roman for miles up to our little hide-out."

"Two hours?" said Cullen. He turned to look at the sun which had traveled a considerable distance into the western sky. He leaned forward, gently parting the branches of a low bush. The fields were empty of people.

"How long have they been gone?"

"Five minutes. Ten, maybe," said Bull.

"Any guards. Roman patrols?"

"None. "

"It's time, then," said Cullen.

"It's time," agreed Bull.

Cullen crept to the other side of the copse where it faced the forest. He picked up the branch to which he'd tied the white cloth and waved it slowly from side to side. On the edge of the forest, small but distant, came the answering wave from the other gladiators. Cullen put down the flag and crept back to Bull.

"They're on their way."

Bull nodded, peering at the house.

"Stay here, Bull," urged Cullen.

"I can walk. Mostly," said Bull

They made their way down the hill, both of them armed with a spear and a sword. They kept as low as they could, using the high grass and wild olive trees as cover. Bull half-walked, half-stumbled his way down. His breath came in short, painful gasps, but he continued on.

As the sun sank, it threw long, grey shadows along the earth. They reached the bottom of the hill and met up with the other gladiators. Dressed in their dull, dark clothes, they were almost invisible. They made their way carefully up to the house. Bull pointed to a long, low building beyond the main residence.

"Servants and slaves in there."

Pugnax, Lister and Maduro walked over to where Bull pointed.

"How long will you need?" asked Pugnax to Cullen.

"Not long," said Cullen. "As soon as they're calmed down, bring them over."

Pugnax nodded and led the other two gladiators away.

Sixty four

"There'll be someone just inside," said Bull. Cullen took out his sword and walked up the steps to the wooden door. He pushed gently on it, but it was locked. He looked at Bull and shook his head. Bull raised his good arm and motioned for Cullen to knock. Cullen rapped softly on the door. He pressed his ear close against the wood, listening intently. From inside came the soft shuffling of feet. A latch was moved and the door creaked open. Just as the man's head appeared, Cullen reached in and grabbed his neck. The man, a short slave with a lined, weather-beaten face, made a few choking noises as Cullen and Bull squeezed in the door. The servant beat at Cullen's arm, but Cullen's grip was iron. Cullen forced the man behind a marble column.

Cullen pressed the point of his sword against the man's throat and slowly released his grip.

"One word, one scream from you..." said Cullen.

But the servant could only gasp, desperately breathing in. His eyes were wide with terror, darting from Bull to Cullen, trying to figure out how long they would allow him to live.

"Are they eating?" asked Cullen.

The man looked at Cullen with eyes so large that Cullen thought his eyeballs would pop out of their head.

"The master and his family. Are they dining?"

Three quick nods from the servant confirmed this. The man shut his eyes and pressed his lips close together as if believing that having surrendered this information, these two ruthless barbarians would have no further use for him and gut him like a fish where he stood. Cullen slapped the man's face lightly. The eyes flew open.

"And the dining room?"

Terrified as he was, Cullen saw suspicion cross the man's face. The servant looked down at the floor.

"What's your name?" asked Cullen.

The man clenched his hands which shook beyond his control. So tight was his grip that all the blood seemed to have been squeezed out of them, leaving the fingers as white as a corpse. His mouth worked compulsively, trying to find a measure of control so he could answer Cullen.

"Nerva."

"Nerva," repeated Cullen. "Are you thinking that I'm here to kill your master?"

Nerva looked up at Cullen.

"Are you?" he croaked hoarsely.

"No," said Cullen. "But I need to talk to him. Where's the dining room?"

Nerva glanced down the hallway, past rows of marble columns.

"Show us," ordered Cullen, shoving Nerva ahead of him, while keeping a tight grip on the terrified man's shirt.

They could hear laughter from someplace in the house. It was impossible to tell from where, as the noise bounced off the marble floors and fresco covered walls.

"Your life," said Cullen, "depends on you, and all who live in this house, staying as calm as you possibly can. There are others of us here. If they hear yelling or shouting then blood will be spilled. Am I making myself understood?"

Nerva nodded.

A shadow crossed a hallway ahead of them and Cullen urged Nerva against a wall, behind a statue of Bacchus, stone grapes dangling over its open mouth. Two women walked along the corridor, side by side, carrying steaming dishes of food. They chatted lightly with each other, their voices rising and falling. Cullen's heart almost skipped a beat when he thought one of them might be Rhiannon, but these women had skin as black as night. Cullen breathed out and willed himself to relax. He turned to Bull.

"Are you alright?" asked Cullen.

Bull's face seemed drained of blood, and he leaned against the wall for support. He nodded at Cullen. "I'm fine."

They walked up to where the women had disappeared and followed them down the corridor. They caught sight of them entering a room with two marble columns on either side. There was no need to ask Nerva if this was the dining room. The laughter and talk was louder now. Cullen felt a dry, nervous tingle in his stomach. His feet padded softly over the marble floor, past the flower arrangement in the slender Greek pot. As they came in sight of the door, Cullen saw a dark-haired, twelve-year-old boy dressed in a grey tunic, reaching across the long table for a piece of bread. Beside him, engaged in a whispered conversation, were two girls, ten years old. Their dark hair flowed over heart-shaped faces that looked like they were copies of the other. The rest of the people came into view. Cullen recognized the master of the house at once. General Sulla. He sat at the far end of the table, washing his hands in a silver bowl held for him by a servant girl. To the general's left was an old man, completely bald, shriveled, but sitting erect. Probably his father.

There were two soldiers at the table. One was talking to the twelve-year-old boy across from him; the other picked apart the meat from a chicken leg. They wore the casual clothes of the soldier on leave. Cullen noted their youth and their obvious fitness. His eyes drifted to their faces where he saw at once they were the sons of the master. They shared his pointed chin and aquiline nose. Cullen noted a subtle difference between them: the one talking to the boy was a joker, a hard worker and a good man to have in your army. The other one was a killer.

A better man to have in your army.

It took Cullen less than a second to assess all this as he stepped into the room, prodding Nerva ahead of him. They did it so quietly that it took the diners another four seconds to realize something was wrong.

One of the twin girls saw him first. She gasped and her hands flew to her mouth. General Sulla glanced up. When his eyes rested on Nerva a look of confusion crossed his face. His eyes shifted to Cullen. No look of recognition registered. He saw the sword that Cullen raised and pressed against Nerva's neck.

"What...?" he said in a whisper.

The other twin turned, saw Cullen's sword at Nerva's throat and screamed, cowering back against her sister. The two soldiers turned. Their assessment of the situation took a few seconds. The first one, the Joker, put his hands up in a placating gesture. *We can work this out,* his demeanor said. *We're all reasonable people.* The other one, the Killer, didn't move. Or at least he didn't appear to. But his right hand, which had held the leg of the chicken, was gone, having moved down to his right foot.

Cullen knew what he was thinking. He would attack while Cullen held only Nerva at sword point. What was the life of a slave? Nerva was expendable. Cullen saw the muscles in the soldier's neck tense.

He looked at the Killer and shook his head from side to side. He gestured with his sword to the mistress of the house, the Killer's mother, who sat closest to Cullen. He moved Nerva so that Bull was revealed in the doorway, his spear held ahead of him. Bull shuffled forward and pressed the back of the spear into the soft fabric of the woman's clothes.

"Toss it over here," said Cullen to the Killer.

The Killer's eyes shifted to Bull, noting his wounds, his pale face. He also saw that Bull would not hesitate to impale his mother on the end of a spear. Cullen saw the corded tension in the Killer's neck relax as he drew the dagger from the hilt tied to his leg and slide it across the table toward Cullen. Now Cullen felt he had control of the room. He looked at the master.

"Do you know me?" he asked.

The General stared at his face, his brows furrowed.

"I don't know you," he replied haltingly. "If its money you want we have treasures here that are worth—"

"Keep your money, General," said Cullen.

"Then what?"

"My wife and child. You have my wife and child. I'd like them back."

Cullen saw the recognition in the General's eyes. He saw the blood flow from the General's face, leaving his pallor as pale as moonlight on alabaster walls. The General and his son—the Killer—exchanged a look. Their faces betrayed nothing, but the fact their eyes met, as if they shared a deep knowledge, told Cullen more than he wanted to know, and he was aware of a cold, icy feeling gnawing at the pit of his stomach.

"What's your boy's name, General?" said Cullen. The General's eyes hardened, becoming dark slits through which flashed murderous thoughts.

"My son has nothing to do with this."

"What's your name, boy?" asked Cullen, speaking directly to the petrified looking 12-year-old child.

"Antonius," whispered the boy.

"How old are you?"

Antonius muttered something that Cullen couldn't hear.

"Speak up, boy."

"Twe...Twelve, sir."

"Same age as my boy. Do you know him, Antonius? His name's Finn and he was brought here by your father two months ago."

"Finn?" said Antonius, brightening. For a second his fear receded. "We'd play swords together. We'd practice fighting like soldiers. I knew him."

Cullen's heart skipped a beat. He stared at the boy for a few moments. "You *knew* him?"

Antonius nodded. Something about the way the man asked the question scared him. It seemed the man's voice grew cold or hard. It was as if something he said angered the man, or made him...scared? But that couldn't be. What had he said to make the man's eyes turn so harsh, the way his father's eyes turned if one of the servants had done something really bad? Tears sprang at the corners of Antonius's eyes and he had to jut his chin out to stop it from trembling.

Cullen looked over at the General who kept his gaze firmly on the edge of the table. The General's wife was staring at her husband, a look of terror on her face. A look that told Cullen they all shared a terrible secret. A dark secret.

Was Finn dead?

I *knew* him.

He looked at Bull who had picked up on all the un-said words, all the words that these Romans were afraid of saying, because saying those words would undoubtedly mean their deaths.

"I hope," whispered Cullen, "I hope my family is well, General. I hope they live, because if they are dead or damaged, then I don't know what I will do, General."

"Listen to me," said the General intensely. "There are things I need to tell you. But you must promise not to harm my family. They are innocent of –"

He was interrupted by the echoes of doors opening in the house. The sound of a crowd walking through the house grew louder.

"Cullen! Bull!" yelled Pugnax.

"In here," growled Bull.

"Innocent of what?" asked Cullen, his voice low and clipped.

"Listen to me," said the General. "Listen…"

Cullen just stared at him. The General faltered, trying to find the words, the right words, to tell Cullen…what?

Pugnax, Listor and Maduro strode into the room, followed by the people from Cullen's village: Bron, with his labored walk, Art, Sayeva—who had somehow managed to look as young and innocent as the day she'd been kidnapped from the village, Kinburga, Aylith, Gretel and Rufus. Bringing up the rear was Brendel.

Pugnax, Listor and Maduro spread out, each of them standing behind a seated member of General Sulla's family.

There was no sign of Rhiannon or Finn.

"Cullen," gasped Brendel. He ran to him and they embraced. The villagers crowded around Cullen, grasping his arms, touching him, assuring themselves if he was really there.

"You were supposed to be dead!"

"How did you escape?"

"How did you find us?"

They peppered him with questions but Cullen could only search among them again, looking for his family. Brendel grabbed those closest to Cullen and pulled them back.

"Give him space, he's got work to do."

The villagers moved back, stepping behind the gladiators. Cullen's eyes fixed on Brendel, asking an unspoken question. Brendel, with what looked like a supreme effort, met his gaze. Brendel took a deep breath.

"Finn was sold three days ago. To someone in Rome."

Cullen blinked in surprise.

"Sold? So…he's alive?"

"Last I saw. Very much alive."

Brendel's eyes lowered to the ground. He opened his mouth as if about to speak, by his breath faded out as the words escaped him.

Cullen closed his eyes, struggling to find the strength to hear the words that he must know, the words that would send a dagger through his heart and soul.

God, not this. Not this. I've done what You wanted. I've done what Your priest wanted. So many times I could have killed my enemies but I didn't. For You, I turned my life around. For my family, not for me, I did what You required of me. My enemies still live. My son is still alive. If he is, I give You thanks. But my Rhiannon, is part of the deal. My Rhiannon is part of our deal. Did You forget? Were You, in all your Glory, and with all Your power, were You unable to keep Your part of the deal?

"She's dead, isn't she?"

He raised his eyes to Brendel, and this time, Brendel was not able to meet them.

"Yes."

The word came from Brendel's mouth as a whisper. That single word sliced through the core of Cullen's being.

Yes.

In a voice that seemed somehow detached from his body, Cullen asked, "How?"

"When they took Finn away, Rhiannon…she tried to stop them…she fought them. They were outside in the fields and she grabbed a knife from the overseer and—she attacked the soldier who had Finn and he—the other soldier who was near him, he…he ran his sword through her."

Cullen looked at the two soldiers at the table.

"Was it these two?"

Brendel glanced up, locking eyes with the two soldiers.

"Yes."

A hush descended on the table. The General's wife had her face in her hands, sobbing gently to herself. Cullen stared at Brendel who met his look with eyes filled with shame.

"I'm sorry, Cullen. I should have helped...I couldn't...they would have killed all of us."

He whispered. "How long did it take her to die?"

"Minutes. Two or three. I tried to stop the blood but the wound was mortal."

"And Finn? Did he see everything?"

Brendel nodded.

Cullen needed time. Time to think.

Because something had happened to him just now that he never expected to happen.

He believed in God.

Faith fell upon him like a curse.

Rhiannon was dead and how could Cullen have expected otherwise? This God might be a God of love but he was also a God who exacted a price. And Cullen had been a killer for so long that the price he paid would be minted in the blood of those he loved. The price of belief was everything you had.

God had just given him a terrible gift.

Faith.

The certainty that He existed, that He saw into every dark corner of every dark heart on Earth descended upon Cullen. How he wanted to reject this gift. How he wished he could let loose the anger that flowed through his body so that every member of this Roman family would die by his sword. The young ones, blameless in his wife's murder, would be killed first. The older ones would watch, then they would die. And the last to go would be the General and his wife, forced to watch everyone they loved, their entire family, butchered before them. How sweet it would be to watch their faces as he ripped their hearts asunder.

How delicious his vengeance would taste.

Just because I believe in God doesn't mean I can't hate Him. I can spite this God of Love that has killed my wife. I can murder this rich family before me that has not lost a moment's sleep over the killing of my wife. I can reject His love and pity for me as I send their souls up to Him to judge.

Would God accept these murderers into His kingdom in the sky? Or would He cast them into the cold, lonely river of death, the Hell where dark souls go to spend eternity? If He truly were a God of Love, surely He would take pity on their souls and take them into His bosom. And if so, what would Cullen have accomplished, except to doom his own soul into Hell?

Faith.

It had come swiftly.

It had come at a terrible price.

Sixty five

"My name is Aulus."

The words broke through Cullen's thoughts. He looked over at the soldier—the Joker—who had uttered the words. Aulus rose to his feet.

"I know who you are. I saw you fight last month in the arena. You bested Dracon. Your name is Cullen, the one they call Thirty-seven. It is my fault your wife is dead. When I saw her try to stab my brother I reacted without thinking. I killed her." He spread his arms wide, and seemed at a loss for words.

"I...I am sorry." The words trailed off, as if Aulus realized how hollow they sounded.

"Aulus, sit down," hissed his father.

"If my wife was killed," continued Aulus, ignoring his father, "I would want her killer's head on a spear."

No!" sobbed his mother. Her cry was cut short by a scream of pain—Bull prodded her with his spear—and she choked back her panic, preferring to keep silent rather than risk impalement.

"Let me stick her, Cullen," pleaded Bull.

"Not yet," he said quietly.

Aulus glanced at his mother, then back at Cullen. He spoke with desperation.

"Please, take me. Soldier to soldier, kill me. But I beg you. Let my family live."

Cullen barely glanced at the man. If he made eye contact all he'd want to do was carve out those eyes from their sockets.

"Please, I offer my life."

"Oh, we'll take your life, whether it's offered or not," said Bull.

Cullen held up a hand. Aulus breathed out in short, trembling gasps.

"Where is she?" asked Cullen quietly.

Aulus glanced at Brendel.

"We buried her beside a hill, near an oak tree," said Brendel.

Cullen nodded and was silent for a few seconds.

"Cullen," growled Bull. "What do you want us to do?" Bull's tone indicated that he would be delighted to start butchering.

"The longer we stay here," insisted Bull, "the better chance we have of something going wrong. Let's do them all now. Let's finish it and get out of here."

"Who bought my son?" said Cullen, looking at Aulus.

"If I tell you," said Aulus, his tongue darting out to lick his lips, "Will you let my family live?"

"Bull, run her through," said Cullen.

"No!" screamed Aulus. His hands flew up, and the family seemed to draw in a collective breath. Aulus blinked rapidly, his mouth working feverishly as if the movement would trigger his memory.

"It was a servant of a house, an old man, he never told us who he represented or who was his master."

"You don't know?" asked Cullen.

"The Bill of Sale," said Aulus, "If I could—"

"It was Dracon."

All eyes looked down at the brother, the one Cullen thought of as the Killer. He had spoken softly, but his voice stilled everyone in the room.

"Dracon the gladiator?" asked Bull.

The soldier nodded.

The Killer had joined his hands together and was tipping the fingers of each hand against each other.

This bastard's cold as ice, thought Cullen, *for one about to die.*

Dracon had Finn. So many images and thoughts ran through Cullen's head that he had to push them all aside, just so he could get the full story out of the soldier.

Cullen walked around the table to Aulus. He laid the flat of the blade on Aulus's shoulder and eased him back down in the chair. The soldier was dripping sweat, and already a dark band ringed the collar of his tunic. Cullen tapped the sword against the Killer's upper arm.

"Go on."

"Dracon's emissary asked specifically for your son," said the Killer. He paused, looking up at Cullen. "You made him mad, beating him like that, humiliating him like you did."

Cullen moved the sword's edge to the Killer's throat. He held it there for a few moments, then slowly drew it lightly across the skin, causing a thin line of blood to peek out. There was a gasp from the other end of the table, followed by a thump. Cullen looked over.

The mother had fainted, her face landing squarely on a plate of quail's eggs.

Idiotic woman, thought Cullen. Spoiled, greedy bitch of a woman. You deserve to see your children die. You deserve to be the only one allowed to live, so you can dream of their deaths every night until the despair grows so great that you fling yourself off a cliff into the sea.

He looked back down at the Killer, who seemed as if he fully expected his throat to be sliced open. To his credit, he kept his composure. Only a thin sheen of perspiration at his hairline betrayed any fear.

So Dracon had bought Finn. Why? Was it to kill the boy if Cullen defeated Dracon in the arena? Was it to torture Finn, to make him pay for Cullen humiliating Dracon before the Emperor?

"Let me see the Bill of Sale," he said.

"Nerva has the paperwork," said the Killer.

"Bull," said Cullen, not taking his eyes off the Killer, "Move behind the children."

Bull limped over to the side where the children sat. He cuffed Antonius on the head, causing the boy to yelp. A flash of anger surged through the Killer's eyes.

"Brendel, take Nerva and find the Bill of Sale," said Cullen.

Brendel took the old man's arm and urged him out of the room. Nerva cast fearful glances back as he left.

Cullen didn't need to see the Bill of Sale. These people were telling the truth. Dracon had his boy. But he needed time to think. *How could Rhiannon be dead?* Up until a few days ago, according to Brendel, she was alive. But Dracon, by taking Finn away from her, had doomed her to death. If Dracon hadn't tried to find his family, Rhiannon would be standing here, they would be hugging each other, they would be happy, and Cullen would feel so good about keeping his promise to find her and bring her home that he would gladly let this Roman family live.

But she was dead. It would have been so easy for God to keep her safe. So easy to wave a hand and ensure that Dracon didn't think about taking Finn away. God existed, and He let this happen. And yet, He fully expected Cullen to keep his promise.

How could he let these Roman pigs live when she was dead?

"Antonius," he said.

The boy jumped as if bitten by a viper. He stared at Cullen with wide, darting eyes.

"Find me some rope. Enough to tie them up," said Cullen.

Antonius scampered out of the room. Cullen's gaze fell to the floor. Marble tiles joined together in complex patterns. Cullen could see four or five different colors, each complementing the other, giving the feeling of warmth and luxury and wealth. How he longed for his dirt floor back home. But that simple dirt floor would never feel the footfalls of his wife. Maybe not even his son. They were not a family anymore.

Cullen squeezed his eyes shut.

No. You can't think of them yet. You must not. There were still things to be done, decisions to be made.

He opened his eyes and they fell on the dagger that the Killer had dropped on the table. He stooped down and picked it up. It was a simple weapon, but well made. There were no adornments on it, no jewels encrusted in the handle or the hand-guard. Just a razor-sharp blade, nine inches long. A thin length of leather was wrapped around the handle. The iron work was not typically Roman.

"I took it off a German barbarian. He tried to slit my throat with it." The Killer held up a palm to Cullen. There was a deep gash running across the skin, now covered over with a raised line of white skin.

"I held him off long enough to gut him with my sword."

Aulus shot his brother a warning glance that was ignored.

"If you kill us," continued the soldier, "every soldier in Rome will hunt you down. They'll find your family, what's left of it, and they'll kill you."

"Calvus, hold your tongue," said the General, between clenched teeth. The Killer—Calvus—glanced at his father, an amused, almost insolent look in his eyes.

"What pleasure will their deaths bring you?" asked Calvus the Killer, nodding to his family.

Cullen was silent, his eyes cast down to the dagger.

"I love my brother," said Calvus, gesturing to Aulus, "but he's an idiot. Even his demise, however long and torturous you make it, will mean nothing."

Calvus's voice lowered to a whisper.

"If its revenge you want, take me. Kill me. No other death will mean anything to you."

Bull looked at the young soldier.

"Maybe we'll kill them all, but let you live. I think that would mean something."

Calvus's eyes, which had feigned nonchalance, flashed with anger and fear.

"That way," continued Bull, "Cullen will know there's someone in this world that carries a rage to match his own. A rage that will eat you up until the day you die."

Calvus kept his mouth shut, breathing heavily. His fists clenched unconsciously. Bull, his voice weakened with exhaustion, still had a cruel smile on his face.

"Don't try to be clever, bastard. If Cullen decides to kill you, you'll die. If Cullen decides to let you live, you'll live."

Rufus, his tall frame stooped as if he wanted to conceal his height, stepped forward, his face drawn with barely concealed terror. His fingers tugged as his scraggly red beard. Cullen noted that his fingernails were bitten to the quick, as if Rufus had been living in constant terror.

"If we're doing this, Cullen, if we're escaping, we should go."

"We'll leave soon enough."

There was a shuffling outside the room, and Brendel led Nerva, the General's servant, back inside. Clutched in Nerva's hand was a parchment. Brendel took it from him and gave it to Cullen. Cullen unrolled it, and scanned the list of purchases and audits written down.

He saw Finn's name near the bottom, written neatly in black ink. It said: Finn; servant boy; age 11—2500 sestercii. Sold to Dracon Marius Gordianus.

If Dracon had Finn now, then Finn's life was in mortal danger. Dracon would be in a rage after having been defeated and tricked by Cullen. He'd want revenge. And if Cullen wasn't available, then Finn would become the target of his wrath. Unless, and this was a hope he clung fiercely to, unless Dracon knew Cullen would try to rescue his son.

Which meant Cullen would have to go back to Rome.

Antonius walked back into the dining room, his arms draped in lengths of rope. He laid them on the floor next to Cullen and hastily crossed over to the General.

Bull stared contemptuously at the rope.

"They killed your wife, Cullen, and you're going to let them live?"

Cullen ignored Bull.

"Is there a cellar in the house, Nerva?"

"Yes," replied the servant. "In a room off the kitchen."

Cullen turned to Aulus.

"Tie up your bastard of a brother."

The two soldiers looked at each other and Cullen could see the same thought flash between them. *Now is our last chance if we are to attack.* But he also saw that maybe, just maybe, this gladiator meant for them to live. He saw Calvus shift his eyes to the dagger in Cullen's hand. If Calvus had a weapon, he would attack, no question. But he had nothing, and so turned his back to his brother, put his wrists together behind his back and gritted his teeth as Aulus tied a firm knot, binding Calvus's wrists together.

Aulus went around the table binding everyone's hands behind them. The last to be done was the general, but as Aulus selected an end of rope with which to bind him, Cullen raised a hand.

"Stop." Cullen pointed the knife in Aulus's direction. "General, bind the wrists of your son."

The two men looked at Cullen, trying to read the mind behind the dark, hooded eyes. The General laid a hand on Aulus's shoulder, turned him gently around and bound his arms together.

"Sit down, general."

The general sat.

"Nerva, the cellar, show me."

Ten minutes later the General's family climbed down the steps into a large cellar with a dirt floor, compacted by many feet over many years. It held the family's wine. Shelves of earthenware jars lined the walls. A check of the walls revealed there was no way out except up the steps and through the trapdoor in the floor.

Aulus and Calvus knelt on the floor, waiting for their turn to go down into the cellar. Pugnax held a sword to Calvus's neck, waiting for the slightest movement as an excuse to run him through. Cullen lifted Aulus, the Joker, to his feet and led him to the steps.

Cullen pushed him.

The soldier fell down the steps, knees striking the stones, arms snapping with impact, nose shattering as it smashed against stone.

Cullen was curious to see if the Roman would live. If he did happen to snap his neck and die, then so be it. This one had killed Rhiannon. Let God decide his fate.

He lived. Cullen saw the young soldier land on the dirt floor. His bindings had become undone, but his arms were useless. Both were broken, bones protruding from broken skin. He groaned in half-consciousness.

Calvus—the Killer—attacked.

Cullen expected this. He welcomed it.

He drove the dagger deep into the Killer's knee. The Killer screamed and fell. Cullen withdrew the dagger and stabbed his other knee, twisting the knife in deep, shredding the ligaments and tendons. This one would never be a soldier again. Cullen rolled him to the steps and pushed. The Killer tumbled down. He fell on his brother and both of them howled in agony.

From his chair the General hissed in anger.

Cullen allowed himself a smile.

Cullen let the trapdoor fall and directed the villagers to haul anything made of stone or marble over and lay it in a heap over the trapdoor. After much heaving and sweating, the trapdoor was covered in stone benches, overturned statues, some tables and chests and the upper half of a fountain.

A thin sheen of perspiration covered Cullen's face as he turned to Pugnax.

"The other slaves and servants, there in the building, tell them we have slaughtered the Romans and will do the same to them if they remain. Tell them to run to the mountains and spend the night there. Tell them to talk to no one or they will be killed."

Pugnax nodded, and left the room.

"Bull," Cullen said, walking over to the gladiator who lay slumped in a chair. "I need you to take my villagers to the boat at the port of Centumcellae. Go with them back to Briton. Look after them. I need you to be their leader until I return."

"Damn this shoulder. I'd go with you, you know that."

"I know it."

"I'm no leader."

"Become one."

Bull got to his feet and grasped Cullen's arm. The gladiator's grip was weak, but insistent.

"Your son's alive. Go find him."

Bull walked out to the atrium where the villagers waited with Pugnax, Listor and Maduro. He stopped beside Genera Sulla, who stood beside the jumble of stone and marble that lay on top of the trapdoor.

"What about this one, Cullen. He thinks if he stands quietly here, you'll forget about him."

The general's face flashed with anger, but he said nothing.

Bull spat in the general's face. The older man flinched back, closing his eyes. He slowly raised a robed arm and wiped the spittle away. Bull shoved past the general and walked out of the room, leaving Cullen and the general alone. Cullen waited until he heard the villagers' whispered chatter die out as they left the villa and the distant *thunk* of the door shutting.

Sixty six

For a full minute the two men stood silently in the room. The general kept his eyes fixed on the floor, while Cullen turned the dagger in his hand, the handle spinning around his fingers. The General tried to imagine what was churning in Cullen's mind. He glanced up, but the Hibernian's face betrayed nothing. General Sulla knew he was going to die. He prayed that somehow his family would be spared. He didn't understand why this man was taking so long to exact his revenge. Every moment he stood there increased the chances that a Roman patrol might reach their farm. Every moment he stood there was a moment where he could be inflicting torture on the General and his family.

It was disconcerting, to say the least.

"My God forbids me to kill you," said Cullen, eyes downcast.

The General had to strain to hear the whispered words. He wanted to reply, but any answer that came to his tongue seemed either flippant or pleading.

"Do you believe in your God?" he asked finally.

Cullen raised his eyes to the General.

"Unfortunately, yes."

In a blur of motion, Cullen let the dagger fly directly at the general. It struck the old man above his right knee, smashing through bone and ligaments, separating muscles. The general gasped and collapsed on the ground, his face wide in shock. Cullen crossed over to him, grasped the knife and wrenched it out. The general tried vainly to hold back the cry of pain that escaped from his lips. Cullen took a handful of the old man's white hair and yanked his head back, exposing a throat through which the muscles danced like rope, tensing and moving up and down along the stretched, dried skin.

Cullen pressed the point of the blade against the leathery skin of the Roman. A pin prick of blood sprang up as the flesh was broken.

Do it, he urged himself. Be a man and do it.

What was stopping him? God? Just because he believed in God didn't mean he still couldn't kill this man. He still had free will. How easy it would be to slice through this bastard's throat, this man whose sons murdered his wife, who sold Finn into slavery. What ecstasy there would be in taking revenge.

So why was he hesitating?

He hated God for giving him faith. It would be so much easier not to believe. So much easier to kill.

Again he willed himself to carve a line deep across the man's neck. To hear him gasp in shock, to feel his legs and arms scramble and jerk in panic as his lungs quickly filled so that he would drown in his own vile, Roman blood.

Then came a thought that filled him with equal parts horror and delight.

Why stop with this man?

Once he killed the General then he would be as one dead to God. And God to him. He would have defied the God of Love, the God who knew how to force a man beyond the limits of all he could endure.

Cullen knew if he killed the General, he would remove all the tables, chairs, chests and stones that held the trapdoor shut. He would open it and descend into the darkness of the cellar.

He would kill all down there. He would butcher them mercilessly, ecstatically, reveling in their screams, lusting in their terror. He would smear his face with their entrails. How good it would feel to reject God and give in to the revenge that the marrow of his being cried out for.

If he could just make that first cut.

The little pinprick of blood had flowed down the old man's neck, kissing the white collar of his tunic, spreading slowly across the fibers.

Rhiannon, he thought. I would kill all Rome for you. I would slaughter them all.

Cullen, she would say. *Kill no one for me. Do not murder in my name. Find our son.*

"You don't understand, Rhiannon," hissed Cullen through clenched teeth. "You don't know what the world is like."

I understand you love me, Cullen. I understand you love Finn. Save him. Save our boy.

"Why must these Roman's live, while you lie buried in this cursed land?"

She was the only person who had never been afraid of him. She was stronger than he was. Infinitely stronger.

If you kill him, then I will be lost to you forever.

"No, no. We'll never be lost to each other." Cullen shook his head defiantly.

I'm going to ask you to do the hardest thing you'll ever have to do, Cullen. Drop the knife.

"No."

Let this old man live. Walk away. Find our son.

"Finn," whispered Cullen.

Finn.

The General sat with his back against a marble column. He clenched his teeth in pain from the wound above his knee. Sweat dripped from his forehead into his eyes, making them sting.

He could not believe that he was still alive.

When that gladiator, Cullen, had shut his family in the cellar, the General's heart almost leapt for joy knowing it was only he who would pay the price for the death of Cullen's wife. How wonderful to know that Cullen had allowed them to live, that his family would live on. He was prepared to accept the death that Cullen would swiftly bring down upon his head. A life for a life. Rich or poor, Roman or barbarian, General or slave- -none of it mattered. People loved who they loved, and Cullen would take his just revenge. The General's bones would feed the same soil that Cullen's wife fed now.

But death never came.

The knife point had penetrated the skin of his neck less than a quarter of an inch. He expected to feel a sharp pain as Cullen ripped the knife across his throat. The coming death would be excruciating, but it would be swift. He prayed to the Gods that his family would understand that he accepted death with honor. He had closed his eyes and waited for the death that never came.

The gladiator had kept the knife poised at the same spot on his neck, and had flexed his muscles, working himself up to slitting the general's throat. But each time Cullen had faltered, muttering to himself, crying out his wife's name, Rhiannon. For five minutes they had lain together, their bodies close, Cullen's hot anger bearing down on him. It was five minutes of at once the most extreme intimacy and detachment the General had ever experienced. The five minutes extended into a lifetime, an eternity...

And then Cullen was gone.

The General could not remember Cullen leaving his side, or taking the knife away from his neck. He only knew that he had jerked awake, though he had not slept. He heard the front door shut and knew he was alone in the house.

He was tied up. It would take hours for him to free himself. Or until one of the slaves was brave enough to return to the house.

When he'd first looked in Cullen's eyes in Rome, he'd seen the eyes of a killer. He had not been wrong, because the gladiator still had that look. But Cullen had not killed him.

His God had forbade him, and he had listened. This killer, this Gladiator Thirty-seven had shown mercy to the man who had taken, and by extension killed, his wife.

All because his God had forbidden it.

What God had that power?

The General felt something shift in his soul.

Sixty seven

Cullen found a horse in the General's stables. She pawed the ground as Cullen took hold of her bridle, but allowed herself to be led out into the night air. Cullen stroked the mare's head and offered her some honeyed treats that he had grabbed off the table as he left the house. The mare shoved her nose into the palm of his hand, greedily sucking up the delicious morsels. He moved to the mare's side and leapt onto her back in a single, fluid move. At the urging of Cullen's knees pressing into her side, the mare trotted over to the entrance of the estate. Cullen drew the cloak he grabbed from the General's house around him, and lifted the hood over his head.

With luck he would be at Dracon's house in the morning.

Bull, the rest of the surviving gladiators, and all the villagers were on their way to the port of Centumcellae where the Christians had arranged for a ship to take them to Briton. Once there, they would make their way to their old village and see what was left of it. The gladiators would be welcome to stay if they wished. Cullen didn't think he'd see Bull again, even if he did find Finn and bring him home. That wound was terrible. But Bull had survived this long, and he was still as much of a bastard as he ever was, so there was always hope.

Cullen slowed the horse down from a trot to a walk as he neared the Roman patrol. There were eight of them, hard experienced soldiers, and they looked at Cullen as he approached. Cullen bowed to them as he passed, hoping that they would ignore him and continue on, but the *Decurion*, the cavalry leader, guided his horse across the road, stopping in front of Cullen. He was a large man, with thick forearms that seemed to sprout from his chest like branches from the trunk of a tree. A dark beard covered his lower face in thick curls.

"Have you been on the road long, sir?"

"About two hours," said Cullen truthfully.

"Where are you going?"

"Rome, sir."

"In the dark of night?"

"I must get there before morning."

"What's your name?"

"Sulla Atticus Scaurus," said Cullen, blurting out the name of the Roman soldier who terrorized the land with his father.

"What business do you have in Rome, Scaurus?"

Cullen's mind went blank. For one absurd moment he wanted to tell these Romans the truth, that he must return to Rome to rescue his son from a madman.

Cullen started to speak, then shook his head in apparent embarrassment.

"My brother..."

"What about him?"

"He..." Again, his mind went blank. He thought of Bull, always talking and whining like an imbecile. *What would he say? What bullshit story would he make up?*

"He, my brother, trades in gold. Brooches, rings, necklaces—that kind of thing. And he sold everything to a rich man's wife, somewhere near the Palatine—or was it the Forum? No, it was the Aventine, yes, where all the shops are. So, he was only supposed to be gone two days. That was a week ago. And my brother always had a fondness for prostitutes. And this despite all my...anyway, I have to reach the whorehouses before he wakes up and avoids me again."

The Decurion waved a hand impatiently. Cullen stopped, thanking his luck, because he had no idea where he was going with the story.

"It'll take you a year to check all the whorehouses in Rome. What I need to know is if you have seen a group of men. Half of them are from the north, half from the east. Some are injured."

"What did they do?" asked Cullen.

The Decurion rolled his eyes.

"Have you seen them?"

Cullen slowly shook his head.

"I wish I could help you. I haven't seen them."

"Where did you spend the night?" asked the soldier.

"The port of Centumcellae." Cullen named the seaport town where Bull and the others had hopefully arrived at.

"And it was quiet," he said. "Peaceful. Beautiful town. Doesn't smell the way Rome smells, you know with the garbage, the rotten food, people doing their business of the streets, and I don't mean business as in money, I mean people actually move their bowels and—"

The Decurion drew in a deep breath as if to interrupt Cullen's speech.

"Oh, oh," said Cullen, snapping his fingers. "At the inn I stayed at last night, a traveler came in from a town near the mountains."

Cullen stopped and looked at the soldiers. They stared back, waiting for him to finish his thought. Cullen stared at them with a serious look on his face. The Decurion shrugged his shoulders.

"So?"

"The traveler," said Cullen, lowering his voice and leaning closer to the soldiers. "He said he saw..." Cullen looked from side to side as if others might be listening. "He said he saw a shooting star."

Cullen sat back, a triumphant look on his face.

"A shooting star?" replied the Decurion, a look of impatience spreading over his face.

"He said it portends great danger. Great danger."

The Decurion glared at Cullen, and guided his horse around him, now staring more intently at Cullen.

"Lower your hood."

Cullen hesitated, then reached up and pulled his hood clear of his head. He plastered an awkward grin on his face.

"You don't think I'm one of them, do you?"

The Roman stared hard at Cullen, his black eyes seeming to bore through him. "Anyone recognize him?"

From the back of the patrol, a young soldier urged his horse forward.

"I do."

The young soldier's face was hidden by dark shadows as he weaved through the other soldiers on their horses. He stopped beside the Decurion and as he turned, Cullen knew who it was before his face was revealed in the moonlight.

It was Lucius, son of Gaius, the young soldier who Finn slashed at with his sword, and whom Cullen saved from falling to his death after the stag pushed him over the cliff.

Lucius stared at Cullen, his eyes cold and hard, betraying nothing. Cullen's hand drifted to his side where his sword lay hidden by his cloak. He could probably take two, maybe three of them before they overpowered him. He was finished. Finn was finished and Rhiannon had died in vain. He should have killed the General when he had the chance. Should have butchered his family. Was this the final joke God would play on him, sending Lucius to unmask him?

The Decurion already had his sword drawn and Cullen realized with a sinking heart that he probably wouldn't be able to get by this single soldier never mind the other seven. If he were to survive, he'd have to let himself be taken by these soldiers and pray that he'd have a chance to escape before they inevitably took him back to the arena to be killed like a common criminal. No, more likely they'd crucify him in the morning. Hadrian wouldn't look kindly on him for escaping and making a fool of Rome. He had outstayed his welcome and he wouldn't be treated as the newest warrior to grace the sands of the Flavian Amphitheater. He would be meat for the animals. Or the cross.

"Well," demanded the leader, "is he one of them?"

"He's lying," said Lucius.

The Decurion snapped his sword forward, its point catching Cullen under the chin. Lucius guided his horse over to Cullen.

"He's not looking for his brother in the brothels," said Lucius, as his horse walked around Cullen. "He's going to them himself."

"Explain," demanded the leader, his sword point pressing the skin in, almost to breaking point.

Lucius turned to the Decurion. "I've bargained with this idiot for a gold necklace for my mother. He couldn't wait to finish the deal because all he could think of was a flaxen-haired wench that would spread herself wide for him for a handful of coins."

Cullen realized that Lucius had just saved his hide. Sweat popped on his face, despite the cold.

The Decurion relaxed his arm slightly.

"So he's not one of them?"

"No," said Lucius, walking his horse to the back of the patrol.

"Well, why didn't you just say so?" growled the Decurion, sliding his sword back into its scabbard. Lucius shrugged, and Cullen saw his mouth lift at the edges in a smile. The Decurion glared at Cullen for a few moments, and Cullen didn't have to act the part of a normal businessman who just had a sword at his throat. He found that he was shaking. What was wrong with him? He never shook like this, never felt as if he had almost died and then been handed his life back.

"Whoring dog," said the Decurion, turning his attention to the road ahead. The soldiers filed past him, steam from their mounts rising in the cool night air.

Cullen bowed his head as the soldiers passed by him. He glanced up at Lucius as he passed. The young soldier met his gaze, his expression unreadable. Cullen felt an urge to whisper 'thank you' under his breath, but he let the thought hang in the air. Lucius looked forward, and in seconds the Roman patrol melted into the darkness.

Cullen turned, lightly tapping his heels against the sides of the black mare. She walked on.

When he was sure the Romans had gone out of earshot, he leaned over the side of the horse and vomited on the ground.

Sixty eight

Dracon's house was built near the edge of a cliff, facing out toward the Mediterranean. There was a drop of over one hundred feet to the sea below. During the winter storms, the waves broke so high that droplets of water reached the top of the cliff. The garden on the cliff side was enormous, with the southern end formed into a series of terraces between which grew vines of grapes, tomatoes and sweet peas. Separating the north side of the garden from the south was an orchard of peach trees, planted randomly among the grass. They were weeks away from full bloom and the fruit that hung on the trees was abundant, but still hard and green. It would be a good crop this year. Beyond the orchard, on the north side of the garden, Dracon had cleared it of any vegetation except for a thick, lustrous layer of grass, which swept from the back of the villa, out past a large marble fountain through which water bubbled gently, curved between two eight-foot-high statues of Romulus and Remus that Dracon had specially made for him by a sculptor in the Forum. The grass continued to grow in waves until it met the edge of the cliff. Part of the garden jutted out further than the rest. A bridge of rock, forming a little peninsula.

At the end of the peninsula stood a lone tree, gnarled, stooped and twisted. A few leaves still clung to its branches, as if defying the elements, determined to eke out an existence no matter how hard the effort, no matter what the cost.

The villa was a long, low structure with white walls topped by a roof of overlapping tiles the color of burnt umber. Blocking the view of the villa, from the dirt road that led up to the house, was a wall, twelve feet high, whose alabaster color was almost obscured by the climbing wisteria vines that crawled up the wall, finding purchase in the small cracks and contours of the plaster.

Cullen had arrived at the area two hours earlier. He had studied it from every direction possible, looking for signs of a trap or an ambush. He had circled the surrounding fields looking for a Roman patrol, or a peasant working the fields who maybe was not a peasant, but a well-armed soldier.

He had climbed a hill that overlooked the property and tried to gauge the mood of the house. If there had been a tension in the air, maybe servants scuttling about, anything that said something was different from what was normal, then he would know that Dracon had enlisted the help of Roman soldiers to ambush Cullen when he arrived.

But Cullen saw no evidence of this.

He counted two servants. One was an old man who sauntered among the tomato plants just after sunrise, slowly picking the best fruits from the crop. He took these inside and reappeared fifteen minutes later and started to prune the already immaculate rosebushes that grew in one corner of the garden. The other servant was a large woman who strode into the garden from the villa, toward the old man. She appeared to yell at him for some job not done. As she talked she gestured to the house. In return, he waved a hand dismissively at her. She turned and walked back inside. He continued pruning the roses.

Normal household happenings. No ambush. No hidden soldiers. Cullen had never thought there would be but he had to be sure.

It would be just Cullen and Dracon.

A fight to the end, with Finn's life hanging in the balance.

The man finished pruning the roses and ambled back into the villa. He came out again in less than a minute carrying two simple wooden chairs. He carried them down the length of the back garden toward the peninsula. Huffing and cursing, he dragged the chairs the last part of the way, placing them on either side of the tree that clung tenaciously to the end of the promontory. The man walked to the edge and looked down at the water below. Waves were breaking over the rocks all along the shore. The old man spat over the edge and watched his spittle fall until it dropped out of sight. Appearing satisfied, he turned and went back into the house.

Two figures emerged from the villa. One tall man with long hair and wide shoulders.

Dracon.

One shorter figure, thin and scrawny.

Finn.

They walked toward the promontory, to the chairs the servant had put there. Finn hung back slightly, as if in deference to Dracon. As they reached the chairs, Dracon sat in one and gestured for Finn to take the other.

Finn sat down, looking around, trying to see over the edge of the cliff. He seemed to glance at Dracon, then quickly looked away. Dracon ignored the boy, and sat forward in his chair, elbows resting on knees. If he had been closer, Cullen was sure he'd have seen that Dracon's eyebrows were furrowed, his mouth would be compressed in a grim line, and his eyes would be dark, forbidding or vengeful.

Cullen shifted his gaze back to his son. *He's alive. Thank God he's alive.* He tried to study the boy's movements, his body language, to see if he was hurt or scared, but Finn's movements were neutral. Normal. He appeared to be well.

Cullen's heart felt it would burst with the love he had for his boy.

It was time to end this.

Sixty nine

Cullen rode the mare out from the trees, back onto the path, and kept going until they stood outside the gates of the villa.

The open gates.

Dracon was doing all but issuing Cullen a written invitation to go inside.

He clicked his heels into the mare's side and she walked through the gates.

"Papa!"

Dracon glanced up, pulled out of his reverie by the boy's exclamation. He had been staring at his hands, re-playing the battle in his head, watching his fists clench and unclench as he silently berated himself for allowing the gladiators to escape. For allowing Cullen to slip through his fingers.

It hadn't worked out the way he wanted. It hadn't worked out at all. His soldiers had failed in their job and had been humiliated. *He* had been humiliated, guilty of completely underestimating his opponent.

The Emperor had been humiliated. For the first time Dracon was not invited back to the Emperor's palace after the games. Not because he lost, but because of the *way* he'd lost.

Dracon's face flushed with the memory of the Roman citizens filing out of the arena, throwing jeers down upon him and his surviving men. Even their disrespect was apathetic. He was over for them now. Cullen had refused to play by the rules and had won their undying love in the process. Cullen had rendered Dracon…

…irrelevant?

But Dracon had one thing that Cullen didn't have. The one thing Cullen wanted more than anything in the world. Dracon had the cunning, the foresight, to dig into Cullen's past and get the one thing that Cullen loved above all else in the world.

His son.

If Cullen had died in the battle, Dracon would have been able to savor the victory for years to come by ordering the young boy about his household. Eventually, of course, he'd have to kill the boy before any ideas of revenge entered his head. Dracon didn't want to wake up with a dagger sticking in this heart.

But now the boy had a role to play.

He was the flame to Cullen's moth. He would draw the father in, so that Dracon would fight him one last time. To the death.

So when Finn gasped the word 'papa', Dracon looked up.

And there he was, sitting astride a large, black mare. The horse stopped at the edge of the grass area about seventy yards away. Cullen was staring at Finn with a gaze that Dracon didn't recognize as Cullen's. It was a look of love and affection. It transformed his face from the hardened look of a gladiator to the look of simply a father.

Let's see how long that lasts.

He watched Cullen dismount. In his belt were two swords, standard soldier issue. He came ready to fight. Good.

Finn leapt from his chair, determined to run to his father, but Dracon grabbed the boy's arm and forced him back to his seat. He watched Cullen's eyes and saw anger surge to the surface, almost turning those green eyes red with fury. But Finn yelled out again, with unsuppressed joy.

"Papa!"

Cullen's gaze shifted back to his son, the anger gone from his eyes as if it had never existed.

"Finn, are you alright?"

Finn wiped tears from his eyes with the palms of his hands.

"I'm not hurt."

Dracon sat back, still holding onto Finn, but content to watch Cullen in this new role of loving father.

"I promised I'd find you, son, didn't I?" said Cullen.

Finn's reply was a sound formed from a half-laugh, half-strangled sob. His tears flowed freely now, and Finn used the sleeve of his shirt to wipe his eyes. He looked at Cullen with haunted eyes.

"They killed her, papa."

"I know, Finn," said Cullen. "I know they killed her."

"It's my fault," said Finn. "If I hadn't cried, then Mama wouldn't be dead."

Cullen had slowly approached until he was twenty feet away. He knelt down on one knee.

"Finn, look at me."

Finn buried his face in the crook of his elbow, wiping this fresh batch of tears away. With considerable effort he choked off his sobs and raised his head to Cullen.

"You're the best son a mother could have. It wasn't your fault that she was killed."

"But—"

"It wasn't your fault."

Cullen moved forward, but Dracon raised his sword a few inches in the boy's direction and gave Cullen a warning look.

"Finn, listen to me. There is nothing you could have done to stop what happened. No matter how big you were, no matter how many weapons you had, there was nothing you could have done."

"But if I'd only—"

"Finn," said Cullen, a slow smile forming on his face, "I think she spoke to me."

Finn's eyes blinked and he looked at his father with rapt attention.

"I had my knife at the throat of the General, the man whose son killed mama. I wanted more than anything to finish him. To kill him. But your mother's voice spoke in my head. *Let the old man live*, she said. *And find Finn. Find Finn.*"

Dracon burst out in a short laugh. "Don't tell me you let him live?" he asked in disbelief.

Cullen looked at Finn and smiled.

"Did…did you kill him?" asked Finn.

"No," said Cullen. "He's alive. So are his sons and the rest of his family. If I'd killed them your mother would have been really mad at me."

Finn laughed. "You kept your promise."

"I kept my promise. And I solved the riddle."

A smile broke out on Finn's face.

"Mother Miriam's riddle! I've been thinking about it all the time." Finn stopped, and frowned. "But I could never figure out which of the two sons I was. Which one are you?"

Dracon looked from Cullen to his son, confusion written on his face.

"What in Hades are you two talking about?"

"I'm both of them, Finn. We're all both of them."

A quizzical smile formed on the boy's face. He stared at his father in confusion.

"I don't understand what that means."

"It's like this, Finn. When I was young, I was sure of myself. I had the world at my feet. I had a plan. I was kind of like the older brother in Mother Miriam's story. I obeyed my father, I fought side by side with him, and if something came into my life to mess it up, then I'd get angry and upset, and I'd fix it with the fists or my sword. I was arrogant and selfish, and thought I deserved what I deserved. I'd earned it. Like the older brother."

Finn nodded staring intently at Cullen.

"But then I grew older. I took a wife, and we had you, and we had all your sisters. And one by one, they were taken from me. My daughters, Grainne, Edra and Fern, my Aisling, my Rhiannon, all taken. All gone, except for you, my boy. I have nothing left except the love I have for you. Now I'm on my knees, and all I can do is hope that God, this desert God that your mother loved, that he forgives me. Now I have nowhere left to turn. Now I'm the younger son."

"We're both of them," said Finn.

"We're all both of them," said Cullen.

A deep, shuddering breath escaped from Finn as if a great weight had been lifted off his shoulders.

"Are we going home, papa?

"Yes, son. We're going home."

Finn looked slowly at Dracon, who leaned forward and ruffled Finn's hair.

"You want to go home, boy?" he asked.

"Yes," said Finn, his voice small.

"Then your father has a job to do."

"A job?"

"He has to kill me."

Finn frowned, not understanding Dracon.

"And...you'll let him?"

"Oh no. I'll be too busy trying to kill him."

Dracon rose to his feet, grabbed Finn by the back of his shirt and dragged him to a standing position. Cullen slipped the two swords out of his belt.

"Careful, Dracon, be very careful." Cullen's voice had dropped to a whisper, but Dracon had no trouble catching every word.

"You think I mean to hurt him?" said Dracon in a mock-hurtful tone. "No, I won't kill him. Not yet anyway."

He placed a sword to Finn's neck and dragged him back up the promontory to the old, twisted tree. Cullen stepped forward, hatred filling his heart like bile corroding his throat.

"I need you to do something for me, Cullen. Swear to me that you will try to kill me, that if the opportunity presents itself, you will slit my throat."

"I swear, on my life, that I will try to kill you," said Cullen.

"Your God doesn't tolerate liars, Cullen. Swear on your desert God."

"I swear it," whispered Cullen.

Dracon grinned as they reached the tree. He thrust his sword into the ground, and forced Finn's hands around a low, thick branch. He whipped out a length of rope that was tucked into his belt, and quickly bound the boy's wrists together. He withdrew his sword from the ground.

"There," he said, wiping the blade of his sword on his jacket. "Safe and sound. But the only way for him to remain that way is for you to fight me. And kill me. Because if you don't, if I live," Dracon laid the blade of the sword against Finn's throat, "I'll kill him."

"Then let's go," said Cullen quietly.

Dracon walked down the promontory, taking another sword from his belt.

"Such a pity," he said, "that there are only two old servants to witness this battle."

Cullen flexed his knees and lowered his arms.

"This battle should be witnessed by all of Rome. I shall have to invent a story of a titanic battle when I deliver your head to the Emperor Hadrian. Of course," admitted Dracon, "judging by the last two times we've fought each other, it might be my head that separates from my body. But at least I'll know."

Cullen stood still. Silent. Watching. Dracon walked closer. Fifteen yards, then ten.

"Not much for idle talk, are you, Cullen? You'll have to forgive my banter. We Romans are known for our incessant prattle. Also, I confess to an emotion I haven't felt in years. I believe I feel something approaching nervousness. Even fear. Not since I was a soldier in Hadrian's army has the adrenaline surged through my bones. It's almost delicious. Shall we get to it then?"

Dracon was five yards away when he rushed forward. Cullen feinted left then darted right.

Dracon wasn't fooled and sliced his sword in a swinging arc from left to right. It was an impossible move to defend, so fast, so brutal, it would knock any defensive sword away and slice through whatever flesh happened to be in the way. Dracon had the move planned even before he rushed, and as soon as Cullen feinted left, then Dracon knew he had the battle won, knew this savage from the north had fallen, finally, to a superior warrior, a Roman. He would walk through Rome with Cullen's head high on a spear, letting them know, letting his fickle admirers know, that Dracon had killed the Hibernian. And he would announce to the Emperor that the leader of the escape had been captured and killed by Rome's greatest warrior.

He would offer the head to Hadrian—*humbly* offer the head to the Emperor. Then he would apologize for letting the gladiators escape and beg—*beg*—for the Emperor's forgiveness. Hadrian would be so touched, so astounded at Cullen's capture and death that he would invite Dracon in to dine with him. He would demand that Dracon tell his story over and over again. Maybe there would be some Senators and their wives at the palace and they would crowd around, listening intently to Dracon's tale, interjecting a question here and there which Dracon would answer with a witty, deprecating remark. And all before him would thank the Gods that Rome still had soldiers—*citizens*—like Dracon. They would marvel at his prowess and think that, in hundreds of years' time, his story would still be told to young boys at night who would dream of growing up like Dracon.

His sword sliced through the air.

No flesh, no bone. Just air.

For an instant, Dracon was confused. It seemed the Hibernian had vanished. A split second later it was too late. Cullen had not darted right after feinting left.

He had dropped to the ground.

Dracon felt a searing pain in his right shin, as if someone had plunged a red-hot poker into the marrow of his bone, and was trying to ram it as far up his leg as possible, splitting the bone. The pain shot up through his body, needles, thousands of hot needles, surging up through his spine, along the length of his arms to his fingertips, up through his neck and seeming to break out of his eyes. A thin, high scream came from deep in this throat as the momentum of his swing carried him to the ground.

He hit the dirt realizing his right foot had been sheared clean off just above the ankle.

He lashed out, hoping to catch Cullen off guard, but before his arm reached the apex of its swing, it stopped. Cullen had caught hold of his right wrist and with a vicious motion, snapped it forward.

The force was so great that the resulting crunch of bone was audible to both of them. Cullen turned Dracon over, grinding his face into the fresh grass. He placed his other hand on Dracon's left elbow, twisting the Roman's arm back as hard as he could.

Dracon screamed. Cullen placed a knee in the back of his head and bore down with such force that Dracon thought his neck would break. The pain in his body was unbearable. Black dots exploded in front of his eyes. He couldn't even blink them away because his face was so far down in the dirt that—

—Craaacck!

Cullen broke his left arm at the elbow. Dracon had thought that if the pain had gotten any worse he would surely pass out. He was wrong. The pain had gotten worse, but every nerve in Dracon's body seemed to be on fire.

And he was very much awake.

Dracon could feel the bones shatter inside, and the ligaments whipping back through the muscles of his arms.

No, he thought, no, it couldn't happen like this. His leg. Gods, his leg had been cut off, his right wrist was broken and his left elbow was shattered.

The pressure on his neck suddenly lessened as he felt Cullen rising to his feet. Dracon turned his head, sucking in air. Then he pitched forward, retching into the grass, vomiting up the bread, cheese and tea he had for breakfast.

He had been defeated. Totally defeated.

It had taken seven seconds.

He tried to sit up, but succeeded only in turning on his back. He lay there, looking up at the sky, his body in more pain than he could have thought possible. If Cullen had any mercy he would end his life. He would drive the sword into his chest, rupturing his heart. Cullen had crippled him. Death was only seconds away and Dracon welcomed it.

But the sword never descended. Dracon moved his arms in front of him, and the effort made him scream in agony. He forced himself to lift his head and face Cullen.

Where was he? A shadow loomed over him and Dracon closed his eyes, relieved that Cullen had come to finish the job. But he felt only a pair of hands wrap something around his leg. Opening his eyes he saw Cinna tying a tourniquet around his lower leg, which sprayed the ground with an arterial pulse of blood. The old man pulled tight. Dracon almost fainted from the pain. He turned toward the promontory and saw Cullen slice though the ropes that held his son. He watched father and son embrace. Cullen picked up Finn and carried him to the mare who had retreated to the edge of the grass, disturbed by the sudden violence and scent of blood.

"You," hissed Dracon, blinking away the sweat that streamed into his eyes. "You were supposed to kill me."

"I lied," said Cullen.

"You people," said Dracon, his voice hoarse with pain, "you Christians, whatever you are, you're not supposed to lie."

"We're also not supposed to kill," said Cullen.

"You think it's merciful to let me live like this? Kill me, like you said. Like you swore on your God you'd do."

But Cullen ignored him, lifting Finn onto his horse, then swinging up behind him. Dracon reached for one of his swords that lay under him, but his wrist flopped uselessly against the handle, his fingers only able to paw the weapon.

"Damn you," roared Dracon.

Cullen kept his eyes fixed on Dracon as he and Finn rode silently away.

Please, thought Dracon. *Let it end now, while I still have the courage to die.*

"Cinna, kill me now," he said to the old man who had just finished staunching the flow of blood from his leg. "End my life with this sword. I beg you. I order you."

The old man lay a soothing hand on Dracon's brow.

"No master," replied his servant in a calm voice. The servant looked up, and took something from the woman who had scurried up to them. In her hand was an iron bar.

"Please," said Dracon, "I can't live like this."

The old man touched something against Dracon's lips. It was a rolled-up belt, and the old man was trying to force it between Dracon's teeth.

"Open wide, master. Bite on this."

Dracon took the belt between his teeth, not knowing why he was doing so. He saw the end of the iron bar glowed with an orange color. He could feel the heat radiating from it. He tried to spit the belt out, so he could scream at them to end his life, but the servant, with appalling ease, lay on top of him while the woman knelt down beside his foot.

"Bite down, master. This is going to hurt."

Cinna, as always, was right.

Seventy

The old fisherman's bones creaked as he pulled in the net. It was full of mackerel and cod, their bodies flopping and leaping, and it took all his strength to haul the catch into his boat. His breath hung in the air, as it always did in the mornings, the tiny water droplets dissipating slowly into the damp atmosphere. The sun was a mere glow through the mist, a soft orb that reached tentatively through the shroud of morning, reflecting on the still surface of the water with the merest of touches.

The last few months had been good to him. After that terrifying encounter with the Roman boat he had a newfound appreciation for his life, even learning to embrace his aching joints, his hacking cough and his unreliable bladder. He had befriended the Widow Grace, who lost her husband the same year his beloved wife lost her battle with death. She came to his house every day, and brought vegetables and milk, and they cooked the fish with carrots, cabbage and leeks. He was able to sell the leftover fish at market and had some coins put aside. Soon he would buy a cow. Maybe two. If he got any richer he could become a farmer. But it would be hard to leave the sea behind. Despite the aches in his bones from the early morning chill, and the strain on his muscles from hauling up the catch, he realized he still loved the open water, still loved the silence and the feeling of being alone in the world.

Whoosh.

He knew that sound. He knew it even though he'd heard it only once before. With a final heave he pulled in the net, crossed quickly to his seat and set the oars in the water. He waited.

Whoosh.

To his left. He drove the oars into the water and pulled his boat away from the sound. His eyes stared at the mist, waiting.

The prow appeared and the old man noticed that there were no eyes drawn on it. It was the practical prow of a merchant vessel. The boat passed thirty feet away from him, and there was no danger of his boat getting caught between the hull and the oars this time, getting tossed around like a child's boat on the water.

He saw two figures standing at the edge of the boat, mere silhouettes in the mist. One was tall, with broad, imposing shoulders. The other was smaller, a child. They looked out toward him and suddenly the child pointed excitedly.

"There, papa. A light. Like I told you!"

The old man's lantern cast a barely discernable glow, but it was good enough to attract the fish and good enough for this child with the excellent eyesight to spot it. He raised a withered hand and waved at the boy.

"Hello, boy," he yelled, his voice raspy with age.

"Hello, fisherman," replied the boy, his voice just beginning to break, on the cusp between boyhood and manhood.

"What's your purpose?" called the old man.

The boy cupped his hand to his mouth.

"We're going home," said the boy.

The fisherman cleared his throat to reply, but by the time he found his voice the ship had started to disappear into the mist. The wake from the merchant vessel reached his boat, rocking it gently side to side. By the time the rocking subsided, the ship was gone, swallowed by the mist as if it had never existed. He settled back into his boat, and surveyed his catch. Another good one, God be praised. His day's work was already done. He grasped the oars in his hands and started to row to shore, thinking that home would be a pretty nice place for him to be too.

It felt good to be alive.

About the Author

Patrick Gleeson is an animator currently working in Los Angeles. He lives in South Pasadena with his wife and two children.

Check out the animated book trailer on YouTube: Gladiator 37 book trailer

Contact: patrickgleesonauthor@gmail.com

www.ingramcontent.com/pod-product-compliance
Lightning Source LLC
Chambersburg PA
CBHW031944260626
47157CB00017B/2194